# THE GLEAMING PATH

People swarmed through the plaza—soldiers, messengers, firemen, and revelers determined to celebrate, no matter that a fire was raging around them. But when the skinny fellow in the dark tunic got within a couple of paces of the emperor, he pulled out a dagger and screamed, "Phos bless the gleaming path!"

He stabbed overhand.

Krispos threw up an arm, catching the fellow's wrist before the blade struck home. The would-be assassin twisted and tried to break free, screaming about the gleaming path. But Krispos had learned wrestling from an army veteran, years ago; he'd gained his first fame by outgrappling a champion. Shouting and twisting were not enough to break away from him.

He bore the knifeman to the cobbles and squeezed hard on the tendons inside his wrist. Involuntarily, the heretic's hand opened. When the knife fell out, Krispos brought up a knee, hard, between his legs. It was unsporting but extremely effective. The fellow stopped screaming about the gleaming path and started screaming in good earnest.

By Harry Turtledove
*Published by Ballantine Books:*

*The Videssos Cycle:*
    THE MISPLACED LEGION
    AN EMPEROR FOR THE LEGION
    THE LEGION OF VIDESSOS
    SWORDS OF THE LEGION

*The Tale of Krispos:*
    KRISPOS RISING
    KRISPOS OF VIDESSOS
    KRISPOS THE EMPEROR

NONINTERFERENCE
A WORLD OF DIFFERENCE
KALEIDOSCOPE
EARTHGRIP
DEPARTURES

THE GUNS OF THE SOUTH

WORLDWAR: IN THE BALANCE

# KRISPOS
# THE
# EMPEROR

### Book Three of
### *The Tale of Krispos*

## Harry Turtledove

A Del Rey® Book
BALLANTINE BOOKS • NEW YORK

A Del Rey® Book
Published by Ballantine Books

Copyright © 1994 by Harry Turtledove

Library of Congress Catalog Card Number: 94-94028

ISBN 0-345-38046-0

Manufactured in the United States of America

First Edition: June 1994

10  9  8  7  6  5  4  3

# KRISPOS
# THE
# EMPEROR

VIDESSOS
AND THE
SURROUNDING LANDS
LATE IN THE
REIGN OF KRISPOS

N

PARDRAYA

MYLASA RIVER

MYLASA

SEA

PEGIAN

MAKURAN

MASHIZ

VIDESSIAN

SEA

PAKRIODOCON
RESAINA
GARSAVRA

EMPIRE

ARANDOS R.

SEA
OF
SALT

SAILORS'

# I

KRISPOS SOPPED A HEEL OF BREAD IN THE FERMENTED FISH SAUCE that had gone over his mutton. He ate the bread in two bites, washed it down with a final swallow of sweet, golden Vaspurakaner wine, set the silver goblet back on the table.

Before he could even let out a contented sigh, Barsymes came into the little dining chamber to clear away his dishes. Krispos cocked an eyebrow at the eunuch chamberlain. "How do you time that so perfectly, esteemed sir?" he asked. "It's not sorcery, I know, but it always strikes me as magical."

The vestiarios hardly paused as he answered, "Your Majesty, attention to your needs is the proper business of every palace servitor." His voice was a tone for which Videssian had no name, halfway between tenor and contralto. His long, pale fingers deftly scooped up plates and goblet, knife and fork and spoon, set them on a vermeil tray.

As Barsymes worked, Krispos studied his face. Like any eunuch gelded before puberty, the vestiarios had no beard. That was part of what made him look younger than he was, but not all. His skin was very fine, and had hardly wrinkled or sagged through the many years Krispos had known him. Being a eunuch, he still had a boy's hairline, and his hair was still black (though that, at least, might have come from a bottle).

Suddenly curious, Krispos said, "How old are you, Barsymes? Do you mind my asking? When I became Avtokrator of the Videssians, I would have sworn on Phos' holy name that

1

you had more years than I. Now, though, I'd take oath the other way round."

"I would not have your Majesty forsworn either way," Barsymes answered seriously. "As a matter of fact, I do not know my exact age. If I were forced to guess, I would say we were not far apart. And, if your Majesty would be so gracious as to forgive me, memories are apt to shift with time, and you have sat on the imperial throne for—is it twenty-two years now? Yes, of course; the twenty-year jubilee was summer before last."

"Twenty-two years," Krispos murmured. Sometimes the day when he walked down to Videssos the city to seek his fortune after being taxed off his farm seemed like last week. He'd had more muscle than brains back then—what young man doesn't? The only trait he was sure he kept from his peasant days was a hard stubbornness.

Sometimes, like tonight, that trek down from his village seemed so distant, it might have happened to someone else. He was past fifty now, though like Barsymes he wasn't sure just how old he was. The imperial robes concealed a comfortable potbelly. His hair had gone no worse than iron gray, but white frosted his beard, his mustache, even his eyebrows. Perverse vanity kept him from the dye pot—he knew he was no boy any more, so why pretend to anyone else?

"Will your Majesty forgive what might perhaps be perceived as an indiscretion?" Barsymes asked.

"Esteemed sir, these days I'd *welcome* an indiscretion," Krispos declared. "One of the things I do miss about my early days is having people come right out and tell me what they think instead of what they think will please me or what's to their own advantage. Go on; say what you will."

"Nothing of any great moment," the vestiarios said. "It merely crossed my mind that you might find it lonely, eating by yourself at so many meals."

"Banquets can be dull, too," Krispos said. But that wasn't what Barsymes meant, and he knew it. Here in the residence where the Avtokrator and his family had more privacy than anywhere else (not much, by anyone else's standard— Barsymes, for instance, was in the habit of dressing Krispos every morning), meals should have been a time when everyone could just sit around and talk. Krispos remembered many such meals—happy even if sometimes short on food—in the peasant huts where he'd grown to manhood.

Maybe if Dara were still alive . . . His marriage to his predecessor's widow began as an alliance of convenience for both of them, but despite some quarrels and rocky times it had grown into more than that. And Dara had always got on well with their sons, too. But Dara had gone to Phos' light, or so Krispos sincerely hoped, almost ten years before. Since then . . .

"Evripos and Katakolon, I suppose, are out prowling for women," Krispos said. "That's what they usually do of nights, anyhow, being the ages they are."

"Yes," Barsymes said tonelessly. He had never prowled for women, nor would he. Sometimes he took a sort of melancholy pride in being above desire. Krispos often thought he must have wondered what he was missing, but he'd never have the nerve to ask. Only those far from the palace quarter imagined the Avtokrator as serene and undisputed master of his household.

Krispos sighed. "As for Phostis, well, I just don't know what Phostis is up to right now."

He sighed again. Phostis, his eldest, his heir—his cuckoo's egg? He'd never known for sure whether Dara had conceived by him or by Anthimos, whom he'd overthrown. The boy's—no, young man's now—looks were no help, for he looked like Dara. Krispos' doubts had always made it hard for him to warm up to the child he'd named for his own father.

And now . . . Now he wondered if he'd been so nearly intolerable as he was growing into manhood. He didn't think so, but who does, looking back on his own youth? Of course, his own younger years were full of poverty and hunger and fear and backbreaking work. He'd spared Phostis all that, but he wondered if his son was the better for it.

He probably was. There were those in Videssos the city who praised the hard, simple life the Empire's peasants led, who even put into verse the virtues that life imbued into those peasants. Krispos thought they were full of the manure they'd surely never touched with their own daintily manicured fingers.

Barsymes said, "The young Majesty will yet make you proud." Fondness touched his usually cool voice. Since he could have no children of his own, he doted on the ones he'd helped raise from infancy.

"I hope you're right," Krispos said. He worried still. Was Phostis as he was because of Anthimos' blood coming through? The man Krispos had supplanted in Dara's bed and then in the palaces had had a sort of hectic brilliance to him, but applied it chiefly in pursuit of pleasure. Whenever Phostis did something extravagantly foolish, Krispos worried about his paternity.

Was Phostis really spoiled from growing up soft? Or, asked the cold, suspicious part of Krispos that never quite slept and that had helped keep him on the throne for more than two decades, was he just getting tired of watching his father rule vigorously? Did he want to take the Empire of Videssos into his own young hands?

Krispos looked up at Barsymes. "If a man can't rely on his own son, esteemed sir, upon whom can he rely? Present company excepted, of course."

"Your Majesty is gracious." The vestiarios dipped his head. "As I said, however, I remain confident Phostis will satisfy your every expectation of him."

"Maybe," was all Krispos said.

Accepting his gloom, Barsymes picked up the tray and began to take it back to the kitchens. He paused at the doorway. "Will your Majesty require anything more of me?"

"No, not for now. Just make sure the candles in the study are lit, if you'd be so kind. I have the usual pile of parchments there waiting for review, and I can't do them all by daylight."

"I shall see to it," Barsymes promised. "Er—anything besides that?"

"No, eminent sir, nothing else, thank you," Krispos said. He'd had a few women in the palaces since Dara died, but his most recent mistress had seemed convinced he would make her relatives rich and powerful regardless of their merits, which were slender. He'd sent her packing.

Now—now his desire burned cooler than it had in his younger days. Little by little, he thought, he was beginning to approach Barsymes' status. He had never said that out loud and never would, for fear both of wounding the chamberlain's feelings and of encountering his pungent sarcasm.

Krispos waited a couple of minutes, then walked down the

hall to the study. The cheerful glow of candlelight greeted him from the doorway: As usual, Barsymes gave flawless service. The stack of documents on the desk was less gladsome. Sometimes Krispos likened that stack to an enemy city that had to be besieged and then taken. But a city had to be captured only once. The parchments were never vanquished for good.

He'd watched Anthimos ignore administration for the sake of pleasure. Perhaps in reaction, he ignored pleasure for administration. When the pile of parchments was very high, as tonight, he wondered if Anthimos hadn't known the better way after all. Without a doubt, Anthimos had enjoyed himself more than Krispos did now. But equally without a doubt, the Empire was better served now than it had been during Anthimos' antic reign.

Reed pens and the scarlet ink reserved for the Avtokrator of the Videssians alone, stylus and wax-covered wooden tablets, and sky-blue sealing wax waited in a neat row at the left edge of the desk, like regiments ready to be committed to battle against the implacable enemy. Feeling a moment's foolishness, Krispos saluted them, clenched right fist over his heart. Then he sat down and got to work.

Topping the pile was a tax report from the frontier province of Kubrat, between the Paristrian Mountains and the Istros River, north and east of Videssos the city. When Krispos' reign began, it had been the independent khaganate of Kubrat, a barbarous nation whose horsemen had raided the Empire for centuries. Now herds and farms and mines brought gold rather than terror south of the mountains. Solid progress there, he thought. He scrawled his signature to show he'd read the cadaster and approved its revenue total.

The second report was also from Kubrat. Even after most of a generation under Videssian rule, the prelate of Pliskavos reported, heresy and outright heathenism remained rife in the province. Many of the nomads would not turn aside from their ancestral spirits to worship Phos, the good god the Empire followed. And the folk of Videssian stock, subject for centuries to the invaders from the steppe, had fallen into strange usages and errors because they were so long cut off from the mainstream of doctrine in Videssos.

Krispos reinked the pen, reached into a pigeonhole for a blank parchment. *Krispos Avtokrator to the holy sir Balaneus:*

*Greetings,* he wrote, and then paused for thought. The pen scratched across the sheet as he resumed: *By all means keep on with your efforts to bring Kubrat and its inhabitants back to the true faith. The example of our new, perfectly orthodox colonists should help you. Use compulsion only as a last resort, but in the end do not hesitate: as we have only one Empire, so we must have only one faith within it. May Phos shine his light on your work.*

He sanded the letter dry, lit a stick of sealing wax at one of the candles on the desk, let several drops fall on the letter, and pressed his ring into the blob of wax while it was still soft. A courier would take the letter north tomorrow; Balaneus ought to have it in less than a week. Krispos was pleased with the prelate and his work. He was also pleased with his own writing; he hadn't done much of it before he became Emperor, but had grown fluent with a pen since.

Another tax report followed, this one from a lowland province in the westlands, across the strait called the Cattle-Crossing from Videssos the city. The lowland province yielded four times as much revenue as Kubrat. Krispos nodded, unsurprised. The lowlands had soil and climate good enough for two crops a year, and had been free of invasion for so long that many of the towns there had no walls. That would have been unimaginable—to say nothing of suicidal—in half-barbarous Kubrat.

The next report was sealed; it came from the latest Videssian embassy to Mashiz, the capital of Makuran. Krispos knew he had to handle that one with careful attention: the Kings of Kings of Makuran were the greatest rivals Videssian Avtokrators faced, and the only rulers they recognized as equals.

He smiled when he broke the seal and saw the elegant script within. It was almost as familiar as his own hand. "Iakovitzes to the Avtokrator Krispos: Greetings," he read, moving his lips slightly as he always did. "I trust you are cool and comfortable in the city by the sea. Were Skotos' hell to be charged with fire rather than the eternal ice, Mashiz would let the dark god get a good notion of what he required."

Krispos' smile broadened. He'd first met Iakovitzes when he was nine years old, when the Videssian noble ransomed his family and other peasants from captivity in Kubrat. In the more than forty years since, he'd seldom known the plump little man to have a kind word for anyone or anything.

Warming to his theme (if that was the proper phrase), Iakovitzes continued, "Rubyab King of Kings has gone and done something sneaky. I have not yet learned what it is, but the little waxed tips to his mustaches quiver whenever he deigns to grant me an audience, so I presume it is something not calculated to make you sleep better of nights, your Majesty. I've spread about a few goldpieces—the Makuraners coin only silver, as you know, so they lust for gold as I do after pretty boys—but without success as yet. I keep trying."

The smile left Krispos' face. He'd sent Iakovitzes to Makuran precisely because he was so good at worming information out of unlikely places. He read on: "Other than his mustaches, Rubyab is being reasonably cooperative. I think I shall be able to talk him out of restoring that desert fortress his troops won in our last little skirmish for the donative you have in mind. He also seems willing to lower the tolls he charges caravans for permission to enter Videssos from his realm. That, in turn, may, should, but probably will not, enable those thieves to lower their prices to us."

"Good," Krispos said aloud. He'd been after Makuran to lower those tolls since the days of Rubyab's father Nakhorgan. If the King of Kings finally intended to yield there, and to restore the fortress of Sarmizegetusa, maybe Iakovitzes was reading too much into waggling waxed mustachios.

Another cadaster followed Iakovitzes' letter from Makuran. Krispos wondered if Barsymes deliberately arranged the parchments to keep him from being stupefied by one tax list after another. The vestiarios had served in the palaces a long time now; his definition of perfect service grew broader every year.

After scrawling *I have read it—Krispos* at the bottom of the tax document, Krispos went on to the parchment beneath it. Like Balaneus' missive, this one also came from an ecclesiastic, here a priest from Pityos, a town on the southern coast of the Videssian Sea, just across the Rhamnos River from Vaspurakan.

"The humble priest Taronites to Krispos Avtokrator: Greetings. May it please your Majesty, I regret I must report the outbreak of a new and malignant heresy among the peasants and herders dwelling in the hinterlands of this Phos-forsaken municipality."

Krispos snorted. Why that sort of news was supposed to please him had always been beyond his comprehension. Formal written Videssian, he sometimes thought, was designed to obscure meaning rather than reveal it. His eyes went back to the page.

"This heresy strikes me as one particularly wicked and also as one calculated as if by the foul god Skotos to deceive both the light-minded and those of a certain type of what might in other circumstances be termed piety. As best I can gather, its tenets are—"

The more Krispos read, the less he liked. The heretics, if Taronites had things straight, believed the material world to have been created by Skotos, not Phos. Phos' light, then, inhabited only the soul, not the body in which it dwelt. Thus killing, for example, but liberated the soul from its trap of corrupting flesh. Arson was merely the destruction of that which was already dross. Even robbery had the salutary effect on its victim of lessening his ties to the material. If ever a theology had been made for brigands, this was it.

Taronites wrote, "This wickedness appears first to have been perpetrated and put forward by a certain Thanasios, wherefrom its adherents style themselves Thanasioi. I pray that your Majesty may quickly send both many priests to instruct the populace hereabouts on proper doctrine and many troops to lay low the Thanasioi and protect the fearful orthodox from the depredations. May Phos be with you always in your struggle for the good."

On the petition, Krispos wrote, *Your requests shall be granted.* Then he picked up stylus and tablet and scribbled two notes to himself, for action in the morning: to see Oxeites the ecumenical patriarch on sending a priestly delegation to Pityos, and to write to the provincial governor to get him to shift troops to the environs of the border town.

He read through the note from Taronites again, put it down with a shake of his head. A naturally argumentative folk, the Videssians were never content simply to leave their faith as they had found it. Whenever two of them got together, they tinkered with it: theological argument was as enjoyable a sport as watching the horses run in the Amphitheater. This time, though, the tinkering had gone awry.

He used the third leaf of the waxed tablet for another self-reminder: to draft an imperial edict threatening outlawry for anyone professing the doctrines of Thanasios. *Patriarch, too,* he scribbled. Adding excommunication to outlawry would strengthen the edict nicely.

After that, he was relieved to get back to an ordinary, unthreatening tax register. This one, from the eastern province of Develtos, made him feel good. A band of invading Halogai from the far north had sacked the fortress of Develtos not long after he became Avtokrator. This year, for the first time, revenues from the province exceeded what they'd been before the fortress fell.

*Well done,* he wrote at the bottom of the register. The logothetes and clerks who handled cadasters for the treasury would know he was pleased. Without their patient, usually unloved work, Videssos would crash to the ground. As Emperor, Krispos understood that. When he'd been a peasant, he'd loved tax collectors no better than any other kind of locust.

He got up, stretched, rubbed his eyes. Working by candlelight was hard, and had grown harder the past few years as his sight began to lengthen. He didn't know what he would do if his eyes kept getting worse: would he have to have someone read each petition to him and hope he could remember enough to decide it sensibly? He didn't look forward to that, but had trouble coming up with any better answer.

He stretched again, yawned until his jaw creaked. "The best answer right now is some sleep," he said aloud. He lit a little lamp at one of the candles, then blew them out. The smell of hot wax filled his nostrils.

Most of the torches in the hallway had gone out. The guttering flames of those that still burned made Krispos' shadow writhe and swoop like something with a life of its own. The lamp he carried cast a small, wan pool of light around him.

He walked past Barsymes' chamber. He'd lived there once himself, when he'd been one of the rare vestiarioi who were not eunuchs. Now he occupied the room next door, the imperial bedchamber. He'd slept there longer than in any other quarters he'd ever had. Sometimes that just seemed a simple part of the way his world worked. Tonight, though, as often happened when he thought about it, he found it very strange.

He opened the double doors. Inside the bedchamber, someone stirred. Ice ran up his back. He stooped to pluck a dagger from his scarlet boot, filled his lungs to shout for help from the Haloga guards at the entranceway to the imperial residence. Avtokrators of the Videssins too often died in unpeaceful ways.

The shout died unuttered; Krispos quickly straightened. This was no assassin in his bed, only one of the palace serving maids. She smiled an invitation at him.

He shook his head. "Not tonight, Drina," he said. "I told the esteemed sir I intended to go straight to sleep."

"That's not what he said to me, your Majesty," Drina answered, shrugging. Her bare shoulders gleamed in the lamplight as she sat up taller in bed. The lamp left most of the rest of her in shadow, making her an even greater mystery than woman ordinarily is. "He said to come make you happy, so here I am."

"He must have misheard." Krispos didn't believe that, not for a minute. Barsymes did not mishear his instructions. Every so often he simply decided not to listen to them. This seemed to be one of those nights. "It's all right, Drina. You may go."

In a small voice, the maid said, "May it please your Majesty, I'd truly sooner not. The vestiarios would be most displeased if I left you."

*Who rules here, Barsymes or I?* But Krispos did not say that, not out loud. He ruled the Empire, but around the palaces what was pleasing to the vestiarios had the force of law. Some eunuch chamberlains used their intimacy with the Avtokrator for their own advantage or that of their relatives. Barsymes, to his credit, had never done that. In exchange, Krispos deferred to him on matters affecting only the palaces.

So now he yielded with such grace as he could: "Very well, stay if you care to. No one need know we'll sleep on opposite sides of the bed."

Drina still looked worried but, like any good servant, knew how far she could safely push her master. "As you say, your Majesty." She scurried over to the far side of the bed. "Here, you rest where I've been lying. I'll have warmed it for you."

"It's not winter yet, by the good god, and I'm no invalid," Krispos said with a snort. But he pulled his robe off over his head and draped it on a bedpost. Then he stepped out of his sandals, blew out the lamp, and got into bed. The warm silk of the sheets was kind to his skin. As his head met the down-filled pillow, he smelled the faint sweetness that said Drina had rested there before him.

For a moment, he wanted her in spite of his own weariness. But when he opened his mouth to tell her so, what came out was an enormous yawn. He thought he excused himself, but fell asleep so fast he was never sure.

He woke up some time in the middle of the night. That happened more and more often as the years went by. He needed a few seconds to realize what the round smoothness pressed against his side was. Drina breathed smoothly, easily, carefree as a sleeping child. Krispo envied her lack of worry, then smiled when he thought he was partly responsible for it.

Now he did want her. When he reached over her shoulder to cup her breast in his hand, she muttered something drowsy and happy and rolled onto her back. She hardly woke up as he caressed her and then took her. He found that kind of trust strangely touching, and tried hard to be as gentle as he could.

Afterward, she quickly slipped back into deep sleep. Krispos got out of bed to use the chamber pot, then lay down beside her again. He, too, was almost asleep when he suddenly wondered, not for the first time, whether Barsymes knew him better than he knew himself.

The trouble with the Hall of the Nineteen Couches, Phostis thought, was that the windows were too big. The ceremonial hall, named back in the days when Videssian nobles actually ate reclining, was cooler in summer than most, thanks to those large windows. But the torches, lamps, and candles needed for nighttime feasts were lodestones for moths, mosquitoes, water bugs, even bats and birds. Watching a crisped moth land in the middle of a bowl of pickled octopus tentacles did not inflame the appetite. Watching a nightjar swoop down and snatch the moth out of the bowl made Phostis wish he'd never summoned his friends to the feast in the first place.

He thought about announcing it was over, but that wouldn't do, either. Inevitably, word would get back to his father. He could already hear Krispos' peasant-accented voice ringing in his ears: *The least you could do, son, is make up your mind.*

The imagined scolding seemed so real that he whipped his head around in alarm, wondering if Krispos had somehow snuck up behind him. But no—save for his own companions, he was alone here.

He felt very much alone. One thing his father had succeeded in doing was to make him wonder who cared for him because he was himself and who merely because he was junior Avtokrator and heir to the Videssian throne. Asking the question, though, often proved easier than answering it, so he had lingering suspicions about almost everyone he knew.

"You won't need to look over your shoulder like that forever, your Majesty," said Vatatzes, who was sitting at Phostis' right hand. He trusted Vatatzes further than most of his friends; being only the son of a mid-level logothete, the youth was unlikely to have designs on the crown himself. Now he slapped Krispos on the shoulder and went on, "Surely one day before too long, you'll be able to hold your feasts when and as you like."

One more word and he would have spoken treason. Phostis' friends frequently walked that fine line. So far, to his relief, nobody had forced him to pretend not to hear something. He, too, wondered—how could he help but wonder?—how long his father would stay vigorous. It might be another day, it might be another twenty years. No way to tell without magic, and even that held risks greater than he cared to take. For one thing, as was but fitting, the finest sorcerous talent in the Empire shielded the Avtokrator's fate from those who would spy it out. For another, seeking to divine an Emperor's future was in and of itself a capital crime.

Phostis wondered what Krispos was doing now. Administering affairs, probably; that was what his father usually did. A couple of years before, Krispos had tried to get him to share some of the burden. He'd tried, too, but it hadn't been pleasant work, especially because Krispos stood behind him while he shuffled through parchments.

Again, he could almost hear his father: "Hurry up, boy! One way or another, you have to decide. If you don't do it, who will?"

And his own wail: "But what if I'm wrong?"

"You will be, sometimes." Krispos had spoken with such maddening certainty that he wanted to hit him. "You try to do a couple of things: You try not to make the same mistake twice, and you take the chance to set one right later if it comes along."

Put that way, it sounded so easy. But after a couple of days of case after complex case, Phostis concluded ease in anything—fishing, sword-swallowing, running an empire, anything—came only with having done the job for years and years. As most young men do, he suspected he was brighter than his father. He certainly had a better education: He was good at ciphering, he could quote secular poets and historians as well as Phos' holy scriptures, and he didn't talk as if he'd just stepped away from a plow.

But Krispos had one thing he lacked: experience. His father did what needed doing almost without thinking about it, then went on to the next thing and took care of that, too. Meanwhile Phostis himself floundered and bit his lip, wondering where proper action lay. By the time he made one choice, three more had grown up to stare him in the face.

He knew he'd disappointed his father when he asked to be excused from his share of imperial business. "How will you learn what you need to know, save by this work?" Krispos had asked.

"But I can't do it properly," he'd answered. To him, that explained everything—if something didn't come easy, why not work at something else instead?

Krispos had shaken his head. "Wouldn't you sooner find that out now, while I'm here to show you what you need, then after I'm gone and you find the whole sack of barley on your back at once?"

The rustic metaphor hadn't helped persuade Phostis. He wished his family's nobility ran back farther than his father, wished he wasn't named for a poor farmer dead of cholera.

Vatatzes snapped him out of his gloomy reverie. "What say we go find us some girls, eh, your Majesty?"

"Go on if you care to. You'll probably run into my brothers if you do." Phostis laughed without much mirth, as much at himself as at Evripos and Katakolon. He couldn't even enjoy the perquisites of imperial life as they did. Ever since he'd discovered how many women would lie down with him merely on account of the title he bore, much of the enjoyment had gone out of the game.

Some nobles kept little enclosures where they hand-raised deer and boar until the animals grew tame as pets. Then they'd shoot them. Phostis had never seen the sport in that, or in bedding girls who either didn't dare say no or else turned sleeping with him into as cold-blooded a calculation as any Krispos made in the age-long struggle between Videssos and Makuran.

He'd tried explaining that to his brothers once, not long after Katakolon, then fourteen, seduced—or was seduced by—one of the women who did the palace laundry. Exalted by his own youthful prowess, he'd paid no heed whatever to Phostis. As for Evripos, he'd said only, "Do you want to don the blue robe and live out your life as a monk? Suit yourself, big brother, but it's not the life for me."

Had he wanted a monastic life, it would have been easy to arrange. But the sole reason he'd ever considered it was to get away from his father. He lacked both a monkish vocation and a monkish temperament. It wasn't that he sought to mortify his flesh, but rather that he—usually—found loveless or mercenary coupling more mortifying than none.

He often wondered how he would do when Krispos decided to marry him off. He was just glad that day had not yet arrived. When it did, he was sure his father would pick him a bride with more of an eye toward advantage for the imperial house than toward his happiness. Sometimes marriages of that sort worked as well as any others. Sometimes—

He turned to Vatatzes. "My friend, you know not how fortunate you are, coming from a family of but middling rank. All too often, I feel my birth more as a cage or a curse than as something in which to rejoice."

"Ah, your Majesty, you've drunk yourself sad, that's all it is." Vatatzes turned to the panpiper and pandoura player who made soft music as a background against which to talk. He snapped his fingers and raised his voice. "Here, you fellows, give us something lively now, to lift the young Majesty's spirits."

The musicians put their heads together for a moment. The man with the panpipes set them down and picked up a kettle-shaped drum. Heads came up all through the Hall of the Nineteen Couches as his hands evoked thunder from the drumhead. The pandoura player struck a ringing, fiery chord. Phostis recognized the Vaspurakaner dance they played, but it failed to gladden him.

Before long, almost all the feasters snaked along in a dance line, clapping their hands and shouting in time to the tune. Phostis sat in his place even when Vatatzes tugged at the sleeve of his robe. Finally, with a shrug, Vatatzes gave up and joined the dance. *He prescribed for me the medicine that works for him,* Phostis thought. He didn't want to be joyous, though. Discontent suited him.

When he got to his feet, the dancers cheered. But he did not join their line. He walked through the open bronze doors of the Hall of the Nineteen Couches, down the low, broad marble stairs. He looked up at the sky, gauging the time by how high the waning gibbous moon had risen. Somewhere in the fifth hour of the night, he judged—not far from midnight.

He lowered his eyes. The imperial residence was separated from the rest of the buildings of the palace compound and screened off by a grove of cherry trees, to give the Avtokrator and his family at least the illusion of privacy. Through the trees, Phostis saw one window brightly lit by candles or lamps. He nodded to himself. Yes, Krispos was at work there. With peasant persistence, his father kept on fighting against the immensity of the Empire he ruled.

As Phostis watched, the window went dark. Even Krispos occasionally yielded to sleep, though Phostis was sure he would have evaded it if he could.

Somebody stuck his head out through one of the Hall's many big windows. "Come on back, your Majesty," he called, voice blurry with wine. "It's just starting to get bouncy in here."

"Go on without me," Phostis said. He wished he'd never gathered the feasters together. The ease with which they enjoyed themselves only made his own unhappiness seem worse by comparison.

He absently swatted at a mosquito; there weren't as many out here, away from the lights. With the last lamps extinguished in the imperial residence, it fell into invisibility behind the cherry grove. He started walking slowly in that direction; he didn't want to get there until he was sure his father had gone to bed.

Haloga guardsmen stood outside the doorway. The big blond

northerners raised their axes in salute as they recognized Phostis. Had he been a miscreant, the axes would have gone up, too, but not as a gesture of respect.

As always, one of the palace eunuchs waited just inside the entrance. "Good evening, young Majesty," he said, bowing politely to Phostis.

"Good evening, Mystakon," Phostis answered. Of all the eunuch chamberlains, Mystakon was closest to his own age and hence the one he thought most likely to understand and sympathize with him. It hadn't occurred to him to wonder how Mystakon felt, going through what should have been ripe young manhood already withered on the vine, so to speak. "Is my father asleep?"

"He is in bed, yes," Mystakon answered with the peculiarly toneless voice eunuchs could affect to communicate subtle double meanings.

Phostis, however, noticed no subtleties tonight. All he felt was a surge of relief at having got through another day without having to confront his father—or having his father confront him. "I will go to bed, too, prominent sir," he said, using Mystakon's special title in the eunuch hierarchy.

"Everything is in readiness for you, young Majesty," Mystakon said, a tautology: Phostis would have been shocked were his chamber not ready whenever he needed it. "If you would be so kind as to accompany me—"

Phostis let the chamberlain guide him down the hallways he could have navigated blindfolded. In the torchlight, the souvenirs of long centuries of imperial triumph seemed somehow faded, indistinct. The conical helmet that had once belonged to a King of Kings of Makuran was just a lump of iron, the painting of Videssian troops pouring over the walls of Mashiz was a daub that could have depicted any squabble. Phostis shook his head. Was he merely tired, or was the light playing tricks on his eyes?

His bedchamber lay as far from Krispos' as it could, in a tucked-away corner of the imperial residence. It had stood empty for years, maybe centuries, until he chose it as a refuge from his father not long after his beard began to sprout.

The door to the chamber stood ajar. Butter-yellow light trickling through the opening said a lamp had been kindled. "Do you require anything further, young Majesty?" Mystakon asked. "Some wine, perhaps, or some bread and cheese? Or I could inquire if any mutton is left from that which was served to your father."

"No, don't bother," Phostis said, more sharply than he'd intended. He tried to soften his voice. "I'm content, thank you. I just want to get some rest."

"As you say, young Majesty." Mystakon glided away. Like many eunuchs, he was soft and plump. He walked in soft slippers, silently and with little mincing steps. With his robes swirling around him as he moved, he reminded Phostis of a beamy merchant ship under full sail.

Phostis closed and barred the door behind him. He took off his robe and got out of his sandals. They were all-red, like his father's—about the only imperial prerogative he shared with Krispos, he thought bitterly. He threw himself down on the bed and blew out the lamp. The bedchamber plunged into blackness, and Phostis into sleep.

He dreamed. He'd always been given to vivid dreams, and this one was more so than most. In it he found himself pacing, naked and fat, through a small enclosure. Food was everywhere—mutton, bread and cheese, jar upon jar of wine.

His father peered at him from over the top of a wooden fence. Phostis watched Krispos nod in sober satisfaction . . . and reach for a hunting bow.

Next thing he knew, he was awake, his heart pounding, his body bathed with cold sweat. For a moment, he thought the darkness that filled his sight meant death. Then full awareness returned. He sketched Phos' sun-circle above his chest in thanks as he realized his nightmare was not truth.

That helped calm him, until he thought of his place at court. He shivered. Maybe the dream held some reality after all.

Zaidas went down on his knees before Krispos, then to his belly, letting his forehead knock against the bright tesserae of the mosaic floor in full proskynesis. "Up, up," Krispos said impatiently. "You know I have no great use for ceremonial."

The wizard rose as smoothly as he had prostrated himself. "Yes, your Majesty, but *you* know the respect a mage will show to ritual. Without ritual, our art would fall to nothing."

"So you've said, many times these past many years," Krispos answered. "Now the ritual is over. Sit, relax; let us talk." He waved Zaidas to a chair in the chamber where he'd been working the night before.

Barsymes came in with a jar of wine and two crystal goblets. The vestiarios poured for Emperor and mage, then bowed himself out. Zaidas savored his wine's bouquet for a moment before he sipped. He smiled. "That's a fine vintage, your Majesty."

Krispos drank, too. "Aye, it is pleasant. I fear I'll never make a proper connoisseur, though. It's all so much better than what I grew up drinking that I have trouble telling what's just good from the best."

Zaidas took another, longer, pull at his goblet. "What we have here, your Majesty, is among the best, let me assure you." The mage was a tall, slim man, about a dozen years younger than Krispos—the first white threads were appearing in the dark fabric of his beard. Krispos remembered him as a skinny, excitable youth, already full of talent. It had not shrunk with his maturity.

Barsymes returned, now with a tureen and two bowls. "Porridge with salted anchovies to break your fast, your Majesty, excellent sir."

The porridge was of wheat, silky smooth, and rich with cream. The anchovies added piquancy. Krispos knew that if he asked his cook for plain, lumpy barley porridge, the man would quit in disgust. As with the wine, he knew this was better, but sometimes he craved the tastes with which he'd grown up.

When his bowl was about half empty, he said to Zaidas, "The reason I asked you here today was a report I've had from the westlands about a new heresy that seems to have arisen there. By this account, it's an unpleasant one." He passed the mage the letter from the priest Taronites.

Zaidas read it through, his brow furrowing in concentration. When he was done, he looked up at Krispos. "Yes, your Majesty, if the holy sir's tale is to be fully credited, these Thanasioi seem most unpleasant heretics indeed. But while there is some considerable connection between religion and sorcery, I'd have thought you'd go first to the ecclesiastical authorities rather than to a layman like me."

"In most cases, I would have. In fact, I've already directed the ecumenical patriarch to send priests to Pityos. But these

heretics sound so vile—if, as you say, Taronites is to be
believed—that I wondered if they have any connection to our
old friend Harvas."

Zaidas pursed his lips, then let air hiss out between.
Harvas—or perhaps his proper name was Rhavas—had dealt
the Empire fierce blows in the north and east in the first years
of Krispos' reign. He was, or seemed to be, a renegade priest
of Phos who had gone over to the dark god Skotos and thus
prolonged his own wicked life more than two centuries beyond
its natural terms. With help from Zaidas, among others,
Videssian forces had vanquished the Halogai that Harvas led at
Pliskavos in Kubrat; his own power was brought to nothing
there. But he had not been taken, alive or dead.

"What precisely do you wish me to do, your Majesty?"
Zaidas asked.

"You head the Sorcerers' Collegium these days, my friend,
and you were always sensitive to Harvas' style of magic. If
anyone can tell through sorcery whether Harvas is the one behind these Thanasioi, I expect you're the man. Is such a thing
possible, what with the little we have to go on here?" Krispos
tapped Taronites' letter with a forefinger.

"An interesting question." Zaidas looked through rather than
at Krispos as he considered. At last he said, "Perhaps it may
be done, your Majesty, though the sorcery required will be
most delicate. A basic magical principle is the law of similar-
ity, which is to say, like causes yield like effects. Most effective in this case, I believe, would be an inversion of the law in
an effort to determine whether like effects—the disruption and
devastation of the Empire now and from Harvas' past
depredations—spring from like causes."

"You know your business best," Krispos said. He'd never
tried to learn magical theory himself; what mattered to him
were the results he might attain through sorcery.

Zaidas, however, kept right on explaining, perhaps to fix his
ideas in his own mind. "The law of contagion might also prove
relevant. If Harvas was in physical contact with any of these
Thanasioi who then came into contact with the priest Taronites,
directly or indirectly, such a trace might appear on the parchment here. Under normal circumstances, two or three interme-
diate contacts would blur the originator beyond hope of
detection. Such was Harvas' power, however, and such was

our comprehension of the nature of that power, that it ought to be detectable at several more removes."

"Just as you say," Krispos answered agreeably. Perhaps because of his lectures at the Sorcerers' Collegium, Zaidas had a knack for expounding magecraft so clearly that it made sense to the Avtokrator, even if he lacked both ability and interest in practicing it himself. He asked, "How long before you will be ready to try your sorcery?"

That faraway look returned to Zaidas' eyes. "I shall of course require the parchment here. Then the research required to frame the precise terms of the spell to be employed and the gathering of the necessary materials ... not that those can't proceed concurrently, of course. Your Majesty, were it war, I could try tomorrow, or perhaps even tonight. I would be more confident of the results obtained, though, if I had another couple of days to refine my original formulation."

"Take the time you need to be right," Krispos said. "If Harvas is at the bottom of this, we must know it. And if he appears not to be, we must be certain he's not concealing himself through his own magic."

"All true, your Majesty." Zaidas tucked the letter from Taronites into the leather pouch he wore on his belt. He rose and began to prostrate himself again, as one did before leaving the Avtokrator's presence. Krispos waved a hand to tell him not to bother. Nodding, the wizard said, "I shall begin work at once."

"Thanks, Zaidas. If Harvas *is* on the loose—" Krispos let the sentence slide to an awkward halt. If Harvas was stirring up trouble again, he wouldn't sleep well until the wizard-prince was beaten ... or until he was beaten himself. In the latter case, his sleep would be eternal.

Zaidas knew that as well as he did. "One way or the other, your Majesty, we shall know," he promised. He bustled off to begin shaping the enchantments he would use to seek Harvas' presence.

Krispos listened to his footfalls fade down the corridor. He counted himself lucky to be served by men of the quality of Zaidas. In his less modest moments, he also thought their presence reflected well on his rule: would such good and able men have served a wicked, foolish master?

He got up from his seat, stretched, and went out into the

corridor himself. Coming his way was Phostis. Both men, young and not so young, stopped in their tracks, Krispos in the doorway, his heir in the middle of the hall.

Among all the other things Phostis was, he served as a living reminder that Krispos' rule would not endure forever. Krispos remembered taking him from the midwife's arms and holding him in the crook of his elbow. Now they were almost of a height; Phostis still lacked an inch, maybe two, of Krispos' stature, but Dara had been short.

Phostis was also a living reminder of his mother. Take away his neatly trimmed dark beard—these days thick and wiry, youth's downiness almost gone—and he wore Dara's face: his features were not as craggy as Krispos', and his eyes had the same distinctive small fold of skin at the inner corner that Dara's had.

"Good morning, Father," he said.

"Good morning," Krispos answered, wondering as always if he *was* Phostis' father. The young man did not look like him, but he did not look like Anthimos, either. Phostis did not have Krispos' native obstinacy, that was certain; the one time he'd tried showing the lad how the Empire worked, Phostis quickly lost interest. Krispos' heart ached over that, but he'd seen enough with Anthimos to know a man could not be forced to govern against his will.

*Good morning* was as much as Krispos and Phostis usually had to say to each other. Krispos waited for his eldest son to walk by without another word, as was his habit. But Phostis surprised him by asking, "Why were you closeted with Zaidas so early, Father?"

"There's some trouble with heresy out in the westlands." Krispos spoke matter-of-factly to keep Phostis from knowing he was startled. If the youngster did want to learn, he would teach him. More likely, though, Krispos thought with a touch of sadness, Phostis asked just for Zaidas' sake; the wizard was like a favorite uncle to him.

"What sort of heresy?" Phostis asked.

Krispos explained the tenets of the Thanasioi as well as he could from Taronites' description of them. This question surprised him less than the previous one; theology was Videssos' favorite intellectual sport. Laymen who pored over Phos' holy scriptures were not afraid to try conclusions with the ecumenical patriarch himself.

Phostis rubbed his chin as he thought, a gesture he shared with Krispos. Then he said, "In the abstract, Father, the doctrines sound rigorous, yes, but not necessarily inspired by Skotos. Their followers may have misinterpreted how these doctrines are to be applied, but—"

"To the ice with the abstract," Krispos growled. "What matters is that these maniacs are laying the countryside to waste and murdering anyone who doesn't happen to agree with them. Save your precious abstract for the schoolroom, son."

"I simply started to say—" Phostis threw his hands in the air. "Oh, what's the use? You wouldn't listen anyhow." Muttering angrily under his breath, he marched down the corridor past Krispos.

The senior Avtokrator sighed as he watched his son's retreating back. Maybe it was better when they just mouthed platitudes at each other: then they didn't fight. But how Phostis could find anything good to say about heretics who were also bandits was beyond Krispos. Only when his heir had turned a corner and disappeared did Krispos remember that he'd interrupted the lad before he finished talking about the Thanasioi.

He sighed again. He'd have to apologize to Phostis the next time he saw him. All too likely, Phostis would take the apology the wrong way and that would start another fight. Well, if it did, it did. Krispos was willing to take the chance. By the time he thought of going down the corridor and apologizing on the spot, though, it was too late. Phostis had already left the imperial residence.

Krispos went about the business of governing with only about three-fourths of his attention for the next couple of days. Every time a messenger or a chamberlain came in, the Avtokrator forgot what he was doing in the hope the fellow would announce Zaidas' sorcery was ready. Every time he was disappointed, he went back to work in an evil temper. No miscreants were pardoned while Zaidas prepared his magic.

When at last—within the promised two days, though Krispos tried not to notice that—Zaidas was on the point of beginning, he came himself to let the Emperor know. Krispos set aside with relief the cadaster he was reading. "Lead on, excellent sir!" he exclaimed.

One difficulty with being Avtokrator was that going anywhere automatically became complicated. Krispos could not simply walk with Zaidas over to the Sorcerers' Collegium. No, he had to be accompanied by a squad of Haloga bodyguards, which made sense, and by the dozen parasol bearers whose bright silk canopies proclaimed his office—which, to his way of thinking, didn't. Throughout his reign, he'd fought hard to do away with as much useless ceremonial as he could. He knew he was losing the fight; custom was a tougher foe than Harvas' blood-maddened barbarians had ever been.

At last, though, not too interminably much later, he stood inside Zaidas' chamber on the second story of the Sorcerers' Collegium. One big blond axeman went in there with him and the wizard; two more guarded the doorway. The rest waited outside the building with the parasol bearers.

Zaidas drew forth the parchment on which Taronites had written his accusations against the Thanasioi. He also produced another parchment, this one yellowed with age. Seeing Krispos' raised eyebrow, he explained, "I took the liberty of visiting the archives, your Majesty, to secure a document indited personally by Harvas. My first spell will compare them against each other to determine whether a common malice informs both."

"I see," Krispos said, more or less truthfully. "By all means carry on as if I were not here."

"Oh, I shall, your Majesty, for my own safety's sake above any other reason," Zaidas said. Krispos nodded. That he understood completely; he'd seized the crown after Anthimos, intent on destroying him by sorcery, botched an incantation and slew himself instead.

Zaidas intoned a low-voiced prayer to Phos, ending by sketching the sun-circle over his heart. Krispos imitated the gesture. The Haloga guard did not; like most of his fellows in Videssos the city, he still followed his own nation's fierce and gloomy gods.

The wizard took from a covered dish a couple of red-brown, shriveled objects. "The dried heart and tongue of a porpoise," he said. "They shall confer invincible effect on my charm." He cut strips off them with a knife, as if he were whittling soft wood, then tossed those strips into a squat bowl of bluish liquid. With each additional fragment, the blue deepened.

Stirring his mix left-handed with a silver rod, Zaidas chanted over the bowl and used his right hand to make passes above it. He frowned. "I can feel the wickedness we face here," he said, his voice tight and tense. "Now to learn whether it comes from one parchment or both."

He took the stirring rod and let a couple of drops of the mixture in the bowl fall on a corner of the letter from the archives, the one Harvas had written. The liquid flared bright red, just the color of fresh-spilled blood.

Zaidas drew back a pace. Though he was a layman, he drew the sun-circle again, even so. "By the good god," he murmured, now sounding shocked and shaken. "I never imagined a response as intense as that. Green, even perhaps yellow, but—" He broke off, staring at Harvas' letter as if it were displaying its fangs.

"I take it you expect the petition from Taronites to do the same if Harvas has a hand in turning the Thanasioi loose on us," Krispos said.

"I sincerely hope the solution does not turn crimson, your Majesty," Zaidas said. "That would in effect mean Harvas lurked just outside the temple wherein Taronites was writing. But the change of color will indicate the degree of relationship between Harvas and these new heretics."

More cautiously than he had before, the wizard daubed some of the liquid onto Taronites' letter. Krispos leaned forward, waiting to see what color the stuff turned. He did not know whether it would go red, but he expected some change, and probably not a small one. By Zaidas' choice of words, so did he.

But the liquid stayed blue.

Both men stared at it; for that matter, so did the bodyguard. Krispos asked, "How long must we wait for the change to take place?"

"Your Majesty, if it was going to occur, it would have done so by now," Zaidas answered. Then he checked himself. "I must always bear in mind that Harvas is a master of concealment and obfuscation. Being such, he might be able to evade this test, porpoise heart or no. But there is a cross check I do not think he can escape, try as he might."

The wizard picked up the two parchments, touched the damp spots on them together. "Being directly present in the one letter, Harvas' essence cannot fail to draw forth from the other any lingering trace of him." He held the two parchments against each other long enough to let a man draw five or six breaths, then separated them.

The blue smear on Taronites' petition remained blue, not green, yellow, orange, red, or even pink. Zaidas looked astonished. Krispos was not only astonished but also profoundly suspicious. He said, "Are you saying this means Harvas has nothing whatever to do with the Thanasioi? I find that hard to believe."

"So do I, your Majesty," Zaidas said. "If you ask what I say, I say the connection between the two is all too likely. My magic, however, seems to be saying something else again."

"But is your magic right, or have you just been deceived?" Krispos demanded. "Can you tell me for certain, one way or the other? I know you understand how important this is, not just to me but to Videssos now and in the future."

"Yes, your Majesty. Having faced Harvas once, having seen the evils he worked and those to which he inspired his followers, I know you want to be as positive as possible as to whether you—and we—confront him yet again."

"That is well put," Krispos said. He doubted he could have been so judicious himself. Truth was, as soon as he'd seen Taronites' letter, the fear of Harvas rose up in his mind like a ghost in one of the romances that the booksellers hawked in the plaza of Palamas. No matter what Zaidas' magical tests said about the Thanasioi, his own terror spoke louder to him. So he went on, "Excellent sir, have you any other sorceries you might use to find out whether this one is mistaken?"

"Let me think," Zaidas said, and proceeded to do just that for the next several minutes, standing still as a statue in the center of his study. Suddenly he brightened. "I know something which may serve." He hurried over to a cabinet set against one wall and began opening its small drawers and rummaging through them.

The Haloga guardsmen moved to place himself between Krispos and Zaidas, in case the wizard suddenly whipped out a dagger and tried to murder the Avtokrator. This he did though Zaidas was a longtime trusted friend, and though the chamber doubtless held weapons far more fell than mere

knives. Krispos smiled but did not seek to dissuade the northerner, who was but doing his duty as he reckoned best.

Zaidas let out a happy grunt. "Here we are." He turned
around, displaying not a dagger but rather a piece of highly
polished, translucent white stone. "This is nicomar, your Majesty, a variety of alabaster. When properly evoked, it has the
virtue of generating both victory and amity. Thus we shall see
if any amity, so to speak, lies between the two letters now in
our possession. If so, we shall know Harvas indeed has a hand
in the heresy of the Thanasioi."

"Alabaster, you say?" Krispos waited for Zaidas to nod,
then continued: "Some of the ceiling panels in the imperial
residence are also of alabaster, to let in more light. Why don't,
ah, victory and amity always dwell under my roof?" He
thought of his unending disagreements with Phostis.

"When properly evoked, I said, the stone brings forth those
virtues," Zaidas answered, smiling. "The evocation is not easy,
nor is the effect lasting."

"Oh." Krispos hoped he didn't sound too disappointed.
"Well, go ahead and do what you need to do, then."

The wizard prayed over the gleaming slab of nicomar and
anointed it with sweet-smelling oil, as if it were being made a
prelate or an Emperor. Krispos wondered if he would be able
to feel the change in the stone, as even a person of no sorcerous talent could feel the curative current that passed between
a healer-priest and his patient. To him, though, the nicomar remained simply a stone. He had to trust that Zaidas knew what
he was about.

With a final pass that seemed to require nearly jointless fingers, Zaidas said, "The good god willing, we are now ready to
proceed. First I shall examine the letter known to have been
written by Harvas."

He set the nicomar over the place where he had previously
splashed his magical liquid. Fierce red light blazed through the
stone. Krispos said, "This tells us what we already knew."

"So it does, your Majesty," Zaidas answered. "It also tells
me the nicomar is performing as it should." He lifted the thin
slab of stone and held it over a brass brazier from which the
pungent smoke of frankincense coiled slowly toward the ceiling. Before Krispos could ask what he was doing, he explained: "I fumigate the nicomar to remove from it the

influence of the parchment it just touched. Thus on the crucial test to come, the workings of the law of contagion shall not be permitted to influence the result. Do you see?"

Without waiting for Krispos' reply, the wizard set the polished alabaser down on the letter from Taronites. Krispos waited for another flash of red. But only a steady blue light penetrated the nicomar. "What does that mean?" Krispos asked, half hoping, half dreading Zaidas would tell him something other than the obvious.

But the wizard did not. "Your Majesty, it means that, so far as my sorcery can determine, no relationship whatever exists between the Thanasioi and Harvas."

"I still find that hard to believe," Krispos said.

"As I told you before, so do I," Zaidas answered. "But if you have a choice between believing whatever you happen to feel at the moment and that which has evidence to support it, which course will you take? I trust I know you well enough to know what you would say were it a matter of law rather than one of magic."

"There you have me," Krispos admitted. "You are so confident in what these conjurations tell you, then?"

"I am, your Majesty. Were it anyone but Harvas, the first test alone would have contented me. With the confirmation of its import by the nicomar, I would stake my life on the accuracy of what I have divined today."

"You may be doing just that, you know," Krispos said with a grim edge to his voice.

Zaidas looked startled for a moment, then nodded. "Yes, that's so, isn't it? Harvas on the loose once more would terrify the bravest." He spat on the floor between his feet to show his rejection of the evil god Skotos, the god Harvas had for a patron. "But by Phos, the lord with the great and good mind, I tell you again that Harvas is in no way connected to the Thanasioi. Misguided they may be; guided amiss by Harvas they are not."

He sounded so certain that Krispos had to believe him despite his own misgivings. As the sorcerer had said, evidence counted for more than vague feelings. And if Harvas' dread hand did not lie behind the Thanasioi, why, how dangerous could they possibly be? The Avtokrator smiled. Over the past couple of decades, he'd faced and overcome enough merely human foes to trust he had their measure.

"Thank you for relieving my mind, excellent sir. Your reward will not be small," he told Zaidas. Then, because the wizard had a habit of putting such rewards into the treasury of the Sorcerers' Collegium, he added, "Keep some for yourself this time, my friend. I command it."

"You needn't fear for that, your Majesty," Zaidas said. "In fact, I have already received the same instruction from one I reckon higher in rank than you."

Normally, the only entity a Videssian would reckon higher in rank than his Avtokrator was Phos. Krispos, though, knew perfectly well about whom Zaidas was talking. Chuckling, he said, "Tell Aulissa I say she is a good, sensible woman and makes you an excellent wife. Be sure you listen to her, too."

"I will pass your words to her as you say them," Zaidas promised. "With some other women, I might not, for fear of inflaming their notions of how important they are in the scheme of things. But since my dear Aulissa is as sensible as you say, I know she'll accept the compliment for what it's worth and not a copper more."

"The two of you are a good deal alike that way," Krispos said. "You're lucky to have each other."

Even when Dara was still alive, he'd sometimes envied Zaidas and Aulissa their tranquil happiness. They seemed to know each other's needs and adjust to each other's foibles as if they were two halves of the same person. His own marriage had not been like that. He and Dara got along well enough on the whole, but they'd always had their fall storms and wintry blizzards along with the warmth of summer. Zaidas and his wife seemed to live in late spring the year round.

The wizard said, "Besides, your Majesty, Aulissa has noted that Sotades is now twelve years old. The boy will soon begin his serious schooling, which, as she pointed out, requires serious quantities of gold."

"Ah, yes," Krispos said wisely, though as Avtokrator he had not had to worry about the expense of educating his sons: every scholar in the city was eager to have any or all of them as his pupils. Having taught the Emperor's child could only improve a savant's reputation . . . and one of those children would likely be Avtokrator himself one day. In Krispos' experience, scholars were no more immune to seeking influence than any other men.

"I am relieved for you, your Majesty, and for the Empire of Videssos," Zaidas said, nodding toward the table where he'd carried out his magic.

"I'm relieved, too." Krispos picked up the letter from Harvas which the wizard had used and quickly read it. It was the one wherein Harvas declared he had cut out Iakovitzes' tongue because the diplomat's freedom with it displeased him. Krispos was not sorry to put down the parchment. That had been far from the worst of Harvas' atrocities. Being spared the worry of another round of them was worth a goodly sum of gold.

When the Avtokrator left the conjuration chamber, the Haloga guard fell in behind him. The two axemen who had stood watch at the doorway preceded him out of the Sorcerers' Collegium. The parasol bearers had been sitting around outside the building and passing the time with the rest of the squad of imperial guards. Their canopies fluttered in agitation when the Avtokrator reappeared. After a moment, though, they formed themselves into the neat pairs that always accompanied Krispos in public.

On the trip back to the palace compound, their presence was pure ostentation, for almost the entire short journey was under covered colonnades. Not for the first time—not for the hundredth—Krispos wished he'd been able to get away with cutting the stifling ceremonial that surrounded him every hour of the day and night. But by the horror that thought evoked in the palace staff, in officials of the government, and even among his guards, he might have proposed offering sacrifice to Skotos on the altar of the High Temple. Fights against custom just were not winnable.

He turned around, glanced back north toward the Sorcerers' Collegium. He would reward Zaidas well indeed, not least for relieving his mind. If the Thanasioi had come up with their foolish heresy all on their own, he was sure he would have no trouble putting them down. In his two decades and more as Avtokrator, after all, he'd gone from one triumph to another. Why should this struggle be any different?

# II

From the outside, Phos' High Temple seemed more massive than beautiful. The heavy buttresses that carried the weight of the great central dome to the ground reminded Phostis of the thick, columnar legs of an elephant; one of the immense beasts had been imported to Videssos the city from the southern shore of the Sailors' Sea when he was a boy. It hadn't lived long, save in his memory.

A poem he'd read likened the High Temple to a glowing pearl concealed within an oyster. He didn't care as much for that comparison. The Temple's exterior was not rough and ugly, as oysters were, just plain. And its interior outshone any pearl.

Phostis climbed the stairway from the paved courtyard surrounding the High Temple up to the narthex or outer hall. Being only a junior Avtokrator, he was less hemmed round with ceremony than his father; only a pair of Haloga guardsmen flanked him on the stairs.

Many nobles hired bodyguards; none of the other people heading for the service paid Phostis any special heed. The High Temple was not crowded in any case, not for an early afternoon liturgy on a day of no particular ritual import. Instead of going up the narrow way to the screened-off imperial niche, Phostis decided to worship with everyone else in the main hall surrounding the altar. The Halogai shrugged and marched in with him.

He'd been going into the High Temple for as long as his

memory reached, and longer. He'd been just a baby when he was proclaimed Avtokrator here. For all that infinite familiarity, though, the Temple never failed to awe him.

The lavish use of gold and silver sheeting; the polished moss-agate columns with the acanthus capitals; the jewels and mother-of-pearl inserts set into the blond oak of the pews; the slabs of turquoise, pure white crystal, and rose quartz laid into the walls to simulate the sky at morning, noon, and eventide—for all these he had perspective; he had grown up among similar riches and lived with them still. But they served only to lead the eye up and up to the great dome that surmounted the altar and the mosaicwork image of Phos in its center.

The dome itself had the feel of a special miracle. Thanks to the sunbeams that penetrated the many small windows set into its base, it seemed to float above the rest of the Temple rather than being a part of it. The play of light off the gold-faced tesserae set at irregular angles made its surface sparkle and shift as one walked along far beneath it. Phostis could not imagine how the merely material might better represent the transcendence of Phos' heaven.

But even the glittering surround of the dome was secondary to Phos himself. The lord with the great and good mind stared down at his worshipers with eyes that not only never closed but also seemed to follow as they moved. If anyone concealed a sin, that Phos would see it. His long, bearded visage was stern in judgment. In his left hand, the good god held the book of life, wherein he recorded each man's every action. With death came the accounting: those whose evil deeds outweighed the good would fall to the eternal ice, while those who had worked more good than wickedness shared heaven with their god.

Phostis felt the weight of Phos' gaze each time he entered the High Temple. The lord with the great and good mind shown in the dome would surely grant justice, but mercy? Few men are arrogant enough to demand perfect justice, for fear they might get it.

The power of that image reached even the heathen Halogai. They looked up, trying to test their stares against the eternal eyes in the dome. As generations of men and women had learned before them, the test was more than any a mere man could successfully undertake. When they had to lower their gaze, they did so almost furtively, as if hoping no one had noticed them withdrawing from a struggle.

"It's all right, Bragi, Nokkvi," Phostis murmured as he sat between them. "No man can count himself worthy to confront the good god."

The big blond northerners scowled. Bragi's cheeks went red; with his fair, pale skin, the flush was easy to track. Nokkvi said, "We are Halogai, young Majesty. Our life is to fear nothing, to let nothing overawe us. In this picture dwells magic, to make us reckon ourselves less than what we are." His fingers writhed in an apotropaic sign.

"Measured against the good god, we are all less than we think ourselves to be," Phostis answered quietly. "That is what the image in the dome shows us."

Both his guards shook their heads. Before they could argue further, though, a pair of blue-robed priests, their pates shaven, their beards bushy and untrimmed, advanced down the aisle toward the altar. Each wore on his left breast a cloth-of-gold circlet, symbol of the sun, the greatest source of Phos' lights. The gem-encrusted thuribles they swung emitted great clouds of sweetly fragrant smoke.

As the priests passed each row of pews, the congregants sitting in it rose to their feet to salute Oxeites, ecumenical patriarch of the Videssians, who followed close behind them. His robe was of gold tissue, heavily overlain with pearls and precious stones. In all the Empire, only the Avtokrator himself possessed more splendid raiment. And, just as footgear all of red was reserved for the Emperor alone, so only the patriarch had the privilege of wearing sky-blue boots.

A choir of men and boys sang a hymn of praise to Phos as Oxeites took his place behind the altar. Their sweet notes echoed and reechoed from the dome, as if emanating straight from the good god's lips. The patriarch raised both hands over his head, looked up toward the image of Phos. Along with everyone in the High Temple save only his own two bodyguards, Phostis imitated him.

"We bless thee, Phos, lord with the great and good mind," Oxeites intoned, "by thy grace our protector, watchful beforehand that the great test of life may be decided in our favor."

All the worshipers repeated Phos' creed. It was the first prayer a Videssian heard, being commonly uttered over a new-born babe; it was the first prayer a child learned; it was the last utterance a believer gasped out before dying. To Phostis, it was as utterly familiar as the shape of his own hands.

More prayers and hymns followed. Phostis continued to make his responses without much conscious thought. The ritual was comforting; it lifted him out of himself and his petty cares of the moment, transformed him into part of something great and wise and for all practical purposes immortal. He cherished that feeling of belonging, perhaps because he found it here so much more easily than in the palaces.

Oxeites had the congregation repeat the creed with him one last time, then motioned for the worshipers to be seated. Phostis almost left the High Temple before the patriarch began his sermon. Sermons, being by their nature individual and specific, took him out of the sense of belonging he sought from worship. But since he had nowhere to go except back to the palaces, he decided to stay and listen. Not even his father could rebuke him for piety.

The ecumenical patriarch said, "I would like to have all of you gathered together with me today pause for a moment and contemplate the many and various ways in which the pursuit of wealth puts us in peril of the eternal ice. For in acquiring great stores of gold and gems and goods, we too easily come to consider their accumulation an end in itself rather than a means through which we may provide for our own bodily survival and prepare a path for our progeny."

*Our progeny?* Phostis thought, smiling. The Videssian clergy was celibate; if Oxeites was preparing a path for *his* progeny, he had more sins than greed with which to concern himself.

The patriarch continued, "Not only do we too readily value goldpieces for their own sake, those of us who do gain riches, whether honestly or no, often also endanger ourselves and our hope of joyous afterlife by grudging those who lack a share, however small, of our own good fortune."

He went on in that vein for some time, until Phostis felt ashamed to have a belly that was never empty, shoes on his feet, and thick robes and hypocausts to warm him through the winter. He raised his eyes to the Phos in the dome and prayed to the lord with the great and good mind to forgive him his prosperity.

But as his gaze descended from the good god to the ecumenical patriarch, he suddenly saw the High Temple in a new, disquieting light. Till this moment, he'd always taken for granted the flood of goldpieces that had been required to erect the Temple in the first place and the further flood that had gone into the precious stones and metals that made it the marvel it was. If those uncounted thousands of goldpieces had instead fed the hungry, shod the barefoot, clothed and warmed the shivering, how much better their lot would have been!

He knew the temples aided the poor; his own father told and retold the story of spending his first night in Videssos the city in the common room of a monastery. But for Oxeites, who wore cloth-of-gold, to urge his listeners to give up what they had to aid those who had not struck Phostis as nothing less than hypocrisy. And worse still, Oxeites himself seemed to have no sense of that hypocrisy.

Anger drove shame from Phostis. How did the ecumenical patriarch have the crust to propose that others give up their worldly goods when he said not a word about those goods the temples owned? Did he think they somehow acquired immunity from being put to good use—being put to the very use he himself advocated—because they were called holy?

By the tone of his sermon, he very likely did. Phostis tried to understand his way of thinking, tried and failed. The junior Avtokrator again glanced up toward the famous image of Phos. How did the lord with the great and good mind view calls to poverty from a man who undoubtedly possessed not just one but many sets of regalia, the value of any of which could have supported a poor family for years?

Phostis decided the good god would set down grim words for Oxeites in his book of judgment.

The patriarch kept preaching. That he did not realize the contradiction inherent in his own views irked Phostis more with every word he heard. He hadn't enjoyed the courses in logic Krispos ordained for him, but they'd left their mark. He wondered if next he would hear a raddled whore extolling the virtues of virginity. It would, he thought, be hardly less foolish than what he was listening to now.

"We bless thee, Phos, lord with the great and good mind, by thy grace our protector, watchful beforehand that the great test of life may be decided in our favor," Oxeites proclaimed for the last time. Even without his robes, he would have been tall and slim and distinguished, with a pure white beard and silky eyebrows he surely combed. When he wore the patriarchal vestments, he seemed to the eye the very image of holiness. But his words rang hollow in Phostis' heart.

Most of the worshipers filed out of the High Temple after the liturgy was over. A few, though, went up to the ecumenical patriarch to congratulate him on his sermon. Phostis shook his head, bemused. Were they deaf and blind, or merely out to curry favor? Either way, Phos would judge them in due course.

As he walked down the steps from the Temple to the surrounding courtyard, Phostis turned to one of his guardsmen and said, "Tell me, Nokkvi, do you Halogai house your gods so richly in your own country?"

Nokkvi's ice-blue eyes went wide. He threw back his head and boomed laughter; the long blond braid he wore bounced up and down as his shoulders shook. When he could speak again, he answered, "Young Majesty, in Halogaland we have not so much for ourselves that we can give our gods such spoils as you fashion for your Phos. In any case, our gods care more for blood than for gold. There we feed them well."

Phostis knew of the northern gods' thirst for gore. The holy Kveldulf, a Haloga who came to revere Phos, was reckoned a martyr in Videssos: his own countrymen had slaughtered him when he tried to convert them to worshiping the lord with the great and good mind. Indeed, the Halogai would have been far more dangerous foes to the Empire did they not incessantly shed one another's blood.

Nokkvi stepped down on the flat flagstones of the courtyard. When he turned to look back at the High Temple, his gaze went wolfish. He said, "I tell you this, too, young Majesty: let but a few shiploads full of my folk free to reive in Videssos the city, and your god, too, will know less of gold and more of blood. Maybe that savor will better satisfy him."

Phostis gestured to turn aside the northerner's words. The Empire was still rebuilding and repeopling towns that Harvas' Halogai had sacked around the time he was born. But even having such a store of riches here in the imperial capital was a temptation not just to the fierce barbarians from the north, but also to avaricious men within the Empire. Any store of riches was such, in fact.

He stopped, his mouth falling open. All at once, he began to understand how the Thanasioi came by their doctrines.

The great bronze valves of the doorway to the Grand Courtroom slowly swung open. Seated on the imperial throne, Krispos got a sudden small glimpse of the outside world. He smiled; the outside world seemed only most distantly connected to what went on here.

He sometimes wondered whether the Grand Courtroom wasn't even more splendid than the High Temple. Its ornaments were less florid, true, but to them was added the ever-changing spectacle of the rich robes worn by the nobles and bureaucrats who lined either side of the colonnade leading from the bronze doors to Krispos' throne. The way between the two columns was a hundred yards of emptiness that let any petitioner think on his own insignificance and the awesome might of the Avtokrator.

In front of the throne stood half a dozen Haloga guardsmen in full battle gear. Krispos had read in the histories of previous reigns that one Emperor had been assassinated on the throne and three others wounded. He did not aim to provide similarly edifying reading for any distant successor.

A herald, distinguished by a white-painted staff, had his place beside the northerners. He took one step forward. The courtiers left off their own chattering. Into the silence, the herald said, "Tribo, the envoy from Nobad, son of Gumush, the khagan of Khatrish, begs leave to approach the Avtokrator of the Videssians." His trained voice was easily audible from one end of the Grand Courtroom to the Other.

"Let Tribo of Khatrish approach," Krispos said.

"Let Tribo of Khatrish approach!" Sprung from the herald's thick chest, the words might have been a command straight from the mouth of Phos.

From a small silhouette in the bright but distant doorway, Tribo grew to man-size as he sauntered up the aisle toward the throne. He slowed every so often to exchange a smile or a couple of words with someone he knew, thereby largely defeating the intimidation built into that walk.

Krispos had expected nothing less; Khatrishers seemed born to subvert any existing order. Even their nation was less than three centuries old, born when Khamorth nomads from the plains of Pardraya overran what had been Videssian provinces. To some degree, they aped the Empire these days, but their ways remained looser than those that were in good form among Videssians.

Tribo paused the prescribed distance from the imperial throne, sinking down to his knees and then to his belly in full proskynesis: some Videssian rituals could not be scanted. As the envoy remained with his forehead pressed against the polished marble of the floor, Krispos tapped the left arm of the throne. With a squeal of gears, it rose several feet in the air. The marvel was calculated to overawe barbarians. From his new height, Krispos said, "You may rise, Tribo of Khatrish."

"Thank you, your Majesty." Like most of his folk, the ambassador spoke Videssian with a slight lisping accent. In Videssian robes, he could have passed for an imperial but for his beard, which was longer and more unkempt than even a priest would wear. The khagans of Khatrish encouraged that style among their upper classes, to remind them of the nomad raiders from whom they had sprung. Tribo was also un-Videssian in his lack of concern for the imperial dignity. Cocking his head to one side, he remarked, "I think your chair needs oiling, your Majesty."

"You may be right," Krispos admitted with a sigh. He tapped the arm of the throne again. With more metallic squeaks, servitors behind the courtroom wall returned him to his former place.

Tribo did not quite smirk, but the expression he assumed shouted that he would have, in any other company. He definitely was less than overawed. Krispos wondered if that meant he couldn't be reckoned a barbarian. Perhaps so: Khatrish's usages were not those of Videssos, but they had their own kind of understated sophistication.

All that was by the way—though Krispos did make a mental note that he need not put the crew of musclemen behind the wall next time he granted Tribo a formal audience. The Avtokrator said, "Shall we to business, then?"

"By all means, your Majesty." Tribo was not rude, certainly not by his own people's standards and not really by the Empire's, either. He just had a hard time taking seriously the elaborate ceremonial in which Videssos delighted. The moment

matters turned substantive, his half-lazy, half-insolent manner
dropped away like a discarded cloak.

As Avtokrator, Krispos had the privilege of speaking first: "I
am not pleased that your master the khagan Nobad son of
Gumush has permitted herders from Khatrish to come with
their flocks into territory rightfully Videssian, and to drive our
farmers away from the lands near the border. I have written to
him twice about this matter, with no improvement. Now I
bring it to your attention."

"I shall convey your concern to his mighty Highness," Tribo
promised. "He in turn complains that the recently announced
Videssian tariff on amber is outrageously high and is being col-
lected with overharsh rigor."

"The second point may perhaps concern him more than the
first," Krispos said. Amber from Khatrish was a monopoly of
the khagan's; his profits on its sale to Videssos helped fatten
his treasury. The tariff let the Empire profit, too. Krispos had
also beefed up customs patrols to discourage smuggling. In his
younger days, he'd been to Opsikion near the border with
Khatrish and seen amber smugglers in action. The firsthand
knowledge helped combat them.

Tribo assumed an expression of outraged innocence. "The
khagan Nobad son of Gumush wonders at the justice of a sovereign who seeks lower tolls from the King of Kings on his
western border at the same time as he imposes higher ones to
the detriment of Khatrish."

A low mutter ran through the courtiers; few Videssians
would have spoken so freely to the Avtokrator. Krispos
doubted whether Nobad knew about his discussions with
Rubyab of Makuran over caravan tolls. Tribo, however, all too
obviously did, and served his khagan well thereby.

"I might reply that any soverign's chief duty is to promote
the advantage of his own realm," Krispos said slowly.

"So you might, were you not Phos' vicegerent on earth,"
Tribo replied.

The mutter from the nobles got louder. Krispos said, "I do
not find it just, eminent envoy, for you who are a heretic to use
to your own ends my position in the faith as practice within
Videssos."

"I crave your Majesty's pardon," Tribo said at once. Krispos
stared suspiciously; he hadn't thought things would be that

easy. They weren't. Tribo resumed, "Since you reminded me I am a heretic in your eyes, I will employ my own usages and ask you where in the Balance justice lies."

Videssian orthodoxy held that Phos would at the end of time surely vanquish Skotos. Theologians in the eastern lands of Khatrish and Thatagush, however, had needed to account for the eruption of the barbarous and ferocious Khamorth into their lands and the devastation resulting therefrom. They proclaimed that good and evil lay in perfect balance, and no man could be certain which would triumph in the end. Anathemas from Videssos the city failed to bring them back to what the Empire reckoned the true faith; abetted by the eastern khagans, they hurled anathemas of their own.

Krispos had no use for the Balancer heresy, but he had trouble denying that it was just for Khatrish to expect consistency from him. Concealing a sigh, he said, "Room for discussion about how we impose the tariffs may possibly exist."

"Your Majesty is gracious." Tribo sounded sincere; maybe he even was.

"As may be," Krispos said. "I also have complaints that ships from out of Khatrish have stopped and robbed several fishing boats off the coast of our dominions, and even taken a cargo of furs and wine off a merchantman. If such piracy goes on, Khatrish will face the Empire's displeasure. Is that clear?"

"Yes, your Majesty," Tribo said, again sincerely. Videssos' navy was vastly stronger than Khatrish's. If the Avtokrator so desired, he could ruin the khaganate's sea commerce without much effort.

"Good," Krispos said. "Mind you, I'll expect to see a change in what your people do; fancy promises won't be enough." Anyone who didn't spell that out in large letters to a Khatrisher deserved the disappointment he would get. But Tribo nodded; Krispos had reason to hope the message was fully understood. He asked, "Have you any more matters to raise at this time, eminent envoy?"

"Yes, your Majesty, may it please you, I do."

The reply caught Krispos by surprise; the agenda he'd agreed upon with the Khatrisher before the audience was complete. But he said, as he had to, "Speak, then."

"Thank you for your patience, your Majesty. But for the theological, er, discussion we just had, I would not presume to mention this. However: I know you believe that we who follow the Balance are heretics. Still, I must question the justice of inflicting upon us your own different and, if I may say so, more pernicious heresies."

"Eminent sir, I hope you in turn will forgive me, but I haven't the faintest idea of what you're talking about," Krispos answered.

Tribo's look said he'd thought the Emperor above stooping to such tawdry denials. That only perplexed Krispos the more; as far as he knew, he was telling the truth. Then the ambassador said, as scornfully as he could to a sovereign stronger than his own, "Do you truly try to tell me you have never heard of the murderous wretches who call themselves Thanasioi? Ah, I see by your face that you have."

"Yes, I have; at my command, the most holy sir the ecumenical patriarch Oxeites is even now convening a synod to condemn them. But how do you know of their heresy? So far as I have learned, it's confined to the westlands, near our frontier with Makuraner-held Vaspurakan. Few places in the Empire of Videssos lie farther from Khatrish."

"That may be so, your Majesty, but merchants learn the goods most worth shipping a long way are those with the least bulk," Tribo said. "Ideas, so far as I know, have no bulk at all. Perhaps some seamen picked up the taint in Pityos. Be that as it may, we have bands of Thanasioi in a couple of our coastal towns."

Krispos ground his teeth. If Khatrish held Thanasioi, their doctrines had undoubtedly spread to Videssian ports, as well. And that meant Videssos the city probably—no, certainly—had Thanasioi prowling its streets. "By the good god, eminent envoy, I swear we've not tried to spread this heresy to your land. Very much the opposite, in fact."

"Your Majesty has said it," Tribo said, by which Krispos knew that were he addressing anyone save the Avtokrator of the Videssians, he would have called him a liar. Perhaps realizing that even by Khatrisher standards he'd been overblunt, the envoy went on, "I pray your forgiveness, your Majesty, but you must understand that, from the perspective of my master Nobad son of Gumush, stirring up religious strife within our bounds is a ploy Videssos might well attempt."

"Yes, I can see that it might be," Krispos admitted. "You

may tell your master, though, that it's a ploy I don't care to use. Since Videssos should have only one faith, I'm not surprised to find other sovereigns holding the same view."

"Please note I intend it for a compliment when I say that, for an Avtokrator of the Videssians, you are a moderate man," Tribo said. "Most men who wear the red buskins would say there should be only one faith through all the world, and that the one which emanates from Videssos the city."

Krispos hesitated before he answered; Tribo's "compliment" had teeth in it. Because Videssos had once ruled all the civilized world east of Makuran, universality was a cornerstone of its dealings with other states and of its theology. To deny that universality would give Krispos' nobles an excuse to mutter among themselves. He wanted them to have no such excuses.

At last he said, "Of course there should be only one faith; how else may a realm count on its folk remaining loyal to it? But since we have not met that ideal in Videssos, we would be in a poor position to pursue it elsewhere. Besides, eminent envoy, if you accuse us of introducing a new heresy into Khatrish, you can hardly at the same time accuse us of trying to force your people into orthodoxy."

Tribo's mouth twisted into a smile that lifted only one corner of it. "The first argument has some weight, your Majesty. As for the second one, I'd like it better in a school of logic than I do in the world. You could well hope to throw us into such religious strife that your folk might enter Khatrish and be acclaimed as rescuers."

"Your master Nobad son of Gumush is well served in you, eminent envoy," Krispos said. "You see more facets in a matter than a jeweler could carve."

"Thank you, your Majesty!" Tribo actually beamed. "Coming from a man with twenty-two years on the throne of Videssos, there's praise indeed. I shall convey to his mighty Highness that Videssos is itself plagued by these Thanasioi and not responsible for visiting them upon my country."

"I hope you do, for that is the truth."

"Your Majesty." Tribo prostrated himself once more, then rose and backed away from the throne until he had gone far enough to turn around without offending the Avtokrator of the Videssians. As far as Krispos was concerned, the ambassador could simply have turned his back and walked away, but the imperial dignity did not permit such ordinary behavior in his presence. He sometimes thought of his office as having a personality of its own, and a stuffy one at that.

Before he left the Grand Courtroom, he reminded himself to have the gear train behind his throne oiled.

"Good morning, your Majesty." With a mocking smile on his face, Evripos made as if to perform a proskynesis right in the middle of the corridor.

"By the good god, little brother, let it be," Phostis said wearily. "You're just as much—and just as little—Avtokrator as I am."

"That's true, for now. But I'll forever be just as little Avtokrator as you are, where after a while I won't be just as much. Do you expect me to be happy about that, just because you were born first? I'm sorry, your Majesty—" The scorn Evripos put into the title was withering. "—but you ask too much."

Phostis wished he could punch his brother in the face, as he had when they were boys. But Evripos was his little brother now only in age; he had most of a palm on Phostis in height and was thicker through the shoulders to boot. These days, he'd be the one to do most of the punching in a fight.

"I can't help being eldest, any more than you can help being born second," Phostis said. "Only one of us will be able to rule when the time comes; that's just the way things are. But who better than my brothers to—"

"—be your lapdogs," Evripos broke in, looking down his long nose at Phostis. Like Phostis, he had his mother's distinctive eyes, but the rest of his features were those of Krispos. Phostis also suspected Evripos had more of their father's driving ambition than he himself had . . . or perhaps it was simply that Evripos was in a position where ambition stood out more. If events continued in their expected course, Phostis would be *the* Avtokrator of the Videssians. Evripos wanted the job, but was unlikely to get it by any legitimate means.

Phostis said, "Little brother, you and Katakolon can be my mainstays on the throne. Better to have family aid a man than outsiders—safer, too." *If I can trust you,* he added to himself.

"So you say now," Evripos retorted. "But I've had to read the historians just as you have. Once one son becomes Emperor, what's left for the others? Nothing, maybe less. They only show up in the books because they've raised a rebellion or else because they get a name for debauchery."

"Who gets a name for debauchery?" Katakolon asked as he came down the corridor of the imperial residence. He grinned at his two grim-faced brothers. "Me, I hope."

"You're well on your way to it, that's certain," Phostis told him. The remark should have been cutting; instead, it came out with an unmistakable ring of envy. Katakolon's grin got wider.

Phostis felt like punching him, too, but he was Evripos' size or bigger. Like Evripos, he favored Krispos in looks. Of the three of them, though, he had the sunny disposition. Being the heir set heavy responsibilities on Phostis. Evripos saw only Phostis standing between him and what he wanted. Both older brothers had better claims to the throne than Katakolon, who didn't seem interested in sitting on it, anyhow. All he wanted was to enjoy himself, which he did.

Evripos said, "His imperial Majesty here is deigning to parcel out to us our subordinate duties once he becomes senior Avtokrator."

"Well, why not?" Katakolon said. "That's how it's going to be, unless Father ties him in a weighted sack and flings him into the Cattle-Crossing. Father might, too, the way they go at each other."

Had Evripos said that, Phostis probably would have hit him. From Katakolon, it was just so many words. Not only was the youngest brother slow to take offense, he had trouble giving it, too.

Katakolon went on, "I know one of the subordinate duties I'd like, come the day: supervising the treasury subbureau that collects taxes from within the city walls."

"By the good god, why?" Evripos said, beating Phostis to the punch. "Isn't that rather too much like work for your taste?"

"That subbureau of the treasury collects tax receipts from and generally has charge of the city's brothels." Katakolon licked his lips. "I'm certain any Avtokrator would appreciate the careful inspection I'd give them."

For once, Phostis and Evripos looked equally disgusted. It wasn't that Evripos failed to delight in venery; he was at least as bold a man of his lance as Katakolon. But Evripos did what he did without chortling about it to all and sundry afterward. Phostis suspected he was disgusted with Katakolon more for revealing a potential vulnerability than for his choice of supervisory position.

Phostis said, "If we don't stick together, brothers, there are plenty in the city who would turn us against one another, for their own benefit rather than ours."

"I'm too busy with my own tool to become anyone else's," Katakolon declared, at which Phostis threw up his hands and stalked away.

He thought about going to the High Temple to ask Phos to grant his brothers some common sense, but decided not to. After Oxeites' hypocritical sermon, the High Temple, an edifice in which he had taken pride like almost every other citizen of Videssos the city and indeed of the Videssian Empire, now seemed only a repository for mountains of gold that could have been better spent in countless other ways. He could hate the ecumenical patriarch for that alone, for destroying the beauty and grandeur of the Temple in his mind.

As he stamped out of the imperial residence, a pair of Halogai from the squadron at the entrance attached themselves to him. He didn't want them, but knew the futility of ordering them back to their post—they would just answer, in their slow, serious northern voices, that *he* was their post.

Instead, he tried to shake them off. They were, after all, encumbered with mail shirts, helms, and two-handed axes. For a little while, he thought he might succeed; sweat poured down their faces as they sped up to match his own quick walk, and their fair skins grew pink with exertion. But they were warriors, in fine fettle, and refused to wilt in heat worse than any for which their northern home had prepared them. They clung to him like limpets.

He slowed down as he reached the borders of the palace compound and started across the crowded plaza of Palamas. He thought of losing himself among the swarms of people there, but, before he could transform thought to deed, the Halogai moved up on either side of him and made a break impossible.

He was even glad of their presence as he traversed the square. Their broad, mailed shoulders and forbidding expressions helped clear a path through the hucksters, soldiers, housewives, scribes, whores, artists, priests, and folk of every other sort who used the plaza as a place wherein to sell, to buy, to gossip, to cheat, to proclaim, or simply to gawp.

Once Phostis got to the far side of the plaza of Palamas, he headed east along Middle Street without even thinking about it. He walked past the red granite pile of the government office building before he consciously realized what he'd done: a few more blocks, a left turn, and his feet would have taken him to the High Temple even though the rest of him didn't want to go there.

He glared down at his red boots, as if wondering if his brothers had somehow suborned them. With slow deliberation, he turned right rather than left at the next corner. He made a few more turns at random, leaving behind the familiar main street of Videssos the city for whatever its interior might bring him.

The Halogai muttered back and forth in their own language. Phostis could guess what they were saying: something to the effect that two guards might not be enough to keep him out of trouble in this part of town. He pushed ahead anyhow, reasoning that although bad things could happen, odds were they wouldn't.

Away from Middle Street and a few other thoroughfares, Videssos the city's streets—lanes might have been a better word, or even alleys—forgot whatever they might have known about the idea of a straight line. The narrow little ways were made to seem narrower still because the upper stories of buildings extended out over the cobblestones toward each other. The city had laws regulating how close together they could come, but if any inspector had been through this section lately, he'd been bribed to look up with a blind eye toward the scrawny strip of blue that showed between balconies.

People on the streets gave Phostis curious looks as he walked along: it was not a district in which nobles in fine robes commonly appeared. No one bothered him, though; evidently two big Haloga guards *were* enough. A barmaid-pretty girl of about his own age stopped and smiled at him. She drew up one hand to toy with her hair and incidentally show off her breasts to the best advantage. When he didn't pause, she gave him the two-fingered street gesture that implied he was effeminate.

The shops in this part of town kept their doors closed. When a customer opened one, Phostis saw its timbers were thick enough to grace a citadel. But for their doors, probably just as thick, houses presented blank fronts of stucco or brick to the street. Though that was normal in Videssos the city, most dwellings being built around courtyards, here it seemed as if they were making a point of concealing whatever they had.

Phostis was on the point of trying to make his way back to Middle Street and his own part of town when he came upon men in ragged cloaks and worker's tunics and women in cheap, faded dresses filing into a building that at first looked no more prepossessing than any other hereabouts. But on its roof was a wooden tower topped with a globe whose gilding had seen better days: this, too, was a temple to Phos, though as different from the High Temple as could be imagined.

He smiled and made for the entrance. He'd wanted to pray when he left the palaces, but hadn't been able to stomach listening to Oxeites celebrate the liturgy again. Maybe the good god had guided his footsteps hither.

The ordinary people going in to pray didn't seem to think Phos had anything to do with it. The stares they gave Phostis weren't curious; they were downright hostile. A man wearing the bloodstained leather apron of a butcher said, "Here, friend, don't you think you'd be more content praying somewheres else?"

"Somewhere fancy, like you are?" a woman added. She didn't sound admiring; to her the word was one of reproach.

Some of the shabby band of worshipers carried knives on their belts. In a rundown part of the city like this, snatching up paving stones to hurl would be the work of a moment. The Halogai realized that before Phostis did, and moved to put themselves between him and what could become a mob.

"Wait," he said. Neither northerner even turned to look at him. Keeping their eyes on the crowd in front of the little temple, they wordlessly shook their heads. He was barely tall enough to peer at the people over their armored shoulders. Pitching his voice to carry to the Videssians, he declared, "I've had my fill of worshiping Phos at fancy temples. How can we hope the good god will hear us if we talk about helping the poor in a building richer than even the Avtokrator enjoys?"

No one had noticed his red boots. Behind the Halogai, they

would be all but invisible. Like the people in the streets, the congregants must have taken him for merely a noble out slumming. His words made the city folk pause and murmur among themselves.

After a small pause, the butcher said, "You really mean that, friend?"

"I do," Phostis answered loudly. "By the lord with the great and good mind, I swear it."

Either his words or his tone must have carried conviction, for the band of worshipers stopped scowling and began to beam. The butcher, who seemed to be their spokesman, said, "Friend, if you do mean that, you can hear what our priest, the good god bless him, has to say. We don't even ask that you keep quiet about it afterward, for it's sound doctrine. Am I right, my friends?"

Everyone around him nodded. Phostis wondered whether this congregation employed *friend* as a general term or if it was just the man's way of speaking. He rather hoped the former was true. The usage might be unusual among Phos' followers, but he liked its spirit.

Still grumbling, the Halogai grudgingly let him go into the temple, though one preceded him and the other followed close behind. A few icons with images of Phos hung on the roughly plastered walls; otherwise, the place was bare of ornament. The altar behind which the priest stood was of carven pine. His blue robe, of the plainest wool, lacked even a cloth-of-gold circle above his heart to symbolize Phos' sun.

The good god's creed and liturgy, though, remained the same regardless of setting. Phostis followed this priest as easily as he had the ecumenical patriarch. The only difference was that this ecclesiastic spoke with an upcountry accent even stronger than that of Krispos, who had worked hard to shed his peasant intonation. The priest came from the west, Phostis judged, not from the north like his father.

When the required prayers were over, the priest surveyed his congregants. "I rejoice that the lord with the great and good mind has brought you back to me once more, friends," he said. His eyes fixed on Phostis and the Haloga guards as he uttered that last word, as if he wondered whether they deserved to come under it.

Giving them the benefit of the doubt, he continued:

"Friends, we have not been cursed with much in the way of material abundance." Again he gave Phostis a measuring stare. "I praise the lord with the great and good mind for that, for we have not much to give away before we come to be judged in front of his holy throne."

Phostis blinked; this was not the sort of theological reasoning he was used to hearing. This priest took off from the point at which Oxeites had halted. But he, unlike the patriarch, lacked hypocrisy. He was plainly as poor as his temple and his congregation. That in and of itself inclined Phostis to take him seriously.

He went on, "How can we hope to rise to the heavens while weighted down with gold in our belt pouches? I will not say it cannot be, friends, but I say that few of the rich live lives sufficiently saintly to rise above the dross they value more than their souls."

"That's right, holy sir!" a woman exclaimed. Someone else, a man this time, added, "Tell the truth!"

The priest picked that up and set it into his sermon as neatly as a mason taking a brick from a new pile. "Tell the truth I shall, friends. The truth is that everything the foolish rich run after is but a snare from Skotos, a lure to drag them down to his eternal ice. If Phos is the patron of our souls, as we know him to be, then how can material things be his concern? The answer is simple, friends: they cannot. The material world is Skotos' plaything. Rejoice if you have but little share therein; would it were true for all of us. The greatest service we can render to one who knows not this truth is to deprive him of that which ties him to Skotos, thereby liberating his soul to contemplate the higher good."

"Yes," a woman cried, her voice high and breathy, as if in ecstasy. "Oh, yes!"

The butcher who had spoken to Phostis still sounded solid and matter-of-fact. "I pray that you guide us in our renunciation of the material, holy sir."

"Let your own knowledge of moving toward Phos' holy light be your guide, friend," the priest answered. "What you renounce is yours only in this world at best. Will you risk an eternity in Skotos' ice for its sake? Only a fool would act so."

"We're no fools," the butcher said. "We know—" He broke off to give Phostis yet another measuring stare; by this time,

Phostis was sick of them. Whatever he had been about to say, he reconsidered, starting again after a barely noticeable pause: "We know what we know, by the good god."

The rest of the people in the shabby temple knew whatever it was the butcher knew. They called out in agreement, some loudly, some softly, all with more belief and piety in their voices than Phostis had ever heard from the prominent folk who most often prayed in the High Temple. His brief anger at being excluded from whatever they knew soon faded. He wished he could find something to believe in with as much force as these people gave to their faith.

The priest raised his hands to the heavens, then spat between his feet in ritual rejection of Skotos. He led the worshipers in Phos' creed one last time, then announced the end of the liturgy. As Phostis turned and left the temple, once more bracketed fore and aft by his bodyguards, he felt a sense of loss and regret on returning to the mundane world that he'd never known when departing from the superficially more awesome setting of the High Temple. An impious comparison crossed his mind: it was almost as if he were returning to himself after the piercing pleasure of the act of love.

He shook his head. As the priest had said, what were those thrashings and moanings, what were any earthly delights, if they imperiled his soul?

"Excuse me," someone said from behind him: the butcher. Phostis turned. So did the Halogai with him. The axes twitched in their hands, as if hungry for blood. The butcher ignored them; he spoke to Phostis as if they were not there: "Friend, you seem to have thought well of what you heard in the temple. That's just a hunch of mine, mind you—if I'm wrong, you tell me and I'll go my way."

"No, good sir, you're not wrong." Phostis wished he'd thought to say "friend," too. Well, too late now. He continued, "Your priest there preaches well, and has a fiery heart like few I've heard. What good is wealth if it hides in a hoard or is wantonly wasted when so many stand in need?"

"What good is wealth?" the butcher said, and let it go at that. If his eye flicked over the fine robe Phostis wore, they did so too fast for the younger man to notice. The butcher went on, "Maybe you would like to hear more of what the holy sir—his name's Digenis, by the way—has to say, and hear it in a more private setting?"

Phostis thought about that. "Maybe I would," he said at last, for he did want to hear the priest again.

Had the butcher smiled or shown triumph, his court-sharpened suspicions would have kindled. But the fellow only gave a sober nod. That convinced Phostis of his sincerity, if nothing more. He decided he would indeed try to have that more private audience with Digenis. He'd found this morning that shaking off his bodyguards was anything but easy. Still, there might be ways . . .

Katakolon stood in the doorway to the study, waiting until Krispos chanced to look up from the tax register he was examining. Eventually Krispos did. He put down his pen. "What is it, son? Come in if you have something on your mind."

By the nervous way in which Katakolon approached his desk, Krispos could make a pretty good guess as to what "it" might be. His youngest son confirmed that guess when he said, "May it please you, Father, I should like to request another advance on my allowance." His smile, usually so sunny, had the hangdog air it assumed whenever he had to beg money from his father.

Krispos rolled his eyes. "*Another* advance? What did you spend it on this time?"

"An amber-and-emerald bracelet for Nitria," Katakolon said sheepishly.

"Who's Nitria?" Krispos asked. "I thought you were sleeping with Varina these days."

"Oh, I still am, Father," Katakolon assured him. "The other one's new. That's why I got her something special."

"I see," Krispos said. He did, too, in a strange sort of way. Katakolon was a lad who generally liked to be liked. With a youth's enthusiasm and stamina, he also led a love life more complicated than any bureaucratic document. Krispos knew a small measure of relief that he'd managed to remember the name of his son's current—or, by the sound of things, soon to be current but one—favorite. He sighed. "How much of an allowance do you get every month?"

"Twenty goldpieces, Father."

"That's right, twenty goldpieces. Do you have any idea how

old I was, son, before I had twenty goldpieces to my name, let alone twenty every month of the year? When I was your age, I—"

"—lived on a farm that grew only nettles, and you ate worms three meals a day," Katakolon finished for him. Krispos glared. His son said, "You make that same speech every time I ask you for money, Father."

"Maybe I do," Krispos said. Thinking about it, he was suddenly certain he did. That annoyed him; was he getting predictable as he got older? Being predictable could also be dangerous. But he added, "You'd be better off if you hadn't heard it so many times you've committed it to memory."

"Yes, Father," Katakolon said dutifully. "May I please have the advance?"

Sometimes Krispos gave in, sometimes he didn't. The cadaster he'd put down so he could talk with his son brought good news: the fisc had gained more revenue than expected from the province just south of the Paristrian Mountains, the province where he'd been born. Gruffly he said, "Very well. I suppose you haven't managed to bankrupt us yet, boy. But not another copper ahead of time till after Midwinter's Day, do you understand me?"

"Yes, Father. Thank you, Father." Little by little, Katakolon's merry expression turned apprehensive. "Midwinter's Day is still a long way off, Father." Like anyone who knew Krispos well, the Avtokrator's third son also knew he was not in the habit of making warnings just to hear himself talk. When he said something, he meant it.

"Try living within your means," Krispos suggested. "I didn't say I was cutting you off without a copper, only that I wouldn't give you any more money ahead of time till then. The good god willing, I won't have to do it afterward, either. But you notice I didn't demand that."

"Yes, Father." Katakolon's voice tolled like a mourning bell.

Krispos fought to keep his face straight; he remembered how much he'd hated to be laughed at when he was a youth. "Cheer up, son. By anyone's standards, twenty goldpieces a month is a lot of money for a young man to get his hands on. You'll be able to entertain your lady friends in fine style during that little while when you're not in bed with them." Katakolon looked so flabbergasted, Krispos had to smile. "I recall how many rounds I could manage back in my own younger days, boy. I can't match that now, but believe me, I've not forgotten."

"Whatever you say, Father. I do thank you for the advance, though I'd be even more grateful if you'd not tied that string round its leg." Katakolon dipped his head and went off to pursue his own affairs—very likely, Krispos thought, in the most literal sense of the word.

As soon as his son was out of earshot, Krispos did laugh. Young men could not imagine what being older was like; they lacked the experience. Perhaps because of that, they didn't believe older men retained the slightest notion of what being young meant. But Krispos knew that wasn't so; his younger self dwelt within him yet, covered over with years but still emphatically there.

He wasn't always proud of the young man he had been. He'd done a lot of foolish things, as young men will. It wasn't because he'd been stupid; he'd just been callow. If he'd known then what he knew now ... He laughed again, this time at himself. Graybeards had been singing that song since the world began.

He went back to his desk and finished working through the tax register. He wrote *I have read and approved—Krispos* in scarlet ink at the bottom of the parchment. Then, without so much as looking at the report that lay beneath it, he got up from the desk, stretched, and walked out into the hallway.

When he got near the entrance to the imperial residence, he almost bumped into Barsymes, who was coming out of the small audience chamber there. The vestiarios' eyes widened slightly. "I'd expected you would still be hard at the morning's assemblage of documents, your Majesty."

"To the ice with the morning's assemblage of documents, Barsymes," Krispos declared. "I'm going fishing."

"Very well, your Majesty. I shall set the preparations in train directly."

"Thank you, esteemed sir," Krispos said. Even something as simple as a trip to the nearest pier was not free from ceremony for an Avtokrator of the Videssians. The requisite twelve parasol bearers had to be rounded up; the Haloga captain had to be alerted so he could provide the even more requisite squadron of bodyguards.

Krispos endured the wait with the patience that years of waiting had taught him. He chose several flexible cane rods, each a little taller than he was, from a rack in a storage room, and a rather greater number of similar lengths of horsehair line. In the tackle box beside the rack of fishing poles were a good many barbed hooks of bronze. He preferred that metal to iron; though softer, it needed less care after being dunked in salt water.

Off in the kitchens, a servant would be catching him cockroaches for bait. He'd done it himself once, but only once; it scandalized people worse than any of Anthimos' ingenious perversions had ever managed to do.

"All is in readiness, your Majesty," Barsymes announced after a delay shorter than Krispos had expected. He held out to the Emperor an elaborately chased brass box from Makuran. Krispos accepted it with a grave nod. Only tiny skittering noises revealed that inside the elegant artifact were frantic brown-black bugs about the size of the last joint of his thumb.

The palace compound boasted several piers at widely spaced points along the sea wall; Krispos sometimes wondered if they'd been built to give an overthrown Avtokrator the best chance for escape by sea. As he and his retinue paraded toward the one closest to the imperial residence, though, he stopped worrying about blows against the state or against his person. When he stepped down into the little rowboat tied there, he was as nearly free as an Emperor could be.

Oh, true, a couple of Halogai got into another rowboat and followed him as he rowed out into the lightly choppy waters of the Cattle-Crossing. Their strokes were strong and sure; scores of narrow inlets pierced the rocky soil of Halogaland, so its sons naturally took to the ocean.

And true, a light war galley would also put to sea, in case conspirators mounted an attack on the Avtokrator too deadly for a pair of northern men to withstand. But the galley stayed a good quarter mile from Krispos' rowboat, and even the houndlike Halogai let him separate himself from them by close to a furlong. He could imagine he sat alone on the waves.

In his younger days, he had never thought of fishing as a sport he might favor. It was something he occasionally did to help feed himself when he had the time. Now, though, it gave him the chance to escape not only from his duties but also from his servitors, something he simply could not do on land.

Being the man he was, he'd also become a skillful fisherman over the years; whatever he did, for whatever reasons, he tried to do well. He tied a cork float to his line to keep his hook at the depth he wanted it. To that hook he wired several little pieces of lead from the tackle box to help it have the semblance of natural motion in the water. Then he opened the bait box Barsymes had given him, seized a roach between thumb and forefinger, and impaled it on the hook's barbed tip.

While he was catching the roach, a couple of others leapt out of box and scuttled around the bottom of the rowboat. For the moment, he ignored them. If he needed them later, he'd get them. They weren't going anywhere far.

He tossed the line over the side. The float bobbed in the green-blue water. Krispos sat holding the rod and let his thoughts drift freely. Sea mist softened the outline of the far shore of the Cattle-Crossing, but he could still make out the taller buildings of the suburb known simply as Across.

He turned his head. Behind him, Videssos the city bulked enormous. Past the Grand Courtroom and the Hall of the Nineteen Couches stood the great mass of the High Temple. It dominated the capital's skyline from every angle. Also leaping above the rooftops of other buildings was the red granite shaft of the Milestone at the edge of the plaza of Palamas, from which all distances in the Empire were reckoned.

Sunlight sparked from the gilded domes that topped the dozens—perhaps hundreds—of temples to Phos in the city. Krispos thought back to his own first glimpse of the imperial capital, and the globes flashing like suns themselves under the good god's sun.

The Cattle-Crossing was full of ships: lean war galleys like the one that watched him; trading ships full of grain or building stone or cargoes more diverse and expensive; little fishing boats whose crews scoured the sea not for sport but for survival. Watching them pull their nets up over the side, Krispos wondered whether they might not work harder even than farmers, a question that had never crossed his mind about any other trade.

His float suddenly jerked under the water. He yanked up the

rod and pulled in the line. A shimmering blue flying fish twisted at the end of it. He smiled, grabbed it, and tossed it into the bottom of the boat. It wasn't very big, but it would be tasty. Maybe his cook could make it stretch in a stew—or maybe he'd catch another one.

He foraged in the bait box, grabbed another cockroach, and skewered it on the hook to replace the one that had been the luckless flying fish's last meal. The roach's little legs still flailed as it sank beneath the sea.

After that, Krispos spent a good stretch of time staring at the float and waiting for something to happen. Fishing was like that sometimes. He had sometimes thought about asking Zaidas if sorcery could help the business along, but always decided not to. Catching fish was only part of the reason he came out here in the little boat. The other part, the bigger part, was to get away from everyone around him. Making himself a more efficient fisherman might net him more fish, but it would cost him some of the precious time he had to himself.

Besides, if fishing magic were possible, the horny-handed, sun-browned sailors who made their living from their catch would surely employ it. No, maybe not: it might be feasible, but too expensive to make it worthwhile for anyone not already rich to afford it. Zaidas would know. Maybe he *would* ask him. And maybe he wouldn't. Now that he thought about it, he probably wouldn't.

His float disappeared again. When he tried to pull up the rod this time, it bent like a bow. He pulled once more, and once more the fish fought back. He walked his hands up to the tip of the rod, then pulled in the line hand over hand. "By the good god, here's a treat indeed!" he exclaimed when he saw the fat red mullet writhing on his hook.

He snatched up a net and slid it up over the fish from below. The mullet was as large as his forearm, and meaty enough to feed several. Had he fished for a living, he could have sold it in the plaza of Palamas for a fine price: Videssos the city's gourmets reckoned it their favorite, even to the point of nicknaming it the emperor of fishes.

Though called red, the mullet had been brownish with yellow stripes when he took it from the sea. It turned a crimson almost the color of his boots, however, as it struggled for its life, then slowly began to fade toward gray.

Mullets were famous for their spectacular color changes. Krispos remembered one of Anthimos' revels, where his predecessor had ordered several of them slowly boiled alive in a large glass vessel so the feasters could appreciate their shifting hues as they cooked. He'd watched with as much interest as anyone else; only looking back on it did it seem cruel.

Perhaps a sauce with garlic-flavored egg whites would do this one justice, he thought; even the head of a mullet pickled in brine was esteemed a delicacy. He'd have to talk with the cook when he went back to the imperial residence.

He gently set the prized catch in the bottom of the rowboat, treating it with far more care than he had the flying fish. If he'd used fishing as anything but an excuse to get away from the palaces, he would have rowed back to the pier with as much celerity as his arms could give him. Instead, he caught another cockroach, rebaited the hook, and dropped the line into the water again.

He quickly made another catch, but it was only an ugly, tasteless croaker. He pulled the barbed hook out of its mouth and tossed it back into the water, then opened the bait box for another bug.

After that, he sat and sat for a long time, waiting for something to happen and accepting with almost trancelike calm the nothing that fate was giving him. The boat shifted gently in the waves. His stomach had been a bit uncertain the first few times he went to sea. With greater familiarity, the motion had come to soothe him; it was as if he sat in a chair that not only rocked but also swiveled. Of course, he did not take the rowboat out on stormy days, either.

"Your majesty!" The call across the water snapped Krispos out of his reverie. He looked back toward the dock from which he'd rowed out, expecting to see someone standing there with a megaphone. Instead, a rowboat was approaching his own as fast as the man in it could ply the blades. He wondered how long the fellow had been hailing him before he noticed.

The Halogai, who had been fishing, too, grabbed for their oars and moved to block the newcomer's path. He paused in his exertion long enough to snatch up a sealed roll of parchment and wave it in their direction. After that, Krispos' bodyguards let him come on, but rowed beside him to make sure he could try nothing untoward if his precious message proved a ruse.

Proskynesis in a rowboat was impractical; the fellow with the parchment contented himself with dipping his head to Krispos. Panting, he said, "May it please your Majesty, I bring a dispatch just arrived from the environs of Pityos." He handed Krispos the parchment across the palm's breadth of water that separated their boats.

As often happened, Krispos had the bad feeling his Majesty was not going to be pleased. Scrawled on the outside of the parchment in a hasty hand was *For Krispos Avtokrator—vital that he read the instant received.* No wonder the messenger had leapt into a rowboat, then.

Krispos flicked off the wax seal with his thumbnail, then used a scaling knife from the tackle box to slice through the ribbon that held the parchment closed. When he unrolled it, he found the message inside written in the same hand as the warning of urgency on the outer surface. It was also to the point:

*Troop Leader Gainas to Krispos Avtokrator: Greetings. We were attacked by Thanasioi two days' march southeast of Pityos. I grieve to report to your Majesty that most of the forces sent there not only yielded themselves up to the heretics and rebels but indeed took their cause against the rest. The leader of this action was the merarch Livanios, the chief aide to our commander Briso.*

*Because of this, those loyal to you were utterly defeated; the priests we were escorting to Pityos were captured and most piteously massacred. May the good god redeem their souls. Forgive one of my lowly rank for writing to you directly, your Majesty, but I fear I am the senior loyal officer left alive. The Thanasioi must now be reckoned to control the whole of this province. Skotos surely awaits them in the world to come.*

Krispos read through the message twice to make sure he'd missed nothing. He started to toss it down with the fish he'd caught, but decided it was too likely to be ruined by seawater. He stowed it in the tackle box instead. Then he seized the rowboat's oars and headed back for the pier. The messenger and the Halogai followed in his wake.

As soon as he reached the dock, he tossed the tackle box up onto the tarred timbers, then scrambled up after it. He grabbed the box and headed for the imperial residence at a trot that left the parasol bearers hurrying after him and complaining loudly as they did their futile best to catch up. Even the Halogai who hadn't gone to sea needed a hundred yards and more before they could assume their protective places around him.

He'd taken the Thanasioi too lightly before. That wouldn't happen now. He wrote and dictated orders far into the night; the only pauses he made were to gulp smoked pork and hard cheese—campaigning food—and pour down a couple of goblets of wine to keep his voice from going raw.

Not until he'd got into bed, his thoughts whirling wildly as he tried without much luck to sleep, did he remember that he'd left the mullet of which he'd been so proud lying in the bottom of the boat.

# III

CIVIL WAR. RELIGIOUS WAR. KRISPOS DIDN'T KNOW WHICH OF the two was worse. Now he had them both, wrapped around each other. Worse yet, fall was not far away. If he didn't move quickly, rain would turn the westlands' dirt roads to gluey mud that made travel difficult and campaigning impossible. That would give the heretics the winter to consolidate their hold on Pityos and the surrounding territory.

But if he did move quickly, with a scratch force, he risked another defeat. Defeat was more dangerous in civil war than against a foreign foe; it tempted troops to switch sides. Figuring out which course to take required calculations more exacting than he'd needed in years.

"I wish Iakovitzes were here," he told Barsymes and Zaidas as he weighed his choices. "Come to that, I wish Mammianos were still alive. When it came to civil war, he always had a feel for what to do when."

"He was not young even in the first days of your Majesty's reign," Zaidas said, "and he was always fat as a tun. Such men are prime candidates for fits of apoplexy."

"So the healer-priests advised me when he died up in Pliskavos," Krispos said. "I understand that. I miss him all the same. Most of these young soldiers I deal with lack sense, it seems to me."

"This is a common complaint of the older against the young," Zaidas said. "Moreover, most of the younger officers in your army have spent more time at peace than was usual in the tenure of previous Avtokrators."

Barsymes said, "Perhaps your Majesty might do more to involve the young Majesties in the preparations against the Thanasioi."

"I wish I knew how to do that," Krispos said. "If they were more like me at the same age, there'd be no problem. But—" His own first taste of combat had come at seventeen, against Kubrati raiders. He'd done well enough in the fighting, then puked up his guts afterward.

"But," he said again, shaking his head as if it were a complete sentence. He made himself amplify it. "Phostis has chosen now to get drunk on the lord with the great and good mind and on the words of this priest he's been seeing."

"Will you reprove piety?" Barsymes asked, his own voice reproving.

"Not at all, esteemed sir. Along with our common Videssian language, our common orthodox faith glues the Empire together. That, among other things, is what makes the Thanasioi so deadly dangerous: they seek to soak away the glue that keeps all Videssos' citizens loyal to her. But neither would I have my heir make himself into a monk, not when Emperors find themselves forced to do unmonkish things."

"Forbid him to see this priest, then," Zaidas suggested.

"How can I?" Krispos said. "Phostis is a man in years and a man in spirit, even if not exactly the man I might have wished him to be. He would defy me, and he would be in the right. One of the things you learn if you want to stay Avtokrator is not to fight wars you have no hope of winning."

"You have three sons, your Majesty," Barsymes said. The vestiarios was subtle even by Videssian standards, but could be as stubborn in his deviousness as any blunt, straightforward, ironheaded barbarian.

"Aye, I have three sons." Krispos raised an eyebrow. "Katakolon would no doubt be willing enough to go on campaign for the sake of the camp followers, but how much use he'd be in the field is another question. Evripos, now, Evripos is a puzzle even to me. He doesn't want to be like his brother, but envies him his place as eldest."

Zaidas spoke in musing tones: "If you ordered him to accompany the army you send forth, and gave him, say, spatharios' rank and a place at your side, that might make Phostis—what's the word I want?—thoughtful, perhaps."

"Worried, you mean." Krispos found himself smiling. Spatharios was about the most general title in the imperial hierarchy; though it literally meant *sword bearer*, *aide* more accurately reflected its import. An Emperor's spatharios, even when not also the Emperor's son, was a very prominent personage indeed. Krispos' smile got wider. "Zaidas, perhaps I'll dispatch you instead of Iakovitzes on our next embassy to the King of Kings. You have the plotter's instinct."

"I'd not mind going, your Majesty, if you think I could serve you properly," the wizard answered. "Mashiz is the home of many clever mages, of a school different from our own. I'd learn a great deal on such a journey, I'm certain." He sounded ready to leave on the instant.

"One of these years, then, I may send you," Krispos said. "You needn't go pack, though; as things stand, I need you too much by my side."

"It shall be as your Majesty wishes, of course," Zaidas murmured.

"Shall it?" Krispos said. "On the whole, I'll not deny it has been as I wish, more often than not. But I have the feeling that if I ever start to take success for granted, it will run away from me and I'll never see it again."

"That feeling may be the reason you've held the throne so long, your Majesty," Barsymes said. "An Avtokrator who takes anything for granted soon finds the high seat slipping out from under his fundament. I watched it happen with Anthimos."

Krispos glanced at the eunuch in some surprise; Barsymes seldom reminded him of having served his predecessor. He cast about for what Barsymes, in his usual oblique way, might be trying to tell him. At last he said, "Anthimos' example taught me a lot about how best not to be an Avtokrator."

"Then you have drawn the proper lesson from it," Barsymes said approvingly. "In that regard, his career had a textbook perfection whose like would be difficult to find."

"So it did." Krispos' voice was dry. Had Anthimos granted to ruling even a tithe of the attention he gave to wine, wenching, and revelry, Krispos might never have tried to supplant him—and if he had, he likely would have failed. But that was grist for the historians now, too. He said, "Esteemed sir, draft for me a letter of appointment for Evripos, naming him my spatharios for the upcoming campaign against the Thanasioi."

"Not one for Phostis as well, your Majesty?" the vestiarios asked.

"Oh, yes, go ahead and draft that one, too. But don't give it to him until he finds out his brother was named to the post. Stewing him in his own juices is the point of the exercise, eh?"

"As you say," Barsymes answered. "Both documents will be ready for your signature this afternoon."

"Excellent. I rely on your discretion, Barsymes. I've never known that reliance to be misplaced." When he was new on the throne, Krispos would have added that it had better not be misplaced here, either. Now he let Barsymes add those last words for himself, as he knew the vestiarios would. Little by little, over the years, he'd picked up some deviousness himself.

Phostis bowed low before Digenis. Gulping a little, he told the priest, "Holy sir, I regret I will not be able to hear your wisdom for some time to come. I depart soon with my father and the armament he has readied against the Thanasioi."

"If it suited you, lad, you could remain in the city and learn despite his wishes." Digenis studied him. The priest's thin shoulders moved in a silent sigh. "But I see the world and its things still hold you in their grip. Do as you feel you must, then; all shall surely result as the lord with the great and good mind desires."

Phostis accepted the priest's calling him merely *lad*, though by now Digenis of course knew who he was. He'd thought about telling Digenis to address him as *your Majesty* or *young Majesty*, but one of the reasons he visited the priest again and again was to rid himself of the taint of sordid materialism and learn humility. Humility did not go hand in hand with ordering a priest about.

But even though he sought humility, he embraced it only so far. Trying to justify himself, he said earnestly, "Holy sir, if I let Evripos serve as my father's aide, it might give my father cause to have him succeed, rather than me."

"And so?" Digenis said. "Would the Empire crumble to pieces on account of that? Is your brother so wicked and depraved that he would cast it all into the fire to feed his own iniquity? Better even perhaps that he should, so the generations which come after us would have fewer material possessions with which to concern themselves."

"Evripos isn't wicked," Phostis said. "It's just that—"

"That you have become accustomed to the idea of one day setting your baser parts on the throne," the priest interrupted. "Not only accustomed to it, lad, but infatuated with it. Do I speak the truth or a lie?"

"The truth, but only after a fashion," Phostis said. Digenis' eyebrow was silent but nonetheless eloquent. Flustered, Phostis floundered for justification: "And remember, holy sir, if I succeed, you will already have imbued me with your doctrines, which I will be able to disseminate throughout the Empire. Evripos, though, remains attached to the sordid matter that Skotos set before our souls to entice them away from Phos' light."

"This is also a truth, however small," Digenis admitted, with the air of a man making a large concession. "Still, lad, you must bear in mind that any compromise with Skotos that you form in your mind will result in compromising your soul. Well, let it be; each man must determine for himself the proper path to renunciation, and that path is often—always—strait. If you do accompany your father on this expedition of his, what shall your duties be?"

"For a good part of it, probably nothing at all," Phostis answered, explaining, "We'll go by ship to Nakoleia, to reach the borders of the revolted province as quickly as we can. Then we march overland to Harasos, Rogmor, and Aptos; my father is arranging for supplies to be ingathered at each. From Aptos we'll strike toward Pityos. That's the leg of the journey where we'll most likely start real fighting."

In spite of his efforts to sound disapproving, he heard the excitement in his own voice. War, to a young man who has never seen it face to face, owns a certain glamour. Krispos never talked about fighting, save to condemn it. To Phostis, that was but another reason to look forward to it.

The priest just shook his head. "How your grand cavalcade of those who love too well their riches shall progress concerns me not at all. I fear for your soul, lad, the only piece of you truly deserving of our care. Without a doubt you will abandon my teachings and return to your old corrupt ways, just as a moth seeks a flame or a fly, a cow turd."

"I'll do no such thing," Phostis said indignantly. "I've discovered a great deal from you, holy sir, and would not think of turning aside from your golden words."

"Ha!" Digenis said. "Do you see? Even your promises of piety betray the greed that remains yet in your heart. Golden words? To the ice with gold! Yet still it holds you in its honeyed grip, sticking you down so Skotos may seize you."

"I'm sorry," Phostis said, humble now. "It was only a figure of speech. I meant no harm by it."

"Ha!" Digenis repeated. "There are tests to see whether you have truly embraced piety or are but dissembling, perhaps even to yourself."

"Give me one of those tests, then," Phostis said. "By the lord with the great and good mind, holy sir, I'll show you what I'm made of."

"You are less easy to test than many might be, you know, lad," the priest said. At Phostis' puzzled look, he explained: "Another young man I might send past a chamber wherein lay some rich store of gold or gems. For those who came to manhood in hunger and want, such would be plenty to let me look into their hearts. But you? Gold and jewels have been your baubles since you were still pissing on your father's floor. You might easily remain ensnared in spiritual error and yet pass them by."

"So I might," Phostis admitted. Almost in despair, he cried out, "But I would prove myself to you, holy sir, if only I knew how."

Digenis smiled. He pointed to a curtained doorway in the rear wall of the dingy temple over which he presided. "Go through there, then, and it may be you shall learn something of yourself."

"By the good god, I will!" But when Phostis pulled aside the curtain, only blank blackness awaited him. He hesitated. His guardsmen waited for him outside the temple, the greatest concession they would make. Assassins might await him in the darkness. He steadied himself: Digenis would not betray him so. Very conscious of the weight of the priest's gaze on his back, he plunged ahead.

The curtain fell back into place behind him. As soon as he turned a corner, the inside of the passage was so absolutely black that he whispered Phos' creed to hold away any supernatural evils that might dwell there. He took a step, then another. The passage sloped steeply down. To keep from breaking his neck, he put his arms out to either side and shifted this way and that until one outstretched finger brushed a wall.

That wall was rough brick. It scraped his fingertips, but he was glad to feel it, even so; without it, he would have groped around as helplessly as a blind man. In effect, he *was* a blind man here.

He walked slowly down the corridor. In the darkness, he could not be sure whether it was straight or followed a gently curving path. He was certain it ran under more buildings than just the temple to Phos. He wondered how old it was and why it had been built. He also wondered if even Digenis knew the answers to those questions.

His eyes imagined they saw shifting, swirling colored shapes, as if he had shut them and pressed knuckles hard against his eyelids. If any beings phantasmagorical did lurk down here, they could be upon him before he decided they were something more than figments of his imagination. He said the creed under his breath again.

He had gone—well, he didn't know how far he had gone, but it was a goodly way—when he saw a tiny bit of light that neither shifted nor swirled. It spilled out from under the bottom of a door and faintly illuminated the floor just in front of it. Had the tunnel been lit, he never would have noticed the glow. As things were, it shouted its presence like an imperial herald.

Phostis' fingers slid across planed boards. After so long scratching over brick, the smoothness was welcome. Whoever was on the other side of the door must have had unusually keen ears, for no sooner had his hand whispered over it than she called, "Enter in friendship, by the lord with the great and good mind."

He groped for a latch, found it, and lifted it. The door moved smoothly on its hinges. Though but a single lamp burned in the chamber, its glow seemed bright as the noonday sun to his light-starved eyes. What he saw, though, left him wondering if those eyes were playing tricks on him: a lovely young woman bare on a bed, her arms stretched his way in open invitation.

"Enter in friendship," she repeated, though he was already

inside. Her voice was low and throaty. As he took an almost involuntary step toward her, the scent she wore reached him. Had it had a voice, that would have been low and throaty, too.

A second, longer look told him she was not quite bare after all: a thin gold chain girded her slim waist. Its glint in the lamplight made him take another step toward the bed. She smiled and moved a little to make room beside her.

His foot was already uplifted for a third step—which would have been the last one he needed—when he caught himself, almost literally, by the scruff of the neck. He swayed off balance for a moment, but in the end that third step went back rather than ahead.

"You are the test against which Digenis warned me," he said, and felt himself turn red at how hoarse and eager he sounded.

"Well, what if I am?" The girl's slow shrug was a marvel to behold. So was the long, slow stretch that followed it. "The holy sir promised me you would be comely, and he told the truth. Do as you will with me; he shall never know, one way or the other."

"How not?" he demanded, his suspicions aroused now along with his lust. "If I have you here, of course you'll bear the tale back to the holy sir."

"By the lord with the great and good mind, I swear I will not," she said. Her tone carried conviction. He knew he should not believe her, but he did. She smiled, seeing she'd got through to him. "We're all alone, only the two of us down here. Whatever happens, happens, and no one else will ever be the wiser."

He thought about that, decided he believed her again. "What's your name?" he asked. It was not quite a question out of the blue.

The girl seemed to understand that. "Olyvria," she answered. Her smile grew broader. As if by their own will rather than hers, her legs parted a little.

When Phostis raised his left foot, he did not know whether he would go toward her or away. He turned, took two quick strides out of the chamber, and closed the door behind him. He knew that if he looked on her for even another heartbeat, he would take her.

As he leaned against the bricks of the passageway and tried

to find a scrap of his composure, her voice pursued him: "Why do you flee from pleasure?"

Not until she asked him did he fully comprehend the answer. Digenis' test was marvelous in its simplicity: only his own conscience stood between himself and an act that, however sweet, went square against everything the priest had been telling him. Digenis' teaching must have had its effect, too: regardless of whether the priest learned what he'd been up to, Phostis knew *he* would always know. Since he found that reason enough to abstain, he supposed he had met the challenge.

Even so, he made as much haste as he could away from that dangerous doorway, although Olyvria did not call to him again. When he looked back to find out whether he could still see the light trickling under the bottom of the door, he discovered he could not. The passage did have a curve to it, then.

A little while later, he came upon another door with a lighted lamp behind it. This time, he tiptoed past as quietly as he could. If anyone in the chamber heard him, she—or perhaps he—gave no sign. Not all tests, Phostis told himself as he pressed ahead, had to be met straight on.

Pitch darkness or no, he could see Olyvria's lovely body with his mind's eye. He was sure both his brothers would have enjoyed themselves immensely while failing Digenis' test. Had he not become dubious of the pleasures of the flesh exactly because they were so easy for him to gain, he might well have failed, too, in spite of all the priest's inspiring words.

Moving along without light made him realize how very much he depended on his eyes. He could not tell whether he was going uphill or down, left or right. Just when he began to wonder if the passage under the city ran on forever, he saw a faint gleam of light ahead. He hurried toward it. When he pulled aside the curtain that covered the entrance to the tunnel, he found himself back in the temple again.

He stood blinking for a few seconds as he got used to seeing once more. Digenis did not seem to have moved while he was gone. He wondered how long that had been; his sense of time seemed to have been cast into darkness down in the tunnel along with his vision.

Digenis studied him. The priest's eyes were so sharp and penetrating that Phostis suspected he might have been able to see even in the black night of the underground passage. After a moment, Digenis said, "The man who is truly holy turns aside from no test, but triumphantly surmounts it."

Quite against his conscious will, Phostis thought of himself triumphantly surmounting Olyvria. Turning his back on the distracting mental image, he answered, "Holy sir, I make no special claim to holiness of my own. I am merely as I am. If I fail to please you, drive me hence."

"Your father, or rather your acceptance of his will, has already sufficed in that regard. But while not a man destined to be renowned among Phos' holy elite, you have not done badly, I admit," Digenis said. That was as near to praise as he was in the habit of coming. Phostis grinned in involuntary relief. The priest added, "I know it is no simple matter for a young man to reject carnality and its delights."

"That's true, holy sir." Only after Phostis had replied did he notice that, this once, Digenis sounded remarkably like his father. His opinion of the priest went down a notch. Why couldn't old men leave off prating about what young men did or didn't do? What did they know about it, anyhow? They hadn't been young since before Videssos was a city, as the saying went.

Digenis said, "May the good god turn his countenance—and his continence—upon you during your wanderings, lad, and may you remember his truths and what you have learned from me in the hour when you will be tested all in earnest."

"May it be so, holy sir," Phostis answered, though he didn't understand just what the priest meant by his last comment. Weren't his lessons Phos' truth in and of themselves? He set that aside for later consideration, bowed deeply to Digenis, and walked out of the little temple.

His Haloga guards were down on one knee in the street, shooting dice. They paid off the last bet and got to their feet. "Back to the palaces, young Majesty?" one asked.

"That's right, Snorri," Phostis answered. "I have to ready myself to sail west." He let the northerners escort him out of the unsavory part of the capital. As they turned onto Middle Street, he said, "Tell me, Snorri, how are you better for having your mail shirt gilded?"

The Haloga turned back, puzzlement spread across his blunt features. "Better, young Majesty? I don't follow the track of your thought."

"Does the gilding make you fight better? Are you braver on account of it? Does it keep the iron links of the shirt from rusting better than some cheap paint might?"

"None of those, young Majesty." Snorri's massive head shook slowly back and forth as if he thought Phostis ought to be able to see that much for himself. In fact, he likely was thinking something of the sort.

Phostis didn't care. Buoyed by Digenis' inspiring word and by pride at turning down what Olyvria had so temptingly offered, he had at the moment no use for the material things of the world, for everything which had throughout his life stood between him and hunger, discomfort, and fear. As if fencing with a rapier of logic, he thrust home. "Why have the gilding, then?"

He didn't know what he'd expected—maybe for Snorri to rush out and buy a jug of turpentine so he could remove the offending pigment from his byrnie. But whether the gilding helped the Haloga or not, he was armored against reasoned argument. He answered, "Why, young Majesty? I like it; I think it's pretty. That's plenty for me."

The rest of the trip to the palaces passed in silence.

Lines creaked as they ran through pulleys. The big square sail swung to catch the breeze from a new angle. Waves slapped against the bow of the *Triumphant* as the imperial flagship turned toward shore.

Krispos knew more than a little relief at the prospect of being on dry land to stay. The voyage west from Videssos the city had been smooth enough; he'd needed to use the lee rail only once. The galleys and transport ships never sailed out of sight of land, and beached themselves every evening. That wasn't why Krispos looked forward to putting in at Nakoleia.

The trouble was, he'd grown to feel isolated, cut off from the world around him, in his week at sea. No new reports stacked up on his desk. His cabin, in fact, had no desk, only a little folding table. He felt like a healer-priest forced to remove his fingers from a sick man's wrist in the middle of taking his pulse.

He knew that was foolish. A week was not a long time to be away from events; Anthimos, even while physically remaining in Videssos the city, had neglected his duties for months on end. The bureaucracy kept he Empire more or less on an even keel; that was what bureaucracy was for.

But Krispos would be glad to return to a location more definite than *somewhere on the Videssian Sea*. Once he landed, the lodestone that was the imperial dignity would attract to his person all the minutiae on which he depended for his understanding of what was going on in Videssos.

"You can't let go, even for a second," he murmured.

"What's that, Father?" Katakolon asked.

Embarrassed at getting caught talking to himself, Krispos just grunted by way of reply. Katakolon gave him a quizzical look and walked on by. Katakolon had spent a lot of time pacing the deck of the *Triumphant*; the week at sea was no doubt his longest period of celibacy since his beard began to sprout. He'd likely do his best to make up for lost time in the joyhouses of Nakoleia.

The port was getting close now. Its gray stone wall was drab against the green-gold of ripening grain in the hinterland. Behind it, blue in the distance, hills rose up against the sky. The fertile strip was narrow along the northern coast of the westlands; the plateau country that made up the bulk of the big peninsula began to rise less than twenty miles from the sea.

Katakolon went by again. Krispos didn't want him, not right now. "Phostis!" he called.

Phostis came, not quite fast enough to suit Krispos, not quite slow enough for him to make an issue out of it. "How may I serve you, Father?" he asked. The question was properly deferential, the tone was not.

Again, Krispos decided to let it lie. He stuck to the purpose for which he'd called his son. "When we dock, I want you to visit all merarchs and officers of higher rank. Remind them they have to take extra care on this campaign because they may have Thanasioi in their ranks. We don't want to risk betrayal at a time when it could hurt us most."

"Yes, Father," Phostis said unenthusiastically. Then he asked, "Why couldn't you simply have your scribes write out as many copies of the order as you need and distribute them to the officers?"

"Because I just told you to do this, by the good god," Krispos snapped. Phostis' glare made him realize that was taking authority too far. He added, "Besides, I have good practical reasons for doing it this way. Officers get too many parchments as is; who but Phos can say which ones they'll read and which ones they'll toss into a pigeonhole or into a well without ever unsealing them? But a visit from the Avtokrator's son—that they'll remember, and what he says to them. And this is an important order. Do you see?"

"I suppose so," Phostis said, again without great spirit. But he did nod. "I'll do as you say, Father."

"Well, I thank your gracious Majesty for that," Krispos said. Phostis jerked as if a mosquito had just bitten him in a tender place. He spun round and stalked away. Krispos immediately regretted his sarcasm, but nothing could recall a word once spoken. He'd learned that a long time before, and should have had it down pat by now. He stamped his foot, angry at himself and Phostis both.

He peered out toward the docks. The fleet had come close enough to let him pick out individuals. The fat fellow with six parasol bearers around him would be Strabonis, the provincial governor; the scrawny one with three, Asdrouvallos, the city eparch. He wondered how long they'd been standing there, waiting for the fleet to arrive. The longer it was, the more ceremony they'd insist on once he actually got his feet on dry land. He intended to endure as much as he could, but sometimes that wasn't much.

Along with the dignitaries stood a lean, wiry fellow in nondescript clothes and a broad-brimmed leather traveler's hat. Krispos was much more interested in seeing him than either Strabonis or Asdrouvallos: imperial scouts and couriers had an air about them that, once recognized, was unmistakable. The governor and the eparch would make speeches. From the courier, Krispos would get real news.

He called for Evripos. His second son was no quicker appearing than Phostis had been. Frowning, Krispos said, "If I'd wanted slowcoaches, I'd have made snails my spatharioi, not you two."

"Sorry, Father," Evripos said, though he didn't sound particularly sorry.

At the moment, Krispos wished Dara had borne girls. Sons-in-law might have been properly grateful to him for their elevation in life, where his own boys seemed to take status for granted. On the other hand, sons-in-law might also have wanted to elevate themselves further, regardless of whether Krispos was ready to depart this life.

He made himself remember why he'd summoned Evripos. "When we land, I want you to check the number and quality of remounts available here, and also to make sure the arsenal has enough arrows in it to let us go out and fight. Is that martial enough for you?"

"Yes, Father. I'll see to it," Evripos said.

"Good. I want you back with what I need to know before you sleep tonight. Make sure you take special notice of anything lacking, so we can get word ahead to our other supply dumps and have their people lay hold of it for us."

"Tonight?" Now Evripos didn't try to hide his dismay. "I was hoping to—"

"To find someone soft and cuddly?" Krispos shook his head. "I don't care what you do along those lines after you take care of what I ask of you. If you work fast, you'll have plenty of time for other things. But business first."

"You don't tell Katakolon that," Evripos said darkly.

"You complain because I don't treat you the same as Phostis, and now you complain because I don't treat you the same as Katakolon. You can't have it both ways, son. If you want the authority that comes with power, you have to take the responsibility that comes with it, too." When Evripos didn't answer, Krispos added, "Don't scant the job. Men's lives ride on it."

"Oh, I'll take care of it, Father. I said I would, after all. And besides, you'll probably have someone else taking care of it, too, so you can check his answers against mine. That's your style, isn't it?" Evripos departed without giving Krispos a chance to answer.

Krispos wondered whether he should have left his sons back in Videssos the city. They quarreled with one another, they quarreled with him, and they didn't do half as much as might some youngster from no particular family who hoped to be noticed. But no—they needed to learn what war was about, and they needed to let the army see them. An Avtokrator who could not control his soldiers would end up with soldiers controlling him.

The *Triumphant* eased into place alongside the dock. Strabonis peered down into the ship. Seen close up, he looked as if he'd yield gallons of oil if rendered down. Even his voice was greasy. "Welcome, welcome, thrice welcome, your imperial Majesty," he declared. "We honor you for coming to the defense of our province, and are confident you shall succeed in utterly crushing the impious heretics who scourge us."

"I'm glad of your confidence, and I hope I will deserve it," Krispos answered as sailors stretched a gangplank painted with imperial crimson from his vessel to the dock. He, too, remained confident he would beat the Thanasioi. He'd beaten every enemy he'd faced in a long reign save only Makuran—and no Avtokrator since the fierce Stavrakios had ever really beaten Makuran, while even Stavrakios' victory did not prove lasting. But Strabonis sounded as if defeating the heretics would be easy as a promenade down Middle Street. Krispos knew better than that.

He walked across the gangplank to the dock. Strabonis folded his fat form into a proskynesis. "Rise," Krispos said. After a week aboard the rolling ship, solid ground seemed to sway beneath his feet.

Asdrouvallos prostrated himself next. As he got back to his feet, he started to cough, and kept on coughing till his wizened face turned almost as gray as his beard. A tiny fleck of blood-streaked foam appeared at one corner of his mouth. A quick flick of his tongue swept it away. "Phos grant your Majesty a pleasant stay in Nakoleia," he said, his voice gravelly. "Success against the foe as well."

"Thank you, excellent eparch," Krispos said. "I hope you've seen a healer-priest for that cough?"

"Oh, aye, your Majesty; more than one, as a matter of fact." Asdrouvallos' bony shoulders moved up and down in a shrug. "They've done the best they can for me, but it's not enough. I'll go on as long as the good god wills, and afterward, well, afterward I hope to see him face to face."

"May that day be years away," Krispos said, though Asdrouvallos, who was not much above his own age, looked as if he might expire at any moment. Krispos added, "By all means consider your oration as given. I do not require you to tax your lungs. Videssos has quite enough taxes without that."

"Your Majesty is gracious," Asdrouvallos said. In truth, Krispos was concerned for the eparch's health. And in showing that concern, he'd also managed to take a formidable bite out of speeches yet to come.

He wished he could have found some equally effective and polite way to make Strabonis shut up. The provincial governor's speech was long and florid, modeled after the rhetoric-soaked orations that had been the style in Videssos the city before Krispos' time—and probably would be again, once his peasant-bred impatience for fancy talk was safely gone. He tried clearing his throat; Strabonis ignored him. At last he started shifting from foot to foot as if he urgently needed to visit the jakes. That got Strabonis' attention. As soon as he subsided, so did Krispos' wiggles. The governor sent the Avtokrator an injured look Krispos pretended not to see.

After that, he had to endure only an invocation from the hierarch of Nakoleia, who proved himself a man able to take a hint by making it mercifully brief. Then Krispos could at last talk with the courier, who had waited through the folderol with more apparent patience than the Avtokrator could muster.

The fellow started to prostrate himself. "Never mind that," Krispos said. "Any more nonsense and I'll die of old age before I get anything done. By the good god, just tell me what you have to say."

"Aye, your Majesty." The courier's skin was brown and leathery from years in the sun, which only made his surprised smile seem brighter. That smile, however, quickly faded. "Your Majesty, the news isn't good. I have to tell you that the Thanasioi put your supply dumps at Harasos and Rogmor to the torch, the one three days ago, the other night before last. Damage—mm, there's a lot of it, I'm sorry to say."

Krispos' right hand clenched into a fist. "A pestilence," he ground out between his teeth. "That won't make the campaign against them any easier."

"No, your Majesty," the courier said. "I'm sorry to be the one who gives you that word, but it's one you have to have."

"You're right. I know it's not your fault." Krispos had never made a habit of condemning messengers for bad news. "See to yourself, see to your horse. No—tell me your name first, so I can commend you to your chief for good service."

The courier's flashing smile returned. "I'm called Evlalios, your Majesty."

"He'll hear from me, Evlalios," Krispos promised. As the

courier turned away, Krispos started thinking about his own next step. If he hadn't already known the Thanasioi now had a real soldier at their head, the raids on his depots would have told him as much. Bandits might have attacked the dumps to steal what they needed for themselves, but only an experienced officer would have deliberately wrecked them to deny his foes what they held. Soldiers knew armies did more traveling, encamping, and eating than fighting. If they couldn't get where they needed to go, or if they arrived half starved, they wouldn't be able to fight.

He'd already sent Phostis and Evripos on errands. That left— "Katakolon!" he called. Ceremonial had trapped his youngest son, who'd been unable to sneak off and start sampling the fleshly pleasures Nakoleia had to offer.

"What is it, Father?" Katakolon sounded like a martyr about to be slain for the true faith.

"I'm afraid you'll have to keep your trousers on a bit longer, my boy," Krispos said, at which his son looked as if the fatal dart had just struck home. Ignoring the virtuoso mime performance, Krispos went on, "I need an accounting of the contents of all the storehouses in this town, and I need it tonight. See the excellent Asdrouvallos here; no doubt he'll have a map to send you on your way from one to the next as fast as you can go."

"Oh, yes, your Majesty," Asdrouvallos said. Even the short sentence was enough to set him coughing again. By his expression, Katakolon hoped the eparch wouldn't stop. Unfortunately for him, Asdrouvallos drew in a couple of deep, sobbing breaths and managed to break the spasm. "If the young Majesty will just accompany me—"

Trapped, Katakolon accompanied him. Krispos watched him go with a certain amount of satisfaction—which, he thought, was more in the way of satisfaction than Katakolon would get tonight: now all three of his sons, however unwillingly, were doing something useful. If only the Thanasioi would yield so readily.

He feared they wouldn't. That they'd known just where he was storing his supplies forced him to relearn a lesson in civil war he hadn't had to worry about since he vanquished Anthimos' uncle Petronas at the start of his reign: the enemy, thanks to spies in his camp, would know everything he decided

almost as soon as he decided it. He'd have to keep moves secret until just before he made them, and so would his officers.
He'd have to remind them about that.

Forgetting his thought of a moment before that all his sons
were usefully engaged, he looked around for one to yell at.
Then he remembered, and laughed at himself. He also remembered he'd sent Phostis out on precisely that mission. His
laugh turned sour. How was he supposed to beat the Thanasioi
if he found himself turning senile before he ever met them in
battle?

Sarkis reminded Phostis of a plump bird of prey. The
Vaspurakaner cavalry commander was one of Krispos' longtime cronies, and close to Krispos in years—which, to Phostis'
way of thinking, made him about ready for the boneyard. A
great hooked beak of a nose protruded from his doughy face
like a big rock sticking out of a mud flat. He was munching
candied apricots when Phostis came into his quarters, too,
which did not improve the young man's opinion of him.

As he already had a score of times that afternoon and evening, Phostis repeated the message with which Krispos had
charged him; he'd give Krispos no chance to accuse him of
shirking a task once accepted. Sarkis paused in his methodical
chewing only long enough to shove the bowl of apricots toward him. He shook his head, not quite in disgust but not quite
politely, either.

Sarkis' heavy-lidded eyes—piggy little eyes, Phostis thought
distastefully—glinted in mirth. "Your first campaign, isn't it,
young Majesty?" he said.

"Yes," Phostis said shortly. Half the officers he'd seen had
asked the same question. Most of them seemed to want to
score points off his inexperience.

But Sarkis just smiled, showing orange bits of apricot between his heavy teeth. "I wasn't much older than you are now
when I first served under your father. He was still learning
how to command then; he'd never done it before, you know.
And he had to start at the top and make soldiers who'd been
leading armies for years obey him. It couldn't have been easy,
but he managed. If he hadn't, you wouldn't be here listening
to me flapping my gums."

"No, I suppose not," Phostis said. He knew Krispos had

started with nothing and made his way upward largely on his own; his father went on about it often enough. But from his father, it had just seemed like boasting. Sarkis made it feel as if Krispos had accomplished something remarkable, and that he deserved credit for it. Phostis, however, was not inclined to give Krispos credit for anything.

The Vaspurakaner general went on, "Aye, he's a fine man, your father. Take after him and you'll do well." He swigged from a goblet of wine at his elbow, then breathed potent fumes into Phostis' face. The throaty accent of his native land grew thicker. "Phos made a mistake when he didn't let Krispos be born a prince."

The folk of Vaspurakan followed Phos, but heretically; they believed the good god had created them first among mankind, and thus they styled themselves princes and princesses. The anathemas Videssian prelates flung their way were one reason most of them were well enough content to see their mountainous land controlled by Markuran, which judged all forms of Phos worship equally false and did not single out Vaspurakaners for persecution. Even so, many folk from Vaspurakan sought their fortune in Videssos as merchants, musicians, and warriors.

Phostis said, "Sarkis, has my father ever asked you to conform to Videssian usages when you worship?"

"What's that?" Sarkis dug a finger into his ear. "Conform, you say? No, never once. If the world won't conform to us princes, why should we conform ourselves to it?"

"For the same reason he seeks to bring the Thanasioi to orthodoxy?" By the doubt in his voice, Phostis knew he was asking the question as much of himself as of Sarkis.

But Sarkis answered it: "He doesn't persecute princes because we give no trouble outside of our faith. You ask me, the Thanasioi are using religion as an excuse for brigandage. That's evil on the face of it."

*Not if the material world is itself the evil,* Phostis thought. He kept that to himself. Instead, he said, "I know some Vaspurakaners do take on orthodoxy to help further their careers. You call them Tzatoi in your language, don't you?"

"So we do," Sarkis said. "And do you know what that means?" He waited for Phostis to shake his head, then grinned and boomed, "It means 'traitors,' that's what. We of Vaspura-kan are a stubborn breed, and our memories long."

"Videssians are much the same," Phostis said. "When my father set out to reconquer Kubrat, didn't he take his maps from the imperial archives where they'd lain unused for three hundred years?" He blinked when he noticed he'd used Krispos as an example.

If Sarkis also noticed, he didn't remark on it. He said, "Young Majesty, he did just that; I saw those maps with my own eyes when we were planning the campaign, and faded, rat-chewed things they were—though useful nonetheless. But three hundred years—young Majesty, three hundred years are but a fleabite on the arse of time. It's likely been three hundred eons since Phos shaped Vaspur the Firstborn from the fabric of his will."

He grinned impudently at Phostis, as if daring him to cry heresy. Phostis kept his mouth shut; Krispos had baited him too often to make it so easy to get a rise out of him. He did say, "Three hundred years seems a long enough time to me."

"Ah, that's because you're young," Sarkis exclaimed. "When I was your age, the years seemed to stretch like chewy candy, and I thought each one would never end. Now I haven't so much sand left in my glass, and I resent every grain that runs out."

"Yes," Phostis said, though he'd pretty much stopped listening when Sarkis started going on about his being young. He wondered why old men did that so much; it wasn't as if he could help being the age he was. But if he had a goldpiece for every time he'd heard *that's because you're young*, he was sure he could remit a year's worth of taxes to every peasant in the Empire.

Sarkis said, "Well, I've kept you here long enough, young Majesty. When you get bored with chatter, just press on. That's the advantage of rank, you know: you don't have to put up with people you find tedious."

*Only my father,* Phostis thought: a single exception that covered a lot of ground. But that was not the sort of thought he could share with Sarkis, or indeed with anyone save possibly Digenis. He was somehow sure the priest would understand, though to him any concern not directly related to Phos and the world to come was of secondary importance.

Having been given an excuse to depart, he took advantage of it.

Even with an army newly arrived and crowding its streets, Nakoleia seemed a tiny town to anyone used to Videssos the city. Tiny, backwater, provincial ... the scornful adjectives came readily to Phostis' mind. Whether or not they were true, they would stick.

Nakoleia was sensibly laid out in a grid. He made his way back to Krispos through deepening dusk and streaming soldiers without undue difficulty. His father's quarters were at the eparch's residence, across the town square from the chief temple to Phos. Like many throughout the Empire, that building was modeled after the High Temple in the capital. Phostis' first reaction was that it was a poor, cheap copy. His second, contrary one was to wish fewer goldpieces had been spent on the structure.

He stopped in his tracks halfway across the square. "By the good god," he exclaimed, careless of who might hear him, "I'm on my way to being a Thanasiot myself."

He wondered why that hadn't occurred to him sooner. Much of what Digenis preached was identical to the doctrines of the heretical sect, save that he made those doctrines seem virtuous, whereas to Krispos they were base and vicious. Given a choice between his father's opinions and those of anyone else, Phostis automatically inclined to the latter.

The irony of his position suddenly struck him. What business had he sallying forth to crush the vicious heretics when he agreed with most of what they taught? He imagined going to Krispos and telling him that. It was the quickest way he could think of to unburden himself of all his worldly goods.

It would also forfeit the succession if anything would. Suddenly that mattered a great deal. The Avtokrator was a great power in the ecclesiastical hierarchy. If *he* were Avtokrator, he could guide Videssos toward Digenis' teachings. If someone stodgy or orthodox—Evripos sprang to mind—began to wear the red boots, persecution would continue. It behooved him, then, not to give Krispos any reason to supplant him.

With that thought in mind, he hurried across the cobblestones toward the eparch's mansion. The Halogai newly posted outside it stared suspiciously until they recognized him, then swung up their axes in salute.

His father, as usual, was wading through documents when he came into the chamber. Krispos looked up with an irritated frown. "What are you doing back here already? I sent you out to—"

"I know what you sent me out to do," Phostis said. "I have done it. Here." He pulled a parchment from the pouch on his belt and threw it down on the desk in front of Krispos. "These are the signatures of the officers to whom I transmitted your order."

Krispos leaned back in his seat so he could more easily scan the names. When he looked up, the frown had disappeared. "You did well. Thank you, son. Take the rest of the evening as your own; I have no more tasks for you."

"As you say, Father." Phostis started to walk away.

The Avtokrator called him back. "Wait. Don't go off angry. How do you think I've slighted you now?"

The way Krispos put the question only annoyed Phostis more. Forgetting he intended to keep on his father's good side, he growled, "You might sound happier that I did what you wanted."

"Why should I?" Krispos answered. "You did your duty well; I said as much. But the task was not that demanding. Do you want special praise every time you piddle without getting your boots wet?"

They glowered at each other in mutual incomprehension. Phostis wished he'd just shown Krispos the parchment instead of giving it to him. Then he could have torn it up and thrown it in his face. As it was, he had to content himself with slamming the door behind him as he stamped out.

Full darkness had fallen by the time he was out on the plaza again. The Haloga guards gave him curious looks, but his face did not encourage questions. Only when he'd put the eparch's residence well behind him did he realize he had no place to go. He paused, plucked at his beard—a gesture very like his father's—and tried to figure out what to do next.

Drinking himself insensible was one obvious answer. Torches blazed in front of all the taverns he could see, and doubtless on ones he couldn't, as well. He wondered if the inn-keepers had imported extra wine from the countryside while the imperial army's quartermasters brought their supplies into Nakoleia. It wouldn't have surprised him; to sordid materialists, the arrival of so many thirsty soldiers had to look like a bonanza.

He didn't take long to decide against the taverns. He had nothing against wine in its place; it was healthier to drink than water, and less likely to give you the flux. But drunkenness tore the soul away from Phos and left it base and animalistic, easy meat for the temptations of Skotos. The state of his soul mattered a great deal to him at the moment. The less he did to corrupt it, the surer his hope of heaven.

He glanced across the square to the temple. Its entrance was also lit, and men filed in to pray. Some, by the way they walked, had got drunk first. Phostis' lip curled in contempt. He didn't want to pray with drunks. He didn't want to pray in a building modeled after the High Temple, either, not when he discovered himself in sympathy with the Thanasioi.

A breeze from off the Videssian Sea had picked up with the coming of evening. It was not what sent a chill through him. So long as his father held the throne, he was in deadly danger—had placed himself there, in fact, the instant he understood what Digenis' preaching implied. The odds that Krispos would turn away from materialism were about as slim as those of oranges sprouting from stalks of barley. Having been born with nothing—as he never tired of repeating—Krispos put about as much faith in things as he did in Phos.

So what did that leave? Phostis didn't want to drink and he didn't want to pray. He didn't feel like fornicating, either, though the whores of Nakoleia were probably working even harder than the taverners—and probably cheating their customers less.

In the end, he went back aboard the *Triumphant* and curled up in the bunk inside his tiny cabin. After a few hours ashore, even the small motion of the ship as it rocked back and forth beside the dock felt strange. Before long, though, it lulled him to sleep.

Horns blared, pipes shrilled, and deep-toned drums thumped. Videssos' banner, gold sunburst on blue, flew tall and proud at the head of the army as it marched forth from Nakoleia's land gate. Many of the horsemen had tied blue and yellow strips of cloth to their mounts' manes. The sea breeze stirred them into a fine martial display.

People packed the walls of Nakoleia. They cheered as the army rode out of the city. Some of the cheers, Krispos thought, had to be sincere. Some were probably even regretful, from tavernkeepers and merchants whose business had soared thanks to the soldiers. And a few—Krispos hoped only a few—were lies from the throats of Thanasioi spying out his strength.

He turned to Phostis, whose horse stood beside his as they watched the troops ride past. "Go back to Noetos, who commands the rear guard. Tell him to have his men be especially alert to anyone sneaking out of Nakoleia. We don't want the heretics to know exactly what all we have along with us."

"Not everyone leaving the city is sneaking out," Phostis answered.

"I know," Krispos said sourly. Like every army, this one had its camp followers, women and occasional men of easy virtue. Also following the imperial force was a larger number of sutlers and traders than Krispos was happy about. He went on, "What can I do? With our bases at Harasos and Rogmor burned out, I'll need all the help I can get feeding the troops."

"Harasos *and* Rogmor?" Phostis said, raising an eyebrow. "I'd not heard that."

"Then you might be the only one in the whole army who hasn't." Krispos gave his eldest an exasperated glare. "Don't you take any notice of what's going on around you? They hit both caches while we were still asea; by the good god, they seemed to know what we were up to almost before we did."

"How do you suppose they managed to learn where we were storing supplies?" Phostis asked in a curiously neutral voice.

"As I've said over and over—" Krispos rubbed Phostis' nose in his inattention. "—we have traitors among us, too. I wish I knew who they were, by Phos; I'd make them regret their treachery. But that's the great curse of civil war: the foe looks just like you, and so can hide in your midst. D'you see?"

"Hm? Oh, yes. Of course, Father."

Krispos sniffed. Phostis hadn't looked as if he was paying attention; his face had a withdrawn, preoccupied expression. If he wouldn't give heed to something that was liable to get him killed, what *would* hold his interest? Krispos said, "I really wish I knew how the heretics heard about my plans. They'd have needed some time to plan their attacks, so they must have

known my route of march about as soon as I decided on it—
maybe even before I decided on it."

He'd hoped the little joke would draw some kind of reaction
from Phostis, but the youngster only nodded. He turned his
horse toward the rear of the army. "I'll deliver your order to
Noetos."

"Repeat it back to me first," Krispos said, wanting to make
sure Phostis had done any listening to him at all.

His eldest reacted to that, with a scowl. He gave back the
order in a precise, emotionless voice, then rode away. Krispos
stared after him—something about the set of his back wasn't
quite right. Krispos told himself he was imagining things. He'd
pushed Phostis too far there, asking him to repeat a command
as if he were a raw peasant recruit with manure on his boots.

Of course, raw peasant recruits had more incentive to remember accurately than did someone who could aspire to
no higher station than the one he already held. It was, in fact,
difficult to aspire to a lower station than raw peasant recruit: about the only thing lower than peasant recruit was peasant. Krispos knew about that. Sometimes he wished his sons
did, too.

The army was riding forward, Phostis back. That brought
him toward Noetos twice as fast as he would have gone otherwise and cut in half his time to think. He had a pretty good
idea how the Thanasioi had learned where the imperial army
would set up its supply dumps: he'd named them for Digenis.
He hadn't intended to betray his father's campaign, but would
Krispos believe that?

Phostis didn't for a moment imagine Krispos wouldn't find
out. He did not see eye to eye with his father, but he did not
underestimate him, either. Nobody incapable stayed on the
throne of Videssos for more than twenty years. When Krispos
set his mind to learning something, sooner or later he would.
And when he did . . .

Phostis wasn't sure what the consequences of that would be,
but he was sure they'd be unpleasant—for him. They wouldn't
stop at scolding, either. Ruining a campaign was worse than a
scolding matter. It was the sort of matter that would put his
head on the block were he anyone but a junior Avtokrator.
Given his father's penchant for evenhanded—at the moment,

Phostis thought of it as heavyhanded—justice, it might put his head on the block anyway.

He wondered whether he ought to pass his father's order on to Noetos. If he truly adhered to the principles of the Thanasioi, how could he hinder the cause of his fellow believers? But if he had any thought for his own safety, how could he not transmit the order? Krispos would descend on him like an avalanche for that. And if his father's suspicions were aroused, his own role in the matter of the supply dumps grew more likely to emerge.

What to do? No more time for thought—there was the rearguard commander's banner, blue sunburst on gold. The reversed imperial colors marked the rear of the army, and out from under the banner, straight toward him, rode Noetos, a solid, middle-aged officer like so many who served under Krispos, unflappable rather than brilliant. He saluted and called out in a ringing voice, "How may I serve you, young Majesty?"

"Uh," Phostis said, and then "Uh" again; he still hadn't made up his mind. In the end, his mouth answered, not his brain. "My father bids you to be especially alert for anyone sneaking out of Nakoleia, lest the stranger prove a Thanasiot spy." He hated himself as soon as he had spoken, but that was too late—the words were gone.

They proved not to matter, though. Noetos saluted again, clenched fist over his heart, and said, "You may tell his imperial Majesty the matter is already being attended to." Then one of the officer's eyelids fell and rose in an unmistakable wink. "You can also tell Krispos not to go trying to teach an old fox how to rob henhouses."

"I'll—pass on both those messages," Phostis said faintly.

He must have looked a trifle wall-eyed, for Noetos threw back his head and let go with one of those deep, manly chortles that never failed to turn Phostis' stomach. "You do that, young Majesty," he boomed. "This'd be your first campaign, wouldn't it? Aye, of course it would. Good for you. You'll learn some things you'd never find out in the palaces."

"Yes, I'm discovering that," Phostis said. He started back toward the front of the army. That was a slower trip than the one from the front to the rear guard, for now he was moving with the stream and gaining more slowly on any point within it. He had the time to think he could have used before. He certainly was learning new things away from the palaces, not least among them how to be afraid much of the time. He doubted that was what Noetos had meant.

The baggage train traveled in the center of the strung-out army, the safest position against attack. Beeves shambled along, lowing. Wagons rattled and squeaked and jounced; ungreased axles squealed loud and shrill enough to set Phostis' teeth on edge. Some of the wagons carried hard-baked bread; others fodder for the horses; others arrows tied in neat sheaves of twenty, ready to be popped into empty quivers; still others carried the metal parts and tackle for siege engines whose timbers would be cut and trimmed on the spot under direction of the military engineers.

Noncombatants traveled with the baggage train. Healer-priests in robes of blue rode mules that alternated between walk and trot to keep up with the longer-legged horses. A few merchants with stocks of fancy goods for officers who could afford them preferred buggies to horseback. So did some of the loose women any army attracts, though others rode astride with as much aplomb as any man.

Some of the courtesans gave Phostis professionally interested smiles. He was used to that, and found it unsurprising: after all, he was young, reasonably well favored, rode a fine horse, and dressed richly. If a woman was mercenary or desperate enough to sell her body to live, he made a logical customer. As for buying such a woman, though—he left that to his brothers.

Then one of the women not only waved but smiled and called out to him. He intended to ignore her as he had all the others, but something about her—maybe the unusual combination of creamy skin and black, black hair that framed her face in ringlets—seemed familiar. He took a longer look . . . and almost steered his horse into a boulder by the side of the road. He'd seen Olyvria, naked and stretched out on a bed, somewhere under Videssos the city.

He felt himself turn crimson. What did she expect him to do, ride over and ask how she'd been since she put some clothes on? Maybe she did, because she kept on waving. He looked straight ahead and dug his knees into his horse's ribs, urging the beast up into a fast canter that hurried it away from the baggage train and the now-dressed wench.

He thought hard as he drew near Krispos. What *was* Olyvria doing here, anyhow? The only answer that occurred to him was spying for Digenis. He wondered if she'd somehow sailed with the imperial army. If not, she'd made better time overland than he'd have thought possible for anyone but a courier.

He wondered if he ought to tell his father about her—she certainly was the sort of person about whom Krispos worried. But his father had no reason to believe he knew anything about her, and she was likely a Thanasiot herself. He had no reason to give her away, not even his own advantage.

Krispos rode at the head of the army. Phostis came up and delivered both messages from Noetos. Krispos laughed when he heard the second one. "He is an old fox, by the good god," he said. Then he turned serious again. "I would have failed in my duty, though, if I'd failed to give him that order. There's a lesson you need to remember, son: an Avtokrator can't count on things happening without him. He has to make sure they happen."

"Yes, Father," Phostis said, he hoped dutifully. He knew Krispos lived by the principles he espoused. His father had given the Empire of Videssos two decades of stable government, but at the cost of turning fussy, driven, and suspicious.

He'd also developed an alarming facility for picking thoughts out of Phostis' head. "You no doubt have in mind that you'll do it all differently when your backside warms the throne. I tell you, lad, there are but two ways, mine and Anthimos'. Better you should shoulder the burden yourself than let it fall on the Empire."

"So you've said, more than once," Phostis agreed: more than a thousand times, he meant. Hearing the resignation in his voice, Krispos sighed and returned his attention to the road ahead.

Phostis started to carry the argument further, but forbore. He'd been about to put forward the wisdom and reliability of a small group of trusted advisors who might carry enough of the administrative burden to keep it from overwhelming an Avtokrator. Before he spoke, though, he remembered the false friends and sycophants he'd already had to dismiss, people who sought to use him for their own gain. Just because advisors were trusted did not mean they wouldn't be venal.

He jerked on the reins; his horse snorted indignantly as he pulled its head away from that of Krispos' mount. But conceding his father a point always annoyed him. By riding away from Krispos, he wouldn't have to concede anything, either to his father or to himself.

By the end of the day, the imperial army had moved far enough inland to make sunset a spectacle very different from what Phostis was used to. Having land all around seemed suddenly confining, as if he were closed off from the infinite possibilities for travel available at Videssos the city. Even the sounds were strange: night birds unknown in the imperial capital announced their presence with trills and strange drumming noises.

Krispos' tent, however, did its best to recreate the splendor of the imperial palaces, using canvas rather than stone. Torches and bonfires held night at bay; officers going in and out took the place of the usual run of petitioners. Some emerged glum, others pleased, again as it would have been back in the city.

As in the capital, Phostis had no choice but to establish his own lodging uncomfortably close to that of his father. Also as in Videssos the city, he did choose to stay as far from Krispos as he could. The servitors who raised his tent carefully did not raise their eyebrows when he ordered them to place it to the rear and off to one side of Krispos' larger, grander shelter.

Phostis ate from the cookpot the Halogai set up in front of Krispos' pavilion. He ran no risk of bumping into his father there; by all accounts, Krispos' habit on campaign was to share the rations of his common soldiers, so he was probably off somewhere standing in line with a bowl and a spoon like any cavalry trooper.

Had he sampled his own guards' stew that evening, he would not have been happy with it. It had a sharp, bitter undertaste that made Phostis' tongue want to shrivel up. The Halogai liked it no better than he, and were less restrained in suggesting appropriate redress.

"Maybe if so bad next time, we cut up cook and mingle his meat with the mush," one of them said. The rest of the northerners nodded so soberly that Phostis, who had at first smiled, began to wonder if the Haloga was joking.

He'd hardly finished supper when his guts knotted and cramped. He made for the latrines at a dead run and barely managed to hike up his robes and squat over a slit trench before he was noisomely ill. Wrinkling his nose at the stench, he got painfully to his feet. A Haloga crouched a few feet away. Another came hurrying up a moment later. Before he could tear down his breeches, he cried in deep disgust, "Oh, by the gods of the north, I've gone and shit myself!"

Phostis made several more trips out to the slit trenches as the night wore on. He began to count himself lucky that he hadn't had to echo the Haloga's melancholy wail. More often than not, several guardsmen were at the latrine with him.

Finally, some time past midnight, he found himself alone in the darkness out there. He'd gone a good ways away from his tent in the hope of finding untrodden, unbefouled ground. Just as he started to squat, someone called from beyond the slit trenches: "Young Majesty!"

His head went up in alarm—it was a woman's voice. But what he had to do was more urgent than any embarrassment. When he'd finished, he wiped sick sweat from his forehead and started slowly back toward his tent.

"Young Majesty!" The call came again.

This time he recognized the voice: it was Olyvria's. "What do you want with me?" he growled. "Haven't you seen me mortified enough, here and back in the city?"

"You misunderstand, young Majesty," she said in injured tones. She held up something; in the dark, he couldn't tell what it was. "I have here a decoction of the wild plum and black pepper that will help relieve your distress."

Had she offered him her body, he would have laughed at her. He'd already declined that when he was feeling perfectly fine. But at the moment, he would have crowned her Empress for something that stopped his insides from turning inside out.

He hurried over to her, skipping across slit trenches as he went. She held a small glass vial out to him; distant torchlight reflected faintly from it. He yanked off the stopper, raised the vial to his lips, and drank.

"Thank you," he said—or started to. For some reason, his mouth didn't want to work right. He stared at the vial he still held in his hand. All at once, it seemed very far away, and receding quickly. Agonizingly slow, a thought trickled across his brain: *I've been tricked.* He turned and tried to run, but felt himself falling instead. *I've been—* Unconsciousness seized him before he could find the word *stupid.*

# IV

"LET'S GET MOVING," KRISPOS SAID IRRITABLY. "WHERE'S Phostis taken himself off to, anyhow? If he thinks I'll hold up the whole army for his sake, he's wrong."

"Maybe he's fallen into the latrine," Evripos said. Bad food was a risk on campaign; plenty of Halogai had been running back and forth in the night. The gibe might have been funny had Evripos sounded less hopeful it was true.

Krispos said, "I haven't time for anyone's nonsense today, son—his or yours." He turned to one of his guardsmen. "Skalla, stick your head into his tent and rout him out."

"Aye, Majesty." Like a lot of his fellows, Skalla looked even fairer—paler was probably a better word—than usual this morning. He strode off to do Krispos' bidding, but returned to the imperial pavilion a moment later with a puzzled expression on his face. "Majesty, he is not there. The coverlet is thrown back as if he'd got out of his cot, but he is not there."

"Well, the ice take it, where is he, then?" Krispos snapped. What Evripos had said sparked a thought. He told Skalla, "Pick a squad of guards and go up and down the slit trenches in a hurry, to make sure he wasn't taken ill there."

"Aye, Majesty." Skalla's voice was doleful. For one thing, now that morning had come, the latrines were busy. Anyone who spotted Phostis there would have raised an uproar. For another . . .

"Pick men the flux missed," Krispos said. "I wouldn't want the stink to make them sick all over again."

"I thank you, Majesty." The Halogai were not what one would call a cheerful folk, but Skalla seemed more pleased with the world.

That did not mean he and the squad of guardsmen had any luck turning up Phostis. When he came back to report failure to Krispos, the Avtokrator said, "I'm not going to wait for him, by the good god. Let's get everyone moving. He'll turn up— where else is he going to go? And when he does, I shall have a word or two with him—a pungent word or two."

Skalla nodded; from everything Krispos had gleaned of how life worked in Halogaland, sons there knew better than to give already grizzled fathers more gray hair. He let out a mordant chuckle—it sounded too good to be true.

The imperial army did not get moving as fast as he would have wanted; it was newly mustered and still shaking down. He'd been sure Phostis would appear before the troops really started heading south and west. But his eldest did not appear. Evripos opened his mouth to say something that surely would have proved ill-advised. Krispos' glare made certain it never crossed the barrier of his son's lips.

By the time the army had been an hour on the road, Krispos' anger melted into worry. He sent couriers to each regiment to summon Phostis by name. The couriers returned to him. Phostis did not. Krispos turned to Evripos. "Fetch me Zaidas, at once." Evripos did not argue.

The wizard, not surprisingly, had a good notion of why he'd been summoned. He came straight to the point. "When was the young man last seen?"

"I've been trying to find out," Krispos answered. "He seems to have been taken with the same flux that seized a fair number of the Halogai last night. Several of them saw him once, or more than once, squatting over a latrine trench. No one, though, has any clear memory of spotting him there after about the seventh hour of the night."

"An hour or so past midnight, then? Hmm." Zaidas' eyes went far away, into a place Krispos could not follow. Despite that, though, he was a thoroughly practical man. "The first thing to determine, your Majesty, is whether he be alive or dead."

"You're right, of course." Krispos bit his lip. For all his quarrels with his eldest, for all his doubts as to whether Phostis *was* his eldest, he discovered he feared for Phostis' life as might any father, true or adoptive. "Can you do that at once, eminent and sorcerous sir?"

"A hedge wizard could do as much, your Majesty, with the abundance of Phostis' effects present here," the mage answered, smiling. "An elementary use of the law of contagion: these effects, once handled by the young Majesty, retain an affinity for him and will demonstrate it under sorcerous prodding . . . assuming, of course, that he yet remains among the living."

"Aye, assuming," Krispos said harshly. "Find out at once, then, if we can go on making that assumption."

"Of course, your Majesty. Have you some artifact of your son's that I might use?"

Krispos pointed. "There's his bedding, slung over the back of the horse he should be riding. Will that do?"

"Excellently." Zaidas rode over to the animal at which Krispos had pointed and pulled a coverlet from the lump of cinched-down bedding. "This is a very basic spell, your Majesty, one that requires no apparatus, merely a concentration of my will to increase the strength of the link between the blanket here and the young Majesty."

"Just get on with it," Krispos said.

"As you say." Zaidas laid the blanket across his knees, as he switched the reins to his left hand. He chanted briefly in the archaic dialect of Videssian most often used in the liturgy for Phos' Temple, at the same time moving his right hand in small, swift passes above the coverlet.

The square of soft wool rippled gently, like the surface of the sea when stirred by a soft breeze. "Phostis is alive," Zaidas declared in a voice that brooked no contradiction. "Had he left mankind, the coverlet would have lain quiescent, as it did before I completed the incantation."

"Thank you, eminent and sorcerous sir," Krispos said. Some of the great weight of worry he'd borne rolled off his shoulders—some, but far from all. The next question followed like one winter storm rolling into Videssos the city hard on the heels of another: "Having found that he is among the living, can you now learn among which living folk he is at the moment?"

Zaidas nodded, not in answer, Krispos thought, but to show he'd expected the Avtokrator would ask that. "Yes, your Majesty, I can do so," he said. "It's not quite so simple a spell as the one I just used, but like it springs from the workings of the law of contagion."

"I don't care if it springs from the ground when you pour pig manure around the place where you planted it," Krispos answered. "If you can work your magic while we move, so much the better. If not, I'll give you all the guards you need for as long as you need them."

"That shouldn't be necessary," Zaidas said. "I think I have with me all I shall require." He drew from a saddlebag a short, thin stick and a small silver cup. From his canteen, he poured wine into the cup until it was nearly full, then passed it to Krispos. "Hold this a moment, your Majesty, if you would be so kind." As soon as he had both hands free, he teased a fuzzy length of wool loose from Phostis' blanket, then wrapped it around the stick.

He held out a hand for the silver cup, which Krispos returned to him. When he had it back, he dropped in the stick so it floated on the wine. "This spell may also be accomplished with water, your Majesty, but I am of the opinion that the spirituous component of the wine improves its efficacy."

"However you think best," Krispos said. Listening to Zaidas cheerfully explain how he did what he did helped the Emperor not think about all the things that could have happened to Phostis.

The wizard said, "Once I have chanted, the little stick here, by virtue of its connection to the wool that was once connected to your son, will turn in the cup to reveal the direction in which he lies."

This spell, as Zaidas had said, was more intricate than the first one he'd used. He needed both hands for the passes, and he guided his horse by the pressure of his knees. At the climax of the incantation, he stabbed down at the floating stick with a rigid forefinger, crying out at the same time in a loud, commanding voice.

Krispos waited for the stick to quiver and point like a well-trained hunting dog. Instead, it spun wildly in the cup, splashing wine up over the edge and then sinking out of sight in the rich ruby liquid. Krispos stared. "What does *that* mean?"

"Your Majesty, if I knew, I would tell you." Zaidas sounded even more surprised than the Avtokrator had. He paused for a moment to think, then went on, "It might mean this blanket was in fact never in direct contact with Phostis. But no—" He shook his head. "That cannot be, either. Had the blanket no affinity for your son, it would not have responded to the spell that showed us he is alive."

"Yes, I follow your reasoning," Krispos said. "What other choices have we?"

"Next most likely, or so it seems to me, is that my sorcerous efforts are somehow being blocked, to keep me from learning where the young Majesty is," Zaidas said.

"But you are a master mage, one of the leaders of the Sorcerers' Collegium," Krispos protested. "How can anyone keep you from working what you wish?"

"Several ways, your Majesty. I am not the only sorcerer of my grade within the Empire of Videssos. Another master, or perhaps even a team of lesser wizards, may be working to keep the truth from me. Notice the spell did not send us off in a direction that later proved false, but merely prevented us from learning the true one. That is an easier magic."

"I see," Krispos said slowly. "You named one way, or possibly even two, in which you could be deceived. Are there others?"

"Yes," Zaidas answered. "I am a master in wizardry based on our faith in Phos and rejection of his dark foe Skotos." The mage paused to spit. "This is, you might say, a two-poled system of magic. The Halogai with their many gods, or the Khamorth of the steppe with their belief in supernatural powers animating each rock or stream or sheep or blade of grass, view the world from such a different perspective that their sorcery is more difficult for a mage of my school to detect or counter. The same applies in lesser degree to the Makuraners, who filter the power of what they term the God through the intermediary of the Prophets Four."

"Assuming this blocking magic is from some school other than ours, can you fight through it?" Krispos asked.

"Your Majesty, there I am imperfectly certain. In theory, since ours is the only true faith, magic developed from it will in the end prove mightier than that based on any other system. In practice, man's creations being the makeshifts they are, a great deal depends on the strength and skill of the mages involved, regardless of the school to which they belong. I can try my utmost, but I cannot guarantee success."

"Do your utmost," Krispos said. "I suppose you will need to halt for your more complicated spells. I'll leave you a courier; send word the moment you have results of any sort."

"I shall, your Majesty," Zaidas promised. He looked as if he wanted to say something more. Krispos waved for him to go on. He did: "I pray you forgive me, your Majesty, but you might also be wise to send out riders to beat the countryside."

"I'll do that," Krispos said with a sinking feeling. Zaidas was warning him not to expect success in a hurry, if at all.

The squads of horsemen clattered forth, some ahead of the army, some back toward Nakoleia, others out to either side of the track. No encouraging word came from them by sundown. Krispos and the main body of his force rode on, leaving Zaidas behind to set up his search magic. A company stayed with him to protect him from Thanasioi or simple robbers. Krispos waited and waited for the courier to return. At last, just as weariness was about to drive him to his cot, the fellow rode into the encampment. Seeing the question in the Emperor's eyes, he just shook his head.

"No luck?" Krispos said, for the sake of being sure.

"No luck," the courier answered. "I'm sorry, your Majesty. The wizard's magic failed again: more than once, from what he told me."

Grimacing, Krispos thanked the man and sent him to his own rest. He hadn't really believed Zaidas would stay baffled. He lay down on the cot as he'd intended, but found sleep a long time coming.

*Stupid.* The word slid sluggishly through Phostis' mind. Because he saw only darkness, he thought for a confused moment that he was still back at the latrines. Then he realized a bandage covered his eyes. He reached up to pull it off, only to discover his hands had been efficiently tied behind his back, his legs at knees and ankles.

He groaned. The sound came out muffled—he was also gagged. He groaned again anyhow. His head felt like an anvil on which a smith about as tall as the top of the High Temple's dome was hammering out a complicated piece of ironwork. He was lying on something hard—boards, he found out when a splinter dug into the thin strip of flesh between blindfold and gag.

Adding to the pounding agony behind his eyes were squeaks and jolts. *I'm in a wagon, or maybe a cart,* he thought, amazed and impressed that his poor benighted brain functioned at all. He groaned one more time.

"He's coming around," said somebody—a man—above and in front of him. The fellow laughed, loudly and raucously. "It's took him long enough, it has, it has."

"Shall we let him see where he's going?" another voice, a woman's, asked. After a moment, Phostis recognized it: Olyvria's. He ground his teeth in helpless fury; he felt he'd already used up all the groans in him.

The man—the driver?—said, "Nah, our orders was to bring him the first stage of the way to Livanios without him knowin' nothin' about it. That's what your pa done said, and that's what we does. So don't go untyin' him, either, you hear me?"

"I hear you, Syagrios," Olyvria answered. "It's too bad. We'd all be happier if we could get him cleaned up a bit."

"I've smelled worse, out in the fields at manuring time," Syagrios said. "The stink won't kill him, and it won't kill you, neither."

Phostis had been aware of a foul smell since his wits returned. He hadn't realized he was the cause of it. He must have gone on fouling himself after Olyvria's potion—the one that was supposed to end his internal turmoil—forced him down into oblivion. *I'll have revenge for that, by the good god,* he thought. *I'll—* He gave up. No vengeance seemed savage enough to suit him.

Olyvria said, "I wish he would have come and talked with me when he saw me by the baggage train. He recognized me, I know he did. I think I could have persuaded him to come with us of his own will. I know he follows Thanasios' gleaming path, at least in large measure."

Syagrios gave a loud, skeptical grunt. "How d'you know that?"

"He wouldn't bed me when he had the chance," Olyvria answered.

Her companion grunted again, in a slightly different tone. "Well, maybe. It don't matter, though. Our orders was to snatch him fast as we could, and we done did it. Livanios will be happy with us."

"So he will," Olyvria said.

She and Syagrios went on talking, but Phostis stopped heeding them. He hadn't figured out for himself—though he supposed he should have—that his kidnappers were Thanasioi. As it did Olyvria, the irony of that struck him, though in his case the impact was far more forcible. Given any sort of choice in the matter, he would have picked a different way of coming into their number. But they had not given him any choice.

He closed his lips on the gag and tried to draw a tiny bit of the cloth into his mouth. He needed several tries before he nipped it between upper and lower front teeth. After working awhile on chewing through it, he decided that was easier said than done. He labored instead to get it down so his mouth would be free. Just when he thought he'd succeed about the time he got to wherever Livanios was, the top edge of the gag slid down over his upper lip. Not only could he talk now if he had to, he could also breathe much more easily.

Even though he could talk, he resolved not to, lest his captors gag him more securely. But his body tested his resolve in ways he hadn't anticipated. At last he said, "Could you people please stop long enough to let me make water?"

Syagrios' startled jerk shook the whole wagon. "By the ice, how'd he get his mouth loose?" He turned around, then growled, "Well, why should we bother? You already stink."

"We aren't just stealing him, Syagrios, we're bringing him to us," Olyvria said. "There's no one on the road; why shouldn't we just stand him up and let him do what needs doing? It won't take long."

"Why should we? You didn't lift him in there, and you won't have to lift him out." The man grumbled a little longer, then said, "All right, have it your way." He must have pulled on the reins; the jingle of harness ceased as the wagon stopped. Phostis felt himself lifted by arms as thick and powerful as any Haloga's. He leaned against the side of the wagon on legs that did not want to hold him up. Syagrios said, "Go ahead and piss. Be quick about it."

"It's not that simple for him, you know," Olyvria said. "Here, wait—I'll help." The wagon shifted behind Phostis as she got down. He listened to her come around and stand by him. She hiked up his robe so he wouldn't wet it. As if that weren't mortification enough, she took him in hand and said, "Go on; now you won't splash on your boots."

Syagrios laughed coarsely. "You hold him like that for very long and he'll be too stiff to piss at all."

Phostis hadn't even thought about that aspect of things; what rang through his mind was his father's voice back at Nakoleia, asking him if he wanted praise for piddling without getting his feet wet. At the moment, such praise would have been welcome. He relieved himself as fast as he could; never before had the phrase possessed such real and immediate meaning for him. His sigh when he was through was involuntary but heartfelt.

The robe fluttered down around his tied ankles. Syagrios picked him up and, grunting, lifted him back into the wagon. The fellow talked like a villain and, without Phostis' excuse for filth, was none too clean, but he had brute strength to spare. He set Phostis down flat in the wagon bed, then returned to his place and got his team moving once more.

"You want to gag him again?" he asked Olyvria.

"No," Phostis said—quietly, so they would see he did not have to be gagged. Then he used a word most often perfunctory for an Avtokrator's son: "Please." It was not perfunctory now.

"I think I'd better," Olyvria said after a brief pause. She must have swung round on the seat; her feet came down in the wagon close by Phostis' head. "I'm sorry," she told him as she slipped the gag over his mouth and tied it behind his neck, "but we just can't trust you yet."

Her fingers were smooth and warm and briskly capable; had she given him the chance, he would have bitten them to the bone. He didn't get the chance. He was already discovering she knew how to do much more than lie temptingly naked on a bed.

That discovery would have surprised his brothers even more than it did him. Evripos and Katakolon were convinced lying naked on a bed was all women were good for. Since he was less concerned about finding them there, he found it easier to envision them doing other things. But not even he had imagined finding one who made such an effective kidnapper.

Olyvria got back up beside Syagrios. She remarked, apparently to no one in particular, "If he gets that one off, he'll regret it."

"I'll *make* him regret it." Syagrios sounded as if he looked forward to doing just that. Phostis, who had already started working on the new gag, decided not to go on. He chose to believe Olyvria had given him a hint.

The day was the longest, driest, hungriest, and generally most miserable he'd ever endured. After some endless while, he began to see real black rather than gray through the blindfold. The air grew cooler, almost chilly. *Night,* he thought. He wondered if Syagrios would drive straight on till dawn. If Syagrios did, Phostis wondered if he would still be alive by the time his eyes saw gray once more.

But not long after dark, Syagrios stopped. He picked Phostis up, leaned him against the side of the wagon, then descended, picked him up again, and slung him over his shoulder like a sack of chickpeas. Behind him, Olyvria got the horses moving at a slow walk.

From ahead came a metallic squawk of rusty hinges, then the scrape of something moving against resistance from dirt and gravel: *a gate opening,* Phostis thought. "Hurry up," an unfamiliar male voice said.

"Here we go," Syagrios answered. He picked up his pace. By their hoofbeats, so did the horses behind him. As soon as they stopped, the gate went scrape-squeak. *Closing,* Phostis thought. The slam of a bar falling into place confirmed that. "Ah, good," Syagrios said. "Think we can untie him for now and take the rag off his eyes?"

"I don't see why not," the other man said. "If he gets away from this place, by the good god, he's earned it. And didn't I hear he's halfway set foot on the gleaming path himself?"

"Aye, I've heard that, too." Syagrios laughed. "Thing is, I didn't get to be as old as I am believing everything I hear."

"Set him down so I can cut the ropes easier," Olyvria said. Syagrios put Phostis onto the ground more carefully than if he'd been chickpeas, but not much. Somebody—presumably Olyvria—slit his bonds, then slid the blindfold from his face.

He blinked; his eyes filled with tears. After a day in enforced darkness, even torchlight seemed shockingly bright. When he tried to lever himself up, neither arms nor legs would

obey him. He set his teeth against the pain of returning blood.
Pins and needles was too mild a phrase for it; it felt more like
nails and spikes. They got worse with every passing moment,
until he wondered if the maltreated members would fall off.

"It will ease soon," Olyvria assured him.

He wondered how she could know—had she ever been
trussed up like a suckling pig on its way to market? But she
was right. After a little while, he tried again to stand. This time
he made it, though he swayed like a tree in a windstorm.

"He don't look too good," said the fellow who went with
this ... farmhouse, Phostis supposed it was, though the man,
lean, pale, and furtive, looked more like a sneakthief than a
farmer.

"He'll be hungry," Syagrios said, "and tired." Syagrios
seemed very much the stalwart bruiser Phostis had expected.
He wasn't even of average height for a Videssian, but had
shoulders as wide as any Haloga's and arms thick with corded
muscle. At some time in the unknown past, his nose had inter-
cepted a chair or other instrument of strong opinion.

A big gold hoop dangled piratically from his left ear. Phostis
pointed at it. "I thought folk who followed the gleaming path
didn't wear ornaments like that."

Syagrios' startled stare quickly slid into a scowl. "None of
your cursed business what I wear or don't—" he began, folding one big hand into a fist.

"Wait," Olyvria said. "This is something he needs to know."
She turned to Phostis. "You're right and yet you're wrong.
When we go among men not of our kind, sometimes lack of
ostentation can betray us. We have the right to disguise our ap-
pearance, just as we may deny our creed to save ourselves."

Phostis bit down hard on that one. A Videssian's faith was
his proudest possession; many had been martyred for refusing
to compromise the creed. Letting a man—or a woman—
dissemble in time of danger went square against everything
he'd ever been taught ... but also made good sense from a
practical standpoint.

Slowly he said, "My father will have a hard time sifting
those who follow Thanasios' ways from the generality, then."
Krispos wouldn't have looked for that. Most heresies, believing themselves orthodox, trumpeted their tenets and made
themselves easy targets. But suppressing the Thanasioi would

be like striking smoke, which gave way before blows yet was not destroyed.

"That's right," Olyvria said. "We'll give the imperial army more trouble than it can handle. Before long, we'll give the whole Empire more trouble than it can handle." Her eyes sparkled at the prospect.

Syagrios turned to the fellow who'd let them into the courtyard. "Where's the food?" he boomed, slapping his bulging belly with the palm of one hand. No matter what Olyvria said, Phostis had trouble picturing him as an ascetic.

"I'll get it," the skinny man said, and went into the house.

"Phostis needs it more than you," Olyvria said to Syagrios.

"So?" he answered. "I was the one with the wit to ask for it. Of course, our friend here wasn't likely to listen to the likes of him." Phostis thought he deliberately avoided naming the other man. That showed more wit than he'd credited Syagrios with having. If he ever escaped . . . but did he want to escape? He shook his head, bewildered. He didn't know what he wanted.

He didn't know what he wanted, that is, until the fellow who looked like a thief came out with a loaf of black bread, some runny yellow cheese, and a jar of the sort that commonly held cheap wine. Then his growling stomach and spit-filled mouth loudly made their wishes known.

He ate like a starving badger. The wine mounted from his belly to his head. He felt more nearly human that he had since he was drugged, but that wasn't saying much. He asked, "May I have a cloth or a sponge and some water to wash myself? And some clean clothes, if there are any?"

The skinny fellow looked at Syagrios. Syagrios, for all his bluster, looked at Olyvria. She nodded. The skinny fellow said to Phostis, "You're my size, near enough. You can wear one of my old tunics. I'll get it. There's a pitcher and a sponge on a stick in the privy."

Phostis waited until he had the rough, colorless homespun garment in his hands, then headed for the privy. The robe he wore was worth dozens of the one he put on, but he made the exchange with nothing but delight.

He looked down at himself as he came out of the privy. He was no peacock, like some of the young men who swaggered around Videssos the city displaying themselves and their finery on holidays. Even if he'd had such longings—as Katakolon did, to some degree—Krispos wouldn't have let him indulge them. Having been born on a farm, Krispos still kept the poor man's scorn for fancy clothes he couldn't afford himself. Nonetheless, Phostis was sure he'd never worn anything so plain in his whole life.

The thin man pointed at him. "See! Without the embroidered robes, he looks like anybody else. That's what Thanasios says, bless him—take away the riches that separate one man from another and we're all pretty much the same. What we have to do is make sure *nobody* has riches. The lord with the great and good mind will love us for that."

"Other way to make us all the same is let everybody have riches." Syagrios cast a covetous eye on the befouled robe Phostis had been so happy to remove. "Clean that up and it'd bring a pretty piece of change."

"No," Olyvria said. "Try to sell it and you shout 'Here I am!' to Krispos' spies. Livanios ordered us to destroy everything Phostis had when we took him, and that's what we'll do."

"All right, all right," Syagrios said, voice surly. "Still seems a waste, though."

The skinny man rounded on him. "Your theology's not all it should be. The goal is the destruction of riches, says Thanasios, not the equality, for Phos best loves those who give up all they have for the sake of his truth."

"Oh, I don't know about that," Syagrios said. "If all were alike, poor or rich, we wouldn't be jealous of each other, and if jealousy ain't a sin, what is, eh?" He set hands on hips and smiled triumphantly at the thin man.

"I'll tell you what," the other answered hotly, ready as any Videssian to do battle for the sake of his dogmas.

"No, you won't." Olyvria's tone reminded Phostis of the one Krispos used when delivering judgment from the imperial throne. "The forces of materialism are stronger than we are. If we quarrel among ourselves, we are lost . . . so we shall not quarrel."

Syagrios and the skinny fellow both glared at her, but neither one of them carried the argument any further. Phostis was impressed. He wondered what power Olyvria had over her henchmen. Whatever it was, it worked. Maybe she carried an amulet ... or would a heretic's charm be efficacious? Then again, were the Thanasioi heretics or the most perfect of the orthodox?

Before Phostis could formulate an answer to either of those questions, the skinny man jerked a thumb in his direction and said, "What do we do with this one tonight?"

"Keep watch on him," Olyvria said. "Tomorrow we move on."

"I'm going to tie him up, too, just in case," the skinny fellow said. "If he gets loose, the imperial executioners have a lot of ways to keep you alive when you'd rather be dead."

"I don't think we need to do that," Olyvria said. This time, though, her tone was doubtful, and she looked to Syagrios for support. The short, muscular man shook his head; he sided with the thin fellow. Olyvria's mouth twisted, but she gave over arguing. With a shrug, she turned to Phostis and said, "I think you'd be safe unbound, but they don't trust you enough yet. Try not to hate us for it."

Phostis also shrugged. "I won't deny I've thought long and hard about becoming one of you Thanasioi, but I never thought I'd be ... recruited ... this way. If you expect me to be happy about it, I fear you're in for disappointment."

"You're honest, at any rate," Olyvria said.

Syagrios snorted. "He's but a babe, same as you, lass. He don't believe nothin' bad can happen to him, not in his guts, not in his balls. You're young, you say what you want and don't give a fart for what happens next on account of you think you're gonna live forever anyways."

That was the most words Phostis had heard from Syagrios at any one time. Try as he would, he couldn't keep his face straight. His laughter had a high, hysterical edge to it, but it was laughter.

"What's so funny?" Syagrios growled. "You laugh at me, you'll go to the ice. I've sent better and tougher men there than you, by the good god."

When Phostis tried to stop laughing, he found it wasn't easy. He had to take a deep breath, hold it, and let it out slowly before the fit would pass. At last, carefully, he said, "I will apologize, Syagrios. It's just that—that—I never expected you to talk like—like—my father." He held his breath again to stave off another wild attack of laughter.

"Huh." Syagrios' smile revealed several broken teeth and a couple of gaps. "Yeah, maybe that is funny. I guess if you've been around awhile, you start thinkin' one kind o' way."

Before Phostis could answer that or even think about it very much, the skinny man came up to him with a fresh length of rope. "Put your hands behind you," he said. "I won't tie 'em as tight as they was before. I—"

Phostis made his move. The romances he'd read insisted a man whose cause was just could overcome several villains. The writers of those romances had never run into the skinny fellow. Phostis' eyes must have given him away, for the thin man kicked him square in the crotch almost before he managed to raise an arm. He fell in a moaning heap and threw up most of the food he'd eaten. He knew he ought not to writhe and clutch at himself, but he could not help it. He'd never known such pain.

"You were right," Olyvria told the skinny man, her voice curiously neutral. "He needs to be tied tonight."

Skinny nodded. He waited for Phostis' thrashings to cease, then said, "Get up, you. Don't be stupid about it, either, or I'll give you another dose."

Swiping at his mouth with the sleeve of his homespun tunic, Phostis struggled to his feet. He had needed to get used to Digenis' addressing him as *lad* rather than *young Majesty*; now he hurt too much to bridle at being roughly called *you*. At the thin man's gesture, he put his hands behind his back and let himself be tied. Maybe the rope wasn't as tight as it had been before. It was none too loose, either.

His kidnappers brought out a blanket that smelled of horse and draped it over him once he'd lain down. The two men went inside the farmhouse, leaving Olyvria behind for the first watch. She had both a hunting bow and a knife that would have made a decent shortsword.

"You keep an eye on him," Syagrios called from the doorway. "If he tries to get loose, hurt him and holler for us. We can't let him get away."

"I know," Olyvria said. "He shan't."

By the way she handled the bow, Phostis could see she knew what to do with it. He had no doubt she'd shoot him to keep him from escaping. With the dull, sickening ache still in his stones, he wasn't going anywhere anyhow, not for a while. He said as much to Olyvria.

"You were stupid to try to break away there," she answered, again in that odd, dispassionate tone.

"So I found out." The inside of Phostis' mouth tasted like something that had just been scraped out of a sewer.

"Why did you do it?" she asked.

"I don't know. Because I thought I might succeed, I suppose." Phostis thought a little, then added, "Syagrios would probably say because I'm young and stupid." What he thought about both Syagrios and his opinions he would not repeat to a woman, not even one who'd shown him her nakedness, who'd drugged him and stolen him.

He could, at the moment, think of Olyvria's nakedness with absolute detachment. He knew he wasn't ruined for life, but he certainly was ruined for the evening. He wriggled around a little on the hard-packed ground, trying to find some position less uncomfortable than most of the others.

"I'm sorry," Olyvria said, as contritely as if they were friends. "Did you want to rest?"

"What I want to do and what I can do aren't the same," he answered.

"I'm afraid I can't help that," she said, sharply now. "If you'd not been so foolish, I might have managed something, but since you were—" She shook her head. "Syagrios and our other friend are right—we have to get you safe to Livanios. I know he'll be delighted to see you."

"To have me in his hands, you mean," Phostis retorted. "And what puts you so high in Livanios' council? How can you *know* what he will or won't be?"

"It's not hard," Olyvria answered. "He's my father."

Zaidas looked worn. He'd ridden hard to catch up with the army. Still in the saddle, he bowed his head to Krispos. "I regret, your Majesty, that I have had no success in locating your son by sorcerous means. I shall accept without complaint any penalty you see fit to exact for my failure."

"Very well, then," Krispos said. Zaidas stiffened, awaiting the Avtokrator's judgment. Krispos delivered it in his most imperial voice: "I order you henceforth to be forcibly prevented from mouthing such nonsense." He started talking normally again. "Don't you think I know you're doing everything you know how to do?"

"You're generous, your Majesty," the wizard said, not hiding his relief. He took the reins in his left hand for a moment so he could pound his right fist down onto his thigh. "You can't imagine how this eats at me. I'm used to success, by the lord with the great and good mind. Knowing a mage out there can thwart me makes me furious. I want to find out who he is and where he is so I can thrash him with my bare hands."

His obvious anger made Krispos smile. "A man who believes he can't be beaten is most often proved right." But his grin soon slipped. "Unless, of course, he's up against something rather more than a man. If you were wrong back in the city and we do, in fact, face Harvas—"

"That thought crossed my mind," Zaidas said. "Being beaten by one of that sort would surely salve my self-respect, for who among mortal men could stand alone against him? Before I rejoined you, I ran the same sorcerous tests I'd used at the Sorcerers' Collegium, and others besides. Whoever he may be, my foe is not Harvas."

"Good," Krispos said. "That means Phostis does not lie under Harvas' hands—a fate I'd wish on no one, friend or foe."

"There we agree," Zaidas answered. "We will all be better off if Harvas Black-Robe is never again seen among living men. But knowing he is not the agency of your son's disappearance hardly puts us closer to learning who is responsible."

"Responsible? Who but the Thanasioi? That much I assume. What puzzles me—and you as well, obviously—is how they're able to hide him." Krispos paused, plucked at his beard, and listened over again in his mind to what Zaidas had just said. After a moment's thought, he slowly went on, "Knowing Harvas isn't responsible for stealing Phostis lifts a weight from my heart. Have you any way to learn by sorcery who is to blame?"

The mage bared his teeth in a frustrated grimace that had nothing to do with a smile save in the twist of his lips. "Majesty, my sorcery can't even find your son, let alone who's to blame for absconding with him."

"I understand that," Krispos said. "Not quite what I meant. Sometimes in ruling I find problems where, if I tried to solve them all at once with one big, sweeping law, a lot of people would rise up in revolt. But they still need solving, so I go about it a little at a time, with a small change here, another one there, still another two years later. Anyone who thinks he can solve a complicated mess in one fell swoop is a fool, if you ask me. Problems that grow up over years don't go away in a day."

"True enough, your Majesty, and wise, too."

"Ha!" Krispos said. "If you're a farmer, it's something you'd better know."

"As may be," Zaidas answered. "I wasn't going to go on with flattery, believe me. I was just going to say I didn't see how your principle, though admirable, applies in this case."

"Someone's magic is keeping you from learning where Phostis is—am I right?" Krispos didn't wait for Zaidas' nod; he knew he was right. He continued, "Instead of looking for the lad for the moment, can you use your magic to learn what sort of sorcery shields him from you? If you can find out who's helping to conceal Phostis, that will tell us something we hadn't known and may help our physical search. Well? Can it be done?"

Zaidas hesitated thoughtfully. At last he said, "The art of magecraft lost a great one when you were born without the talent, your Majesty. Your mind, if you will forgive a crude comparison, is as twisty as a couple of mating eels."

"That's what comes of sitting on the imperial throne," Krispos answered. "Either it twists you or it breaks you. Does the idea have merit, then?"

"It . . . may," Zaidas said. "It certainly is a procedure I had not considered. I would not promise results, not before trial and not out here away from the resources of the Sorcerers' Collegium. If it works, it will require sorcery of the most delicate sort, for I would not want to alert my quarry to his being scrutinized in this fashion."

"No, that wouldn't do." Krispos reached out and set a hand on Zaidas' arm for a moment. "If you think this worth pursuing, eminent and sorcerous sir, then do what you can. I have faith in your ability—"

"More than I do, right now," Zaidas said, but Krispos neither believed him nor thought he believed himself.

The Avtokrator said, "If the idea turns out not to work, we're no worse off: am I right?"

"I think so, your Majesty," the wizard answered. "Let me explore what I have here and the techniques I might use. I'm sorry I can't give you a quick answer as to the practicability of your scheme, but it really does require more contemplation and research. I promise I'll inform you as soon as I either see a way to attempt it or discover I have not the skill, knowledge, or tools to undertake it."

"I couldn't ask for more." Halfway through the sentence, Krispos found himself talking to Zaidas' back. The mage had swung his horse away. When he got hold of an idea, he worried it between his teeth—and ceased to worry about protocol or even politeness. In Krispos' mind, his long record of success would have justified far worse lapses of behavior than that.

The Avtokrator soon forced magical schemes and even worry about Phostis to the back of his mind. Early that afternoon, the imperial army rode into Harasos, which let him see firsthand the devastation the Thanasioi had worked on the supply dumps there. In spite of himself, he was impressed. They'd done a job that would have warmed the heart of the most exacting military professional.

Of course, the local quartermasters had made matters easier for them, too. Probably because the warehouses inside the shabby little town's shabby little wall were inadequate, sacks of grain and stacks of cut firewood had been stored outside. Burned black smears on the ground and a lingering smell of smoke showed where they'd rested.

Next to the black smears was an enormous purple one. The broken crockery still in the middle of it said it had been the army's wine ration. Now the men would be reduced to drinking water before long, which would increase both grumbling and diarrhea.

Krispos clicked his tongue between his teeth, sorrowing at the waste. The country hereabouts was not rich; collecting this surplus had taken years of patient effort. It might have seen the district through a famine or, as here, kept the army going without its having to forage on the countryside.

Sarkis rode up and looked over the damage with Krispos.

The cavalry general pointed to what had been a corral. "See? They had beeves waiting for us, too."

"So they did." Krispos sighed. "Now the Thanasioi will eat their share of them."

"I thought they had scruples against feasting on meat," Sarkis said.

"That's right, so they do. Well, they've slaughtered some—" The Avtokrator wrinkled his nose at the stench from the bloated carcasses inside the ruined fence. "—and driven off the rest. We'll have no use from them, that's certain."

"Aye. Too bad." By his tone, Sarkis worried more about filling his own ample belly than the effect of the raid on the army as a whole.

"We'll be able to bring in a certain amount of food by sea at Nakoleia," Krispos said. "By the good god, though, that'll be a long supply line for us to maintain. Will your men be able to protect the wagons as they make their way toward us?"

"Some will get through, your Majesty. Odds are most will get through. If they hit us, though, we'll lose some," Sarkis answered. "And we'll lose men guarding those wagons, too. They'll be gone from your fighting force as sure as if the rebels shot 'em all in the throat."

"Yes, that's true, too. Rude of you to remind me of it, though." Krispos knew how big a force he could bring to bear against the Thanasioi; he'd campaigned enough to make a good estimate of how many men Sarkis would have to pull from that force to protect the supply line against raiders. Less certain was how many warriors the rebels could array in line of battle. When he'd set out from Videssos the city, he'd thought he had enough men to win a quick victory. That looked a lot less likely now.

Sarkis said, "A pity the wars can't be easy all the time, eh, your Majesty?"

"Maybe it's just as well," Krispos answered. Sarkis raised a bushy, gray-flecked eyebrow. Krispos explained. "If they were easy, I'd be tempted to fight more often. Who needs that?"

"Aye, something to what you say."

Krispos raised his eyes from the ruined supply dump to the sky. He gauged the weather with skill honed by years on a farm, when the difference between getting through a winter and facing hunger often rode on deciding just when to start bringing in the crops. He didn't like what his senses told him now. The wind had shifted so it was coming out of the northwest; clouds began piling up, thick and black, along the horizon there.

He pointed to them. "We don't have long to do what needs doing. My guess is, the fall rains start early this year." He scowled. "They would."

"Nothing's ever as simple as we wish, eh, your Majesty?" Sarkis said. "We'll just have to push on as hard as we can. Smash them once and the big worry goes, even if they keep on being a nuisance for years."

"I suppose so." But Sarkis' solution, however practical, left Krispos dissatisfied. "I don't want to have to keep fighting and fighting a war. That will cause nothing but grief for me and for Phostis." He would not say out loud that his kidnapped eldest might not succeed him. "Give a religious quarrel half a chance and it'll fester forever."

"That's true enough, as who should know better than one of the princes?" Sarkis said. "If you imperials would just leave our theology in peace—"

"—the Makuraners would come in and try to convert you by force to the cult of the Four Prophets," Krispos interrupted. "They've done that a few times, down through the years."

"And they've had no better luck than Videssos. We of Vaspurakan are stubborn folk," Sarkis said with a grin that made Krispos remember the lithe young officer he'd once been. He remained solid and capable, but he'd never be lithe again. Well, Krispos wasn't young any more, either, and if he'd put on less weight than his cavalry commander, his bones still ached after a day in the saddle.

He said, "If I had to rush back to Videssos the city from the borders of Kubrat now, I think I'd die before I got there."

Sarkis had been on that ride, too. "We managed it in our puppy days, though, didn't we?" He looked down at his own expanding frontage. "Me, I'd be more likely to kill horses than myself. I'm as fat as old Mammianos was, and I haven't as many years to give me an excuse."

"Time does go on." Krispos looked northwest again. Yes, the clouds were gathering. His face twisted; that thought had too ominous a ring to suit him. "It's moving on the army, same as it is on each of us. If we don't want to get bogged down in the mud, we have to move fast. You're right about that."

He wondered again whether he should have waited till spring to start campaigning against the Thanasioi. Losing a battle to the heretics would be bad enough, but not nearly so dangerous as having to withdraw in mud and humiliation.

With deliberate force of will, he made his mind turn aside from that path. Too late now to concern himself with what he might have done had he made a different choice. He had to live with the consequences of what he had chosen, and do his best to carve those consequences into the shape he desired.

He turned to Sarkis. "With the supply dump as ruined as it is, I see no point to encamping here. Spending a night by the wreckage wouldn't be good for the soldiers' spirit, either. Let's push ahead on the route we've planned."

"Aye, your Majesty. We ought to get to Rogmor day after tomorrow, maybe even tomorrow evening if we drive hard." The cavalry commander hesitated. "Of course, Rogmor's burned out, too, if you remember."

"I know. But from all I've heard, Aptos isn't. If we move fast, we ought to be able to lay hold of the supplies there before we start running out of what we brought from Nakoleia."

"That would be good," Sarkis agreed. "If we don't, we're liable to face the lovely choice between going hungry and pillaging the countryside."

"If we start pillaging our own land one day, we put ten thousand men into the camp of the Thanasioi by the next sunrise," Krispos said, grimacing. "I'd sooner retreat; then I'd just seem cautious, not a villain."

"As you say, your Majesty." Sarkis dipped his head. "Let's hope we have a swift, triumphant advance, so we needn't worry about any of these unpleasant choices."

"That hope is all very well," Krispos said, "but we also have to plan ahead so misfortune, if it comes, doesn't catch us by surprise and strike us in a heap because we were napping instead of thinking."

"Sensible." Sarkis chuckled. "Seems to me I've told you that a good many times over the years—but then, you generally *are* sensible."

"Am I? I've heard what was meant to be greater flattery that I liked less." Krispos tasted the word. " 'He was sensible.' I'd sooner see that than most of the lies stonecutters are apt to put on a memorial stele."

Sarkis made a two-fingered gesture to turn aside even the implied mention of death. "May you outlast another generation of stonecutters, your Majesty."

"And stump around Videssos as a spry eighty-year-old, you mean? It could happen, I suppose, though the lord with the great and good mind knows most men aren't so lucky." Krispos looked around to make sure neither Evripos nor Katakolon was in earshot, then lowered his voice all the same. "If that does prove to be my fate, I doubt it will delight my sons."

"You'd find a way to handle them," Sarkis said confidently. "You've handled everything the good god has set in your path thus far."

"Which is no promise the prize will be mine next time out," Krispos answered. "As long as I remember that, I'm all right, I think. Enough jabbering for now; the sooner we get to Aptos, the happier I'll be."

After serving under Krispos for his whole reign, Sarkis had learned the trick of understanding when the Emperor meant more than he said. He set spurs to his horse—despite advancing years and belly, he still had a fine seat and enjoyed a spirited mount—and hurried away at a bounding canter. A moment later, the horns of the military musicians brayed out a new command. The whole army picked up the pace, as if fleeing the storm clouds piling up behind.

Harasos lay at the inland edge of the coastal plain. From it, the road toward Rogmor climbed onto the central plateau that took up the majority of the westlands: drier, hillier, poorer country than the lowlands. Along riverbanks and in places that drew more rain than most, farmers brought in one crop a year, as they did in the country where Krispos had grown up. Elsewhere on the plateau, grass and scrub grew better than grain, and herds of sheep and cattle ambled over the ground.

Krispos eyed the plateau country ahead with suspicion, not because it was poor but because it was hilly. He much preferred a horizon that stretched out for miles on every side. Attackers had to work to set an ambush in country like that. Here sites for ambuscades came up twice in every mile.

He ordered the vanguard strengthened, lest the Thanasioi delay the army on its push to Rogmor. When the whole strung-out force ascended to the plateau, he breathed a heartfelt sigh of relief and a prayer of thanks to Phos. Had he commanded the heretics, he would have hit the imperial army as early and as hard as he could: delaying it on its march now would be worth as much as a great battle later. Thinking thus, he made sure his own saber slid smoothly from its scabbard. Though no great champion, he fought well enough when combat came his way.

The leader of the Thanasioi thought with him strategically, but not in terms of tactics. Not long after the army from Videssos the city reached the plateau, some sort of disturbance broke out at the rear. Krispos' force stretched for more than a mile. He needed awhile to find out what was happening: as if the army were a long, thin, rather stupid dragon, messages from the tail took too long to get up to the head.

When at last he was sure the disturbance really meant fighting, he ordered the musicians to halt his whole force. No sooner had their peremptory notes rung out than he wondered if he'd made a mistake. But what else could he do? Leaving the rear to fend for itself while the van kept moving forward was an invitation to getting destroyed.

He turned to Katakolon, who sat his horse a few yards away. "Get back there at the gallop, find out what's truly going on, and let me know. At the gallop, now!"

"Aye, Father!" Eyes snapping with excitement, Katakolon dug spurs into the horse's side. It squealed an indignant protest at such treatment, but bounded off with such celerity that Katakolon almost went over its tail.

The Avtokrator's youngest son returned faster than Krispos would have thought possible. His anger faded when he saw Katakolon had in tow a messenger he recognized as one of Noetos' men. "Well?" he barked.

The messenger saluted. "May it please your Majesty, we were attacked by a band of perhaps forty. They came close enough to shoot arrows at us; when we rode out to drive them off, most fled but a few stayed behind and fought with the saber to help the others escape."

"Casualties?" Krispos asked.

"We lost one killed and four wounded, your Majesty," the

messenger answered. "We killed five of theirs, and several more were reeling in the saddle as they rode away."

"Did we capture any of them?" Krispos demanded.

"We were still in pursuit when I left to bring this word to you. I know of no prisoners, but my knowledge, as I say, is incomplete."

"I'll ride back and find out for myself." Krispos turned to Katakolon. "Tell the musicians to order the advance." As his son hurried off to obey, he told the messenger, "Take me to Noetos. I'll hear his report of the action directly."

Krispos fumed as he rode toward the rear of the army. Forty men had held him up for a solid hour. A few more such pinpricks and the army would go hungry before it got to Aptos. *Better cavalry screens,* he told himself. Raiders had to be beaten back before they reached the main body. Screening parties could fight and keep moving, or fall back on their comrades if hard-pressed.

He hoped the rear guard had managed to lay hold of some Thanasioi. One interrogation was worth a thousand guesses, especially when he knew so little about the enemy. He knew the methods his men would use to wring truth out of any captives. They did not please him, but any man taken in arms against the Avtokrator of the Videssians was on the face of it a traitor and rebel, not to be coddled if that meant danger to the Empire.

One of the wounded imperials lay on a wagon, a blue-robed healer-priest bent over him. The soldier thrashed feebly; an arrow protruded from his neck. Krispos reined in to watch the healer-priest at work. He wondered why the blue-robe hadn't drawn the arrow, then decided it was all that kept the wounded man from bleeding to death in moments. This would be anything but an easy healing.

The priest repeated the creed again and again. "We bless thee, Phos, lord with the great and good mind, by thy grace our protector, watchful beforehand that the great test of life may be decided in our favor." As he used the prayers to sink down toward the healing trance, he set one hand on the trooper's neck, the other on the arrow that bobbed back and forth as the fellow fought to breathe.

All at once, the blue-robe jerked the arrow free. The trooper let out a bubbling shriek. Bright blood spurted, splashing against the priest's face. So far as breaking his concentration went, it might have been water, or nothing at all.

As abruptly as if the blue-robe had turned a spigot, the spurting stopped. Awe prickled through Krispos, as it always did when he watched a healer-priest at work. He thought the air above the injured trooper should have shimmered, as if from the heat of a fire, so strong was the force of healing that passed between priest and soldier. But the eye, unlike other, less easily nameable senses, perceived nothing.

The healer-priest released his hold on the injured man and sat up. The blue-robe's face was white and drained, a token of what the healing had cost him. A moment later, the soldier sat, too. A pale scar marred the skin of his neck; by its seeming, he might have worn it for years. Wonder filled his face as he picked up the bloodstained arrow the priest had pulled from his neck.

"Thank you, holy sir," he said, his voice as unhurt as the rest of him. "I thought I was dead."

"As I think I am now," the healer croaked. "Water, I pray you, or wine." The trooper pulled free the flask that still dangled from his belt, handing it to the man who had saved him. The blue-robe's larynx worked as he threw back his head and gulped down great drafts.

Krispos urged his horse forward, glad the soldier was hale. Healer-priests were better suited to dealing with the consequences of skirmishes than battles, for they quickly exhausted their powers—and themselves. In large conflicts, they helped only the most desperately hurt, leaving the rest to those who fought wounds with sutures and bandages rather than magic.

Noetos rode toward Krispos. Saluting, he said, "We drove the bastards off with no trouble, your Majesty. Sorry we had to slow you down to do it."

"Not half so sorry as I am," Krispos answered. "Well, the good god willing, that won't happen again." He explained his plan to extend the cavalry screen around the army. Noetos nodded with sober approval. Krispos went on, "Did your men capture any of the rebels?"

"Aye, we got one in the pursuit after I sent Barisbakourios to you," Noetos said. "Shall we squeeze the Thanasiot cheese till the whey runs out of him?" A couple of his lieutenants were close by; they chuckled grimly at the rearguard commander's truth in jest's clothing.

"Presently, at need," Krispos said. "Let's see what magic can do with him first. Bring him here. I want to see him."

Noetos called orders. Some of his troopers frogmarched a young man in peasant homespun into the Avtokrator's presence. The captive must have taken a fall from his horse. His tunic was out at both elbows and over one knee; he was bloody in all three of those places and a couple of others, as well. Serum oozed down into one eye from a scrape on his forehead.

But he remained defiant. When one of the guards growled, "Down on your belly before his Majesty, wretch," he bent his head, sure enough, but only to spit between his feet as if in rejection of Skotos. All the soldiers snarled then, and roughly forced him into a proskynesis in spite of his struggles.

"Haul him to his feet," Krispos said, thinking the cavalrymen were likely to have done worse to their prisoner had they not been under his eye. When the ragged, battered youth—he might have been Evripos' age, more likely Katakolon's—Krispos asked him, "What have I done to you, that you treat me like the dark god?"

The prisoner worked his jaw, perhaps preparing to spit once more. "You don't want to do that, sonny," one of the troopers said.

The young man spat anyhow. Krispos let his captors shake him a little, but then raised a hand. "Hold on. I want this question answered as freely as may be, given what's happened here. What have I done, to be hated so? We've been at peace most of the years since he was born; taxes are lower now than then. What does he have against me? What *do* you have against me, sirrah? You may as well speak your mind; the headsman's shadow already falls across your fate."

"You think I fear death?" the prisoner said. "By the good god, I laugh at death—it takes me out of this trap of Skotos, the world, and sends me on to Phos' eternal light. Do your worst to me; that's but for a moment. Then I shake free of the dung we call a body, like a butterfly bursting from its cocoon."

His eyes blazed, though he kept blinking the one beneath the scrape. The last set of eyes Krispos had seen burning with such fanaticism had belonged to the priest Pyrrhos, first his benefactor, then his ecumenical patriarch, and at last such a ferocious and inflexible champion of orthodoxy that he'd had to be deposed.

Krispos said, "Very well, young fellow—" He realized he was speaking as if to one of his sons who'd been foolish. "—you despise the world. Why do you despise my place in it?"

"Because you're rich, and wallow in your gold like a hog in mud," the young Thanasiot answered. "Because you choose the material over the spiritual, and give over your soul to Skotos in the process."

"Here, you speak to his Majesty with respect, or it'll go the harder for you," one of the cavalrymen growled. The prisoner spat on the ground again. His captor backhanded him across the face. Blood started from the corner of his mouth.

"Enough of that," Krispos said. "He'll be one of many who feel that way. He's eaten up bad doctrine and sickened on it."

"Liar!" the young man shouted, careless of his own fate. "You're the one with false teachings poisoning your mind. Abandon the world and the things of the world for the true and lasting life, the one yet to come." He could not raise his arms, but lifted his eyes to the heavens. "We bless thee, Phos, lord with the great and good mind—"

Hearing the heretic pray to the good god with the identical words he himself used, Krispos wondered for a moment if the fellow could be right. Pyrrhos, in his day, might have come close to saying yes, but not even the rigorously ascetic Pyrrhos could have countenanced destroying all the things of this world for the sake of the afterlife. How were men and women to live and raise families if they wrecked their farms or shops, abandoned parents or children?

He put the question to the prisoner: "If you Thanasioi had your way, wouldn't you soonest let mankind die out in a single generation's time, so no one would be left alive to commit any sins?"

"Aye, that's so," the youth answered. "It won't be so simple; we know that—most folk are too cowardly, too much in love with materialism—"

"By which it sounds as if you mean a full belly and a roof over one's head," Krispos broke in.

"Anything that ties you to the world is evil, is from Skotos," the prisoner insisted. "The purest among us stop taking food and let themselves starve, the better to join Phos as soon as they may."

Krispos believed him. That streak of fanatic asceticism ran deep in many Videssians, whether orthodox or heretic. The Thanasioi, though, seemed to have found a way to channel that religious energy to their own ends, perhaps more effectively than the comfortable clergy who came from Videssos the city.

"Me, I aim to live in this world as long and as well as I can," the Avtokrator said. The Thanasiot laughed scornfully. Krispos did not care. Having known privation in his youth, he saw no point to embracing it when he did not have to. He turned to the men who had hold of the youngster. "Tie him onto a horse. Don't let him escape or harm himself. When we encamp tonight, I'll have Zaidas the wizard question him. And if magic doesn't get me what I need to know . . ."

The guards nodded. The young heretic just glared. Krispos wondered how long that defiance would last if confronted with fire and barbed iron. He hoped he wouldn't have to find out.

Late in the afternoon, the Thanasioi again tried to raid the imperial army. A courier carried a dripping head back to Krispos. His stomach lurched; the hacking was as crude as that of any farmer who slaughtered a pig, while the iron smell of fresh blood also brought back memories of butchering.

If the courier had any such memories, they didn't bother him. Grinning, he said, "We drove the whoresons off, your Majesty—spreading us wider was a fine plan. Junior here, he didn't run fast enough."

"Good," Krispos said, trying not to meet Junior's sightless eyes. He dug in the pouch at his belt and tossed the courier a goldpiece. "This is for the good news."

"Phos bless you, majesty," the fellow exclaimed. "Shall we put this lad on a pike and carry him ahead of us for a standard?"

"No," Krispos said with a shudder. An army that seemed bent on wanton killing would be just what the countryside needed to throw it into the rebels' camp. Controlling his features as best he could, the Avtokrator went on, "Bury it or toss it in a ditch or do whatever you please, as long as you don't display it. We want the people to know we've come to root out the heretics, not to glory in gore."

"However you'd have it, your Majesty," the courier said cheerfully. He rode off happy enough with his reward, even though the Emperor had turned down the suggestion he'd made. Krispos knew some Avtokrators—not the worst of rulers Videssos had ever had, either—would have taken him up on it, or had the idea for themselves. But he did not have the stomach for it.

After the army made camp, he went over to Zaidas' pavilion. He found the Thanasiot prisoner tied to a folding chair and the mage looking frustrated. Zaidas gestured to the apparatus he'd set up. "You are familiar with the two-mirror spell for determining truth, your Majesty?"

"I've seen it used, yes," Krispos answered. "Why? Are you having trouble with it?"

"That would be putting it mildly. It yields me nothing— nothing, do you hear?" Normally among the gentlest of men, Zaidas looked ready to tear the answer to his failure out of the prisoner with red-hot pincers.

"Can it be shielded against?" Krispos asked.

"Obviously it can." Zaidas gave the Thanasiot another glare before continuing. "This I knew before. But I never thought to find such shielding on a fleabitten trooper like this. If all the rebels are warded in like fashion, interrogation will become less certain and more bloody."

"The good god's truth armors me," the young captive declared. He sounded proud, as if he failed to realize his immunity would only cause him to be given over to torment.

"Any chance he's telling the truth?" Krispos asked.

Zaidas made a scornful noise, then suddenly turned thoughtful. "Maybe his fanaticism does afford some protection," the mage said. "One of the reasons sorcery so often fails in battle is that men at a high pitch of excitement are less vulnerable to its effects. Fervent belief in the righteousness of his cause may raise this fellow to a similar, less vulnerable, plane."

"Can you learn whether this is so?"

"It would take some time." Zaidas pursed his lips and seemed on the point of retreating into one of his brown studies.

Krispos forestalled him. Whenever magic touched the Thanasioi, something went wrong. Zaidas hadn't been able to learn where the heretics had taken Phostis—whose absence, unexpectedly, was an ache that only the endless work of the campaign held at bay—he hadn't been able to learn *why* he couldn't learn that, and now he couldn't even squeeze truth from an ordinary prisoner. To him, that made the young Thanasiot an intriguing challenge. To Krispos, it made the rebel an obstacle to be crushed, since he would not yield to gentler methods.

Harshly the Avtokrator said, "Let the men in red leather have him." Interrogators who used no magic wore red to hide the stains of their trade.

In his youth, Krispos would have been slower to give that order. He knew his years on the throne—and his desire to remain there for more years—had hardened him; even corrupted might not have been too strong a word. But he was also introspective enough to recognize that hardening and resist it save in times of dire need. This, he judged, was one of those times.

The Thanasiot's shrieks kept him awake long into the night. He was a ruler who did what he thought he had to do; he was no monster. Some time past midnight, he downed a beaker of wine and let the grape put a blurry curtain between him and the screaming. At last he slept.

# V

After a lifetime spent within hearing of the sea, Phostis found the hill country he traveled through strange in more ways than he could count. The moaning wind sounded wrong. It even smelled wrong, carrying the odors of dirt and smoke and livestock, but not the salt tang he'd never noticed till he met it no more.

Instead of being able to look out from a tall window and see far across blue water, he now found his horizon limited to a few hundred yards of gray rock, gray-brown dirt, and gray-green brush. The wagon in which he rode bumped along over winding trails so narrow he wouldn't have thought a horse able to use them, let alone a vehicle with wheels.

And, of course, no one had ever used him as Syagrios and Olyvria did now. All through his life, people had jumped to obey, even to anticipate, his every whim. The only exceptions he'd known were his father, his mother when she was alive, and his brothers—and, being the eldest, he was pretty good at getting his way with Evripos and Katakolon. That a rebel officer's daughter and a ruffian could not only disobey him but give orders themselves had never crossed his mind, even in nightmare.

That they could do anything else had never crossed their minds. As the road took another of its innumerable twists, Syagrios said, "Down flat, you. Anybody who sees you is likely to be one of us, but ain't nobody gets old on 'likely.' "

Phostis scrambled down into the wagon bed. The first time

Syagrios told him to do that, he'd balked—whereupon Syagrios clouted him. He couldn't jump out of the wagon and run; a stout rope bound his ankle to a post. He could stand up and yell for help, but as Syagrios had said, most of the people hereabouts were themselves Thanasioi.

Syagrios had said something else, too, when he tried to disobey: "Listen, boy, you may think you can pop up like a spring toy and get us killed. You may even be right. But you better think about this, too: I promise you won't be around to see our heads go up on the Milestone."

Was he bluffing? Phostis didn't think so. A couple of times, other wagons or horsemen had trotted past, but he'd lain quiet. Most of the times he was ordered into the wagon bed, as now, no one came round the blind corner. After a minute or two, Syagrios said, "All right, kid, you can come back up."

Phostis returned to his place between the burly driver and Olyvria. He said, "Where are you taking me, anyhow?"

He'd asked that question ever since he was kidnapped. As usual, Olyvria answered, "What you don't know, you can't tell if you're lucky enough to get away." She brushed back a curl that had slipped out to tickle her cheek. "If you decide you want to try to get away, that is."

"I might be less inclined to, if you'd trust me more," he said. In his theology he was not far from the Thanasioi. But he had a hard time loving people who'd drugged, kidnapped, beaten, and imprisoned him. He considered that from a theological point of view. Should he not approve of them for removing him from the obscenely comfortable world in which he'd dwelt?

No. Maybe he was imperfectly religious, but he still thought of those who tormented him as his enemies.

Olyvria said, "I'm not the one who can decide whether you're to be trusted. My father will do that when you come before him."

"When will that be?" Phostis asked for at least the dozenth time.

Syagrios answered before Olyvria could: "Whenever it is. You ask too bloody many questions, you know that?"

Phostis maintained what he hoped was a dignified silence. He feared hope outran reality. Dignity came easily when backed up with embroidered robes, unquestioned authority, and a fancy palace with scores of servants. It was harder to bring off for someone in a threadbare tunic with a rope round his ankle, and harder still when a few days before he'd fouled himself while in the power of the people he was trying to impress.

The wagon rattled around another bend, which meant Phostis spent more time hiding—or was the proper expression *being hidden*? Even his grammar tutor would have had trouble deciding that—in the back of the wagon. This time, though, Syagrios grunted in satisfaction when the corner was safely turned; Olyvria softly clapped her hands together.

"Come on up, you," Syagrios said. "We're just about there."

Although he couldn't smell the sea, Phostis still thought *there* would be the port of Pityos. He'd never seen Pityos, but imagined it to be something on the order of Nakoleia, though likely even smaller and dingier.

The town ahead was smaller and dingier that Nakoleia, but there its resemblance to Phostis' imaginings ceased. It was no port at all, just a huddle of houses and shops in a valley a little wider than most. A stout fortress with walls of forbidding gray limestone dominated the skyline as thoroughly as did the High Temple in Videssos the city.

"What *is* this place?" Phostis asked. He regretted his tone at once; he'd plainly implied the town was unfit for human habitation. As a matter of fact, that was his opinion—how could anyone want to live out his life trapped in a single valley? And how could anyone trapped in a single valley have a life worth living? But letting his captors know what he thought seemed less that clever.

Syagrios and Olyvria looked at each other across him. When she spoke, it was to her comrade: "He'll find out anyhow." Only when Syagrois reluctantly nodded did she answer Phostis: "The name of this town is Etchmiadzin."

For a moment, he thought she'd sneezed. Then he said, "It sounds like a Vaspurakaner name."

"It is," Olyvria said. "We're hard by the border here, and a fair number of princes still call this town home. More to the point, though, Etchmiadzin is where the pious and holy Thanasios first preached, and the chief center of those who follow his way."

If Etchmiadzin was the chief center of the Thanasioi, Phostis was glad his kidnappers hadn't taken him to some outlying hamlet. Back at Videssos the city, he would have blurted out that thought, had it occurred to him. His friends and hangers-on—sometimes it was hard to tell the one group from the other—would have bawled laughter, probably drunken laughter, too. In his present circumstances, silence again seemed the smarter course.

The people of Etchmiadzin went stolidly about their business, taking no notice of the incognito arrival in their midst of a junior Avtokrator. As Olyvria had said, a good many of them seemed to be of Vaspurakaner blood, broader-shouldered and thicker-chested than their Videssian neighbors. An old Vaspurakaner priest, his robe of different cut and a darker blue than those orthodox clerics wore, stumped down an unpaved street, leaning on a stick.

The men on guard outside the fortress were about as far removed from the Halogai in the gilded mail shirts as was possible while still retaining the name of soldier. Not one fighter's kit matched his comrade's; the guards leaned and slouched at every angle save the perpendicular. But Phostis had seen the measuring stare in these wolves' eyes on the faces of the northern men in the capital as they sized up some new arrival at the palaces.

As soon as the guards recognized Syagrios and Olyvria, though, they came to excited life, whooping, cheering, and pounding one another on the back. "By the good god, you did nab the little bugger!" one of them yelled, pointing toward Phostis. As a form of address, that hit a new low.

"Inform my father that he's here, if you would, friends," Olyvria said; from her lips, as from Digenis', the greeting of the Thanasioi came fresh and sincere.

The rough men hurried to do her bidding. Syagrios reined in and alighted from the wagon. "Give me your foot," he told Phostis. "You ain't gonna run away from here." As if reading his captive's mind, he added, "If you try to kick me in the face, boy, I won't just beat you. I'll stomp you so hard you won't breathe without hurting for the next year. You believe me?"

Phostis did, as fully as he believed in the lord with the great and good mind, not least because Syagrios looked achingly eager to do as he'd threatened. So the heir to the imperial throne sat quietly while the driver cut through the rope. Perhaps he and Syagrios shared the Thanasiot theology. That would never make them friends. Phostis had made orthodox enemies when orthodox himself; he saw no reason why one Thanasiot should not despise another as a man, even if they held to the same dogmas.

The guards came straggling back, one a few paces behind the other. The fellow who got back to his post first waved to usher Olyvria, Syagrios, and even Phostis into the fortress. Syagrios shoved Phostis forward, none too gently. "Get moving, you."

He got moving. More soldiers—no, warriors was probably a better word for them, as they had ferocity but seemed without discipline—traded strokes or shot at propped up bales of hay or simply sat around and chattered in the inner ward. They waved to Syagrios, nodded respectfully to Olyvria, and paid Phostis no attention whatever. In his plain, cheap tunic, he did not look as if he deserved attention.

The iron-fronted door to the keep was open. Propelled by another shove from Syagrios, Phostis plunged into gloom. He stumbled, not sure where he was going and even less sure of his footing. Olyvria murmured, "Turn left at the first opening."

He obeyed gratefully. Only when he was inside the chamber did he think to wonder if Syagrios was really as harsh and Olyvria as kindly as they appeared to be. Snapping him back and forth between them like a ball thrown in a bath house struck him as a good way to weaken whatever resolve he had left.

"Come in, young majesty, come in!" exclaimed the slim little man sitting in a high-backed chair at the far end of the chamber. So this was Livanios, then. He sounded as cordial as if he and Phostis were old friends, not captor and captive. The smile on his face was warm and inviting—was, in fact, Olyvria's smile set in a face framed by a neat, graying beard and marred from a couple of sword cuts. It made Phostis want to trust him—and made him want to distrust himself on account of that.

The chamber itself had been set up to imitate, as closely as was possible in the keep of a fortress in the middle of the back of beyond, the Grand Courtroom in the palace compound back at Videssos the city. To someone who had never seen the real Grand Courtroom, it might have been impressive. Phostis, who'd grown up there, found it ludicrous. Where was the marble double colonnade that led the eye to the distant throne? Where were the elegant and richly clad courtiers who took their place along the way to the Emperor? The handful of rudely staring soldiers made a poor substitute. Nor were the ragged priest and the nondescript fellow in a striped caftan adequate replacements for the ecumenical patriarch and the lofty Sevastos who stood before the Avtokrator's high seat.

Phostis knew a weird mental shift as he reminded himself he'd come to despise the pomp and ostentation that surrounded his father. He also wondered why the leader of the radically egalitarian Thanasioi wanted to mimic that pomp.

He had, however, bigger worries. Livanios brought them into sudden sharp focus, saying, "So how much will your father give to have you back. I don't mean gold; we of the gleaming path despise gold. But surely he will yield land and influence to restore you to his side."

"Will he? I wonder." Phostis' bitterness was not altogether feigned. "We've always quarreled, my father and I. For all I know, he's glad to have me gone. Why not? He has two other sons, both of them more to his liking."

"You undervalue yourself in his eyes," Livanios said. "He's turned the countryside around the imperial army upside down searching for you."

"He searches sorcerously as well, and with the same determination," the man in the caftan said. His Videssian held a vanishing trace of accent.

Phostis shrugged. Maybe what he heard was true, maybe not. Either way, it mattered little. He said, "Besides, what makes you think I want to go back to my father? By all I've heard of you Thanasioi, I'd sooner live out my days with you than smother myself in things back at the palace."

He didn't know whether he was telling the truth, telling part of the truth, or flat-out lying. The doctrines of the Thanasioi drew him powerfully. Of so much he was sure. But would men who observed all those fine-sounding principles stoop to something so sordid as kidnapping? Maybe they would, if their faith let them pretend to be orthodox to preserve themselves. If so, they were the best actors he'd ever run across. They even fooled him.

Livanios said, "I've heard somewhat of this from my daughter and the holy Digenis both. The possibilities are . . . interesting. You'd truly rather live out your days in the want that is our lot than in the luxury you've always known?"

"I fear more for my soul than for my body," Phostis said. "My body is but a garment that will wear out all too soon. When it's tossed on the midden, what difference if it once was stained with fancy dyes? My soul, though—my soul goes on forever." He sketched Phos' sun-sign above his breast.

Livanios, the priest, Olyvria, even Syagrios also traced quick circles. The man in the caftan did not. Phostis wondered about that. An imperfectly pious Thanasiot struck him as a contradiction in terms. Or perhaps not—that label fit him pretty well. Was he claiming more belief than he really felt to get Livanios to treat him mildly? He had trouble reading his own heart.

"What shall we do with you?" Livanios said musingly. By his tone, Phostis would have bet the heretics' leader was wondering about the same questions that had gone through his own mind. Livanios went on, "Are you one of us, or do we treat you merely as a piece in the board game, to be placed in the square of greatest advantage to us at the proper time?"

Phostis nodded at the analogy; whatever else could be said about him, Livanios knew how to compare ideas. Pieces taken off the board in the Videssian game of stylized combat were not gone for good, but could be returned to action on the side of the player who had captured them. That made the board game harder to master, but also made it a better model for the involuted intricacies of Videssian politics and civil strife.

"Father, may I speak?" Olyvria said.

Livanios laughed. "When have I ever been able to tell you no? Aye, say what's in your mind."

"There is a middle way in this, then," she said. "No one of spirit, whether he followed the gleaming path or not, could be happy with us after we stole him away and brought him here against his will. But once here, how could one of good will not see how we truly live our lives in conformity to Phos' holy law?"

"Many might fail to see that," Livanios said dryly. "Among them I can name Krispos, his soldiers, and the priests he has in his retinue. But *I* see you're not yet finished. Say on, by all means."

"What I was going to suggest was not clapping Phostis

straightaway into a cell. If and when we do return him to the board, we don't want him turning back against us the instant he finds the chance."

"Can't just let him run loose, neither," Syagrios put in. "He tried to get away once, likely thought about it a lot more'n that. You're just askin' to have him run back home to his papa if he gets on a horse without nobody around him."

Phostis kicked himself for a fool for trying to make a break at the farm house. The skinny fellow had kicked him, too, a lot harder.

Olyvria said, "I wasn't going to suggest we let him run loose. You're right, Syagrios; that's dangerous. But if we take him around Etchmiadzin and to other places where the gleaming path is strong, we can show him the life he was on the edge of embracing for himself before we lay hold of him. Once he sees it, as I said, once he accepts it, he may become fully one of us regardless of how he got here."

"That might have some hope of working," Livanios said, and Phostis' heart leaped. The heresiarch, however, was very Videssian in his ability to spot betrayal before it sprouted: "It might also give him an excuse for hypocrisy and let him pick his own time and place to flee us."

"Aye, that's so, by the good god," Syagrios growled.

Steepling his fingers, Livanios turned to Phostis. "How say you, young Majesty?" In his mouth the title was, if not mocking, at least imperfectly respectful. "This affects you, after all."

"So it does." Phostis tried to match dry with dry. If he'd thought fulsome promises would have kept him out of a small, dark, dank chamber, he would have used them. But he guessed Livanios would assume fulsome promises to be but fulsome lies. He shrugged and answered, "The choice is yours. If you don't trust me, you won't believe what I say in any case."

"You're clever enough, aren't you?" Sitting in his high-backed chair, Livanios reminded Phostis of a smug cat who'd appointed himself judge of mice. Phostis had never been a mouse before; he didn't care for the sensation. Livanios went on, "Well, we can see how it goes. All right, young majesty, no manacles for you." *Not now,* Photis heard between the words. "We'll let you see us—with suitable keepers, of course—and we'll see you. Later on we'll decide what's to be done with you in the end."

The priest who stood in front of Livanios smiled as widely as his pinched features would permit and made the sun-sign once more. The man in the caftan, who stood at Livanios' right, half turned and said, "Are you sure this is wise?"

"No," Livanios answered frankly; he did not seem annoyed to have his decision questioned. "But I think the reward we may reap repays the risk."

"They would never take such a chance back in—"

Livanios held up a hand. "Never mind what they would do there. You are here, and I hope you will remember it." He might listen to his adviser's opinion, but kept a grip on authority. The man in the caftan put both hands in front of him and bowed almost double, acknowledging that authority.

"If he is to be enlarged, even in part, where shall we house him?" Olyvria asked her father.

"Take him up to a chamber on the highest floor here," Livanios answered. "With a guard in the corridor, he'll not escape from there unless he grows wings. Syagrios, when he is out and about, you'll be his principal keeper. I charge you not to let him flee."

"Oh, he won't." Syagrios looked at Phostis as if he hoped the younger man would try to get away. Phostis had never seen anyone who actually looked forward to hurting him before. His testicles crawled up into his belly.

He said, "I don't want to go anywhere right now, except maybe to sleep."

"Spoken like a soldier," Livanios said with a laugh. Syagrios shook his head, denying Phostis deserved the name. Phostis didn't know if he did or not. He might have found out, had the Thanasioi not kidnapped him. But could he have fought against them? He didn't know that, either. He contented himself with ostentatiously ignoring Syagrios. That made Livanios laugh harder.

"If he wants to sleep, he may as well," Olyvria said. "By your leave, Father, I'll take him up to one of the rooms you suggested."

Livanios waved an airy hand as if he were the Avtokrator granting a boon. Having watched Krispos all his life, Phostis had seen the gesture better done. Olyvria led him toward the spiral stairway. Syagrios pulled an unpleasantly long, unpleasantly sharp knife from his belt and followed the two of them. The ruffian, Phostis thought, was not subtle in his messages.

Doing his best to keep on pretending Syagrios did not exist, Phostis turned to Olyvria and said, "Thank you for keeping me out of the dungeon, at any rate." He wondered why she'd taken his side; from a young man raised in the palaces, calculation of advantage came naturally as breathing.

"It's simple enough: I think that, given the chance, you will take your place on the gleaming path," Olyvria answered. "Once you forgive us for the unkind way we had to grab you, you'll see—I'm sure you'll see—how we live in accord with Phos' teachings, far more so than those who pride themselves on how fat their bellies are or how many horses or mistresses they own."

"How could anyone doubt surfeit is wrong?" Phostis said, and Olyvria beamed. But Phostis wondered if sufficiency was wrong, too: the glutton deserved the scorn he got, but was having a belly not growling with hunger every hour of the day also something to condemn? He knew what his father's answer would have been. Then again, he also remained sure his father did not have all the answers.

In normal circumstances, he might have enjoyed arguing the theology of it, especially with an attractive young woman. The knife Syagrios held a couple of feet from his kidneys reminded him how abnormal these circumstances were. Theological disputation would have to wait.

The way he wobbled by the time he got to the head of the stairs also reminded him he was not all he could have been. His own belly grumbled and cried out for more nourishment than he'd had lately.

The chamber to which Olyvria led him was severely simple. It held a straw pallet covered with linen ticking, a blanket that looked as if it had seen better years, a couple of three-legged stools, and a chamber pot with some torn rags beside it. The rest—floors, wall, ceiling—was blocks of bare gray stone. Livanios did not have to fret about his growing wings, either: even if he did sprout feathers, he couldn't have slipped through the slit window that gave the little room what light it had.

The door had no bar on the outside, but it had none on the inside, either. Syagrios said, "Someone will be in the hall watching you most of the time, boy. You'll never know when.

Even if you do get lucky, someone will catch you in the stairs or in the hall or in the ward. You can't run. Get used to it."

Olyvria added, "Our hope is that you won't want to run, Phostis, that you'll find you've gained by coming here, no matter how little you care for the way you traveled. When you see Etchmiadzin, when you see the gleaming path as it leads toward Phos and his eternal life, we hope you'll become one of us."

She sounded very earnest. Phostis had trouble believing she was acting—but she'd fooled him before. He wondered if her father truly wanted him to take his place on the gleaming path. As things stood, Livanios led the Thanasioi, at least in battle. But an Avtokrator's son had a claim on leadership merely because of who he was. Maybe Livanios thought Phostis would be a pliant puppet. Phostis had his own opinion of that.

"We'll leave you to your rest now," Olyvria said. "Come tomorrow, you'll begin to see how the followers of the pious and holy Thanasios shape their lives."

She and Syagrios walked out. She closed the door after them. It wasn't much of a barrier, but it would have to do. Phostis looked around at his cell—that struck him as a better name for the place than *room*, and in truth no monk would have complained its furnishings were too luxurious. It was, however, not a dungeon. He did indeed have that for which to be grateful to Olyvria.

He lay down on the pallet. Dry straw rustled under his weight. It smelled musty. Straws poked through the thin linen covering, and in a couple of places through his tunic as well. He wiggled till he was no longer being stabbed, then drew the blanket up to his neck. When he did that, his feet stuck out. He wiggled some more and managed to get all of himself covered. Competing fears and worries roared in his head so loudly he could clearly hear none of them. He fell asleep almost at once.

Rain blew into Krispos' face. He cast an unhappy countenance up to the heavens—and got an eyeful of raindrops for his presumption. "Well," he said in a hollow voice, "at least we won't be hungry."

Sarkis rode at his left hand. "That's true, your Majesty. We got the flying column into Aptos just in time to drive off the Thanasiot raiders. It was a victory."

"Why don't I feel victorious?" Krispos said. Rain trickled between his hat and cloak and slithered down the back of his neck. He wondered how well the gilding and grease on his coat of mail repelled rust. He had the feeling he'd find out.

To his right, Evripos and Katakolon looked glum. They looked worse than glum, in fact—they looked like a couple of drowned cats. Katakolon tried to make the best of it. He caught Krispos' eye and said, "I usually like my baths warm, Father."

"If you go out in the field, you have to take that up with Phos, not with me," Krispos said.

"But you're his viceregent on earth. Don't you have his ear?"

"Aye, viceregent on earth—so they say. But nowhere, son, will you find that an Avtokrator has jurisdiction over what the heavens decide to do. Oh, I can tell the clouds not to drop rain on me, but will they listen? They haven't yet, not to me or any of the men who came before me."

Evripos muttered something sullen under his breath. Krispos looked at him. He shook his head, muttered again, and rode a little farther away so he wouldn't have to say anything out loud to his father. Krispos thought about pressing him, decided it wouldn't be worth the argument, and kept his own mouth shut.

Sarkis said, "If you could command the weather, your Majesty, you'd have started doing it your first fall on the throne, when Petronas raised his revolt against you. The rains came early that year, too."

"That's true; they did. I wish you hadn't reminded me," Krispos said. The rains then had kept him from following up a victory and let Petronas regroup and continue the fight the next year. He hoped he'd manage a genuine victory against the Thanasioi before the downpour made warfare impossible.

Katakolon said, "I'd expected the heretics to come out and really fight against us by now." He sounded disappointed that they hadn't; he was only seventeen, with no true notion of what combat was about. Krispos had got his own first taste at about the same age, and sickened on it. He wondered if Katakolon would do the same.

But his son had raised a legitimate point. Krispos said, "I'd thought they would come out and fight, too. But this Livanios of theirs is a canny one, curse him to the ice. He knows he gains if I don't destroy him this campaigning season."

"He doesn't gain if we take back Pityos," Sarkis said.

Krispos' horse put a foot in a hole concealed by water and almost stumbled. When he'd saved his seat and brought the gelding back under control, he said, "I'm starting to think we'll need a break in the rain even to get to Pityos."

"Even if the Thanasioi attack us, it'll be a poor excuse for a battle," Sarkis said. "By the time a man's shot his bow twice, the string'll be too wet to use again. Not much chance for tactics after that—just out saber and slash."

"A soldiers' battle, eh?" Krispos said.

"Aye, that's what they call it," Sarkis said, "the ones who live to call it anything, that is."

"Yes," Krispos said. "What it really means is, some stupid general's fallen asleep on the job." Soldiers' battles were part of the Videssian military tradition, but not a highly esteemed part. Videssos honored cleverness in warfare as in everything else; the point was not simply to win, but to win with minimum damage to oneself. That could make unnecessary what would have been the next battle.

Sarkis said, "In this campaign, a soldiers' battle would favor us. But for the band of turncoats who went over with Livanios, most of the Thanasioi are odds and sods who oughtn't to have the discipline they need to stand up in a long fight."

"From your mouth to the good god's ear," Krispos said.

"Cowardly scum, the lot of them," Evripos growled; he'd been listening after all. By his tone, he hated the Thanasioi less for their doctrinal errors than for making him get cold and wet.

"They won't be cowards, young majesty; that's not what I meant at all," Sarkis said earnestly. "They'll have fire and dash aplenty, unless I miss my guess. What I doubt is their sticking power. If they don't break us at the first onset, they should be ours."

Evripos grunted once more, wordlessly this time. Krispos peered through the rain at the territory ahead. He didn't like it: too many hills to pass between on the way to Pityos. Maybe he would have done better to stick to the coastal plain. He hadn't expected the rains so soon. But he was too far in to withdraw; the best course now was to forge ahead strongly and hope things would come out right in the end.

That was, however, also the least subtle course. Against the odds and sods Sarkis had mentioned, he'd have been confident of success. But Livanios had shown himself to be rather better at the game of war than that. Krispos wondered what he had in mind to counter it, and how well the ploy would work.

"One more thing I'll have to find out the hard way," he murmured. Sarkis, Katakolon, and even Evripos looked curiously at him. He didn't explain. His sons wouldn't have understood, not fully, while the cavalry commander probably followed him only too well.

Camp that night was soaked and miserable. The cooks had trouble starting their fires, which meant the army was reduced to bread, cheese, and onions. Evripos scowled in distaste at the hard, dark little loaf a fellow handed him out of a greased leather sack. After one bite, he threw it down in the mud.

"No more for you this evening," Krispos ordered. "Maybe hunger'll give you a better appetite for breakfast."

Evripos started worse than the rain that beat down on him. Long used to ignoring importunate men pleading their cases at the top of their lungs, Krispos ignored him. The Avtokrator saw nothing particularly wrong with the army bread. Phos had granted him good teeth, so he had no trouble eating it. He didn't like it as well as the white bread he ate in the palaces, but he wasn't in the palaces now. In the field, you made the best of what you had. Evripos hadn't figured that out yet.

Whether from his own good sense or, more likely, fear of igniting his father, Katakolon ate up his ration without complaint. Young face unwontedly thoughtful, he said, "I wonder what Phostis is eating tonight."

"I wonder if he's eating anything tonight," Krispos said. With the evening's orders given, with the morrow's line of march planned, he had nothing to keep him from brooding over the fate of his eldest. He couldn't stand that sort of helplessnes. Trying to hold it at bay, he went over to Zaidas' tent to see what the mage had learned.

When he stuck his head into the tent, he found Zaidas scraping mud off his boots. Chuckling to catch his friend at such untrammeled mundanity, he asked, "Couldn't you do that by magic instead?"

"Oh, hello, your Majesty. Aye, belike I could," the wizard answered. "Likely it would take three times as long and leave me drained for two days afterward, but I could. One of the things you have to learn if you go into magic is when to leave well enough alone."

"That's a hard lesson for any man to learn, let alone a mage," Krispos said. Zaidas got up and unfolded a canvas chair for him; he sank into it. "Perhaps I've not learned it myself in fullness. If I had, I might not come here to tax you on what you've found out about Phostis."

"No one could think ill of you for that, your Majesty." Zaidas spread his hands. "I only wish I had more news—or, indeed, any news—to give you. Your eldest son remains hidden from me."

Krispos wondered whether that showed Phostis was in fact a cuckoo's egg in his nest. But no: the magic Zaidas worked sought Phostis for himself, not on account of his relation—if any—to the Avtokrator. Krispos said, "Have you progressed toward learning what sort of sorcery conceals his whereabouts?"

Zaidas bit his lip; not even a friend casually tells his Avtokrator he has failed to accomplish something. The wizard said, "Your Majesty, I must confess I have continued to devote most of my efforts toward locating Phostis rather than on analyzing why I cannot locate him."

"And what sort of luck have you had in those efforts?" The question was rhetorical; had Zaidas had any luck other than bad, he would have proclaimed it with trumpet and drum. Krispos went on, "Eminent and sorcerous sir, I strongly urge you to give over your direct efforts, exactly because they've not succeeded. Learn what you can about the mage who opposes you. If you have any better fortune there, you can go back to seeking out Phostis."

"It shall of course be as your Majesty suggests," Zaidas said, understanding that an imperial recommendation was tantamount to a command. The wizard hesitated, then continued, "You must be aware I would still have no guarantee of success, especially here in the field. For this delicate work, the tomes and substances accumulated within the Sorcerers' Collegium are priceless assets."

"So you've said," Krispos answered. "Do your best. I can ask no more of any man."

"I shall," Zaidas promised, and reached for a codex as if

about to start incanting on the spot. Before he could demonstrate such diligence, Krispos left the tent and headed back to his own pavilion. He was disappointed in his chief mage, but not enough to say anything more to Zaidas than he'd already said: Zaidas had been doing the best he could, by his own judgment. An emperor who castigated the men he'd chosen for their expert judgment would not long retain such experts around him.

Rain drummed on the oiled silk; mud squelched underfoot. The tent was a joyless place. Krispos felt the weight of every one of his years. Even with the luxuries his rank afforded him—enough room to stand and walk around, a cot rather than just a bed roll—campaigning was hard on a man as old as him. The only trouble was, not campaigning would in the long run prove harder still.

So he told himself, at any rate, as he blew out the lamps, lay down, and tried to sleep. So men always told themselves when they went off to war. So, no doubt, Livanios was telling himself somewhere not far enough away. Only by looking backward through the years could anyone judge who had been right, who wrong.

Outside the entrance to the tent, the Haloga guards chatted back and forth in their own slow, sonorous speech. Krispos wondered if they ever had doubts when they lay down at night. They were less simple than many Videssians made them out to be. But they did actively like to fight, where Krispos avoided battle when he could.

He was still wishing life could be less complicated when at last he surrendered to exhaustion. When he woke up the next morning, his mind bit down on that as if he'd never slept. He dressed and went out to share a breakfast as dank and miserable as the supper the night before.

Getting the army moving helped kick him out of his own gloom, or at least left him too busy to dwell on it. By now the soldiers were more efficient than they had been when they set out from Nakoleia. Knocking down tents, then loading them onto horses and mules and into wagons, took only about half as long as it had earlier. But, as if to make sure no blessing went unmixed, the rain made travel slower and tougher than Krispos had counted on. He'd planned to reach Pityos six or seven days after he set out from Aptos. That would stretch now.

The army rode through a village. But for a couple of dogs splashing through the mud between houses, the place was deserted. The peasants and herders who called it home had fled into the hills. That was what peasants and herders did when a hostile army approached. Krispos bit his lip in frustrated anger and sorrow that his subjects should reckon forces he led hostile.

"They're most of them Thanasioi, is my guess," Evripos answered when he said that aloud. "They know what they have to look forwrd to when we stamp out this heresy of theirs."

"What would you do with them after we win?" Krispos asked, interested to learn how the youth would handle a problem whose solution he did not clearly see himself.

Evripos was confident, if nothing else: "Once we beat the rebel army in the field, we peel this land like a man stripping the rind off an orange. We find out who the worst of the traitors are and give them fates that will make the rest remember for always what opposing the Empire costs." He shook his fist at the empty houses, as if he blamed them for putting him here on horseback in the cold rain.

"It may come to that," Krispos said, nodding slowly. Evripos' answer was one a straightforward soldier might give—was, in fact, not very different from what Sarkis had proposed. The lad could have done worse, Krispos thought.

Confident in his youth that he'd hit on not just an answer but *the* answer, Evripos spoke out in challenge: "How could you do anything but that, Father?"

"If we can lure folk back to the true faith by persuasion rather than fear, we cut the risk of having to fight the war over again in a generation's time," Krispos anwered. Evripos only snorted; he thought in terms of weeks and months, not generations.

Then Krispos had to stop thinking about generations, or even weeks: a scout from the vanguard came splattering back, calling, "The bastards aim to try and hold the pass up ahead against us!"

*Open fighting at last*, Krispos thought—*Phos be praised.* Already, at Sarkis' bawled orders, the musicians were ordering the imperial army to deploy. While it traveled as a strung-out snake, it could not fight that way. It began to stretch out into line of battle.

But, as Krispos saw when he rode forward to examine the ground for himself, the line of battle could not stretch wide. The Thanasioi had cunningly chosen the place for their stand: the sides of the pass were too steep for cavalry, especially in the rain, while at the narrowest point the enemy had erected a rough barricade of logs and rocks. It would not stop the attackers, but it would slow them down . . . and here and there, behind the barrier, cloth-covered awnings sprouted like drab toadstools.

Krispos pointed to those as Sarkis came up beside him. "They'll have archers under there, or I miss my guess. The barricade to hold us in place, the bowmen to hurt us while we're held."

"Likely you're right, your Majesty," the cavalry commander agreed glumly. "Livanios, curse him, is a professional."

"We'll send some infantry around the barricade to either side to see if we can't push them back, then," Krispos decided. It was the only maneuver he could think of, but not one in which he had great confidence. The foot soldiers were the poorest troops in his force, both in fighting quality and literally: they were the men who could not afford to outfit themselves or be outfitted by their villages with horse and cavalry accouterments.

Being a horseman himself, Sarkis shared and more than shared the Avtokrator's distrust of infantry. But he nodded, not having any better plan to offer. A courier hurried off to the musicians. At their call, the infantry went forward to outflank the Thanasioi, who waved spears and yelled threats from behind their barricade.

"We'll send the horse forward at the same time, your Majesty, if that's all right with you," Sarkis said, and Krispos nodded in turn. Keeping as many of the enemy as possible busy would go a long way toward winning the fight.

Shouting "Phos with us!" and "Krispos!" the imperials advanced. As the Emperor and Sarkis had thought they would, bowmen under cover from the rain shot at soldiers who had trouble answering back. Here and there along the line, a man crumpled or a wounded horse screamed and broke away from its rider's control.

Then the enemy's awnings shook, as if in a high breeze—but there was no breeze. Several of them fell over, draping Thanasiot archers in yards of soaked, clinging cloth. The stream of arrows slackened. Krispos' men raised a cheer and advanced. The Avtokrator looked round for Zaidas. He did not see the sorcerer, but had no doubt he'd caused the collapse. Battle magic might have trouble touching men, but things were another matter.

Yet the Thanasioi, even with their strategem spoiled, were far from beaten. Their men swarmed forward to fight the foot soldiers who sought to slide around their barrier. The heretics' war cry was new to Krispos: "The path! The gleaming path!"

Their ferocity was new, too. They fought as if they cared nothing whether they lived or died, so long as they hurt their foes. Their impetuous onslaught halted Krispos' infantry in its tracks. Some of his men kept fighting, but others scrambled out of harm's way, skidding and falling in the muck as they ran.

Krispos cursed. "The ice take them!" he shouted. "The good god knows I didn't expect much from them, but this—" Fury choked him.

"Maybe the rebels will make a mistake," Sarkis said, seeking such solace as he could find. "If they come out to chase our poor sorry lads, the cavalry'll nip in behind 'em and cut 'em off at the knees."

But the Thanasioi seemed content to hold off the imperial army. Again Krispos saw the hand of a well-trained soldier in their restraint: raw recruits, elated at success, might well have swarmed forward to take advantage of it and left themselves open to a counterblow like the one Sarkis had proposed. Not here, though. Not today.

The imperial cavalry tried to force its way through the barrier the rebels had thrown up. On a clear day, they could have plied their poorly armored foes with arrows and made them give ground. With the sky weeping overhead, that didn't work. They fought hand to hand, slashing with sabers and using light spears against similarly armed opponents who, while not mounted, used the barricade as if it were their coat of mail.

"They've got more stick in them than I looked for," Sarkis said with a grimace. "Either they put the real soldiers who de-

fected in the middle or . . ." He let that hang. Krispos finished
it mentally: *or else we're in more trouble than we thought.*

Unlike the infantry, the imperial horsemen stayed and
fought. But they had no better luck at dislodging the stubborn
heretics. Curses rose above the clash of iron on iron and the
steady drumming of the rain. Wounded men and wounded
horses shrieked. Healer-priests labored to succor those sorest
hurt until they themselves dropped exhausted into the mud.

Time seemed stuck. The gray mat of clouds overhead was
so thick, Krispos had no better way to gauge the hour than by
his stomach's growls. If his belly did not lie, afternoon was
well advanced.

Then, not far away, shouts rang out, first in the squadron of
Haloga guards and then from the Thanasioi. Through the confused uproar of battle came a new cry: "To me! For the Empire!"

"By the good god!" Krispos exclaimed. "That's Evripos!"

At the head of a couple of dozen horsemen, the Avtokrator's
second son forced a breach in the heretic's barrier. In amongst
them, he lay about him with his saber, making up in fury what
he lacked in skill. Half the Halogai poured into that gap, as
much to protect him as to take advantage of it in any proper
military sense.

The result was satisfactory enough. At last driven back from
their barricade, the heretics became more vulnerable to the onslaught of the better-disciplined imperial troops. Their confident yells turned suddenly frantic. "Push them hard!" Krispos
shouted. "If we break them here, we have an easy road on to
Pityos!" With its major city taken, he thought, how could the
revolt go on?

But the Thanasioi kept fighting hard, even in obvious defeat.
Krispos thought about the prisoner he'd ordered tortured, about
the contempt the youth had shown for the material world. That,
he saw, had not been so much cant. Rear guards sold themselves more dearly than he would have imagined, fighting to
the death to help their comrades' retreat. Some men who had
safety assured even abandoned it to hurl themselves at the imperials and their weapons, using those to remove themselves
forever from a worldly existence they judged only a trap of
Skotos'.

Because of that fanatical resistance, the imperial army

gained ground more slowly than Krispos wanted. Not even more daredevil charges from Evripos could break the heretics' line.

Sarkis pointed ahead. "Look, your Majesty—they're filing over that bridge there."

"I see," Krispos answered. Ten months out of the year, the stream spanned by that ramshackle wooden bridge would hardly have wet a man's shins as he forded it. But with the fall rains, it not only filled its banks but threatened to overflow them. If Krispos' men could not seize the bridge, they'd have to break off pursuit.

"They took a long chance here, provoking battle with their backs to the river," Sarkis said. "Let's make them pay for it."

More and more of the Thanasioi gained the safety of the far bank. Yet another valiant stand by a few kept the imperial soldiers away from the bridge. Just when they were about to gain it in spite of everything the heretics could do to stop them, the wooden structure exploded into flame in spite of the downpour.

"Magic?" Krispos said, staring in dismay at the heavy black smoke that poured from the bridge.

"It could be, your Majesty," Sarkis answered judiciously. "More likely, though, they painted it with liquid fire and just now touched it off. That stuff doesn't care about water when it gets to burning."

"Aye, you're right, worse luck," Krispos said. Made from naphtha, sulfur, the foul-smelling oil that seeped up between rocks here and there in the Empire, and other ingredients— several of them secret—liquid fire was the most potent incendiary Videssos' arsenal boasted. A floating skin of it would even burn on top of water. No wonder it took no notice of the rain.

The last handful of Thanasioi still on the eastern side of the stream went down. "Come on!" Evripos shouted to the impromptu force he led. "To the ice with this fire! We'll go across anyhow."

Not all the men followed him, and not only men but also horses failed him. His own mount squealed and reared in fright when he forced it near the soddenly crackling flames. He fought the animal back under control, but did not try again to make it cross.

That proved as well, for the bridge collapsed on itself a couple of minutes later. Charred timbers splashed into the river and, some, still burning, were swept away downstream. The Thanasioi jeered from the far bank, then began vanishing behind the curtain of rain.

Krispos sat glumly on his horse, listening to the splash and tinkle of the storm and, through it, the cries of wounded men. He squared his shoulders and did his best to rally. Turning to Sarkis he said, "Send companies out at once to seize any nearby routes east that remain open."

"Aye, your Majesty, I'll see to it at once." After a moment, Sarkis said, "We have a victory here, your Majesty."

"So we do." Krispos' voice was hollow. As a matter of fact, Sarkis' voice was hollow, too. Each seemed to be doing his best to convince the other everything was really all right, but neither appeared to believe it. Krispos put worry into words: "If we don't find another route soon, we'll have a hard time going forward."

"That's true." Sarkis seemed to deflate like a pig's bladder poked with a pin. "A victory that gets us nothing is scarcely worth the having."

"My thought exactly," Krispos said. "Better we should have stayed in Videssos the city and started this campaign in the spring than be forced to cut it off in the middle like this." He forced himself away from recrimination. "Let's make camp, do what we can for our hurt, and decide what we try next."

"A lot of that will depend on what the scouting parties turn up," Sarkis said.

"I know." Krispos did his best to stay optimistic. "Maybe the Thanasioi won't have knocked down every bridge for miles around."

"Maybe." Sarkis sounded dubious. Krispos was dubious, too. Against a revolt made up simply of rebellious peasants, he would have had more hope. But Livanios had already proved himself a thoroughgoing professional. You couldn't count on him to miss an obvious maneuver.

Krispos put the future out of his mind. He couldn't even plan until the scouts came back and gave him the information he needed. He rode slowly through the army, praising his men for fighting well, and congratulating them on the victory. They were not stupid; they could see for themselves that they hadn't accomplished as much as they might have. But he put the best face he could on the fight. "We've driven the bastards back, showed them they can't stand against us. They won't come yapping round our heels again like little scavenger dogs any time soon."

"A cheer for his Majesty!" one of the captians called. The cheer rang out. It was not one to make the hillsides echo, but it was not dispirited or sardonic, either. All things considered, it satisfied Krispos.

He rode up close to the bridge. Some of its smoldering support timbers still stood. Evripos looked across the river toward the now-vanished Thanasioi. He turned his head to see who approached, then nodded, one soldier to another. "I'm sorry, Father. I did my best to get over, but my stupid horse wouldn't obey."

"Maybe it's for the best," Krispos answered. "You would have been trapped on the far side when the bridge went down. I can't afford to lose sons so prodigally." He hesitated, then reached out to whack Evripos on his mailed back. "You fought very well—better than I'd looked for you to do."

"It was—different from what I expected." A grin lightened Evripos' face. "And I wasn't afraid, the way I thought I'd be."

"That's good. I was, my first time in battle. I puked up my guts afterward, as a matter of fact, and I'm not ashamed to admit it." Krispos studied his son in some bemusement. "Have I gone and spawned a new Stavrakios? I've always expected good things from you, but not that you'd prove a fearsome warrior."

"Fearsome?" Evripos' grin got wider; all at once, in spite of his beard and the mud that streaked his face, he reminded Krispos of the little boy he'd been. "Fearsome, you say? By the good god, I like it."

"Don't like it too well," Krispos said. "A taste for blood is more expensive than even an emperor can afford." He realized he laid that on too thick and tried to take some of it off: "But I was glad to see you at the fore. And if you go through the encampments tonight, you'll find out I wasn't the only one who noticed."

"Really?" Krispos could see Evripos wasn't used to the idea of being a hero. By the way the young man straightened up, though, the notion sat well. "Maybe I'll do that."

"Try not to let them get you too drunk," Krispos warned. "You're an officer; you need to keep your head clear when you're in the field." Evripos nodded. Remembering himself at the same age, Krispos doubted his son would pay the admonition too much heed. But he'd planted it in Evripos' mind, which was as much as he could do.

He went off to see how Katakolon had fared in his first big fight. His youngest son had already disappeared among the tents of the camp followers, so Krispos silently shelved the lecture on the virtues of moderation. He did seek out a couple of officers who had seen Katakolon in action. By their accounts, he'd fought well enough, though without his brother's flair. Reassured by that, Krispos decided not to rout him from his pleasures. He'd earned them.

Krispos had urged Evripos to go through the camp to soak up adulation. He made his own second tour for a more pragmatic reason: to gauge the feel of the men after the indecisive fight. He knew a certain amount of relief that none of the regiments had tried to go over to the foe.

A fellow who had his back turned and so did not know the Avtokrator was close by said to his mates, "I tell you, boys, at this rate it's gonna take us about three days less'n forever to make it to Pityos. If the mud don't hold us back, mixing it with the cursed heretics will." His friends nodded in agreement.

Krispos walked away from them less happy than he might have been. He breathed a silent prayer up to Phos that the scouting parties could discover an undefended river crossing. If his men didn't think they could do what he wanted from them, they were all too likely to prove themselves right.

Even though he'd not fought, himself, the battle left him worn. He fell asleep as soon as he lay down on his cot and did not wake until the gray dawn of another wet day. When he came out of the tent, he wished he'd stayed in bed, for Sarkis greeted him with unwelcome news: "Latest count is, we've lost, ah, thirty-seven men, your Majesty."

"What do you mean, lost?" Krispos' wits were not yet at full speed.

The cavalry commander spelled it out in terms he could not misunderstand: "That's how many slipped out of camp in the night, most likely to throw in with the Thanasioi. The number'll only grow, too, as all the officers finish morning roll for their companies." No sooner were the words out of his mouth than a soldier came up to say something to him. He nodded and sent the man away, then turned back to Kripos: "Sorry, your Majesty. Make that forty-one missing."

Krispos scowled. "If we have to use half the army to guard the other half, it'll be only days before we can't fight with any of it."

"Aye, that's so," Sarkis said. "And how will you be able to tell beforehand which half to use to do the guarding?"

"You have a delightful way of looking at things this morning, don't you, Sarkis?" Krispos peered up at the sky from under the broad brim of his hat. "You're as cheery as the weather."

"As may be. I thought you wanted the men around you to tell you what was so, not what sounded sweet. And I tell you this: if we don't find a good road forward today—well, maybe tomorrow, but today would be better—this campaign is as dead and stinking as last week's fish stew."

"I think you're right," Krispos said unhappily. "We've sent out the scouts; that's all we can do for now. But if they don't have any luck . . ." He left the sentence unfinished, not wanting to give rise to any evil omen.

He sent out more scouting parties after breakfast. They splashed forth, vanishing into rain and swirling mist. Along with Krispos, the rest of the soldiers passed a miserable day, staying under canvas as much as they could, doing their best to keep weapons and armor greased against the ravages of rust, and themselves as warm and dry as they could—which is to say, not very warm and not very dry.

The first scouting parties returned to camp late in the afternoon. One look at their faces gave Krispos the bad news. The captains filled in unpleasant details: streams running high, ground getting boggier by the hour, and Thanasioi out in force at any possible crossing points. "If it could have been done, your Majesty, we'd have done it," one of the officers said. "Truth is, it can't be done, not here, not now."

Krispos grunted as if kicked in the belly. Agreeing with Sarkis that he wanted to hear from his subjects what was so was one thing. Listening to an unpalatable truth, one that flew in the face of all he wanted, was something else again. But he had not lasted two decades and more on the throne by substituting his desires for reality: another lesson learned from poor wild dead Anthimos.

"We can't go forward," he said, and the scout commanders chorused agreement. "The lord with the great and good mind knows we can't stay here." This time, if anything, the agreement was louder. Though the bitter words choked him, Krispos said what had to be said: "Then we've no choice but to go back to Videssos the city." The officers agreed once more. That did nothing to salve his feelings.

The Thanasioi tramping into the keep of Etchmiadzin did not look like an army returning in triumph. Phostis had watched—had taken part in—triumphal processions down Middle Street in Videssos the city, testimonials to the might of his father's soldiers and to the guile of his father's generals.

Looking down from his bare little cell in the citadel, he saw none of the gleam and sparkle, none of the arrogance, that had marked the processions with which he was familiar. The fighting men below looked dirty and draggled and tired unto death; several had bandages, clean or not so clean, on arms or legs or heads. And, in fact, they'd not won a battle. In the end, Krispos' army had forced them back from the position they tried to hold.

But even defeat hadn't mattered. Instead of pressing forward, the imperial force was on its way back to the capital.

Phostis was still trying to grasp what that meant. He and Krispos had clashed almost every time they spoke to each other. But Phostis, however much he fought with his father, however much he disagreed with much of what he thought his father stood for, could not ignore Krispos' long record of success. Somewhere down deep, he'd thought Krispos would deal with the Thanasioi as he had with so many other enemies. But no.

The door behind him swung open. He turned away from the window. Syagrios' grin, always unpleasant, seemed especially so now. "Come on down, you," the ruffian said. "Livanios wants a word with you, he does."

Phostis did not particularly want a word with the Thanasiot leader. But Syagrios hadn't offered him a choice. His watchdog stepped aside to let him go first, not out of deference but to keep Phostis from doing anything behind his back. Being thought dangerous felt good; Phostis would have been even happier had reality supported that thought.

The spiral stair had no banister to grab. If he tripped, he'd roll till he hit bottom. Syagrios, he was sure, would laugh the louder for every bone he broke. He planted his feet with special care, resolved to give Syagrios nothing with which to amuse himself.

As he did every time he came safe to the bottom of the stairs, he breathed a prayer of thanks to Phos. As he also did every time, he made certain no one but he knew it. Through the years, Krispos had gained some important successes simply by not letting on that anything was wrong. Even if the tactic was his father's, Phostis had seen that it worked.

Livanios was still out in the inner ward, haranguing his troops about the fine showing they'd made. Phostis could wait on his pleasure. Unused to waiting on anyone's pleasure save his own—and Krispos'—Phostis quietly steamed.

Then Olyvria came out of one of the side halls whose twists Phostis was still learning. She smiled and said to him, "You see, the good god himself has blessed the gleaming path with victory. Isn't it exciting? By being with us as we sweep away the old, you have the chance to fully become the man you were meant to be."

"I'm not the man I would have been, true," Photsis said, temporizing. Had he still been back with the army, half his heart, maybe more than half, would have swayed toward the Thanasioi. Now that he was among them, he was surprised to find so much of his heart leaning back the other way. He put it down to the way in which he'd come to Etchmiadzin.

"Now that our brave soldiers have returned, you'll be able to get out more and see the gleaming path as it truly is," Olyvria went on. If she'd noticed his lukewarm reply, she ignored it.

Syagrios, worse luck, seemed to notice everything. Grinning his snag-toothed grin, he put in, "You'll have a tougher time running off, too."

"The weather's not suited to running," Phostis answered as mildly as he could. "Anyhow, Olyvria is right: I do want to watch life along the gleaming path."

"She's right about more than that," Syagrios said. "Your

cursed father can't hurt us the way he thought he could. Come spring, all these lands'll be flowing smooth as a river under Livanios, you bet they will."

A river that didn't flow smooth had won more for the Thanasioi than their soldiers' might, or so Phostis had heard. He kept that thought to himself, too.

Olyvria said, "It shouldn't be a matter of running in any case. We won't speak of that again, for we want you to remain and be contented among us."

"I'd also like to be contented among you," Phostis answered. "I hope it proves possible."

"Oh, so do I!" Olyvria's face glowed. For about the first time since she'd helped kidnap him, Phostis longingly remembered how she'd looked naked in the lamplight, in the secret chamber under Videssos the city. If he'd gone forward instead of back . . .

Outside in the inner ward, Livanios finished his speech. The Thanasiot soldiers cheered. Syagrios set a strong hand on Phostis' arm. "Come on. Now he'll have time to deal with the likes of you."

Phostis wanted to jerk away, not just from the contempt in his keeper's voice but also from being handled as if he were only a slab of meat. Back at the palaces, anyone who touched him like that would be gone inside the hour, and with stripes on his back to reward his insolence. But Phostis wasn't back at the palaces; every day reminded him of that in a new way.

Olyvria trailed along as Syagrios led him out to Livanios. The Thanasioi who still filled the courtyard made room for the ruffian and for Livanios' daughter to pass. Phostis they eyed with curiosity: some perhaps wondering who he was; and others, who knew *that* much, wondering what he was doing here. He wondered what he was doing here himself.

Livanios' smile instantly changed him from stern soldier to trusted leader. He turned its full warmth on Phostis. "And here's the young majesty!" he exclaimed, as if Phostis were sovereign rather than prisoner. "How fare you, young majesty?"

"Well enough, eminent sir," Phostis answered. He'd seen courtiers who could match Livanios as chameleons, but few who could top him.

The Thanasiot leader said, "Save your fancy titles for the

corrupt old court. I'm but another man making his way along the gleaming path that leads to Phos."

"Yes, sir," Phostis said. He noticed Livanios did not reject that title of respect.

"Father, I do think he'll choose to join you on the gleaming path," Olyvria said.

"I hope he does," Livanios said, and then to Phostis: "I hope you do. Our brave and bright warriors surely kept your father from making life difficult for us this year. We have a whole season now in which to build and grow. We'll use it well, I assure you."

"I don't doubt that," Phostis said. "Your little realm here already reminds me of the way the Empire is run."

"Does it?" Livanios sounded pleased. "Maybe you can help keep it running as it should, as a matter of fact. Knowing your father, he's doubtless made sure you have some of the same skills he uses, though now you'd turn them to the cause of righteousness."

"Well, yes, some," Phostis said, not caring to admit he'd disliked and scanted administering imperial affairs. He wanted Livanios to think of him as someone useful, not as foe or a potential rival to be disposed of.

"Good, good." Livanios beamed. "We'll yet scour greed and miserliness and false doctrine from the face of the earth, and usher in such a reign of virtue that Phos' triumph over Skotos will be soon and certain."

Olyvria clapped her hands in delight at the vision her father put forward. It excited Phostis, too; this was the way Digenis had spoken. Before, Livanios had seemed more an officer out for his own advantage than someone truly committed to Thanasios' preaching. If he meant to put it into effect, Phostis would have more reason to think hard about fully binding himself to the movement.

Syagrios said, "We'll hit the imperials some more licks, too. I want to be in on that, by the good god."

"There'll be slaughter aplenty for you, never fear," Livanios told him. Phostis' newly fired zeal chilled as suddenly as it had heated. How, he wondered, could you get rid of greed and at the same time maintain a red zest for slaughter? And how could the gleaming path simultaneously contain both righteousness and Syagrios?

One thing was clear: he'd have time to find out. Now that his father's push had failed, he'd stay among the Thanasioi indefinitely. Had he really wanted that as much as he'd thought before he got it? He'd find that out, too.

# VI

KRISPOS PACED THE PALACE CORRIDORS LIKE A CAGED ANIMAL. The fall rains were done; now sleet and snow came down from the cold gray heavens. The occasional clear days or even, once or twice, clear weeks were salt in his wounds: If they but lasted, he could fare forth once more against the Thanasioi.

One long stretch of good weather sorely tempted him, but he restrained himself: he knew too well it would not hold. But each successive bright morning gave a fresh twist of the knife. That once, he welcomed the blizzard that blew in. Though it trapped him, it let him feel sagacious.

Now Midwinter's Day, the day of the winter solstice, drew near. Krispos ticked off the passing days on the calendar one by one, but somehow they raced too swiftly even so. He faced the coming solstice with more resignation than joy. Midwinter's Day was the greatest festival of the religious year, but he found himself in no mood to celebrate.

Not even previewing the mime troupes that would perform in the Amphitheater restored his good humor. Among other things, Midwinter's Day gave folk more license than any other festival, and a good many of the skits poked fun at him for failing to put down the Thanasioi. More than one teased him for losing Phostis, too.

Not only would he have to watch this foolishness from the imperial box on the spine of the Amphitheater, he'd have to be seen to laugh. An Avtokrator who couldn't take what the mimes dished out quickly forfeited the city mob's fickle favor.

He took advantage of the imperial dignity to complain loud and often. At last Mystakon, the eunuch chamberlain who had most often served Phostis, said, "May it please your Majesty, I am of the opinion that the young Majesty, were he able, would gladly assume the duty you find onerous."

Krispos felt his cheeks flame. "Yes, no doubt you're right," he mumbled. After that, he bottled his forebodings up inside himself.

Perhaps in one of Barsymes' efforts to cheer him, the serving maid Drina showed up in his bed again after a particularly trying day. This time he actively wanted her, or at least his mind did. His body, however, failed to rise to the occasion despite her ingenuity.

When it became clear nothing was going to happen, she said, "Now don't you fret, your Majesty. It happens to everyone now and again." She spoke so matter-of-factly, he got the idea she was talking from experience. She added, "I'll tell you something else, too: you foolish men make more of a much about it than women ever do. It's just one of those things."

"Just one of those things," Krispos echoed between clenched teeth. Drina wrapped a robe around her and slipped out of the imperial bedchamber, leaving him alone in the darkness. "Just one of those things," he repeated, staring up at the ceiling. "Just one more thing that doesn't work."

Maybe Drina knew better than to gossip, or maybe—and more likely, given the way news of any sort raced through the palaces—the servitors knew better than to show the Avtokrator they knew anything. Back in his own days as vestiarios, he'd chattered about Anthimos, though never where Anthimos could listen. At any rate, he heard no sniggers, which relieved him in a way altogether different from the one he'd sought with Drina.

Compared to failing in bed, the ordeal of facing public mockery on Midwinter's Day suddenly seemed much more bearable. When the day finally dawned, cold and clear, he let Barsymes pour him into his finest ceremonial robe as if it were chain mail to armor him against the taunts he expected.

The procession from the palaces to the Amphitheater took him past bonfires blazing in the plaza of Palamas. People dressed in their holiday best—women with lace at their throat and ankles, perhaps with a couple of bodice buttons undone or skirts slit to show off a pretty calf; men in robes with fur collars and cuffs—leapt over the fires, shouting "Burn, ill-luck!"

"Go on, your Majesty, if you care to," Barsymes urged. "It will make you feel better."

But Krispos shook his head. "I've seen too much to believe ill-luck's so easy to get rid of, worse luck for me."

Preceded by the dozen parasol bearers protocol required, flanked by bodyguards, the Avtokrator crossed the racetrack that circled the floor of the Amphitheater and took his place on the seat at the center of the spine. Looking up to the top of the great oval was like looking up from the bottom of a soup tureen, save that the Amphitheater was filled with people, not soup. To the folk in the top rows, Krispos could have been only a scarlet dot; to anyone shortsighted up there, he was surely invisible.

But everyone in the Amphitheater could hear him. He thought of that as magic of a sort, though in fact it was nothing more—or less—than cleverly crafted acoustics. When he spoke from the Emperor's seat, it was as if he spoke straight into the ear of all the tens of thousands of men, women, and children who packed the arena.

"People of Videssos," he said, and then again, after his first words won quiet, "people of Videssos, after today the sun, the symbol of the lord with the great and good mind, turns to the north once more. Try as Skotos will, he has not the power to pull it from the sky. May the solstice and the days that follow it give everyone a lesson: even when darkness seems deepest, longer, brighter days lie ahead. And when darkness seems deepest, we celebrate to show we know it cannot rule us. Now let the Midwinter's Day festivities begin!"

He knew the cheer that rose had more to do with his opening the festival than with what he'd said. Nonetheless, the noise avalanched down on him from all sides until his head rang with it; just as from the Emperor's seat his voice flew throughout the Amphitheater, so every sound within the stone bowl was focused and magnified there.

Though he'd known in advance his speech would be largely ignored, he spoke, as always, from the center of what most concerned him at the moment. The people would forget his words the moment they were gone; he tried to take them to heart. When things seemed blackest, carrying on was never easy. But if you didn't carry on, how could you make your way to better times?

Squeals of glee greeted the first mime troupe to appear. The crowd's laughter dinned around Krispos as the performers, some dressed as soldiers, others as horses, pretended to be stuck in the mud. Even if they did lampoon his ill-fated campaign in the westlands, he found himself amused at first. Their act was highly polished, as were most that appeared in the Amphitheater. Rotten fruit and sometimes stones greeted troupes that did not live up to what the city folk thought their due.

The next group of mimes put on a skit whose theme puzzled Krispos. One of their number wore a costume that turned him into a skeleton. The other three seemed to be servants. They brought him ever more elaborate meals, finally wheeling out a prop feast that looked sumptuous enough to feed half the people in the Amphitheater. But the fellow in the skeleton suit refused everything with comic vehemence, and finally lay stiff and still in the dirt of the racetrack. His underlings picked him up and hauled him away.

The audience didn't quite know what to make of that show, either. Most of them sat on their hands. A few roared laughter; a couple of shouts of "Blasphemy!" rang out.

Krispos got up and walked over to Oxeites the patriarch, who sat a few yards down the spine from his own place. "Blasphemy?" he asked. "Where is the blasphemy—for that matter, where is the point?—in refusing food, most holy sir? Or does the blasphemy lie in mocking that refusal?"

"Your Majesty, I do not know." The patriarch sounded worried to admit it. Well he might; if he could not untie a theological knot, who in Videssos the city could?

All the performers in the professional mime troupes were male. It wasn't that way in peasant villages like the one where Krispos had grown up; he smiled to remember the village women and girls doing wicked impressions of their husbands and brothers. But the fellow who played a woman in the next troupe seemed so feminine and so voluptuous that the Avtokrator, who knew perfectly well what he was, found lubricious thoughts prancing through his mind all the same.

The performer turned his—or her—wiles on another member of the troupe, one dressed in a robe of priestly blue. The cleric proved slaveringly eager to oblige.

The crowd howled laughter. No one yelled "Blasphemy!" Krispos turned to Oxeites again. He contented himself with raising a questioning eyebrow; if he spoke from the Emperor's seat, the whole Amphitheater would hear him.

Oxeites coughed in embarrassment. "There was, your Majesty, an, ah, unfortunate incident concerning celibacy while you were, ah, on campaign."

Krispos walked over to the patriarch's chair so he could talk without being overheard. "I saw no written reports on this, most holy sir. Did you think it would escape my notice? If so, do not make such a mistake again. When a priest drags the reputation of the temples through the bathhouses, I *will* find out about it. Have I made myself clear enough?"

"Y-yes, your Majesty." The patriarch was as pale as the pearls that ran riot over his regalia. Keeping unsavory secrets secret was part of the game of Videssian bureaucracy, secular and ecclesiastical alike. Getting found out meant you'd lost a round in that game.

The Avtokrator began to hope the mimes, poke fun at him as they might, would largely forget Phostis' kidnapping. That hope lasted until the next troupe came on and lampooned him for misplacing his eldest son; by the way the actor in fancy robes portrayed Krispos, his heir might have been a gold coin that had fallen through a hole in his belt pouch. The fellow kept looking behind prop bushes and under stones, as if certain he'd turn up the vanished heir in a moment.

The audience thought it all very funny. Krispos looked over to see how his other two sons were taking the mimes. He'd seldom seen such rage on Katakolon's face; his youngest son seemed ready to grab a bow and do his best to slaughter the whole troupe. The pretty girl next to Katakolon had her face carefully blank, as if she wanted to laugh but didn't dare.

A few seats away, Evripos was laughing as hard as some tinker up near the top row of the Amphitheater. He happened to catch Krispos' eye. He choked and grew sober as abruptly as if he'd been caught in some unnatural act. Krispos nodded grimly, as if to say Evripos had better keep himself quiet. He knew his second son hungered for the throne; in Evripos' shoes, he would have hungered for it, too. But displaying exultation because his brother had disappeared would not do.

By the time the last troupe made its bows and left the Amphitheater, the year's shortest day was almost done. By then, several troupes had satirized Phostis' kidnapping. Krispos endured it as best he could. Evripos sat so still, he might have been carved from stone.

To end the show, Krispos spoke to the crowd. "Tomorrow the sun will come sooner and leave the sky later. Once again Skotos—" He spat in rejection of the evil god. "—has failed to steal the light. May Phos bless you all, and may your days also be long and filled with light."

The crowd cheered, almost universally forgetting they'd giggled at the Avtokrator's expense bare minutes before. That was the way of crowds, Krispos knew. He'd started learning how to manipulate the Videssian mob while still a groom in Petronas' service, to help push out Anthimos' then-vestiarios so he could take the eunuch's place. The decades that had passed since had done little to increase his respect for the people in a collective body.

He got up from the Emperor's seat and took a few steps away from the acoustical focus. Only then could he privately talk aloud, even to himself. "Well, it's over," he said. He'd got through it, his family had got through it, and he didn't think any of the skits had done him permanent harm. Given the way the preceding few months had gone, he could hardly have hoped for better.

Twilight deepened quickly as, in the company of parasol bearers and Haloga bodyguards, he made his way out of the Amphitheater. He, of course, had his own special exit. Had he wanted to, he could have gone straight back to the palaces under a covered way. But walking through the plaza of Palamas, as he had on the way to the mime show in the Amphitheater, gave him a chance to finger the pulse of the city. Ceremonial separated him from his subjects too much as things were. When he got a chance like this, he took it, and so he headed back toward the imperial residence through the square.

More bonfires burned there now than had when he went into the Amphitheater. People coming out of the mime show queued up to jump over them and burn away the year's accumulated misfortune. A few turned their heads as the Emperor and his retinue went by. One or two even called out, "Joy on the day, your Majesty!"

"And to you and yours," he called back. On impulse, he added, "May I beg to steal a place in line?"

Men and women scrambled out of the way to give him what he'd asked for. Some of the Halogai stayed close by him; others, knowing Videssian ways, hurried to the far side of the fire. Krispos took a running start. The scarlet imperial boots were less than perfect footgear for running, but he managed. Leaping with all his strength, he yelled, "Burn, ill-luck!" as he soared over and through the flames. Maybe, as he'd said earlier in the day, it would do no good. But how could it do harm?

He landed heavily, staggering. One of the guardsmen grabbed his arm and steadied him. "Thanks," he said. His heart pounded, his breath came quick. A run and a jump—was that exerting himself? When he first took the throne, he'd have laughed at the idea. Now it seemed less funny. He shrugged. The only alternative to getting older was *not* getting any older. This wasn't perfect, but it was better.

A couple of bonfires over, a young man stooped to ignite a torch. He waved it over his head. Sparks flew through the night. The young man weaved among slower-moving people in the square. Still waving his torch, he shouted, "The gleaming path! Phos bless the gleaming path!"

For a moment, the cry did not register with Krispos. Then he stopped in midstride, stared, and pointed toward the young man. "That is a Thanasiot. Arrest him!"

Thinking back afterward, he realized he could have handled things better. Some of his guards dashed after the Thanasiot. So did some people in the crowd. Others, mistaking Krispos' target, chased the wrong man—several wrong men—and got in the way of those pursuing the right one. Shouts and fistfights erupted.

The young heretic kept right on running and kept right on chanting the Thanasiot war cry. To Krispos' horror, he cast his torch into one of the wood-and-canvas market stalls that were closed for the Midwinter's Day celebration. Flames clung and began to grow.

All at once Krispos, a lump of ice in his belly, wished the holiday had seen a blizzard or, better yet, a driving rainstorm.

*Rain in the westlands when I didn't want it,* he thought wildly, *but none now when I can really use it.* The weather was not playing fair.

Neither were the Thanasioi. That first arsonist, no longer obvious for what he was as soon as he'd thrown his torch, vanished into the crowd. But others of his kind dashed here and there, waving torches and yelling acclaim for the gleaming path. In fewer than half a dozen minutes, more than half a dozen fires began to burn.

The people in the plaza of Palamas surged like the sea in storm, some toward the blazes but many more away from them. Fire in Videssos the city—fire in any town—was a great terror, for the means of fighting it were so pitifully few. Great fires, with winds whipping walls of flame ahead of them, had slain thousands and burned out whole quarters of the city. Most of those—all of them, as far as Krispos knew—sprang from lightning or accident. To use fire in a city—in *the* city—as a weapon . . . Krispos shivered. The Thanasioi were not playing fair, either.

He tried to pull himself together. "Bucket and siphon men!" he yelled to one of the chamberlain. "Fetch them on the double!"

"Aye, your Majesty." The eunuch pelted into the palace compound. A company of firemen was stationed there, attached to the imperial guards. Several other companies had bases in other parts of the city. They were brave, they were skilled, they were even useful if they could get to a fire before it went wild. But if the Thanasioi were throwing torches around in the Forum of the Ox as well as the plaza of Palamas, and in the coppersmiths' district, and over by the High Temple, some of those blazes would surely get loose.

Krispos shouted, "Twenty goldpieces for every arsonist slain, fifty for every one taken alive!" With luck, the price differential would keep cutthroats from murdering innocent bystanders and then claiming a reward.

"Will you retire to the palaces, your Majesty?" Barsymes asked.

"No." Krispos saw he'd surprised the vestiarios. He explained, "I want to be seen fighting this madness. I'll do it from the plaza here."

"As you say, your Majesty," Barsymes answered in the peculiarly toneless voice he used when he thought Krispos was making a mistake.

Before long, Krispos, too, wondered if he hadn't made a mistake. Messengers who ran to the palaces didn't find him there. Because of that, he learned later than he should have that not only arson but also full-scale rioting had broken out in some of the poorer districts of the city. The two went hand in hand in every Avtokrator's nightmares: arson might leave him without a capital to rule, while riots could keep him from ruling at all.

But setting up his headquarters out where the people could see him had advantages, too. Not only did he shout for men to form a bucket brigade from the nearest fountain, he pitched in and passed buckets himself. "This is my city as well as yours," he told anyone who would listen. "We all have to work together to save it if we can."

For a while, that looked anything but certain. A bucket brigade was hopelessly inadequate to put out a fire once it got going. Even if some excited citizens didn't know that much, Krispos did. At his direction, the fellows at the far end of the brigade concentrated on wetting down the buildings and market stalls around the growing blaze to try to keep it from spreading.

He was beginning to think even that would be beyond their power when someone yelled, "Here's the fire company!"

"Oh, Phos be praised," Krispos panted. Already his shoulders ached from unaccustomed exertion; tomorrow, he suspected, he would be stiff and sore all over. Well, he'd worry about that tomorrow. Tonight, fighting the fire counted for more. He silently thanked the good god that, while he'd put on weight since he came to the throne, he hadn't got so fat as to kill himself if he had to do physical labor.

Instead of a hand bucket, the fire crew carried a great wooden tub on poles like those of a sedan chair. They filled it at the fountain, then—with shouts of "Gangway!"—dashed to the fire. Instead of dumping the big bucket on the blaze, two of the men worked a hand pump mounted in the bucket, while a third directed the stream of water that issued from the nozzle of an oiled canvas hose.

The bucket brigade shifted its efforts to keeping the tub full. Even so, it emptied faster than they could pour water into it.

The firemen snatched it up by its cradle, filled it at the fountain again, then lugged it back with much swearing and grunting. The pumpers worked like men possessed; the fellow at the hose, a gray-haired veteran named Thokyodes, played his stream right at the heart of the blaze.

That second tubful began to give the fire company the upper hand. The blaze had eaten two or three stalls and damaged a couple of others, but it would not turn into a conflagration. Thokyodes came over to Krispos and greeted him with a crisp military salute, clenched fist over heart. "You called us in good time, your Majesty. We've managed to save this lot."

"Not the first service you've done the city—or me," Krispos answered; Thokyodes had served on the fire crews for longer than Krispos had been Emperor. "I wish I could tell you to stand easy the rest of the night, but I fear we'll have more fires set."

"Ah, well, Midwinter's Day is always a nervous time for us." Thokyodes stopped, staring at the Avtokrator. "Set, did you say? This wasn't just one of the bonfires' blowing embers that caught?"

"I wish it had been," Krispos said. "But no, no such luck. The Thanasioi are raising riot, and when they riot, they seem to like to burn, too. The less anyone has, the better they're pleased."

Thokyodes made a horrible face. "They're fornicating crazy, begging your pardon, your Majesty. Those bastards ever see anybody who's burned to death? They ever smelled a burned corpse? They ever try rebuilding what's been burned down?"

"I don't think they care about any of that. All they want is to get out of the material world as fast as they can."

"Send 'em on to me, then," Thokyodes growled. He carried a hatchet at his belt, to break down a wall so he could use his siphon or break through a door if he needed to effect a rescue. Now he grabbed the oak handle as if he had something else in mind for the tool. "Aye, I'll send 'em on to the ice real soon, I will, by the good god. Start their own fires, will they?" Like any fireman, he had a fierce, roaring hatred for arsonists of any sort, religious or secular.

A messenger came up to Krispos. Blood ran down his face from a scalp wound. When Krispos exclaimed over it, the man shook off his concern. "I'll live, your Majesty. The rock glanced off, and my father always told me I had a hard head. Glad the old man was right. But I'm here to tell you it's getting worse than just riots in the poor part of town south of Middle Street. It's regular war—they're fighting with everything they have. Not just rocks like what got me, but bows and shortswords and I don't know what all else."

"Do you know where the barracks are in the palace compound, and can you get there without falling over?" Krispos asked. When he got nods to both questions, he went on, "Rout out Noetos' regiment of regulars. If the Thanasioi want to pretend they're soldiers, let's see how well they do facing soldiers instead of the city watch."

"Aye, your Majesty," the messenger said. "You ought to send some priests out, too, for the heretics have one at their head, leather-lunged blue-robe name of—I think—Digenis."

Krispos frowned; while he knew he'd heard the name before, he needed a little while to place it. When he did, he snarled something that made the messenger's eyes widen. "That's the blue-robe Phostis fell in love with before he got kidnapped," he ground out. "If he's a Thanasiot—"

He stopped. If Digenis was a Thanasiot, did that mean Phostis had joined the heresy, too? Thinking so appalled Krispos, but he also realized that just about everything he did appalled Phostis, if for no other reason than because he did it. And if his eldest had become a Thanasiot, had he really been kidnapped at all? Or had he run off to join the rebels of his own free will?

One way or another, Krispos had to have answers. He said, "Pass the word—a hundred goldpieces for this Digenis alive, and may the lord with the great and good mind have mercy on anyone who slays him, for I'll have none."

"I'll make your wishes—your commands—known, your Majesty." The messenger took off at a dead run.

Krispos had no time to brood on the fellow's news; two men dashed into the plaza of Palamas from different directions, each screaming "Fire!" at the top of his lungs. "Thokyodes!" Krispos yelled. The veteran asked both panicky men a few sharp questions, decided whose plight was more urgent, and went off with that fellow. The other man stamped his feet and looked about ready to burst. Krispos hoped he wouldn't lose all that he owned by the time the fire company got back.

A bitterly cold wind began to blow out of the northwest, the direction from which the winter storms came. Krispos would have welcomed one of those storms, but bright stars glittered in a blue-black sky. No storm tonight; maybe, he thought, tasting the wind, no storm tomorrow, either. Of course not. He needed one.

Some of the palace servitors scurried about the plaza of Palamas, setting up awnings to protect him from whatever weather might come. Since he'd decided to make his headquarters here, the servants would see that he had such comforts as they could provide. Barsymes eyed him, daring him to make something of it. He kept quiet.

Along with the servitors, people of every sort swarmed through the plaza—soldiers, messengers, firemen, and revelers determined to celebrate Midwinter's Day as they pleased no matter what was going on around them. The skinny fellow in the dark tunic didn't look the least out of place as he worked his way up to Krispos. When he got to within a couple of paces of the Avtokrator, he pulled out a dagger and screamed, "Phos bless the gleaming path!"

He stabbed overhand, which was less than wise. Krispos threw up a hand and caught the fellow's wrist before the knife struck home. The would-be assassin twisted and tried to break free, screaming all the while about the gleaming path. But Krispos had learned to wrestle from an army veteran about the time his beard began to sprout, and he had gained his first fame in Videssos the city by outgrappling a Kubrati champion. Shouting and twisting were not nearly enough to break away from him.

He bore the knifeman to the cobbles, squeezing hard on the tendons inside his wrist. Involuntarily, the Thanasiot's hand opened. When the knife fell out, the fellow tried to roll and grab for it. Krispos brought up a knee, hard, between his legs. It was unsporting but extremely effective. The fellow stopped screaming about the gleaming path and started screaming in good earnest.

A Haloga's axe came down with a meaty *thunk*. The screams rose to a brief high note, then stopped. Krispos scrambled to his feet to keep his robes from soaking up the quickly spreading pool of blood.

"I'd like to have asked him some questions," he said mildly.

"Honh!" the bodyguard answered, a northern exclamation full of contempt. "He attacked you, your Majesty; he did not deserve to live, even for a moment."

"All right, Trygve," Krispos said. If he criticized the northerner too harshly, Trygve was liable to decide the knifeman had managed to come so close to the Emperor because of his own failing, and slay himself to make up for it. The Halogai were wonderful guards, but they had to be handled very differently from Videssians. Krispos had spent twenty years groping toward an understanding of their gloomy pride; given another twenty, he thought he might come close.

Thokyodes and his fire company returned to the plaza of Palamas. The fellow whose earlier plea they'd rejected fell on them like a starving bear. Without so much as a chance to draw breath, they hurried away in his wake. Krispos wondered if they'd find anything left to save.

From out of the palace complex, their armor clashing about them, marched the troops who had served as Krispos' rear guard in the ill-fated western campaign. They looked angry, first at being confined to barracks on Midwinter's Day and then at getting called out not to celebrate but to fight. As they grimly tramped through the plaza of Palamas, Krispos reflected that he wouldn't have cared to get in their way this evening.

A few minutes later, the noise floating into the square from the rest of the city suddenly redoubled. It did not sound like happy noise. Happy was the grunt that came from Trygve's throat. "Your soldiers, they go breaking heads." To him, the prospect seemed blissful.

Krispos watched the stars wheel slowly across the sky. He caught himself yawning. Though he was far more likely than most Videssians to stay up well into the night—who, after all, could better afford candles than the Avtokrator?—he still went to bed early by choice. Well, tonight he had no choice.

A trooper came back to report on the fighting south of Middle Street. He didn't seem to notice his iron pot of a helmet had been knocked sideways on his head. Saluting, he confirmed the headgear's mute testimony: "Your Majesty, them whoresons is putting up a regular battle, they is. They's been ready for it awhile, too, or I miss my guess."

"Don't tell me they're beating the regiment," Krispos exclaimed. *You'd better not tell me that,* he thought, *or some of my officers won't be officers by this hour of the night tomorrow.*

But the trooper shook his head. "Oh, nothing like that. They has spunk, aye, and more stay to 'em than I'd have looked for from a mob, but they ain't got armor and they ain't got many shields. We can hurt them a lot more than they can hurt us."

"Tell Noetos to do what he has to do to put them down," Krispos said. "Remind him also to make every effort to seize the priest Digenis, who I've heard is leading the rioters."

"Aye, there's a blue-robe flouncing about, shouting all sorts of daft nonsense. I figures we'd just knock him over the head." Krispos winced; somehow rumor seemed to spread every word but the one he wanted spread. "But if you want him took alive, we'll try and manage that."

"There's a reward," Krispos said, which made the messenger hurry back toward the brawl.

Waiting was hard. Krispos would much rather have been with a fire company or the regiment of soldiers. They were actually doing something. But if he did it with them, he'd lose track of how all his forces in the city were doing, save only the one he was with. Sometimes standing back to look at the whole mosaic was better than walking right up to it and peering closely at one tile. Better, maybe, but not easier.

Without his noticing, the servitors had fetched cots from the imperial residence—or perhaps from a barracks—and set them under the awning they'd erected. Evripos dozed on one, Katakolon on another. The girl who'd come to the Amphitheater with him was gone. Krispos knew his son would sooner have been in her bed than the one he occupied, but he felt a certain amount of amused relief that Katakolon hadn't dared leave. The boy knew better than that, by the good god.

Glancing over at Evripos, Krispos was surprised at how badly he wanted to wake him and put him to work. The lad—no, Evripos had shown himself the fair beginnings of a man—could have given him another pair of eyes, another pair of hands. But Krispos let him sleep.

Even though the fires in the plaza of Palamas were long since extinguished, Krispos smelled smoke from time to time, wafted from blazes elsewhere in the city. The wind, fortunately, had died down. With luck, it would not spread flames and embers in one of those running fires that left whole quarters bare behind them; rebuilding after one like that took years.

Krispos sat down on his cot. *Just for a few minutes,* he told himself. He dimly remembered leaning over sideways, but didn't know he'd fallen asleep until someone yelled, "Your Majesty! Wake up, your Majesty!"

"Wuzzat? I *am* awake," Krispos said indignantly. But the gluey taste in his mouth and the glue that kept trying to stick his eyelids together gave him the lie. "Well, I'm awake now," he amended. "What's toward?"

"We've nailed Digenis, your Majesty," the messenger told him. "Had a couple of lads hurt in the doing, but he's in our hands."

"There's welcome news at last, by the lord with the great and good mind," Krispos breathed. With it, he really did come all the way awake. He must have been out for two hours or so; the buildings to the southeast were silhouetted against the first gray glow of morning twilight. When he got to his feet, twinges in the small of his back and one shoulder announced how awkwardly he'd rested. That wouldn't have happened in his younger days, but it happened now.

"We're bringing the bastard—begging your pardon for speaking so of a priest, your Majesty, but he's a right bastard if ever there was one—anyhow, we're bringing him back here to the plaza," the messenger said. "Where will you want him after that?"

"In the freezingest icepit of Skotos' hell," Krispos said, which jerked a startled laugh from the soldier who'd carried him the news. The Avtokrator thought fast. "He shouldn't come here, anyway—too much chance of his getting loose. Head up Middle Street—he'll be coming that way, yes?—and tell the men to haul him to the government office building there and secure him in one of the underground gaol cells. I'll be there directly myself."

Pausing only long enough to return the messenger's salute, Krispos shook Katakolon awake and ordered him to fetch Zaidas to the government office building. "What? Why?" asked Katakolon, who'd slept through the messenger's arrival. His eyes went wide when his father explained.

Haloga officers booted their men back to consciousness to guard Krispos on the way down Middle Street. With his usual quiet efficiency, Barsymes—who probably had not slept at all—started spreading word of where the Avtokrator would be so any sudden urgent word could quickly reach him.

The government office building was a granite pile of no particular loveliness. It housed bureaucrats of station insufficiently exalted to labor in the palaces, records of antiquity great enough that they were not constantly consulted, and, below-ground, prisoners who rated more than a fine but less than the headsman. It looked like a fortress; in seditions past, it had served as one.

Today's riot, though, did not lap around it. Some of the Halogai deployed at the doorway in case trouble should approach. Others accompanied Krispos into the entry hall, which was quiet and, but for their torches, dark. Krispos took the stairway down.

Noise and light and strong odors of torch smoke, stale food, and unwashed humanity greeted him on the first basement floor. The prison guards hailed him with salutes and welcoming shouts—his coming was enough out of the ordinary to make their labor seem worthwhile again.

A senior guard said, "The one you're after, your Majesty, they're holding him in cell number twelve, down that hallway there." The wine on his breath added a new note to the symphony of smells. It being the morning after Midwinter's Day, Krispos gave no sign he noticed, but made a mental note to check whether the fellow drank on duty other days, as well.

Instead of the usual iron grillwork, cell number twelve had a stout door with a locked bar on the outside. The gaoler inserted a big brass key, twisted, and swung the bar out of the Avtokrator's way. Flanked by a pair of Halogai, Krispos went in.

A couple of soldiers from Noetos' regiment already stood guard over Digenis, who, wrists tied behind him and ankles bound, lay on a straw pallet that had seen better years. "Haul him to his feet," Krispos said roughly.

The guard obeyed. Blood ran down Digenis' face from a small scalp wound. Those always bled badly, and, being a priest, Digenis had no hair to shield his pate from a blow. He glared defiance at Krispos.

Krispos glared back. "Where's Phostis, wretch?"

"Phos willing, he walks the gleaming path," Digenis an-

swered, "and I think Phos may well be willing. Your son
knows truth when he hears it."

"More than I can say for you, if you follow the Thanasiot
lies," Krispos snapped. "Now where is he?"

"I don't know," Digenis said. "And if I did, I'd not tell you,
that's certain."

"What's certain is that your head will go up on the Milestone as belonging to a proved traitor," Krispos said. "Caught
in open revolt, don't think you'll escape because you wear the
blue robe."

"Wealth is worth revolting against, and I don't fear the
headsman because I know the gleaming path will lead me
straight to the lord with the great and good mind," Digenis
said. "But I could be as innocent as any man the temples revere as holy and still die of your malice, for the patriarch, far
from being the true leader of the ecclesiastical hierarchy, is but
your puppet, mouthing your impious words."

Stripped of the venom with which he spoke them, Digenis'
words held a certain amount of truth: if Oxeites turned against
Krispos, he would soon find himself out of the ecumenical patriarch's blue boots. But none of that mattered, not here, not
now. "You're captured for no ecclesiastical offense, sirrah, but
for the purely secular crimes of rebellion and treason. You'll
answer for them as any other rebel would."

"I'll sing hymns to Phos thanking you for freeing me from
the stench-filled world that strives unceasingly to seduce and
corrupt my soul," Digenis said. "But if you do not travel the
gleaming path yourself, no hymns of mine will save you.
You'll go to the ice and suffer for all eternity, lured to destruction by Skotos' honied wiles."

"Given a choice between sharing heaven with you and hell
with Skotos, I believe I'd take Skotos," Krispos said. "He at
least does not pretend to virtues he lacks."

Digenis hissed like a viper and spat at Krispos, whether to
ward off the dark god's name or from simple hatred, the
Avtokrator could not have said. Just then Zaidas came into the
cell. "Hello," he said. "What's all this?" He set down the carpetbag in his left hand.

"This," Krispos said, "is the miserable excuse for a priest
who sucked my son into the slimy arms of the Thanasioi.
Wring what you can from the cesspit he calls a mind."

"I shall of course make every effort, your Majesty, but . . ." Zaidas' voice trailed away. He looked doubtful, an expression Krispos was unused to seeing on his face. "I fear I've not had the best of luck, probing for the heretics' secrets."

"You gold-lovers are the heretics," Digenis said, "casting aside true piety for the sake of profit."

Emperor and wizard both ignored him. "Do your best," Krispos said. He hoped Zaidas would have better fortune with Digenis than he had with other Thanasiot prisoners or with learning what sort of magic screened him away from finding Phostis. Despite the rare sorcerous tools and rarer scrolls and codices in the Sorcerers' Collegium, the chief wizard had been unable to learn why he was unable to seek Phostis out by sorcery.

Zaidas started pulling sorcerous gear from the bag. "I'll try the two-mirror test, your Majesty," he said.

Krispos wanted to hear confidence in his voice, wanted to hear him say he would have the truth out of Digenis no matter what the renegade priest did. What he heard, with ears honed by listening behind the words of thousands of petitioners, officers, and officials, was doubt. Doubt from Zaidas fed his own doubt: because magic drew so strongly from the power of belief, if Zaidas didn't truly believe he could make Digenis speak, he'd likely fail. He'd already failed on a Thanasiot with the two-mirror test.

"What other strings do you have to your bow?" the Emperor asked. "How else can we hope to pull answers from him?" He could hear his own delicacy of phrase. He wanted Zaidas to think about alternatives, but didn't want to demoralize the mage or suggest he'd lost faith in him . . . even if he had.

Zaidas said, "Should the two-mirror test fail, our strongest hope of learning truth goes with it. Oh, a decoction of henbane and other herbs, such as the healers use, might loosen this rascal's tongue, but with it he'd spew as much gibberish as fact."

"One way or another, he'll spew, by the good god," Krispos said grimly, "if not to you, then to the chap in the red leathers."

"Torment my flesh as you will," Digenis said. "It is but the excrement of my being; the sooner it slides down the sewer, the sooner my soul soars past the sun to be with the lord with the great and good mind."

"Go on," Krispos told Zaidas. Worry on his face, the wizard set up his mirrors, one in front of Digenis, the other behind him. He got a brazier going; clouds of fumigants rose in front of the mirrors, some sweet, some harsh.

But when the questioning began, not only did Digenis stand mute, so did his image in the mirror behind him. Had the spell been working as it should have, that second image would have given out truth in spite of his efforts to lie or remain silent.

Zaidas bit his lip in angry, mortified frustration. Krispos sucked in a long, furious breath. He'd had the bad feeling Digenis would remain impervious to interrogation of any sort. The vast majority of men broke under torture. Maybe the priest would, or maybe he'd spill his guts under the influence of one of Zaidas' potions. But Krispos wasn't willing to bet on either.

As if to rub in his determination, Digenis said, "I shall praise Phos' holy name for every pang you inflict on me." He began to sing a hymn at the top of his lungs.

"Oh, shut up," Krispos said. Digenis kept on singing. Someone scratched at the door to the cell. Axe ready to strike, a Haloga pulled it open. A priest started to walk in, then drew back in alarm at the upraised axe blade. "Come on, come on," Krispos told him. "Don't stand there dithering—just tell me what you want."

"May it please your Majesty," the priest began nervously, and Krispos braced for trouble. The blue-robe tried again: "M-may it please your Majesty, I am Soudas, an attendant at the High Temple. The most holy ecumenical patriarch Oxeites, who was commemorating the day by celebrating a special liturgy there, directed me to come to you on hearing that the holy priest Digenis had been captured, so to speak, in arms, and bade me remind your Majesty that ecclesiastics are under all circumstances immune from suffering bodily torment."

"Oh, he did? Oh, they are?" Krispos glared at the priest, who looked as if he wished he could sink through the floor—though that would only have put him in a deeper level of the jail. "Doesn't the most holy ecumenical patriarch recall that I took the head of one of his predecessors for treason no worse than this Digenis has committed?"

"If you mentioned the fate of the formerly most holy Gnatios—may Phos grant his soul mercy—I was instructed to point out that, while capital punishment remains your province, it is a matter altogether distinct from torture."

"Oh, it is?" Krispos made his glare fiercer still. It all but shriveled Soudas, but the priest managed a shaky nod. Krispos dropped his scowl to his red boots; could he have scowled at his own face, he would have done it. The part of him that weighed choices like a grocer weighing out lentils swung into action. Could he afford a row with the regular temple hierarchy while at the same time fighting the Thanasiot heretics? Reluctantly, he decided he could not. Growling like a dog that has reached the end of its chain and so cannot sink its teeth into a man it wants to bite, he said, "Very well, no torture. You may tell the patriarch as much. Generous of him to let me use my own executioners as I see fit."

Soudas bobbed his head in what might have been a nod, then wheeled about and fled. Digenis hadn't missed a note of his hymn. Krispos tried to console himself by doubting whether the renegade would have broken under torment. But he craved the chance to find out.

The Avtokrator swung toward Zaidas. The wizard had listened to his talk with the priest. Zaidas was anything but a fool; he could figure out for himself that the burden on him had just grown heavier. If he couldn't pry secrets from Digenis, those secrets would stay unknown for good. The wizard licked his lips. No, he was not long on confidence.

Digenis ended his hymn. "I care not if you go against the patriarch," he said. "His doctrine is false in any case, and I do not fear your torments."

Krispos knew a strong temptation to break Digenis on the rack, to tear at his flesh with red-hot pincers, not so much in the hope that he would tell where Phostis was—if in fact he knew—but to see if he so loudly despised torment after suffering a good deal of it. Krispos had enough control over himself to recognize the temptation as base and put it aside, but he felt it all the same.

Digenis not only remained defiant but actually seemed to seek out martyrdom. "Your refusal to liberate me from my polluting and polluted envelope of flesh is but another proof of your own foul materialism, your rejection of the spiritual for the sensual, the soul for the penis, the—"

"When you go to the ice, I hope you bore Skotos with your

stupid maunderings," Krispos said, a sally that succeeded in making Digenis splutter in outrage and then, better still, shut up. The Emperor added, "I've wasted enough time on you." He turned to Zaidas. "Try anything and everything you think might work. Bring in whatever colleagues you need to give you aid. One way or another, I will have answers from this one before the dark god takes him forever."

"Aye, your Majesty." Zaidas' voice was low and troubled. "The good god willing, others from the Sorcerers' Collegium will have more success than I at smashing through his protective shell of fanaticism."

Accompanied by his bodyguards, Krispos left the cell and the subterranean jail. About halfway up the stairs to the entrance hall, one of the Halogai said, "Forgive me, Majesty, but may I ask if I heard the blue-robe aright? Did he not blame you there for failing to flay him?"

"Aye, that's just what he did, Frovin," Krispos answered.

The northerner's blue eyes mirrored his confusion. "Majesty, I do not understand. I do not fear hurt and gore; that were unmanly. But neither do I run forth and embrace them like man clasping maid."

"Nor do I," Krispos said. "A streak of martyrdom runs through some of the pious in Videssos, though. Me, I'd sooner live for the good god than die for him."

"Spoken like a man of sense," Frovin said. The other bodyguards rumbled approval, down deep in their chests.

When he went outside, the gray light of winter dawn was building. The air smelled of smoke, but with stoves, fireplaces, and braziers by the tens of thousands, the air of Videssos the city always had a smoky tang to it. No great curtains of black billowed up into the lightening sky. If the Thanasioi had thought to burn down the city, thus far they'd failed.

Back in the plaza of Palamas, Evripos still slept. To Krispos' surprise, he found Katakolon in earnest conversation with Thokyodes the fire captain. "If you're sure everything's out in that district, why don't you get some rest?" his youngest son was saying. "You won't do us or the city any good if you're too worn to answer the next summons."

"Aye, that's good advice, young Majesty," Thokyodes answered, saluting. "We'll kip right out here, if that suits—and if you can find us some blankets."

"Barsymes!" Katakolon called. Krispos nodded approvingly—Katakolon might not know where things were, but he knew who would. His son spotted him. "Hello, Father. Just holding things together as best I could; Barsymes told me you were busy with that madman of a priest."

"So I was. I thank you for the help. Do we have the upper hand?"

"We seem to," Katakolon said, more caution in his voice than Krispos was used to hearing there.

"Good enough," Krispos said. "Now let's see if we can keep it."

Toward midmorning, riot flared again in the quarter south of Middle Street. The soldiers Krispos had sent in the night before stayed loyal, much to his relief. Better still, the wind stayed calm, which gave Thokyodes' crew a fighting chance against the blazes set by the heretics and rioters—not identical groups; some of the brawlers arrested were out for what they reckoned piety, others just for loot.

When messengers reported that spasm spent, Krispos raised cups of wine with both Katakolon and Evripos, convinced the worst was past. Then another messenger arrived, this one a jailer from under the government office building. "What now?" Krispos asked.

"It concerns the matter of the prisoner Digenis the priest," the fellow answered.

"Well, what about him?" Krispos said, wishing the goaler wouldn't talk like what he was now that he'd come away from the cells and into the sun.

"Your Majesty, he has refused alimentation," the man declared. Krispos' upraised eyebrow warned him he'd better talk straighter than that. He did try: "Your Majesty, he won't eat his victuals. He declares his intention to starve himself to death."

For the first time since he grew old enough to jump over a bonfire instead of falling into one, Phostis did no leaping on Midwinter's Day. Whatever ill-luck he'd accumulated over the past year remained unburned. He wasn't mewed up in his monklike cell in the keep of Etchmiadzin; he'd been allowed out and about for some weeks. But no fires blazed on street corners anywhere in the town.

Dark streets on Midwinter's Day struck him as unnatural,

even while he accompanied Olyvria and—inevitably—
Syagrios to one of Etchmiadzin's temples. The service was
timed for sunset, which came early not only became this was
the shortest day of the year but also because the sun, instead
of descending to a smooth horizon, disappeared behind the
mountains to the west.

Night came down like an avalanche. Inside the temple,
whose strong, blocky architecture spoke of Vaspurakaner
builders, darkness seemed absolute; the Thanasio: unlike the
orthodox, did not celebrate the light on Midwinter's Day but
rather confronted their fear of the dark. Not a torch, not a candle burned inside the temple.

Standing there in the midst of blackness, Phostis peered
about, trying to see something, anything. For all the good his
eyes did, he might as well have been blindfolded again. His
shiver had nothing to do with the cold that filled the temple
along with night. Never had the menace of Skotos seemed so
real, so close.

Seeking assurance where sight gave none, he reached out
and clasped Olyvria's hand in his own. She squeezed back
hard; he wondered if this eerie, silent ritual was as hard on her,
on all the Thanasioi, as it was on him.

"Someone will start screaming soon," he whispered, not
least to keep himself from becoming that someone. His breath-
less voice seemed to echo through the temple, though he knew
even Olyvria could hardly hear him.

"Yes," she whispered back. "It happens sometimes. I remember when—"

He didn't find out what she remembered. Her words were
lost in a great exhalation of relief from the whole congregation.
A priest carrying a single candle strode up the aisle toward the
altar. Every eye swung toward that glowing point as if drawn
by a lodestone.

"We bless thee, Phos, lord with the great and good mind,"
the priest intoned, and everyone in the temple joined in the
creed with greater fervor than Phostis had ever known, "by thy
grace our protector, watchful beforehand that the great test of
life may be decided in our favor."

The congregation's amens came echoing back from the conical dome that surmounted the altar. Often, to Phostis, Phos'
creed had become mere words to be quickly gabbled through

without thinking on what they meant. Not now. In the cold and frightening dark, they, like the tiny flame from the candle the priest held on high, took on new meaning, new importance. If they were not, if light was not—what then? Only black, only ice. Phostis shivered again.

The priest moved the candle to and fro and said, "Here is the soul, adrift in a creation not its own, the sole light floating on an ocean of darkness. It moves here, it moves there, always surrounded by—things." Coming out of the gloom that prevailed even at the altar, the word had a frightening power.

"But the soul is not a—thing," the priest went on. "The soul is a spark from the infinite torch of Phos, trapped in a world made by the foe of sparks and the greater foe of greater sparks. The things that surround us distract us from the pursuit of goodness, holiness, and piety, which are all that truly matter.

"For our souls endure forever, and will be judged forever. Shall we then turn toward that which does not endure? Food turns to dung, fire to ash, fine raiment to rags, our bodies to stench and bones and then to dust. What boots it, then, whether we gorge on sweetmeats, toast our homes till we sweat in the midst of winter, drape ourselves with silks and furs, or twitch to the brief deluded passions—miscalled pleasures—that spring from the organs we better use to void ourselves of dross?"

Contemplating infinite judgment, contemplating infinite punishment for the sins he, like any mortal, had surely committed, made Phostis want to tear his grip free from Olyvria's. Anything involving base matter in any way was surely evil, surely sufficient to cast him down to the ice forevermore.

But Olyvria clung to him harder than she had before. Maybe, he told himself, she needed comfort and reassurance. Granting her that spiritual boon might outweigh his guilt for noticing how warm and smooth her skin was. He did not let go of her hand.

The priest said, "Each year, the lord with the great and good mind warns us we cannot presume his mercy will endure forever. Each year, all through fall, Phos' sun sinks lower in the sky. Each year, our prayers call it back to rise higher once more, to grant warmth and light even to the wicked figments of reality that spring from the dark heart of Skotos.

"But beware! No mercy, not even the good god's, endures forever. Phos may yet sicken on our great glut of sins. One year—maybe one year not far from now, given the wretched state of mankind; maybe even next year; maybe even *this* year—one year, I say, the sun may not turn back toward the north the day after Midwinter's Day, but rather go on sinking ever southward, sinking until only a little crimson twilight remains on the horizon, and then—nothing. No light. No hope. No blessings. Forever."

"No!" someone wailed. In an instant, the whole congregation took up the cry. Among the rest was Olyvria, her voice clear and strong. Among them, after a moment, was Phostis himself: the priest had a gift for instilling fright. Among them even was Syagrios. Phostis hadn't thought the ruffian respected Phos or feared Skotos.

Through all the outcry, Olyvria's fingers remained laced with his. He didn't really think about that; he just accepted it gratefully. Instead of feeling alone in the cold blackness that could have come straight from Skotos, he was reminded others fought the dark with him. He needed that reminder. Never in all his years of worshiping at the High Temple had he known such fear of the dark god.

The priest said, "With fasting and lamentation we may yet show Phos that, despite our failings, despite the corruption that springs from the bodies in which we dwell, we remain worthy of the sign of his light for yet another year, that we may advance farther down the gleaming path praised by the holy Thanasios. Pray now, and let the lord with the great and good mind know what is in your hearts!"

If before the temple had echoed to the shouts of the congregation, now, even louder, it was filled with the worshipers' prayers. Phostis' went up with the rest. In the riches and light of the High Temple it was easy to believe, along with the ecumenical patriarch and his plump, contented votaries, that Phos would surely vanquish Skotos at the end of days. Such sublime confidence was harder to maintain in the dark of a chilly temple with a priest preaching of light draining out of the world like water from a tub.

At first, all Phostis heard was the din of people at noisy prayer. Then, little by little, he noticed individual voices in the din. Some repeated Phos' creed over and over: Videssos' universal prayer prevailed among Thanasioi and their foes alike. Others sent up simple requests: "Give us light." "Bless my wife with a son this year, O Phos." "Make me more pious and less lustful!" "Heal my mother's sores, which no salve has aided!"

Prayers like those would not have seemed out of place back in the High Temple. Others, though, had a different ring to them. "Destroy everything that stands in our way!" "To the ice with those who will not walk the gleaming path!" "O Phos, grant me the courage to cast aside the body that befouls my soul!" "Wreck them all, wreck them all, wreck them all!"

He did not care for those; they might have come from the throats of baying wolves rather than men. But before he could do more than notice them, the priest at the altar raised a hand. Any motion within his candle's tiny circle of light was astoundingly noticeable. The congregation fell silent at once, and with it Phostis' concerns.

The priest said, "Prayer alone does not suffice. We do not walk the gleaming path with our tongues; the road that leads beyond the sun is paved with deeds, not words. Go forth now and live as Thanasios would have had you live. Seek Phos' blessings in hunger and want, not the luxuries of this world that are but a single beat of a gnat's wings against the judgment yet to come. Go forth! This liturgy is ended."

No sooner had he spoken than acolytes bearing torches came into the worship area from the narthex to light the congregants' way out. Phostis blinked; his eyes filled with tears at what seemed the savage glare, though a moment later he realized it was not so bright after all.

He'd dropped Olyvria's hand the instant the acolytes entered—or perhaps she'd dropped his. In more light than a single candle flame, he dared not risk angering Syagrios . . . and, even more to the point, angering Livanios.

Then palace calculation surged forward unbidden in his mind. Would Livanios throw his daughter at the heir apparent to the throne? Did he seek influence through the marriage bed? Phostis filed that away for future consideration. But no matter what Livanios intended, the feel of Olyvria's hand in his had been the only warmth he'd known, physical or spiritual, through the Thanasiot service.

He'd thought the temple's interior cold, and so it had been. But there, at least, some hundreds of people crowded together had given a measure, albeit a small one, of animal warmth.

Out on the night-black streets of Etchmiadzin, with the wind whipping knifelike down from the hills, Phostis rediscovered what true cold meant.

The heavy wool cloak he wore might have been made of lace, for all the good it did to keep off the wind. Even Syagrios hissed as the blast struck him. "By the good god," he muttered, "I'd not mind jumping over a bonfire tonight, or even into one, just so as I could get warm."

"You're right." The words were out of Phostis' mouth before he remembered to be surprised at agreeing with Syagrios about anything.

"Fires and displays are not the way of the gleaming path," Olyvria said. "I remember them, too, from the days before my father accepted Thanasios' way. He says it's better to make your soul safe than to worry about what happens to your body."

The priest in the temple had said the same. From him, it sank deep into Phostis' heart. From Livanios, even through Olyvria as intermediary, the words did not mean as much. The heresiarch mouthed Thanasiot slogans, but did he live by them? As far as Phostis could see, he remained sleek, well fed, and worldly.

*Hypocrite.* The word tolled like a warning bell on a rocky coast. Hypocrisy was the crime of which Phostis had in his mind convicted his father, most of the capital's nobles, the ecumenical patriarch, and most of the clergy, as well. The quest for unvarnished truth was what had drawn him to the Thanasioi in the first place. Finding Livanios anything but unvarnished made him doubt the perfection of the gleaming path.

He said, "I wouldn't mind seeing the time of the sun-turning as one of rejoicing as well as sorrow. After all, it does ensure life for another year."

"But life in the world means life in things which are Skotos," Olyvria said. "Where's to rejoice over that?"

"If it weren't for material things, life would come to an end, and so would mankind," Phostis countered. "Is that what you want: to fade away and vanish?"

"Not for myself." Olyvria's shiver, like Phostis' back in the temple, had little to do with the weather. "But there are those who do want exactly that. You'll see some of them soon, I think."

"They're daft, if you ask me," Syagrios said, though his voice lacked its usual biting edge. "We live in this world along with the next one."

Olyvria argued that. If there was one thing Videssians would do at any excuse or none, it was argue theology. Phostis kept out of the argument, not least because he inclined to Syagrios' side of it and did not want to offend Olyvria by saying so out loud.

The memory of her hand remained printed in his mind. It called up that other memory he had of her, the one from the chamber off the passageway under Digenis' temple back in the city. That latter memory was suited for Midwinter's Day, at least as he'd known it before. It was a time of festival, even of license. As the proverb put it, "Anything can happen on Midwinter's Day."

Had this been a holiday of the sort with which he was familiar, he might—somewhere down deep in him, in a place below words, he knew he *would*—have tried to get her off by herself. And he suspected, she would have gone with him, even if only for the one night.

But here in Etchmiadzin, seeking sensual pleasure on Midwinter's Day did not bear thinking about. Rejection was the mildest return he could expect. More likely was some sort of mortification of his flesh. Though he had increasing respect for the asceticism of the gleaming path, his flesh had lately suffered enough mortification to suit him.

Besides, Syagrios would make a eunuch of him—and enjoy doing it—if he got himself into trouble of that sort.

The ruffian broke off his disputation with Olyvria, saying, "However you care to have it, my lady. You know more about this business than me, that's for sure. All I know now is that this here poor old smashed nose of mine is going to freeze off if I don't get to somewheres with a fire."

"There I cannot disagree with you," Olyvria said.

"Let's us head back to the keep, then," Syagrios suggested. "It'll be warm—well, warmer—in there. 'Sides, I can dump his Majestyhood here back in his room and get me a chance to relax a bit."

*To the ice with you, Syagrios.* The thought stood pure and crystalline in the center of Phostis' mind. He wanted to scream it. Only a healthy regard for his own continued survival kept him from screaming it. He was, then, at most an imperfect Thanasiot. Like Olyvria, he remained enamored of the fleshly envelope his soul wore, no matter what the source of that flesh.

The narrow, muddy lanes of Etchmiadzin were almost preternaturally dark. Night travel in Videssos the city was undertaken with torchbearers and guards, if for any legitimate purpose. Only footpads there cherished the black of night. But no one in Etchmiadzin tonight carried a light or seemed concerned over becoming a robber's victim. Cries rose into the dark sky, but they were only the lamentations the priest had commanded of his congregants.

The bulk of the fortress and the stars it obscured helped mark the path back from the temple. Even the torches above the gates were out. Livanios went that far in adhering to the tenets of the Thanasioi.

Syagrios grumbled under his breath. "Don't like that," he said. "Just anybody could come wandering in, and who'd be the wiser till too late?"

"Who's in the town save our own folk and a few Vaspurakaners?" Olyvria said. "They have their own rites and leave ours alone."

"They'd better," Syagrios replied. "More of us than there is of them."

Only inside the keep did light return. Livanios' caftan-wearing advisor sat at a table gnawing the leg of a roasted fowl and whistling a cheery tune Phostis did not know. If he'd heard the order for fasting and lamentation, he was doing a good job of ignoring it.

Syagrios lit a candle from a torch set in a soot-blackened sconce. With it in one hand and his knife in the other, he urged Phostis up the spiral stairway. "Back to your room now," he said. Phostis barely had time to nod to Olyvria before the twist of the stairs made her disappear.

The corridor that led to his little chamber was midnight black. He turned to Syagrios, pointing at the candle. "May I light a lamp in my room from that?"

"Not tonight," Syagrios said. "I got to watch you instead of roisterin', so you get no more enjoyment than me."

Once inside, Phostis drew off his cloak and put it over the blanket on his pallet. He did not take off his tunic as he got under them both and huddled up in a ball to try to warm himself as fast as he could. He looked back toward the door, beyond which Syagrios surely lurked. "Roistering, is it?" he whispered. He might be a poor Thanasiot himself, but he knew a worse one.

# VII

THE MAN'S EYES TWITCHED BACK AND FORTH IN THEIR SOCKETS. It was like no motion Phostis had ever seen before; watching made him queasy. Voice calm but weak, the man said, "I can't see you, not really, but that's all right. It goes away in a few days, I'm told by those who have come this way before me."

"That's g-good." Phostis knew he sounded shaky. It shamed him, but he couldn't help it.

"Fear not," the man said. He'd been introduced to Phostis as Strabon. He smiled radiantly. "Soon, I know, I shall join the lord with the great and good mind and cast aside this flesh that has too long weighed me down."

Strabon had, Phostis thought, already cast aside almost all of his flesh. His face was a skull covered with skin; his neck seemed hardly thicker than a torch. Withered branches might have done for his arms, and claws for his hands. Not only had he no fat left on his bones, he had no muscle, either. He was bone and tendon and skin, nothing more. No, one more thing: the joy that lit his blind eyes.

"Soon," he repeated. "It's been six weeks, a few days over, since last I polluted my soul with aliment. Only a man who was fat to begin with will last much above eight, and never was I in the habit of glutting myself. Soon I shall fare beyond the sun and look on Phos face to face. Soon."

"Does—does it hurt?" Phostis asked. Beside him, Olyvria sat calmly. She'd seen these human skeletons before, often enough so now she was easy with the husk of Strabon.

Syagrios had not come into the hut; Phostis heard him pacing around outside the door.

Strabon said, "No, boy, no; as I told you, fear not. Oh, my belly panged in the early days, I'll not deny, as Skotos' part of me realized I had determined to cut my essential self free of it. But no, I feel no pain, only longing to be free." He smiled again. Save for the faintest tinge of pink, his lips were invisible.

"But to linger so—" Phostis shook his head, though he knew Strabon could not see that. Then he blurted, "Could you not also have refused water, and so made a quicker end of it?"

The corners of Strabon's gash of a mouth turned down. "Some of those who are most holy do as you say. Sinner that I am, I had not the fortitude for it."

Phostis stared at him. Never in his comfortable life back at the palaces had he dreamed he'd be talking with a man in the last stages of deliberately starving himself to death. Even if he had dreamed that, could he have imagined the man would reproach himself for lack of fortitude? No; impossible.

The lids fell over Strabon's twitching eyes; he seemed to doze. "Is he not a miracle of piety?" Olyvria whispered.

"Well, yes, that he is." Phostis scratched his head. Back in Videssos the city, he'd despised the temple hierarchy for wearing bejeweled vestments and venerating Phos in temples built by riches taken—stolen—from the peasantry. Better, he'd thought, a simple but strong worship, one that sprang from within and demanded nothing of anyone save the single pious individual.

Now before him he saw personified, and indeed taken to an extreme he'd never imagined, an example of such worship. He had to respect the religious impulse that had led Strabon to make himself into a collection of twigs and branches, but he was less sure he considered it an ideal.

Yet such self-destruction was implicit in Thanasiot doctrine, for those who had the courage to follow where logic led. If the world of the senses was but a creation of Skotos', what course more logical than to remove one's precious and eternal soul from that swamp of evil and corruption?

Rather hesitantly, he turned toward Olyvria. "However holy he may be, I'd not care to imitate him. Granted, the world is not all it might be, but leaving it this way strikes me as—oh,

I don't know—as running away from the fight against wickedness rather than joining it."

"Ah, but the body itself is evil, boy," Strabon said. He
hadn't been asleep after all. "Because of that, any fight is fore-
doomed to failure." His eyes closed again.

Olyvria spoke in a low voice. "For the many, there may be
much truth in what you say, Phostis. As I told you back on
Midwinter's Day, I'd not have the bravery to do as Strabon
does. But I thought you ought to see him, to celebrate and admire what the soul can do if it so wills."

"I see it," Phostis said. "It is indeed a marvel. But something to celebrate? Of that I'm less certain."

Olyvria looked at him severely. Had she been standing, her
hands would have gone onto her hips. As it was, she breathed
out in exasperation. "Even the dogma you grew up with has
room for asceticism and mortifying the flesh."

"That's true," he said. "Too much care for this world and
you have fat, contented priests who might as well not be
priests at all. But now, seeing Strabon here, I think there may
be too little care for the world, as well." His voice fell to a
whisper, so he would not disturb the fitfully sleeping relic of
a man. This time, Strabon did not respond.

Phostis listened to himself with some surprise. *I sound like
my father,* he thought. How many times, back at the palaces,
had he watched and listened to Krispos steering a middle
course between schemes that might have proved spectacular
successes or even more spectacular disasters? How many times
had he sneered at his father for that moderation?

"What he does affects no one but himself," Olyvria said,
"and will surely earn him eternity in communion with Phos."

"That's true," Phostis repeated. "What he does by himself
affects him alone. But if one man and one woman in four, say,
decided to walk the gleaming path in his exact footprints, that
would affect those who declined to do so very much indeed.
And Strabon's way, if I rightly understand it, is the one
Thanasiot doctrine favors."

"For those whose spirits let them take it, yes," Olyvria said.
Phostis looked from Strabon to her, then back again. He tried
to envision her features ravaged by starvation, her bright eyes
writhing blindly in their sockets. He'd never been the most

imaginative of young men. More often than not, he felt that to be a lack. It seemed a blessing now.

Strabon coughed himself awake. He tried to say something, but the coughs went on and on, deep wet ones that wracked the sack of bones he had become. "Chest fever," Phostis whispered to Olyvria. She shrugged. If it was, he thought, the Thanasiot zealot might be dead by evening, for how could he have any strength in his body to fight off illness?

Olyvria stood to go. Phostis was far from sorry to get up with her. When he no longer saw the wasted figure lying on the bed, he felt more alive himself. Maybe that was illusion sprung from the animal part of him and from Skotos; he could not say. But he knew he would have trouble overcoming that animal part. Was his soul a prisoner of his body, as the Thanasioi proclaimed, or a partner with it? He would have to think long and hard on that.

Outside Strabon's hut, Syagrios paced up and down the muddy street, whistling a tune and spitting through his uneven teeth. Phostis watched him grin and swagger. When he tried to visualize the ruffian starving himself, his thoughts ran headlong into a blank wall. He simply could not see it happening. Syagrios was an ugly specimen, but a vivid one for all that.

"So what did you think of the boneyard?" he asked Phostis, spitting again.

Olyvria rounded on him, tight black curls flying in fury. "Show proper respect for the pious and holy Strabon!" she blazed.

"Why? Soon enough he'll be dead, and then it'll be up to Phos, not to the likes of me, to figure out what he deserves."

Olyvria opened her mouth, then closed it again. Phostis made a mental note that Syagrios, while indubitably uncouth, was far from stupid. *Too bad,* he thought. Aloud, he said, "If a few people choose to make their end that way, I don't see that it much matters to the world around them—and, as Olyvria says, they are pious and holy. But if many decide to end their lives, the Empire will shake."

"And why shouldn't the Empire shake, pray?" Olyvria asked.

Now Phostis had to pause and consider. An unshaken Empire of Videssos was almost as much of an article of faith for him as Phos' creed. And why not? For seven centuries and more, Videssos had given folk in a great swathe of the world reasonable peace and reasonable security. True, there had been disasters, as when steppe nomads took advantage of Videssian civil war to invade the north and east and form their own khaganates in the ruins of imperial provinces. True, every generation or two fought another in the long string of debilitating wars with Makuran. But, on the whole, he remained convinced life within the Empire was likelier to be happy than anywhere outside it.

But when he said as much, Olyvria answered, "So what? If life in this world is but part of Skotos' trap, what matter if you're happy as the jaws close? Better then that we should be unhappy, that we should recognize everything material as part of the lure that draws us down to the ice."

"But—" Phostis felt himself floundering. "Suppose—hmm—suppose everyone in the westlands, or most people, starved themselves to death like Strabon. What would happen after that? The Makuraners would march in unopposed and rule the land forever."

"Well, what if they did?" Olyvria said. "The pious men and women who'd abandoned the world would be safe in Phos' heaven, and the invaders would surely go to the ice when their days were done."

"Yes, and the worship of Phos would go out of the world, for the Makuraners reverence their Four Prophets, not the good god," Phostis said. "No one who worshiped Phos would be left, and Skotos would have the victory in this world. The realm beyond the sun would gain no new recruits, but the dark god would have to carve new caverns into the ice." He spat in ritual rejection of Skotos.

Olyvria frowned. The very tip of her tongue poked out of her mouth for a moment. Her voice was troubled as she said, "This argument has more weight than I would have looked for."

"No it don't," Syagrios said with a raucous laugh. "The two of you's quarreling over whether you'd like your cow's eggs better poached or fried. Truth is, a cow ain't about to lay no eggs—and whole flocks of people ain't about to starve themselves to death, neither. Come to that, is either one o' *you* ready to stop eatin' yet?"

"No," Olyvria said quietly. Phostis shook his head.

"Well, then," Syagrios said, and laughed even louder.

"But if you're not ready to leave the world behind, how can you be a proper Thanasiot?" Phostis asked with the relentless logic of the young.

"That's a bloody good question." Syagrios whacked Phostis on the back, almost hard enough to knock him sprawling into the muck that passed for a street. "You ain't as dumb as you look, kid." The day was gloomy, the sky an inverted bowl full of thick gray clouds. The gold ring in Syagrios' ear glinted nonetheless. In Etchmiadzin he did not wear it to deceive those not of his faith, for the Thanasioi ruled the town. But he did not take it out, either.

"Syagrios, to say one can be a good Thanasiot only through starvation contradicts the faith as the holy Thanasios set it forth, which you know perfectly well." Olyvria sounded as if she were holding onto patience with both hands.

Syagrios caught the warning in her voice. Suddenly he reverted to being a guardsman rather than an equal. "As you say, my lady," he answered. Had Phostis told him the same thing, the ruffian would have torn into him in argument and likely with fists and booted feet, as well.

But Phostis, though prisoner in Etchmiadzin, was not Olyvria's servitor. Moreover, he actively enjoyed theological disputation. Turning to Olyvria, he said, "But if you choose to live in Skotos' world, surely you compromise with evil, and compromise with evil takes you to the ice, not so?"

"But not everyone is or can be suited to leaving the world of his own will," Olyvria said. "The holy Thanasios teaches that those who feel they must remain in Skotos' realm may yet gain merit along two byroads of the gleaming path. In one, they may lessen the temptations of the material for themselves and for those around them."

"Those who follow that byroad would be the men your father leads," Phostis said.

Olyvria nodded. "Them among others. But it is also virtuous to content yourself with simple things: black bread instead of white, coarse cloth rather than fine. The more you do without, the less you subject yourself to Skotos."

"Yes, I see the point," Phostis said slowly. *The more you burn and destroy, also,* he thought, but kept that to himself. Instead of mentioning it, he asked, "What is the second byroad you spoke of?"

"Why, ministering to those who have chosen the path of greater abnegation," Olyvria answered. "By helping them as they advance along the gleaming path, those who stay behind bask in their reflected piety, so to speak."

"Hmm," Phostis said. At first hearing, that sounded good. But after a moment, he said, "How does that make their dealings with those of greater holiness different from any peasant's dealings with a noble?"

Olyvria gave him an exasperated glare. "It's different because the usual run of noble wallows in corruption, thinking mostly of his purse and his, ah, member, and so a peasant who serves such a man is but drawn deeper into the sensual mire. But our pious heroes reject all the lures of the world and inspire others to do likewise to the degree that is in their power."

"Hmm," Phostis said again. "Something to that, I suppose." He wondered how much. A good noble of the non-Thanasiot sort helped the peasants on his land get through hard times, defended them against raiders if he lived near a frontier, and didn't go around seducing their women. Phostis knew a good many nobles, and knew of a good many more. He wondered how maintaining one's dependents rated against the individual pursuit of piety. The good god knew for certain, but Phostis doubted whether anyone merely human did.

Before he could say as much, a familiar figure from Livanios' miniature court at the keep came stamping up the street: the fellow who seemed to be the heresiarch's chief wizard. Despite all his time in Etchmiadzin, Phostis still had not learned the man's name. Now he wore a thick wool caftan with bright vertical stripes, and on his head a fur cap with earflaps that might have come straight off the plains of Pardraya.

He touched his forehead, lips, and chest in greeting to Olyvria, gave Phostis a measuring stare, and ignored Syagrios. "He's going into Strabon's house," Phostis said. "What does he want with someone who likely won't be here two weeks from now and may not be here tomorrow?"

"He visits everyone he can who chooses to leave the world of evil things," Olyvria answered. "I don't know why; if he's as curious as most mages, perhaps he seeks to learn as much as he can about the world to come while still remaining in this one."

"Maybe." Phostis supposed one did not cease to be a mage, or a tanner, or a tailor, on becoming a Thanasiot. "What *is* he called, anyhow?"

Olyvria paused visibly before she answered. Syagrios stepped into the breach: "He doesn't like people knowin' his name, for fear they'll work magic with it."

"That's silly. He must not be much of a wizard, then," Phostis said. "My father's chief mage is named Zaidas, and he doesn't care who knows it. He says if you can't protect yourself from name magic, you have no business taking up sorcery in the first place."

"Not all wizards have the same ways," Olyvria said. Since that was too obviously true to require comment, Phostis let it go.

The fellow in the caftan came out of Strabon's house a couple of minutes later. He did not look happy, and was muttering under his breath. Not all the muttering sounded like Videssian; Phostis wondered if he was from nearby Vaspurakan. Of what was in the imperial language, Phostis caught only one phrase: "Old bastard's not ripe yet." The wizard stalked away.

"Not ripe yet?" Phostis said after he'd rounded a corner. "Not ripe for what?"

"I don't know," Syagrios said. "Me, I don't mess with mages or their business and I don't want them messin' with me."

That was a sensible attitude for anyone, and especially, Phostis thought, for somebody like Syagrios, who was likely to be "messed with" by mages when said mages were on the track of objects mysteriously vanished. Phostis smiled at his automatic contempt for the bruiser who'd become his keeper. Syagrios saw the smile and gave him a hard, suspicious stare. He did his best to look innocent, which was rendered more difficult because he was guilty.

Syagrios changed the subject. "How's about we go find some food? Standin' on my pins all mornin', me, I could hack steaks off a donkey and eat 'em raw."

"Get out of here, you beast! Out of my sight!" Olyvria snarled, her voice breaking with fury. "Out! Away! How dare you—how could you be so dense, so blockheaded—as to talk about food after we've just seen the pious Strabon dedicating himself to escaping the world and advancing along the gleaming path? Get out!"

"No," Syagrios said. "Your father told me to keep an eye on this one—" He pointed at Phostis. "—and that there's just what I aim to do."

Up till then, that stolid remark had been proof against anything Olyvria would throw at it. Indeed, Olyvria had not tried to contest it. Now, though, she said, "Where will he go? Do you think he'll kidnap *me*?"

"I don't know and I don't care," Syagrios answered. "I just know what I got told to do."

"Well, I tell you to go away. I can't abide the sight or sound of you after what you just said," Olyvria said. When he shook his head, she added, "If you don't, I'll tell my father what you said just now. Do you want to undergo the penance you'd receive for mocking the holy faith?"

"I didn't," Syagrios said, but he seemed suddenly doubtful. Whether he had or he hadn't, Livanios was apt to believe Olyvria rather than him. It was most unfair. All at once, Phostis understood why he himself had not had many friends as a boy. If he ran to tell his father about a quarrel, *his* father was the Avtokrator. If the Avtokrator—or Livanios now—ruled against you, to whom could you appeal?

Bitterness gusted through Phostis. The Avtokrator, in those lost boyhood days, was only too likely to rule against him, not for. His father had never truly warmed to him; from time to time he wondered what he'd done wrong, to make Krispos find fault with everything about him. He doubted he'd ever find out.

Olyvria said to Syagrios, "Go on, I tell you. I'll be responsible for seeing Phostis doesn't run out of Etchmiadzin. And I tell you this, too: if you say me nay once more, you'll be sorry for it."

"All right, then, my lady." The ruffian turned what should have been a title of respect into one of reproach. "On you the blame, and almost I hope you end up wearing it." Syagrios strode off with the straight, proud back of a man who's had the last word.

Watching him go, Phostis felt a burden lift from his spirit, as if the sun had come out to brighten a gloomy day. He also had to stifle a burst of laughter. In spite of having just come out of starving Strabon's house, he was hungry.

Since unlike Strabon he was not about to waste away and die of hunger, he kept that to himself. He didn't want Olyvria rounding on him as she had on Syagrios. If anything was more likely to bring back the watchdog, he couldn't imagine what it might be.

Olyvria was looking at him with a quizzical expression. He realized she was left as much at a loss by Syagrios' departure as was he. "What shall we do now?" she asked, perhaps hoping he could think of something.

Unfortunately, he couldn't. "I don't know," he answered. "I really haven't seen enough of Etchmiadzin to know what you *can* do around here." *Not much before the Thanasioi took over the town, and less now,* he guessed.

"Let's just amble about, then, and see where our feet take us," she said.

"That's all right with me." Short of a trip to the torturer, anything Olyvria suggested would have been all right with Phostis. He looked for grass to sprout in the streets, flowers to burst into bloom, and birds to start singing in winter, all because she'd managed to outbluff Syagrios.

Their feet led them to a street of dyers. That the men there followed the gleaming path didn't keep their shops from smelling of stale piss, just like the establishments of perfectly orthodox dyers back in Videssos the city. In the same way, Thanasiot carpenters had hands crisscrossed with scars and Thanasiot bakers faces permanently reddened from peering into hot ovens.

"It all seems so—ordinary," Phostis said after a while. *Dull* was the other word that came to mind, but he suppressed it. "For most folk, it's as if being a Thanasiot doesn't change much in their lives."

That bothered him. To his way of thinking, heresy and orthodoxy—whichever was which in this dispute—should have been easy to tell apart at a glance. But, on further reflection, he wondered why. Unless they chose Strabon's path out of the world, the Thanasioi had to make their way in it, and only so many ways of doing that were possible. The dyeshops probably stank of urine in Mashiz, too; carpenters would sometimes gouge themselves with chisels; and bakers would need to make sure their loaves didn't burn.

Olyvria said, "The difference is the gleaming path, it's standing aside from the world as well as one can, not thinking riches the only end in life, seeking to satisfy the spirit rather than the baser impulses of the body."

"I suppose so," Phostis said. They walked a little farther while he ruminated on that. Then he said, "May I ask you something? For all the ribbons on my cage, I know I'm pretty much a prisoner here, so I don't mean to make you angry, but there is something I'd like to learn, if giving the answer doesn't offend you."

Olyvria turned toward him. Her eyes were wide with curiosity, her mouth slightly open. She looked very young, and very lovely. "Ask," she said at once. "You're here to learn about the gleaming path, after all. How will you learn if you don't ask?"

"All right, I will." Phostis thought for a little while; the question he had in mind needed to be framed carefully. At last he said, "In the room in the tunnel under Digenis' temple, what you said there—"

"Aha!" Olyvria stuck out her tongue at him. "I thought it would be something about that, just from the way you went all around it like a man feeling for a goldpiece in the middle of a nettle patch."

Phostis felt his face heat. By the way Olyvria giggled, his embarrassment was also plain to the eye. Even so, he stubbornly plowed ahead; in some ways—though he would have hotly denied it—he was very much like Krispos. "What you said under there, when you tried to lure me to you, about the pleasure of love being sweet, and no sin?"

"What about it?" Olyvria lost some—though not all—of her mischievous air as she saw how serious he was.

What he really wanted to ask was how she knew—or, even more to the point, what she would have done had he lain down on the bed beside her and taken her in his arms. But he did not think he was in a position where he could safely put either of those questions. So instead he said, "If you hold to Thanasios' gleaming path as strongly as you say, how could you make such a claim? Doesn't it go straight against everything you profess to believe?"

"I could answer that any number of ways," Olyvria said. "I could tell you, for instance, that it was none of your business."

"So you could, and I would beg your pardon," he said. "I said from the start that I didn't want to offend you."

Olyvria went on as if he had not spoken: "Or I could say I was doing as Digenis and my father bade me do, and trusted them to judge the rights and wrongs of it." Her eyes twinkled again. He knew she was toying with him, but what could he do about it?

"Or," she went on, maddeningly disingenuous, "I could say Thanasios countenanced dissimulation when it serves spreading the truth, and that you have no idea what my true feelings on the subject are."

"I know I don't. That's what I was trying to find out, your true feelings on the subject." Phostis felt like an old, spavined plowhorse trying to trap a dragonfly without benefit of net. He tramped on, straight ahead, while Olyvria flitted, evaded, and occasionally flew so close to the end of his nose that his eyes crossed when he tried to see her clearly.

"Those are just some examples of what I might say," she noted, ticking them off on her fingertips. "If you'd like others, I might also say—"

As if the old plowhorse suddenly snorted and startled the beautiful, glittering insect, he broke in, "What *would* you say that's so, by the good god?"

"I'd say—" But then Olyvria shook her head and looked away from him. "No, I wouldn't say anything at all, Phostis. Better if I don't."

He wanted to shake truth from her, but she was not a salt cellar. "Why?" he howled, months of frustration boiled into a single despairing word.

"Just—better if I don't." Olyvria still held her head averted. In a small voice, she added, "I think we ought to go back to the fortress now."

Phostis didn't think that, nor anything like it, but walked with her all the same. In the inner ward stood Syagrios, talking with someone almost as disreputable-looking as he was. The ruffian left his—partner in crime?—ambled over, and attached himself to Phostis like a shadow returning from a brief holiday. In an unsettling sort of way, Phostis was almost glad to have him back. He'd certainly made a hash of his first little while in Etchmiadzin on his own.

Digenis' robe had fallen open, displaying ribs like ladder rungs. His thighs were thinner than his knees. Even his ears seemed to be wasting away. But his eyes still blazed defiance. "To the ice with you, your false Majesty," he growled when Krispos came into his cell. "Your way would have sent me beyond the sun quicker, but I gain, I gain."

To Krispos, the firebrand priest looked more as if he lost. Lean to begin with, now he looked like a peasant in a village after three years of blighted crops. But for those eerily compelling eyes, he might have been a skeleton that refused to turn back into a man.

"By the good god," Krispos muttered when that thought struck him, "now I understand the mime troupe."

"Which one, your Majesty?" asked Zaidas, who still labored fruitlessly to extract truth from the dwindling Digenis.

"The one with the fellow in the suit of bones," Krispos answered. "He was supposed to be a Thanasiot starving himself to death, that's what he was. Now, were the mimes heretics, too, or just mocking their beliefs?" Something else occurred to him. "And isn't it a fine note when mimes know more about what's going on with the faith than my own ecumenical patriarch?"

Digenis' mocking laugh flayed his ears. "Of Oxeites' ignorance no possible doubt can exist."

"Oh, shut up," Krispos said, though down deep he knew tractability was one of the qualities that had gained Oxeites the blue boots. *If only he'd been more tractable about letting me do what I wanted with this wretch here,* the Avtokrator thought. But Oxeites, like any good bureaucrat, protected his own.

Krispos sat down on a three-legged stool to see if Zaidas would have any better luck today. His chief wizard swore his presence inhibited nothing. Zaidas at least had courage, to be willing to labor on in the presence of his Avtokrator. What he did not have, unfortunately, was success.

He was trying something new today, Krispos saw, or maybe something so old he hoped its time had come round again. At any rate, the implements he took from his carpetbag were unfamiliar. But before the Emperor saw them in action, a panting messenger from the palaces poked his head into Digenis' cell.

"What's happened?" Krispos asked suspiciously; his orders were that he be left undisturbed in his visits here save for only the most important news . . . and the most important news was all too often bad.

"May it please your Majesty," the messenger began, and then paused to pant some more. While he caught his breath, Krispos worried. That opening, lately, had given him good cause to worry. But the fellow surprised him, saying, "May it please your Majesty, the eminent Iakovitzes has returned to Videssos the city from his embassy to Makuran and awaits your pleasure at the imperial residence."

"Well, by the good god, there's word that truly does please me," Krispos exclaimed. He turned to Zaidas. "Carry on here without me, and may Phos grant you good fortune. If you glean anything from this bag of bones, report it to me at once."

"Certainly, your Majesty," Zaidas said.

Digenis laughed again. "The catamite goes off to pleasure his defiler."

"That is a lie, one of so many you spew," Krispos said coldly. The Halogai fell in around him. As he went up the stairs that led to the doorway of the government office building, he found himself laughing. He'd have to tell that one to Iakovitzes. His longtime associate would laugh, too, not least because he'd wish the lie were true. Iakovitzes never made any secret of his fondness for stalwart youths, and had tried again and again to seduce Krispos when Krispos, newly arrived in Videssos the city, was in his service.

Barsymes greeted him when he returned to the imperial residence. "Good day, your Majesty. I've taken the liberty of installing the eminent Iakovitzes in the small dining chamber in the south hallway. He requested hot mulled wine, which was fetched to him."

"I'll have the same," Krispos said. "I can't think of a better way to fight the winter chill."

Iakovitzes rose from his chair as Krispos came into the room where he sat. He started to prostrate himself; Krispos waved for him not to bother. With a smug nod, Iakovitzes returned to his seat. He was a well-preserved seventy, plump, his hair and beard dyed dark to make him seem younger, with a complexion on the florid side and eyes that warned—truly—he had a temper.

"Good to see you, by Phos," Krispos exclaimed. "I've wished you were here a great many times the past few months."

On the table in front of Iakovitzes lay a scribe's three-paneled writing tablet. He opened it, used a stylus to scribble rapid words on the wax, then passed Krispos the tablet. "I've wished I were back a great many times myself. I'm bloody sick of mutton."

"Sup with me this evening, then," Krispos said. "What do they say? 'When in Videssos the city, eat fish.' I'll feast you till you grow fins."

Iakovitzes made a strange gobbling noise that served him for laughter. "Make it tentacles, if you'd be so kind," he wrote. "Squid, octopus . . . lobster, come to think of it, has no tentacles, but then lobster is lobster, in itself a sufficient justification. By the good god, it makes me wish I could lick my lips."

"I wish you could, too, old friend, and taste in fullness as well," Krispos said. Iakovitzes had only the stump of his tongue; twenty years before, Harvas Black-Robe had torn it from his mouth when he was on an embassy to the evil sorcerer.

The wound—and the spell placed on it to defeat healing—had almost been the death of him. But he'd rallied, even thrived. Krispos knew a great part of his own persona would have been lost had he suffered Iakovitzes' mutilation. He wrote well enough, but never had been fluent with a pen in his hand. Iakovitzes, though, wielded pen or stylus with such vim that, reading his words, Krispos still sometimes heard the living voice that had been two decades silent.

Iakovitzes took back the tablet, wrote, and returned it to Krispos. "It's not so bad, your Majesty: not nearly so bad as sitting down to table with a bad cold in your head, for instance. Half your taste, or maybe more, I've found, is in your nose, not in your mouth. Besides, staying in Mashiz turned into a bore. The only folk who read Videssian seemed as old and wrinkled as I am. You have no notion how hard it is to seduce a pretty boy when he can't understand you."

"Gold speaks a lot of languages," Krispos observed.

"Sometimes you're too pragmatic for your own good,"

Iakovitzes wrote, rolling his eyes at his sovereign's obtuseness. "There's no challenge to merely buying it; the pursuit is part of the game. Why do you think I chased you so long and hard when I knew your appetite ran only to women?"

"So that's it, eh?" Krispos said. "At the time, I thought you were just being beastly."

Iakovitzes clapped a hand over his heart and pantomimed a death scene well enough to earn him a place on a professional mime troupe. Then, miraculously recovered, he bent over his tablet and wrote rapidly: "I think I shall make my way back to Mashiz after all. There, being a representative of the enemy, I am treated with the respect I deserve. My alleged friends prefer slander." He rolled his eyes.

Krispos laughed out loud. Iakovitzes' peculiar combination of touchiness and viperish wit never failed to amuse—except when it infuriated. Sometimes it managed both at once. The Avtokrator quickly sobered. He asked, "On your way back from Makuran, did you have any trouble with the Thanasioi?"

Iakovitzes shook his head, then amplified on the tablet. "I returned by the southern route, and saw no trace. They seem to be a perversion centered in the northwest, though I gather you've had your bouts with them here in the city, too."

"Bouts indeed," Krispos said heavily. "A good windstorm and they might have burned down half this place. Not only that, interrogation by sorcery doesn't have any luck with them, and they're so drunk in their beliefs that many take torture more as an honor than a torment."

"And they have your son," Iakovitzes wrote. He spread his hands to show sympathy for Krispos.

"They have him, aye," Krispos said, "certainly in body and perhaps in spirit as well." Iakovitzes raised a questioning eyebrow; his gestures, though wordless, had grown so expressive in the years since he'd lost his tongue as to have almost the quality of speech. Krispos explained, "He was talking with a priest who turned out to be a Thanasiot. For all I know, he's taken the wretch's doctrines as his own."

"Not good," Iakovitzes wrote.

"No. And now this Digenis—the priest—is starving himself in my jail. He thinks he'll end up with Phos when he quits the world. My guess is that Skotos will punish him forevermore." The Emperor spat between his feet in despisal of the dark god.

Iakovitzes wrote, "If you ask me, asceticism is its own punishment, but I'd not heard of its being a capital offense till now." That observation made Krispos nod. It also filled all three leaves of the tablet. Iakovitzes reversed his stylus, smoothed out the wax with the blunt end, wrote again. "These days I can tell very easily when I'm talking too much—as soon as I have to start erasing, I know I've been running on. Would that those who still flap their gums enjoyed such a visible sign of prolixity."

"Ah, but if they did, they'd spend their increased silent time thinking up new ways to commit mischief," Krispos said.

"You're likely right," Iakovitzes answered. He studied Krispos for a few seconds, then reclaimed the tablet. "You're more cynical than you used to be. Is that all good? I do admit it's natural enough, for from the throne you've likely heard more drivel these last twenty years than any other man alive, but is it good?"

Krispos thought about that for a while before he answered. In different forms, the question had arisen several times lately, as when he gave that first Thanasiot prisoner over to torture after Zaidas' magic failed to extract answers from him. He'd not have done that so readily when he was younger. Was he just another Emperor now, holding to power by whatever means came to hand?

"We're none of us what we were awhile ago," he said, but that was not an answer, and he knew it. By the way Iakovitzes raised an eyebrow, cocked his head, and waited for Krispos to go on, he knew it was no answer, too. Floundering, Krispos tried to give one: "The temples will never venerate me as holy, I daresay, but I hope the chroniclers will be able to report I governed Videssos well. I work hard at it, at any rate. If I'm harsh when I have to be, I also think I'm mild when I can be. My sons are turning into men, and not, I can say, the worst of men. Is it enough?" He heard pleading in his voice, a note he'd not found there in some years: the Avtokrator heard pleas; he did not make them.

Iakovitzes bent over the writing tablet. When the stylus was done racing back and forth, he passed the tablet to Krispos, who received it with some anxiety. He knew Iakovitzes well enough to be sure his old companion would be blunt with him. He had no trouble reading it, at any rate; constant poring over documents had kept his sight from lengthening with age as much as most men's.

"That you can ask the question after so long on the throne speaks well for you," Iakovitzes wrote. "Too many Avtokrators forget it exists within days of their anointing. As for the reply you gave, well, Videssos has had the occasional holy man on the throne, and most turned out bad, for the world is not a holy place. So long as you remember now and again what an innocent—and attractive—boy you once were, you'll not turn out too badly."

Krispos nodded slowly. "I'll take that."

"You'd better," Iakovitzes replied after more scribbling. "I flatter only when I hope to entice someone under the sheets with me, and after all our years of acquaintance I'm at last beginning to doubt I'll ever have much luck with you."

"You're incorrigible," Krispos said.

"Now that you mention it, yes," Iakovitzes wrote. He beamed, taking it for a compliment. Then he covered his mouth with a hand while he yawned; the empty cavern within was an unpleasant sight, and he made a point of not displaying it. He wrote some more. "By your leave, your Majesty, I'll take my own leave now, to rest at home after my travels. Do you still take supper just past sunset?"

"I have enough years on me now to have become a creature of habit," Krispos answered, nodding. "And with which of your handsome grooms do you intend to rest until suppertime?"

Iakovitzes assumed a comically innocent look, then bowed his way out of the little dining chamber. Krispos guessed his barb had struck home—or at least given Iakovitzes an idea. Krispos finished his mulled wine, then set the silver goblet down beside Iakovitzes'. The wine hadn't stayed warm, but the ginger and cinnamon stirred into it nipped his tongue pleasantly.

Barsymes came in with a tray on which to carry away the goblets. Krispos said, "Iakovitzes will join me for supper this evening. Please let the cooks know he'll like seafood in as many courses as possible—he says he's tired of Makuraner mutton."

"I shall convey the eminent sir's request," Barsymes agreed

gravely. "His presence will allow the kitchen staff to display their full range of talents."

"Hrmp," Krispos said in mock indignation. "I can't help being raised on a poor farm." While he enjoyed fancy dishes well enough, he more often preferred the simple fare he'd grown up with. More than one cook had complained of having his wings clipped.

Dusk was settling over the city when Iakovitzes returned, resplendent and glittering in a robe shot through with silver thread. Barsymes escorted him and Krispos to the small dining room where they'd taken wine earlier in the day. A fresh jar awaited them, cooling in a silver bucket of snow. The vestiarios poured a cup for each man. Iakovitzes wrote, "Ah, it's pale. Perhaps someone listened to me."

"Perhaps someone did, eminent sir," Barsymes said. "And now, if you will excuse me—" He glided away, to return with a bowl. "A salad of lettuce and endives, dressed with vinegar flavored by rue, dates, pepper, honey, and crushed cumin—a garnish said to promote good health—and topped with anchovies and rings of squid."

Iakovitzes rose from his chair and gave Barsymes a formal military salute, then kissed him on each beardless cheek. The vestiarios retreated in order less good than was his wont. Krispos hid a smile and attacked the salad, which proved tasty. Iakovitzes cut his portion into very small bits. He had to wash each one down with wine and put his head back to swallow.

His smile was blissful. He wrote, "Ah, squid! Were you to offer one of these tentacled lovelies to Rubyab King of Kings, your Majesty, without doubt he would flee faster than from an invading Videssian army. The Makuraners, when it comes to food, live most insular—or perhaps I should say inlandsular—lives."

"The more fools they." Krispos ate slowly, so as not to get ahead of Iakovitzes. Barsymes cleared away the plates. Krispos said, "Tell me, eminent sir, did you ever find out what was making Rubyab's mustaches quiver with secret glee?"

"Do you know, I didn't, not to be sure of it," Iakovitzes answered. He looked thoughtful. "Terrible, isn't it, when a Makuraner outdoes me in deceit? I must be getting old. But I tell you this, your Majesty: one way or another, it concerns us."

"I was sure it would," Krispos said. "Nothing would make Rubyab happier than buggering Videssos." He caught Iakovitzes' eye. "In the metaphorical sense, of course."

Iakovitzes gobbled laughter. "Oh, of course, your Majesty," he wrote.

Barsymes returned with a fresh course. "Here we have leeks boiled in water and olive oil," he declared, "and then stewed in more oil and mullet broth. To accompany them, oysters in a sauce of oil, honey, wine, egg yolks, pepper, and lovage."

Iakovitzes tasted the oysters, then wrote in big letters, "I want to marry the cook."

"He is a man, eminent sir," Barsymes said.

"All the better," Iakovitzes wrote, which sent the vestiarios into rapid retreat. He presently returned with another new platter along with a fresh jar of wine. This dish held peppered mullet liver paste baked in a fish-shaped mold and then sprinkled with virgin olive oil, as well as squashes baked with mint, coriander, and cumin, and stuffed with pine nuts ground with honey and wine.

"I shan't eat for a week," Krispos declared happily.

"But your Majesty, the main courses approach," Barsymes said in anxious tones.

Krispos corrected himself: "Two weeks. Bring 'em on." The tip of his nose was getting numb. How much wine had he drunk, anyhow? The rich flavor of the fish livers nicely complemented the squashes' sweet stuffing.

Barsymes bore away the empty mold from which the liver paste had come and the bowl that had held the squashes. Under the table, Krispos felt something on his leg, just above the knee. It turned out to be Iakovitzes' hand. "By the good god," the Avtokrator exclaimed, "you never give up, do you?"

"I'm still breathing," Iakovitzes wrote. "If I haven't stopped the one, why should I stop the other?"

"Something to that," Krispos admitted. He hadn't had much luck with the other lately, and he'd surely be too gorged after this banquet was done to try to improve that tonight. Just then Barsymes came back again, this time with a tureen and two bowls. Thinking about what the tureen might hold took Krispos' mind off other matters, a sure sign of advancing years.

The vestiarios announced, "Here we have mullets stewed in

wine, with leeks, broth, and vinegar, seasoned with oregano, coriander, and crushed pepper. For your added pleasure, the stew also includes scallops and baby prawns."

After the first taste, Iakovitzes wrote, "The only thing that could further add to my pleasure would be an infinitely distensible stomach, and you may tell the cooks as much."

"I shall, eminent sir," Barsymes promised. "They will take pleasure in knowing they have pleased you."

The next course was lobster meat and spawn chopped fine, mixed with eggs, pepper, and mullet broth, wrapped in grape leaves, and then fried. After that came cuttlefish boiled in wine, honey, celery, and caraway seeds, and stuffed with boiled calves' brains and crumbled hard-cooked eggs. Only the expectant look on Barsymes' face kept Krispos from falling asleep then and there. "One entree yet to come," the vestiarios said. "I assure you, it shall be worth the wait."

"My weight's already gone up considerably," Krispos said, patting his midsection. He could have used an infinitely distensible stomach himself about then.

But Barsymes, as usual, proved right. When he set down the last tray and its serving bowl, he said, "I am bidden by the cooks to describe this dish in detail. Any lapses in the description spring from my lapses of memory, not theirs of talent. I begin: to soaked pine nuts and sea urchins, they added in a casserole layers of mallows, beets, leeks, celery, cabbage, and other vegetables I now forget. Also included are stewed chickens, pigs' brains, blood sausage, chicken gizzards, fried tunny in bits, sea nettles, stewed oysters in pieces, and fresh cheeses. It is spiced with celery seed, lovage, pepper, and asafetida. Over the top was poured milk with beaten egg. It was then stiffened in a hot-water bath, garnished with fresh mussels, and peppered once more. I am only too certain I've left out something or another; I beg you not to report my failing to the cooks."

"Phos have mercy," Krispos exclaimed, eyeing the big casserole dish with something far beyond mere respect. "Should we eat of it or worship it?" After Barsymes served Iakovitzes and him, he had his answer. "Both!" he said with his mouth full.

The feast had stretched far into the night; every so often, Barsymes fed charcoal to a brazier that kept the dining chamber tolerably warm. Iakovitzes held up his tablet. "I hope you have a wheelbarrow in which to roll me home, for I'm certain I can't walk."

"Something shall be arranged, I am certain," the vestiarios said. "Dessert will be coming shortly. I trust you will do it justice?"

Iakovitzes and Krispos both groaned. The Avtokrator said, "We'll deal with it or burst trying. I'd say it's about even money which." He'd taken an army into battle many times with better odds than those.

But the sweet scent of the steam gently rising from the pan Barsymes brought in revived his interest. "Here we have grated apricots cooked in milk until tender, then covered in honey and lightly dusted with ground cinnamon." The vestiarios bowed to Iakovitzes. "Eminent sir, the cooks apologize for their failure to include seafood in this one dish."

"Tell them I forgive their lapse," Iakovitzes wrote. "I've not yet decided whether to sprout fins or tentacles from tonight's fête."

The apricots tasted as good as they smelled. Krispos nonetheless ate them very slowly, being full far past repletion. He was only halfway through his portion when Barsymes hurried into the dining chamber. The Emperor raised an eyebrow; such a lapse was unlike the eunuch.

Barsymes said, "Forgive me, your Majesty, but the mage Zaidas would have speech with you. It is, I gather, a matter of some urgency."

"Maybe he's here to tell me Digenis dropped dead at last," Krispos said hopefully. "Fetch him in, esteemed sir. If he'd come sooner, he could have helped the two of us commit gluttony here, not that we haven't managed well enough on our own."

When Zaidas came to the doorway, he started to prostrate himself. Krispos waved for him not to bother. Nodding his thanks, the wizard greeted Iakovitzes, whom he knew well. "Good to have you back with us, eminent sir. You've been away too long."

"It certainly *seemed* too bloody long," Iakovitzes wrote.

Barsymes carried in a chair for the mage. "Help yourself to apricots," Krispos said. "But first tell me what brings you here so late. It must be getting close to the sixth hour of the night. Has Digenis finally gone to the ice?"

To his surprise, Zaidas answered, "No, your Majesty, or not that I know of. It has rather to do with your son Phostis."

"You found a way to make Digenis talk?" Krispos demanded eagerly.

"Not that either, your Majesty," the mage said. "As you know, till now I've had no success even learning the possible source of the magic that conceals the young Majesty from my search. This has not been from want of effort or diligence, I assure you. Till now, I would have described the trouble as want of skill."

"Till now?" Krispos prompted.

"As you know, your Majesty, my wife Aulissa is a very determined lady." Zaidas gave a small, self-deprecating chuckle. "She has, in fact, determination to spare for herself and me both."

Iakovitzes reached for the stylus, but forbore. Krispos admired Aulissa's beauty and her strength of purpose while remaining content she was his mage's wife, not his own. The two of them had been happy together for many years, though. Now Krispos just said, "Go on, pray."

"Yes, your Majesty. In any case, Aulissa, seeing my discontent at failing to penetrate the shield the Thanasiot sorcerers have thrown up to disguise Phostis' whereabouts, suggested I test that screen at odd times and in odd ways, in the hope of ascertaining its nature while it might be weakest. Having no more likely profitable notions of my own, I fell in with her plan, and this evening I saw it crowned with success."

"There's good news indeed," Krispos said. "I'm in your debt, and in Aulissa's. Tell her when you go home that I'll show I'm grateful with more than words. But for now, by the good god, tell me what you know before I get up and tear it from you."

Iakovitzes let out his gobbling laugh. "It's an idle threat, sorcerous sir," he wrote. "Neither Krispos nor I could rise for anything right now, in any sense of the word."

Zaidas' smile was nervous. "You must understand, your Majesty, I've not broken the screen, merely peeked behind one lifted corner of it, if I may use ordinary words to describe sorcerous operations. But this I can tell you with some confidence: the magic behind the screen is of the school inspired by the Prophets Four."

"*Is* it?" Krispos said. Iakovitzes' eyebrows were eloquent of surprise. The Avtokrator added, "So the wind blows from that quarter, does it? It's not what I expected, I'll say that. Knowing how the screen was made, can you now pierce it?"

"That remains to be seen," Zaidas said, "but I can essay such piercing with more hope than previously was mine."

"Good for you!" Krispos lifted the latest wine jar from its bed of snow. It was distressingly light. "Barsymes!" he called. "I'd intended to make an end of things here, but I find we need more wine after all. Fetch us another, and a cup for Zaidas and one for yourself. Tonight the news is good."

"I shall attend to it directly, your Majesty," Barsymes said, and he did.

Occasional sleet rode the wind outside the little stone house with the thatched roof. Inside, a small fire burned on the hearth, but the chill remained. Phostis chafed his hands one against the other to keep feeling in them.

The priest who had presided over the Midwinter's Day liturgy at the main temple in Etchmiadzin bowed to the middle-age couple who sat side by side at the table where they'd no doubt eaten together for many years. On the table rested a small loaf of black bread and two cups of wine.

"We are met here today with Laonikos and Siderina to celebrate their last meal, their last partaking of the gross substance of the world and their commencement of a new journey on Phos' gleaming path," the priest proclaimed.

Along with Phostis, Olyvria, and Syagrios, the little house was crowded with friends and relatives; the couple's son and daughter and two of Laonikos' brothers were easy to pick out by looks. Everyone, including Laonikos and Siderina, seemed happy and proud of what was about to happen. Phostis looked happy himself, but he'd learned in the palaces how to assume an expression at will. In fact, he didn't know what to think. The man and woman at that table were obviously of sound mind and as obviously eager to begin with what they thought of as the last step of their earthly existence and their first steps toward heaven. *How should I feel about that,* Phostis wondered, *when it's not a choice I'd ever make for myself?*

"Let us pray," the priest said. Phostis bent his head, sketched the sun-circle over his heart. Everyone recited Phos' creed. As he had at Etchmiadzin's temple, Phostis found the creed more moving, more sincere, here than he ever had in the High Temple. These people *meant* their prayers.

They put fervor into a round of Thanasiot hymns, too. Phostis did not know those as well as the rest of the folk gathered here; he kept stumbling over the words and then coming in again a line and a half later. The hymns had different tunes—some borrowed from the orthodox liturgy—but the same message: that loving the good god was all-important, that the next world meant more than this one, and that every earthly pleasure was from Skotos and to be shunned.

The priest turned to Laonikos and Siderina and asked, "Are you now prepared to abandon the wickedness in this world, the dark god's vessel, and to seek the light in the realm beyond the sun?"

They looked at each other, then touched hands. It was a loving gesture, but in no way a sensual one; with it they affirmed that what they did, they did together. Without hesitation, they said, "We are." Phostis could not have told which of them spoke first.

"It's so beautiful," Olyvria whispered, and Phostis had to nod. Dropping her voice still further, so only he heard, she added, "And so frightening." He nodded again.

"Take up the knife," the priest said. "Divide the bread and eat it. Take the wine and drink. Never again shall the stuff of Skotos pass your lips. Soon the bodies that are themselves sinful shall be no more and pass away; soon your souls shall know the true joy of union with the lord with the great and good mind."

Laonikos was a sturdy man with a proud hooked nose and distinctive eyebrows, tufted and bushy. Siderina might have been pretty as a girl; her face was still sweet and strong. *Soon,* Phostis thought, *they'll both look like Strabon.* The idea horrified him. It didn't seem to bother Laonikos and Siderina at all.

Laonikos cut the little loaf in half and gave one piece to his wife. The other he kept himself. He ate it in three or four bites, then tilted back the wine cup until the last drop was gone. His smile lit up the house. "It's done," he said proudly. "Phos be praised."

"Phos be praised," everyone echoed. "May the gleaming path lead you to him!"

Siderina finished her final meal a few seconds after Laonikos. She dabbed at her lips with a linen napkin. Her eyes sparkled. "Now I shan't have to fret about what to cook for supper any more," she said. Her voice was gay and eager; she looked forward to the world to come. Her family laughed with her. Even Phostis found himself smiling, for her manifest happiness communicated itself to him no matter how much trouble he had sharing it.

The couple's son took the plate, knife, and wine cups. "The good god willing, these will inspire us to join you soon," he said.

"I hope they do," Laonikos said. He got up from the table and hugged the young man. In a moment, the whole family was embracing.

"We bless thee, Phos, lord with the great and good mind—" the priest began. Everyone joined him in prayer once more.

Phostis thought the blue-robe had intruded himself on the family's celebration. He thought his own presence an intrusion, too. Turning to Olyvria, he whispered, "We really ought to go."

"Yes, I suppose you're right," she murmured back.

"Phos bless you, friends, and may we see you along his gleaming path," Laonikos called to them as they made their way out the door. Phostis put up his hood and pulled his cloak tight around him to shield against the storm.

"Well," Olyvria said when they'd gone a few yards down the street, "what did you think of that?"

"Very much what you did," Phostis answered. "Terrifying and beautiful at the same time."

"Huh!" Syagrios said. "Where's the beauty in turning into a bag of bones?" It was the same thought Phostis had worried at before, if more pungently put.

Olyvria let out an indignant sniff. Before she could speak, Phostis said, "Seeing faith so fully realized is beautiful, even for someone like me. My own faith, I fear, is not so deep. I cling to life on earth, which is why seeing someone choose to leave it frightens me."

"We'll all leave it sooner or later, so why choose to hurry?" Syagrios said.

"For a proper Thanasiot," Olyvria said, emphasizing *proper*, "the world is corrupt from its creation, and to be shunned and abandoned as soon as possible."

Syagrios remained unmoved. "Somebody has to take care of all the bloody sods leavin' the world, or else they'll leave it faster'n they have in mind, thanks to his old man's soldiers." He jerked a thumb at Phostis. "So I'm not a sheep. I'm a sheepdog. You don't have sheepdogs, my lady, wolves get fat."

The argument was ugly but potent. Olyvria bit her lip and looked to Phostis. He felt he was called to save her from some dreadful fate, even though she and Syagrios were in truth on the same side. He flung the best rhetorical brickbat he could find: "Saving others from sin doesn't excuse sins of your own."

"Boy, you can talk about sin when you find out what it is," Syagrios said scornfully. "You're as milkfed now as when you came out from between your mother's legs. And how do you think you got in there to come out, eh, if there'd been no heavy breathing awhile before?"

Phostis *had* thought about that, as uneasily as most people when making similar contemplations. He started to shoot back that his parents had been honestly married when he was conceived, but he wasn't even sure of that. And rumor in the palace quarter said—whispered, when he was suspected of being in earshot—Krispos and Dara had been lovers while the previous Avtokrator—and Dara's previous husband—Anthimos still held the throne. Glaring at Syagrios wasn't the response Phostis would have liked to make, but seemed the best one available.

As wet will not stick to a duck's oiled feather, so glares slid off Syagrios. He threw back his head and laughed raucously at Phostis' discomfiture. Then he spun on his heel and swaggered away through the slush, as if to say Phostis wouldn't know what to do with a chance to sin if one fell into his lap.

"Cursed ruffian," Phostis growled—but softly, so Syagrios would not hear. "By the good god, he knows enough of sin to spend eternity in the ice; the gleaming path should be ashamed to call him its own."

"He's not a Thanasiot, not really, though he'll quarrel over the workings of the faith like any Videssian." Olyvria's voice was troubled, as if she did not care for the admission she was about to make. "He's much more a creature of my father's."

"Why does that not surprise me?" Phostis freighted the words with as much irony as they would bear. Only after they had passed his lips did he wish he'd held them in. Railing at Livanios would not help him with Olyvria.

She sounded defensive as she answered, "Surely Krispos also has men to do his bidding, no matter what it may be."

"Oh, he does," Phostis said. "But he doesn't wrap himself in piety while he's about it." In some surprise, he listened to himself defending his father. This wasn't the first time he'd had good things to say about Krispos since he'd ended up in Etchmiadzin. He hadn't had many when he was back in the imperial capital under Krispos' eye—and his thumb.

Olyvria said, "My father seeks to liberate Videssos so the gleaming path may become a reality for everyone. Do you deny it's a worthy goal?"

*He seeks power, like any other ambitious man,* Phostis thought. Before he could say it aloud, he started to laugh. Olyvria's eyes raked him. "I wasn't laughing at you," he assured her quickly. "It's just that we sound like a couple of little squabbling children: 'My father can do this.' 'Well, *my* father can do that.' "

"Oh." She smiled back, her good humor restored. "So we do. What would you rather talk about than what our fathers can do?"

The challenging way she threw the question at him reminded him of the first time he'd seen her, in the tunnel under Videssos the city. If he was to become a proper Thanasiot, as Olyvria had put it in her argument with Syagrios, he ought to have forgotten that, or at most remembered it as a test he'd passed. But he'd discovered before he ever heard of Thanasios that he did not have a temper approaching the monastic. He did not remember just the test; he remembered *her.*

And so he did not answer in words. Instead, he reached out and slipped an arm around her waist. If she'd pulled back, he was ready to apologize profusely. He was even ready to produce a convincing stammer. But she didn't pull back. Instead, she let him draw her to him.

In Videssos the city, they would have been nothing out of the ordinary: a young man and a young woman happy with each other and not paying much attention to anything else. Even in Etchmiadzin, a few people on the street smiled as they walked by. Others, though, glowered in pious indignation at such a public display of affection. *Crabs,* he thought.

After a few steps, though, Olyvria pulled away. He thought she'd seen the disapproving faces, too. But she said, "Strolling with you like this is very pleasant, but I can't feel happy about pleasure, if you know what I mean, just after we've come away from the celebration of the Last Meal."

"Oh. That." As it has a way of doing, the wider world intruded itself on Phostis' thoughts. He remembered the joy Laonikos and Siderina had shown when they swallowed the last wine and bread they would taste on earth. "It's still hard to imagine that impinging on me. Like Syagrios, if in lesser measure, I fear I'm a creature of this world."

"In lesser measure," Olyvria agreed. "Well, so am I, if the truth be told. Maybe when I'm older the world will repel me enough to make me want to leave it, but for now, even if everything Thanasios says about it is true, I can't force my flesh to turn altogether away from it."

"Nor I," Phostis said. The fleshly world intruded again, in a different way this time: He stepped up to Olyvria and kissed her. Her lips were for a moment still and startled under his; he was a little startled himself, because he hadn't planned to do it. But then her arms enfolded him as his did her. Her tongue touched his, just for a couple of heartbeats.

At that, they broke apart from each other, so fast Phostis couldn't tell which of them drew back first. "Why did you do that?" Olyvria asked in a voice that was all breath.

"Why? Because—" Phostis stopped. He didn't know why, not in the way he knew how mulberries tasted or where in Videssos the city the High Temple stood. He tried again: "Because—" Another stumble. Once more: "Because of all the folk in Etchmiadzin, you're the only one who's shown me any true kindness." That was indeed part of the truth. The rest Phostis did not care to examine quite so closely; it was as filled with carnality as the upper part of his mind was with the notion that carnality and sinfulness were one and the same.

Olyvria considered what he'd said. Slowly she nodded. "Kindness is a virtue that moves you forward on the gleaming path, a reaching out from one soul to another," she said. But her eyes slipped away from his as she spoke. He watched her lips. They seemed slightly softer, slightly fuller than they had before his touched them. He wondered if she, too, was having trouble reconciling what she believed with what she felt.

They walked on aimlessly for a while, not touching, both of them thoughtful. Then, over a low rooftop, Phostis saw the bulk of the fortress. "We'd better get back," he said. Olyvria nodded, as if relieved to have a definite goal for her feet.

As if he were a conjured demon, Syagrios popped out of a wineshop not far outside the fortress' walls. He might have started shirking his watchdog duties, but he didn't want Livanios finding out about that. The ruffian glanced mockingly at the two of them. "Well, have you settled all the doings of the lord with the great and good mind?"

"That's for Phos to do with us, not we with him," Phostis said.

Syagrios liked that; his laugh blew grapey fumes into Phostis' face. He pointed toward the gates. "Back to your cage now, and you can see how Phos settles you there."

Phostis kept walking toward the fortress. He'd learned that giving any sign Syagrios' jabs hurt guaranteed he'd keep getting them. As he went through the gates, he also noticed how much like home the fortress was becoming in his mind. *Just because it's familiar doesn't mean they can make you belong here,* he told himself.

But were they making him? He still hadn't settled that question in his own mind. If he followed Thanasios' gleaming path, oughtn't he be here of his own free will?

In the inner yard, Livanios was watching some of his recruits throw javelins. The light spears thumped into bales of hay propped against the far wall. Some missed and bounced back.

Ever alert, Livanios turned his head to see who the newcomers were. "Ah, the young Majesty," he said. Phostis didn't care for the way he used the title; it was devoid even of scornful courtesy. The heresiarch sounded as if he wondered whether Phostis, instead of proving useful, might be turning into a liability. That made Phostis nervous. If he wasn't useful to Livanios, how long would he last?

"Take him up to his chamber, Syagrios," Livanios said; he might have been speaking of a dog, or of a sack of flour.

As the door to his little cell closed behind him, Phostis realized that, if he didn't care to abandon his fleshly form as the Thanasioi advocated for their most pious folk, he might have to take some most un-Thanasiot actions. As soon as that thought crossed his mind, he remembered Olyvria's lips sweet against his. The Thanasioi would not have approved of that, not even a little.

He also remembered whose daughter Olyvria was. If he tried to escape, would she betray him? Or might she help? He stamped on the cold floor. He just did not know.

# VIII

Krispos was wading through changes in a law that dealt with tariffs on tallow imported from the northeastern land of Thatagush when Barsymes tapped at the open door of his study with one knuckle. He looked up. The vestiarios said, "May it please your Majesty, a messenger from the mage Zaidas at the government office building."

"Maybe it *will* please me, by the good god," Krispos said. "Send him in."

The messenger quickly prostrated himself, then said, "Your Majesty, Zaidas bids me tell you that he has at last succeeded in commencing a sorcerous interrogation of the rebel priest Digenis."

"Has he? Well, to the ice with tallow."

"Your Majesty?"

"Never mind." The less the messenger knew about the dickering with Thatagush, the happier he'd be. Krispos got up and accompanied him out of the study and out of the imperial residence. Haloga guards fell in with him as he went down the broad steps outside. He felt a childish delight in having caught his parasol bearers napping, as if he'd put one over on Barsymes.

He hadn't gone to listen to Digenis since the day of Iakovitzes' return. He'd seen no point to it: he'd already heard all the Thanasiot platitudes he could stomach, and Digenis refused to yield the truths he wanted to learn.

He was shocked at how the priest had wasted away. In his

peasant days, he'd seen men and women lean with hunger after a bad harvest, but Digenis was long past leanness: everything between his skeleton and his skin seemed to have disappeared. His eyes shifted when Krispos came into his cell, but did not catch fire as they had before.

"He is very weak, your Majesty; his will at last begins to fail," Zaidas said quietly. "Otherwise I doubt even now I could have found a way to coax answers from him."

"What have you done?" Krispos asked. "I see no apparatus for the two-mirror test."

"No." By his expression, Zaidas would have been glad never to try the two-mirror test again. "This is half magic, half healing art. I laced the water he drinks with a decoction of henbane, having first used sorcery to remove the taste so he would notice nothing out of the ordinary."

"Well done." After a moment, Krispos added, "I do hope the technique for that is not so simple as to be available to any poisoner who happens to take a dislike to his neighbor—or to me."

"No, your Majesty," Zaidas said, smiling. "In any case, the spell, because it goes against nature, is easy to detect by sorcery. Digenis, of course, was not in a position to do so."

"And a good thing, too," Krispos said. "All right, let's see if he'll give forth the truth now. What questions have you put to him thus far?"

"None of major import. As soon as I saw he was at last receptive, I sent for you at once. I suggest you keep your questions as simple as you can. The henbane frees his mind, but also clouds it—both far more strongly than wine."

"As you say, sorcerous sir." Krispos raised his voice. "Digenis! Do you hear me, Digenis?"

"Aye, I hear you." Digenis' voice was not only weak from weeks of self-imposed starvation but also dreamy and far away.

"Where's Phostis—my son? The son of the Avtokrator Krispos," Krispos added, in case the priest did not realize who was talking to him.

Digenis answered, "He walks the golden path to true piety, striding ever farther from the perverse materialistic heresy that afflicts too many soulblind folk throughout the Empire." The priest held his convictions all the way down to his heart, not merely on the surface of his mind. Krispos had already been sure of that.

He tried again: "Where is Phostis physically?"

"The physical is unimportant," Digenis declared. Krispos glanced over at Zaidas, who bared his teeth in an agony of frustration. But Digenis went on, "If all went as was planned, Phostis is now with Livanios."

Krispos had thought as much, but hearing the plan had been kidnap rather than murder lifted fear from his heart. Phostis could easily have been dumped in some rocky ravine with his throat cut; only the wolves and ravens would have been likely to discover him. The Avtokrator said, "What does Livanios hope to do with him? Use him as a weapon against me?"

"Phostis has a hope of assuming true piety," Digenis said. Krispos wondered if he'd confused him by asking two questions at once. After a few heartbeats, the priest resumed, "For a youth, Phostis resists carnality well. To my surprise, he declined the body of Livanios' daughter, which she offered to see if he could be tempted from the gleaming path. He could not. He may yet prove suitable for an imminent union with the good god rather than revolting and corruptible flesh."

"An imminent union?" All faiths used words in special ways. Krispos wanted to be sure he understood what Digenis was talking about. "What's an imminent union?"

"That which I am approaching now," Digenis answered. "The voluntary abandonment of the flesh to free the spirit to fly to Phos."

"You mean starving yourself to death," Krispos said. Somehow Digenis used his emaciated neck for a nod. Slow horror trickled through Krispos as he imagined Phostis wasting away like the Thanasiot priest. No matter that he and the young man quarreled, no matter even that Phostis might not be his by blood: he would not have wished such a fate on him.

Digenis began to whisper a Thanasiot hymn. Seeking to rock him out of the holy smugness he maintained even in the face of approaching death, Krispos said, "Did you know Livanios uses magic of the school of the Prophets Four to hide Phostis' whereabouts?"

"He is cursed with ambition," Digenis answered. "I knew the spoor; I recognized the stench. He prates of the golden path, but Skotos has filled his heart with greed for power."

"You worked with him, knowing he was evil by your reckoning?" That surprised Krispos; he'd expected the renegade priest to have sterner standards for himself. "And you still claim you walk Thanasios' gleaming path? Are you not a hypocrite?"

"No, for Livanios' ambition furthers the advance of the holy Thanasios' doctrines, whereas yours leads only to the further aggrandizement of Skotos," Digenis declared. "Thus evil is transmuted into good and the dark god confounded."

"Thus sincerity turns to expedience," Krispos said. He'd already gained the impression that Livanios cared more for Livanios than for the gleaming path. In a way, that made the heresiarch more dangerous, for he was liable to be more flexible than an out-and-out fanatic. But in another way, it weakened Livanios: fanatics, by the strength of their beliefs, could sometimes make their followers transcend difficulties from which an ordinary thoughtful man would flinch.

Krispos thought for a while, but could not come up with any more questions about Phostis or the rebels in the field. Turning to Zaidas, he said, "Squeeze all you can from him about the riots and the city and those involved. And then—" He paused.

"Yes, what then, your Majesty?" the mage asked. "Shall we let him continue his decline until he stops breathing one day before long?"

"I'd sooner strike off his head and put it up on the Milestone," Krispos said grimly. "But if I did that now, with him looking as he does, all the Thanasioi in the city would have themselves a new martyr. I'd just as soon do without that, if I could. Better to let him die in quiet and disappear: the good god willing, folk will just forget about him."

"You are wise and cruel," Digenis said. "Skotos speaks through your lips."

"If I thought that were so, I'd step down from the throne and cast off my crown this instant," Krispos said. "My task is to rule the Empire as well as I can devise, and pass it on to my heir so he may do likewise. Having Videssos torn apart in religious strife doesn't seem to me to be part of that bargain."

"Yield to the truth and there will be no strife." Digenis began whispering hymns again in his dusty voice.

"This talk has no point," Krispos said. "I'd sooner build than destroy, and you Thanasioi feel the opposite. I don't want the land burned over, nor do I want it vacant of Videssians who slew themselves for piety's sake. Other folk would simply steal what we've spent centuries building. I will not have that, not while I live."

Digenis said, "The lord with the great and good mind willing, Phostis will prove a man of better sense and truer piety."

Krispos thought about that. Suppose he got his son back, but as a full-fledged fanatical Thanasiot? What then? *If that's so,* he told himself, *it's as well I had three boys, not one.* If Phostis came back a Thanasiot, he'd live out his days in a monastery, whether he went there of his own free will or not. Krispos promised himself that: he wouldn't turn the Empire over to someone more interesting in wrecking than maintaining it.

Time enough to worry about that if he ever saw Phostis again, though. He turned to Zaidas. "You've done well, sorcerous sir. Knowing what you've learned now, you should have a better chance of pinpointing Phostis' whereabouts."

"I'll bend every effort toward that end," the mage promised.

Nodding, Krispos stepped out of Digenis' cell. The head gaoler came up to him and said, "A question, your Majesty?" Krispos raised an eyebrow and waited. The gaoler said, "That priest in there, he's getting on toward the end. What happens if he decides he doesn't care to starve himself to death and wants to start eating again?"

"I don't think that's likely to happen." If nothing else, Krispos respected Digenis' sense of purpose. "If it does, though, by all means let him eat; this refusal to take food is his affair, not mine. But notify me immediately."

"You'll want to ask him more questions, your Majesty?" the gaoler said.

"No, no; you misunderstand. That priest is a condemned traitor. If he wants to carry out the sentence of death on himself in his own way, I am willing to permit it. But if his will falters, he'll meet the headsman on a full stomach."

"Ah," the gaoler said. "The wind sits so, eh? Very well, your Majesty, it shall be as you say."

In his younger days, Krispos would have come back with something harsh, like *It had better be.* More secure in his power now, he headed upstairs without a backward glance. As long as the gaoler felt no other result than the one he desired was possible, that result was what Krispos would get.

The Halogai who had waited outside the government office building took their places around Krispos and those who had gone down with him into the gaol. "Is the word good, Majesty?" one of the northerners asked.

"Good enough, anyhow," the Avtokrator answered. "I know now Phostis was snatched, not killed, and I have a good notion of where he's been taken. As for getting him back—time will tell about that." *And about what sort of person he'll be when I do get him back,* he added to himself.

The guardsmen cheered, their deep-voiced shouts making passersby's heads turn to find out what news was so gladsome. Some people exclaimed to see Krispos out and about without his retinue of parasol bearers. Others exclaimed at the Halogai. The men from the north—tall, fair, gloomy, and slow-spoken— never failed to fascinate the Videssians, whose opposites they were in almost every way.

Struck by sudden curiosity, Krispos turned to one of the northerners and said, "Tell me, Trygve, what do you make of the folk of Videssos the city?"

Trygve pursed his lips and gave the matter some serious thought. At last, in his deliberate Videssian, he answered, "Majesty, the wine here is very fine, the women looser than they are in Halogaland. But everyone, I t'ink, here talks too much." Several other guardsmen nodded in solemn agreement. Since Krispos had the same opinion of the city folk, he nodded, too.

Back at the imperial residence, he gave the news from Digenis to Barsymes. The vestiarios' smile, unusually broad, filled his face full of fine wrinkles. He said, "Phos be praised that the young Majesty is thought to be alive. The other palace chamberlains, I know, will be as delighted as I am."

Down a side corridor, Krispos came upon Evripos and Katakolon arguing about something or other. He didn't ask what; when the mood struck them, they could argue over the way a lamp flame flickered. He'd had no brothers himself, only two sisters younger than he, both many years dead now. He supposed he should have been glad his sons kept their fights to words and occasional fists rather than hiring knifemen or poisoners or wizards.

Both youths glanced warily in his direction as he approached. Neither one looked conspicuously guilty, so each of them felt the righteousness of his own cause—though Evripos, these days, was developing the beginning of a pretty good stone face.

Krispos said, "Digenis has cracked at last, thank the good god. By what he said, Phostis is held in some Thanasiot stronghold, but is alive and likely to stay that way."

Now he studied Evripos and Katakolon rather than the other way round. Katakolon said, "That's good news. By the time we're done smashing the Thanasioi next summer, we should have him back again." His expression was open and happy; Krispos didn't think he was acting. He was sure he couldn't have done so well at Katakolon's age . . . but then, he hadn't been raised at court, either.

Evripos' features revealed nothing whatever. His eyes were watchful and hooded. Krispos prodded to see what lay behind the mask. "Aren't you glad to be sure your elder brother lives?"

"For blood's sake, aye, but should I rejoice to see my ambition thwarted?" Evripos said. "Would you, in my boots?"

The question cut to the root. Ambition for a better life had driven Krispos from his farm to Videssos; while he was one of Iakovitzes' grooms, ambition had led him to wrestle a Kubrati champion and gained him the notice of the then-Emperor Anthimos' uncle Petronas, who administered Videssos in his nephew's name; ambition led him to let Petronas use him to supplant Anthimos' previous vestiarios; and then, as vestiarios himself, to take ever more power into his own hands, supplanting first Petronas and then Anthimos.

He said, "Son, I know you want the red boots. Well, so does Phostis, and I have but the one set to give. What would you have me do?"

"Give them to me, by Phos," Evripos answered. "I'd wear them better than he would."

"I have no way to be sure of that—nor do you," Krispos said. "For that matter, a day may come when Katakolon here begins to think past the end of his prick. He might prove a better ruler than either of you two. Who can say?"

"Him?" Evripos shook his head. "No, Father, forgive me, but I don't see it."

"Me?" Katakolon seemed as bemused as his brother. "I've never thought much of wearing the crown. I always figured the only way it would come to me was if Phostis and Evripos were dead. I don't want it badly enough to wish for that. And since I'm not likely to be Avtokrator, why shouldn't I enjoy myself?"

As Avtokrator and voluptuary both, Anthimos had been anything but good for the Empire. But as Emperor's brother, Katakolon would be relatively harmless if he devoted himself to pleasure. If he did lack ambition, he might even be safer as a voluptuary. The chronicles had shown Krispos that rulers had a way of turning suspicious of their closest kin: who else was likelier both to accumulate power and to use it against them?

"Maybe it's because I grew up on a farm," Krispos began, and both Evripos and Katakolon rolled their eyes. Nonetheless, the Avtokrator persisted: "Maybe that's why I think waste is a sin Phos won't forgive. We never had much; if we'd wasted anything, we would have starved. The lord with the great and good mind knows I'm glad it isn't so with you boys: being hungry is no fun. But even though you have so much, you should still work to make the most you can of your lives. Pleasure is all very well in its place, but you can do other things when you're not in bed."

Katakolon grinned. "Aye, belike: you can get drunk."

"Another sermon wasted, Father," Evripos said acidly. "How does that fit into your scheme of worths?"

Without answering, Krispos pushed past his two younger sons and down the corridor. Phostis was unenthusiastic about ruling, Evripos embittered, and Katakolon had other things on his mind. What would Videssos come to when the common fate of mankind took his own hand from the steering oar?

Men had been asking that question, on one scale or another, for as long as there were men. If the head of a family died and his relatives were less able then he, the family might fall on hard times, but the rest of the world went on. When an able Emperor passed from the scene, families past counting might suffer because of it.

"What am I supposed to do?" Krispos asked the statues and paintings and relics that lined that hallway. No answer came back to him. All he could think of was to go on himself, as well as he could for as long as he could.

And after that? After that it would be in his sons' hands, and in the good god's. He remained confident Phos would continue to watch over Videssos. Of his sons he was less certain.

Rain poured down in sheets, ran in wide, watery fishtails off the edges of roofs, and turned the inner ward of the fortress of Etchmiadzin into a thin soup of mud. Phostis closed the wooden shutter to the little slit window in his cell; with it open, things were about as wet inside as they were out in the storm.

But with it closed, the bare square room was dark as night; fitfully flickering lamps did little to cut the gloom. Phostis slept as much as he could. Inside the cell in near darkness, he had little else to do.

After a few days of the steady rain, he felt as full of sleep as a new wineskin is of wine. He went into the corridor in search of something other than food.

Syagrios was dozing on a chair down the hall. Perhaps he'd had himself magically attuned to Phostis' door, for he came alert as soon as it opened, though Phostis had been quiet with it. The ruffian yawned, stretched, and said, "I was beginning to think you'd died in there, boy. In a little while, I was going to check for a stink."

*You might have found one,* Phostis thought. Because the Thanasioi reckoned the body Skotos' creation, they neither lavished baths on it nor disguised its odors with sweet scents. Sometimes Phostis didn't notice the resulting stench, as he was part of it. Sometimes it oppressed him dreadfully.

He said, "I'm going downstairs. I've grown too bored even to nap anymore."

"You won't stay bored forever," Syagrios answered. "After the rain comes the clear, and when the clear comes, we go out to fight." He closed a fist and slammed it down on his leg. Syagrios was bored, too, Phostis realized: he hadn't had the chance to go out and hurt anything lately.

A couple of torches had gone out along the corridor, leaving it hardly brighter than Phostis' cell. He lit a taper from the burning torch nearest the stairway and headed down the steep stone spiral. Syagrios followed him. As always, he was sweating by the time he reached the bottom; a misstep on the stairs and he would have got there much faster than he wanted to.

Livanios' soldiers crowded the ground floor of the citadel.

Some of them slept rolled in blankets, their worldly goods either under their heads in leather sacks that served for pillows or somewhere else close by. However much the Thanasioi professed to despise the things of the world, their fighters could still be tempted to take hold of things of the world that were not things of theirs.

Some of the men who were awake threw dice; there coins and other things of the world changed hands in more generally accepted fashion. Phostis had been bemused the first time he saw Thanasiot soldiers gambling. He'd watched the dice many times since and concluded the men were soldiers first and followers of the gleaming path afterward.

Off in a corner, a small knot of men gathered around a game board whereon two of their fellows dueled. Phostis made his way over to them. "If nobody's up for the next game, I challenge the winner," he said.

The players looked up from their pieces. "Hullo, friend," one of them said, a Thanasiot greeting Phostis was still getting used to. "Aye, I'll take you on after I take care of Grypas here."

"Ha!" Grypas returned to the board the prelate he'd captured from his opponent. "Guard your emperor, Astragalos; Phostis here will play *me* next."

Grypas proved right; after some further skirmishing, Astragalos' emperor, beset on all sides, found no square where he could move without threat of capture. Muttering into his beard, the soldier gave up.

Phostis sat in his place. He and Grypas returned the pieces to their proper squares on the first three rows on each man's side of the nine-by-nine board. Grypas glanced over at Phostis. "I've played you before, friend. I'm going to take winner's privilege and keep first move."

"However you like," Phostis answered. Grypas advanced the foot soldier diagonally ahead of his prelate, freeing up the wide-ranging piece for action. Phostis pushed one of his own foot soldiers forward in reply.

Grypas played like the soldier he was. He hurled men into the fight without much worry about where they would be three moves later. Phostis had learned in a subtler school. He lost a little time fortifying his emperor behind an array of goldpieces and silvers, but then started taking advantage of that safety.

Before long, Grypas was gnawing his mustache in consternation. He tried to fight back by returning to the fray pieces he'd taken from Phostis, but Phostis had not left himself as vulnerable as Astragalos had before. He beat the soldier without much trouble.

As the dejected man got up from the board, Syagrios sat down across it from Phostis. He leered at the junior Avtokrator. "All right, youngster, let's see how tough you are."

"I'll keep first move against you, by the good god," Phostis said. Around them, bets crackled back and forth. Over the long winter, they'd shown they were the two best players in the fortress. Which of them was better than the other swung from day to day.

Phostis stared over the grid at his unkempt opponent. Who would have guessed that a man with the looks of a bandit and habits to match made such a cool, precise player? But the pieces on the board cared nothing for how a man looked or even how he acted when he wasn't at the game. And Syagrios had already showed he had more wit behind that battered face than anyone who judged by it alone would guess.

The ruffian had a special knack for returning captured pieces to the board with telling effect. If he set down a horseman, you could be sure it threatened two pieces at once, both of them worth more than it. If a siege engine went into action, your emperor would be in trouble soon.

His manner at the game betrayed his origins. Whenever Phostis made a move he didn't like, he'd growl, "Oh, you son of a whore!" It had been unnerving at first; by now, Phostis took no more notice of it than of the twitches and tics of some of his opponents back in Videssos the city.

He took far fewer chances against Syagrios than he had against Grypas. In fact, he took no chances at all that he could see: give Syagrios an opening and he'd charge right through. Syagrios treated him with similar caution. The game, as a result, was slow and positional.

Finally, with returned foot soldiers paving the way, Syagrios broke up Phostis' fortress and sent his emperor scurrying for safety. When he was trapped in a corner with no hope of escape, Phostis took him off the board and said, "I surrender."

"You made me sweat there, by the good god." Syagrios

thumped his chest with a big fist, then boomed out, "Who else wants a go at me?"

Astragalos said, "Let Phostis take you on again. That'll make a more even match than the rest of us are apt to give you."

Phostis had stood up. He looked around to see if anybody else wanted to play Syagrios. When no one made a move, he sat back down again. Syagrios leered at him. "I ain't gonna give you first move, either, boy."

"I didn't expect you would," Phostis answered, altogether without ironic intent: any man who didn't look out for himself wasn't likely to find anyone to do it for him.

After a game as hard-fought as the first one, he got his revenge. Syagrios leaned over the board and punched him on the meaty part of his arm. "You're a sneaky little bastard, you know that? To the ice with whose son you are. That ain't horse manure between your ears, you know?"

"Whatever you say." Compliments from Syagrios made Phostis even more nervous than the abuse that usually filled the ruffian's mouth. Phostis stood up again and said, "You can take on the next challenger."

"Why's that?" Syagrios demanded. Quitting while you were winning was bad form.

"If I don't leave about now, you'll have to wipe up the floor under me," Phostis answered, which made Syagrios and several of the other men around the game board laugh. With the fortress of Etchmiadzin packed full of fighters, the humor there was decidedly coarse.

In better weather, Phostis would have wandered out into the inner ward to make water against the wall. There was, however, an oversufficiency of water in the inner ward already. He headed off to the garderobe instead. The chamber, connected as it was to a cesspit under the keep, was so noisome that he avoided it when he could. At the moment, however, he had little choice.

Wooden stalls separated one hole in the long stone bench from another, an unusual concession to delicacy but one Phostis appreciated. Three of the four were occupied when he went in; he stepped into the fourth, which was farthest from the doorway.

As he was easing himself, he heard a couple of people come

in behind him. One of them let out an unhappy grunt. "All full," he said. By the slight accent he gave his words, Phostis recognized him as Livanios' pet wizard.

The other was Livanios. "Don't worry, Artapan," he said easily. "You won't burst in the next couple of minutes, and neither shall I."

"Don't use my name," the wizard grumbled.

Livanios laughed at him. "By the good god, if we have spies in the latrine, we're doomed before we start. Here, this fellow's coming out. You go ahead; I'll wait."

Phostis had already set his clothes to rights, but he waited, too, waited until he heard Livanios go into a stall and shut the door. Then he all but jumped out of the one he'd been in and hurried away from the garderobe. He didn't want either Livanios or Artapan to know he'd heard.

Now that he knew the wizard's name, he also recognized the accent that had tantalized him for so long. Artapan was from Makuran. Phostis wondered what a mage from Videssos' perennial enemy was doing in Livanios' camp. Why couldn't Livanios find a proper Thanasiot mage?

After a few seconds, he stopped wondering. To one raised in the palaces, to one who had, however unwillingly, soaked up a good deal of history, the answer fairly shouted at him: Artapan was there serving the interests of Rubyab King of Kings. And how could Rubyab's interest be better served than by keeping Videssos at war with itself?

Two other questions immediately sprang from that one. The first was whether Livanios knew he was being used. Maybe he didn't, maybe he was Makuran's willing cat's-paw, or maybe he was out to exploit Rubyab's help at the same time Rubyab used him. Phostis had a tough time seeing Livanios as a witless dupe. Choosing between the other two alternatives was harder.

Phostis set them aside. To him, the second question carried greater weight: if the Thanasioi were flourishing thanks to aid from Makuran, what did that say about the truth of their teachings? That one was hard enough to break teeth when you bit into it. Would Thanasios' interpretation of the faith have grown and spread without the foreign—no, no mincing words—without the enemy—help? Was it at bottom a religious movement at all, or rather a political one? If it was just political, why did it have such a strong appeal to so many Videssians?

Without even bothering to get a taper, Phostis went upstairs and into his room. All at once, he didn't care how gloomy it was in there. In fact, he hardly noticed. He sat down on the battered old stool. He had a lot to think about.

Somewhere among the gears and levers behind the wall of the Grand Courtroom, a servitor stood in frustrated uselessness. Much to the fellow's dismay, Krispos had ordered him not to raise the throne on high when the ambassador from Khatrish prostrated himself. "But it's the custom!" the man had wailed.

"But the reason behind the custom is to overawe foreign envoys," Krispos had answered. "It doesn't overawe Tribo—it just makes him laugh."

"But it's the custom," the servitor had repeated. To him, reasons were irrelevant. Raising the throne was what he'd always done, so raising the throne was what he had to do forever.

Even now, as Tribo approached the throne and cast himself down on his belly, Krispos wondered if the throne would rise beneath him in spite of orders. Custom died hard in the Empire, when it died at all.

To his relief, he remained at his usual elevation. As the ambassador from Khatrish got to his feet, he asked, "Mechanism in the throne break down?"

*I can't win,* Krispos thought. Khatrishers seemed to specialize in complicating the lives of their Videssian neighbors. Krispos did not reply: he stood—or rather sat—on the imperial dignity, though he had the feeling that would do him about as much good as the climbing throne had before.

Sure enough, Tribo let out a knowing sniff when he saw he wouldn't get an answer. He said, "May it please your Majesty, the Thanasioi are still troubling us."

"They're still troubling us, too, in case you hadn't noticed," Krispos said dryly.

"Well, yes, but it's different for you Videssians, you see, your Majesty. You grew the murrain your very own selves, so of course it's still spreading through your flocks. We don't take kindly to having our cows infected, too, though, if you take my meaning."

A Videssian would have used a comparison from agriculture

rather than herding, but Krispos had no trouble following Tribo. "What would you have me do?" he asked. "Shut the border between our states and ban shipping, too?"

The Khatrisher envoy flinched, as Krispos had known he would: Khatrish needed trade with Videssos much more than Videssos with Khatrish. "Let's not be hasty, your Majesty. All I want is to hear you say again that you and your ministers don't have anything to do with spreading the cursed heresy, so I can take the word to my khagan."

Barsymes and Iakovitzes stood in front of the imperial throne. Krispos could see only their backs and the sides of their faces. He often made a game of trying to figure out from that limited view what they were thinking. He guessed Iakovitzes was amused—he admired effrontery—and Barsymes outraged—the normally self-controlled eunuch was fairly quivering in his place. Krispos needed a moment to realize why: Barsymes reckoned it an insult for him to have to deny anything more than once.

His own notion of what was insulting was more flexible, even after twenty years and more on the throne. If the envoy wanted another guarantee, he could have it. Krispos said, "You can tell Nobad son of Gumush that we aren't exporting this heresy to Khatrish on purpose. We wish it would go away here, and we're trying to get rid of it. But we aren't in the habit of stirring up sectarian strife, even if it might profit us."

"I shall send exactly that word to the puissant khagan, your Majesty, and I thank you for the reassurance," Tribo said. He glanced toward the throne. Under his shaggy beard, a frown twisted his mouth. "Your Majesty? Did you hear me, your Majesty?"

Krispos still didn't answer. He was listening to what he'd just said, not to the ambassador from Khatrish. Videssos might fight shy of turning its neighbors topsy-turvy with religious war, but would Makuran? Didn't the Thanasiot mage who hid Phostis use spells that smelled of Mashiz? No wonder Rubyab's mustaches had twitched!

Iakovitzes spun where he stood so he faced Krispos. The assembled courtiers murmured at the breach of etiquette. Iakovitzes had a fine nose for intrigue. His upraised hand and urgent expression said he'd just smelled some. Krispos would

have bet a counterfeit copper against a year's tax receipts it
was the same odor that had just filled his own nostrils.

He realized he had to say something to Tribo. After a few
more seconds, he managed, "Yes, I'm glad you'll reassure
your sovereign we are doing everything we can to fight the
Thanasiot doctrine, not to spread it. This audience now is
ended."

"But your Majesty—" Tribo began indignantly. Then, with a
glare, he bowed to inflexible Videssian custom. When the
Avtokrator spoke those words, an envoy had no choice but to
prostrate himself once more, back away from the throne until
he had gone far enough that he could turn around, and then depart the Grand Courtroom. He left in a manifest snit; evidently
he'd had a good deal more on his mind than he got the chance
to say.

*I'll have to make it up to him,* Krispos thought; keeping
Khatrish friendly was going to be all the more important in the
months ahead. But for now even the urgency of that paled. As
soon as Tribo left the Grand Courtroom, Krispos also made his
way out, at a pace that set the tongues of the assembled nobles
and prelates and ministers wagging.

Politics was a religion of its own in Videssos; before long,
many of those officials would figure out what was going on.
Something obviously was, or the Avtokrator would not have
left so unceremoniously. For the moment, though, they were at
a loss as to what.

Iakovitzes half trotted along in Krispos' wake. He knew
what was going through the Emperor's mind. Barsymes plainly
didn't, but he would sooner have gone before the torturers in
their red leather than question Krispos where anyone else
could hear him. What he'd have to say in private about cutting
short the Khatrisher's audience was liable to be pointed.

Krispos swept across the rain-slicked flags of the path that
led through the cherry orchard and to the imperial residence.
The cherry trees were still bare-branched, but before too long
they'd grow leaves and then the pink and white blossoms that
would make the orchard fragrant and lovely for a few brief
weeks in spring.

As soon as he was inside, Krispos burst out, "That bastard!
That sneaky, underhanded son of a snake, may he shiver in the
ice for all eternity to come."

"Surely Tribo did not so offend you with his remark concerning the throne?" Barsymes asked. No, he didn't know why Krispos had left on the run.

"I'm not talking about Tribo, I'm talking about Rubyab the fornicating King of Kings," Krispos said. "Unless I've lost all of my mind, he's using the Thanasioi for his stalking horse. How can Videssos hope to deal with Makuran if we tie ourselves up in knots?"

Barsymes had been in the palaces longer than Krispos; he was anything but a stranger to devious machinations. As soon as this one was pointed out to him, he nodded emphatically. "I have no doubt but that you're right, your Majesty. Who would have looked for such elaborate deceit from Makuran?"

Iakovitzes held up a hand to gain a pause while he wrote something in his tablet. He passed it to Krispos. "We Videssians pride ourselves as the sneakiest folk on earth, but down deep somewhere we ought to remember the Makuraners can match us. They're not barbarians we can outmaneuver in our sleep. They've proved it, to our sorrow, too many times in the past."

"That's true," Krispos said as he handed the tablet to Barsymes. The vestiarios quickly read it, then nodded his agreement. Krispos thought back over the histories and chronicles he'd read. He said, "This seems to me to be something new. Aye, the King of Kings and his folk have fooled us many times, but mainly that's meant fooling us about what Makuran intends to do. Here, though, Rubyab's seen deep into our soul, seen how to make ourselves our own worst foes. That's more dangerous than any threat Makuran has posed in a long time."

Iakovitzes wrote, "There was a time, oh, about a hundred fifty years ago, when the men from Mashiz came closer to sacking Videssos the city than any Videssian likes to think about. Of course, we'd been meddling in their affairs before then, so I suppose they were out for revenge."

"Yes, I've seen those tales, too," Krispos said, nodding. "The question, though, is what we do about it now." He eyed Iakovitzes. "Suppose I send you back to Mashiz with a formal note of protest to Rubyab King of Kings?"

"Suppose you don't, your Majesty," Iakovitzes wrote, and underlined the words.

"One thing we ought to do is get this tale told as widely as possible," Barsymes said. "If every official and every priest in every town lets the people know Makuran is behind the Thanasioi, they'll be less inclined to go over to the heretics."

"Some of them will, anyhow," Krispos said. "Others will have heard too many pronouncements from the pulpit and from the city square to take special notice of one more. No, don't look downhearted, esteemed sir. It's a good plan, and we'll use it. I just don't want anyone here expecting miracles."

"No matter what the priests and the officials say, what we must have is victory," Iakovitzes wrote. "If we can make the Thanasioi stop hurting us, people will see us as the stronger side and pretend they never had a heretical notion in all their born days. But if we lose, the rebels' power will grow regardless of who's behind them."

"Not so long till spring, either," Krispos said. "May the good god grant us the victory you rightly say we need." He turned to Barsymes. "Summon the most holy patriarch Oxeites to the palaces, if you please. What words can do, they shall do."

"As you say, your Majesty." The vestiarios turned to go.

"Wait." Krispos stopped him in midstride. "Before you draft the note, why don't you fetch all three of us a jar of something sweet and strong? Today, by the good god, we've earned a taste of celebration."

"So we have, your Majesty," Barsymes said with the hint of a smile that was as much as he allowed himself. "I'll attend to that directly."

The jar of wine became two and then three. Krispos knew he would pay for it in the morning. He'd been a young man when he discovered he couldn't come close to roistering with Anthimos. Older now, he had less capacity than in those days, and less practice at carousing, too. But every so often, once or twice a year, he still enjoyed letting himself go.

Barsymes, abstemious in pleasure as in most things, bowed his way out halfway down the second jar, presumably to write the letter ordering Oxeites to appear at the palace. Iakovitzes stayed and drank: he was always game for a debauch, and held his wine better than Krispos. The only sign he gave of its effects was that the words he wrote grew large and sprawling. Syntax and venom remained unchanged.

"Why don't you write like you're drunk?" Krispos asked some time after dinner; by then he'd forgotten what he'd eaten.

Iakovitzes replied, "You drink with your mouth and then try to talk through it; no wonder you've started mumbling. My hand hasn't touched a drop."

As the night hours advanced, one of the chamberlains sent to Iakovitzes' house. A couple of his muscular grooms came to the imperial residence to escort their master home. He patted them both and went off humming a dirty song.

The hallway swayed around Krispos as he walked back from his farewells to Iakovitzes at the entrance: he felt like a beamy ship trying to cope with quickly shifting winds. In such a storm, the imperial bedchamber seemed a safe harbor.

After he closed the door behind him, he needed a few seconds to notice Drina smiling at him from the bed. The night was chilly; she had the covers drawn up to her neck. "Barsymes is up to his old tricks again," Krispos said slowly, "and he thinks I'm up to mine."

"Why not, your Majesty?" the serving maid said. "You never know till you try." She threw off the bedclothes. The smile was all she was wearing.

Even through the haze of wine, memory stabbed at Krispos: Dara had always been in the habit of sleeping without clothes. Drina was larger, softer, simpler—his wife the Empress had always been prickly as a hedgehog. As he seldom did these days, he let himself remember how much he missed her.

Watching Drina flip away the covers like that took him back almost a quarter of a century to the night he and Dara had joined on this very bed. Even after so long, a remembered thrill of fear ran through him—had Anthimos caught them, he would not be here now, or certain vital parts of him would not. And with the fear came the memory of how excited he'd been.

The memory of past excitement—and Drina there waiting for him—were enough to summon up at least the beginning of excitement now. He pulled off his robe and tugged at the red boots. "We'll see what happens," he said. "I make no promises: I've drunk a lot of wine."

"Whatever happens is all right, your Majesty," Drina said, laughing. "Haven't I told you before that you men worry too much about these things?"

"Women have probably been saying that since the start of

time," he said as he lay down beside her. "My guess is that the next man who believes it will be the first."

But oddly, knowing she had no great expectations helped him perform better than he'd expected himself. He didn't think she was pretending when she gasped and quivered under him; he could feel her secret place clench around him, again and again. Spurred by that, he, too, gasped and quivered a few seconds later.

"There—you see, your Majesty?" Drina said triumphantly.

"I see," Krispos said. "This was already a good day; you've made it better still."

"I'm glad." Drina let out a squeak. "I'd better get up, or else I'll leave stains on the sheet for the washerwomen to giggle at."

"Do they do that?" Krispos asked. He fell asleep in the middle of her answer.

By the time spring drew near in Etchmiadzin, Phostis knew every little winding street in town. He knew where the stonecutters had their shops, and the harnessmakers, and the bakers. He knew the street on which Laonikos and Siderina were busy dying—knew it and kept away from it.

He got more and more chances to wander where he would without Syagrios. Etchmiadzin's wall was too high to jump from without breaking his neck, its single gate too well guarded for him to think of bolting through it and away. And as the weather got better, Syagrios was more and more closeted with Livanios, planning the upcoming summer's campaign.

Phostis did his best to stay out of Livanios' way. The less he reminded the heresiarch of his presence, the less likely Livanios was to think of him, think of the danger he might represent, and put him out of the way.

Just wandering, however, was beginning to pall. When he'd had Syagrios at his elbow every hour of the day and night, he was sure just getting away from the ruffian for a little while would bring peace to his soul. And so it had . . . for a little while. But the taste of freedom, however small, served only to whet his appetite for more. He was no longer a glad explorer of Etchmiadzin's back alleys. He paced them more like a wildcat searching for an opening in its cage.

He hadn't found one yet. *Maybe around the next corner,* he told himself for the hundredth time. He went round the next corner—and almost walked into Olyvria, who was coming around it the other way.

They both sidestepped in the same direction, which meant they almost bumped into each other again. Olyvria started to laugh. "Get out of my way, you," she said, miming a push at his chest.

He made as if to stumble backward from it, then bowed extravagantly. "I humbly crave your pardon, my lady; I had no intention of disturbing your glorious progress," he cried. "I pray that you find it in your heart to forgive me!"

"We'll see about that," she said darkly.

By then they were both laughing. Phostis came back up to her and slipped an arm around her waist. She snuggled against him; her chin fit nicely on the top of his shoulder. He wanted to kiss her, but held back—she was still nervous about it. From her perspective, he supposed she had reason to be.

"What are you doing here?" they both asked in the same breath. That made them laugh again.

"Nothing much," Phostis answered. "Keeping away from mischief as best I can. What about you?"

Olyvria was carrying a canvas bag. She pulled a shoe out of it and held it up so close to Phostis' face that his eyes crossed. "I broke off the heel, see?" she said. "There's a little old Vaspurakaner cobbler down this street who does wonderful work. Why not? He's been doing it longer than both of us put together have been alive. Anyway, I was taking it to him."

"May I accompany you on your journey?" he asked grandly.

"I hoped you would," she answered, and dropped the wounded shoe back into the bag. Arm in arm, they walked down the little lane.

"Oh, this place," Phostis said when they reached the cobbler's shop. "Yes, I went by here." Over the door hung a boot carved from wood. To one side of it the wall bore the word SHOON in Videssian, to the other what was presumably the same message in the square, blocky characters the "princes" of Vaspurakan used to write their language.

Phostis peered through one of the narrow windows set into the front wall, Olyvria into the other. "I don't see anyone in there," she said, frowning.

"Let's find out." Phostis reached for the latch and pulled the door open. A bell rang. The rich smell of leather filled his nose. He motioned for Olyvria to precede him into the cobbler's shop. The door swung shut behind them.

"He's *not* here," Olyvria said disappointedly. All the candles and lamps were out; even with them burning, Phostis would have found the shop too dim. Awls and punches, little hammers and trimming knives hung in neat rows on pegs behind the cobbler's bench. No one came out from the back room to answer the bell.

"Maybe he was taken ill," Phostis said. Something else ran through his mind: *Or maybe he'd rather starve himself to death than work any more.* But no, probably not. She'd said he was a Vaspurakaner, not a Thanasiot.

"Here's a scrap of parchment." Olyvria pounced on it. "See if you can find pen and ink. I'll leave him the shoe and a note." She clicked her tongue between her teeth. "I hope he reads Videssian. I'm not sure. Someone could easily have painted that word on the wall for him."

"Here." Phostis discovered a little clay jar of ink and a reed pen below the tools. "He reads something, anyhow, or I don't think he'd have these."

"That's true. Thanks." Olyvria scribbled a couple of lines, put her broken shoe on the bench, and secured the parchment to it with a long rawhide lace. "There. That should be all right. If he can't read Videssian, he ought to know someone who can. I hope he's well."

A donkey went by outside. Its hooves made little wet sucking noises as it lifted them from the mud one after another. It let out a braying squeal of discontent at being ridden in such dreadful conditions. "Ahh, quit your bellyaching," growled the man on its back, who was plainly used to its complaints. The donkey brayed again as it squelched past the cobbler's shop.

But for the donkey, everything was still save far off in the distance, where a dog barked. Olyvria took a small step toward the door. "I suppose I should get back," she said.

"Wait," Phostis said.

She raised a questioning eyebrow. He put his arms around her and bent his face down to hers. Before their lips touched, she pulled back a little and whispered, "Are you sure?" In the murky light, the pupils of her eyes were enormous.

He wondered how she meant that, but it could have only one answer. "Yes, I'm sure."

"Well, then." Now she moved forward to kiss him.

She hesitated once more, just for a heartbeat, when his hand closed on the firm softness of her breast. But then she molded herself against him. They sank down to the rammed-earth floor of the cobbler's shop together, fumbling at each other's garments.

It was the usual clumsy first time, made more frantic than usual by fear that someone—most likely the cobbler—would walk through the door at the most inopportune moment possible. "Hurry!" Olyvria gasped.

Phostis did his best to oblige. Afterward, because he'd rushed so, he wasn't sure he'd fully satisfied her. At the time, he didn't worry about it. His mouth slid from hers to her breasts and down the rounded slope of her belly. Her hand was urgent on him. She lay on her rumpled dress. A fold of it got distractingly between them when he scrambled above her. He leaned on one elbow to yank it out of the way. He kissed her again as he slid inside.

When he was through, he sat back on his haunches, enormously pleased with the entire world. Olyvria hissed, "Get dressed, you lackwit," which brought him back to himself in a hurry. They both dressed quickly, then spent another minute or so dusting off each other's clothes. Olyvria stirred the dirt of the floor around with her foot to cover up the marks they'd left. She looked Phostis over. "Your elbow's dirty." She licked a fingertip with a catlike dab of her tongue and rubbed it clean.

He held the door for her. They both almost bounded out of the cobbler's shop. Once out on the street again, Phostis said, "Now what?"

"I just don't know," Olyvria answered after a small pause. "I have to think." Her voice was quiet, almost toneless, as if she'd left behind all her exuberance, all her mischief, with the broken shoe. "I didn't—quite—expect to do that."

Phostis hadn't seen her at a loss before; he didn't know what to make of it. "I didn't expect to, either." He knew his grin was foolish, but he couldn't help it. "I'm glad we did, though."

She glared at him. "Of course you are. Men always are." Then she softened, a little, and let her hand rest on his arm for a moment. "I'm not angry, not really. We have to see what happens later, that's all."

Phostis knew what he would like to have happen later, but also had a good notion that mentioning it straight out would make it less likely. Instead, he spoke obliquely. "The flesh is hard to ignore."

"Isn't it?" Olyvria glanced back at the cobbler's shop. "If we . . . well, if we do that again, we'll have to find a better place for it. My heart was in my mouth every second."

"Yes, I know. Mine, too." But they'd joined anyhow. Like Olyvria, Phostis saw he was going to have to do some hard thinking about that. By every Thanasiot standard, they'd just committed a good-sized sin. He didn't feel sinful, though. He felt relaxed and happy and ready to tackle anything the world threw at him.

Olyvria might have plucked that thought right out of his brain. She said, "You don't have to worry if you're with child till the moon spins through its phases."

That sobered him. He didn't have to worry about conceiving, not directly, but if Olyvria's belly started to swell, what would Livanios do? He might force a marriage on them, if that fit into his own schemes. But if it didn't . . . He might act like any outraged father, and beat Phostis within an inch of his life or even kill him. Or he might give him over to the clergy. The priests of the Thanasioi took a very dim view of carnal pleasures. Their punishments might make him wish Livanios had personally attended to the matter—and, to add humiliation to anguish, would have the vociferous approval of most of the townsfolk.

"Whatever happens, I'll take care of you," he said at last.

"How do you propose to manage that?" she asked with a woman's bitter practicality. "You can't even take care of yourself."

Phostis flinched. He knew she spoke the truth, but having his nose rubbed in it stung. As the Avtokrator's son, he'd never really had to worry about taking care of himself. He was taken care of, simply by virtue—or fault—of his birth. Here in Etchmiadzin, he was also taken care of: as a prisoner. The amount of freedom he'd lost was smaller than it seemed at first glance.

At Krispos' insistence, he'd studied logic. He saw only one

possible conclusion. "I'll have to get out. If you like, I'll take you with me."

As soon as the words left his mouth, he knew he should have kept them in there. Having her laugh at him would be bad enough. Having her tell her father would be a thousand times worse.

She didn't laugh. She said, "Don't try to run. You'd just be caught, and then you'd never get another chance."

"But how can I stay here?" he demanded. "Even under the best of circumstances, I'm—" He hesitated, but finished the thought as he'd intended. "—I'm not a Thanasiot, nor likely to become one. I know that now."

"I know what you mean," Olyvria answered unhappily. Phostis noted she had not said she agreed with him. She shook her head. "I'd better go." She hurried away.

He started to call after her, but in the end did not. He kicked at the gluey ground underfoot. In the romances, all your problems were supposed to be over when you made love to the beautiful girl. Olyvria was pretty enough, no doubt about that. But as far as Phostis could see, making love to her had only complicated his life further.

He wondered why the romances were so popular if they were also so far removed from actuality. That notion disturbed him; he thought the popular should match the real. Then he realized that simple paintings in bright colors might be easier to appreciate than more highly detailed ones—and honey was sweeter than the usual mix of flavors life presented.

None of which helped him in his present complexities. Here at last he'd found a woman who, he believed, wanted him only for himself, not because of the rank he held or the advantage she might gain from sleeping with him—and who was she? Not just the woman who had kidnapped him and who was the daughter of the rebel who held him prisoner. That would have been muddle enough by itself. But there was more. For all her fencing with him about it, he knew she took Thanasiot principles seriously—a lot more seriously than Livanios, if Phostis was any judge. And Thanasios, to put it mildly, had not thought well of the flesh.

Phostis still distrusted his own flesh, too. But he was coming to the sometimes reluctant conclusion that it was part of what made him himself, not just an unfortunate adjunct to his spirit that ought to be discarded as quickly as possible.

Almost as vividly as if he were in her arms again, he remembered the feel of Olyvria's warm, sweet body pressed against him. Sometimes he was not so reluctant about that conclusion, too. He knew he wanted her again, when and as he got the chance.

Digenis would not have approved. He knew that, too. Now, though, he hadn't talked with the fiery priest, or come under the spell of his words, for several months. And he'd seen far more of the way the Thanasioi ran their lives than he had when he'd listened to Digenis back in Videssos the city. Much of it he still found admirable—much of it, but a long way from all. Reality had a way of intruding on Digenis' bright word-pictures, no less than on those of the romancers.

If Olyvria was heading back toward the fortress of Etchmiadzin, Phostis decided he ought to stay away awhile longer, so as not to make anyone there draw a connection between them. It was a nice calculation. If he just followed her back, he might arouse suspicion. If he stayed away too long, Syagrios would track him like hound after hare. He didn't want Syagrios to have to do that; it would anger the ruffian, and Phostis cherished the limited freedom he'd so slowly regained.

He had a few coins in his belt pouch, winnings at the battle game. He spent a silver piece on a leg of roasted fowl and a hard roll, then carefully put the coppers from his change back into the pouch. He'd learned about haggling: it was what you did when you were short of money. He'd got good at it. Despite Krispos' firm hand, he'd never been short of money before he ended up in Etchmiadzin.

He was chewing on the roll when Artapan strode by. The wizard, full of his own affairs, didn't notice him. Phostis decided to try to find out where he was going in such a hurry. Ever since he'd realized Artapan was from Makuran, he'd wondered just how the mage fit into Livanios' plans ... or perhaps how Livanios fit into Artapan's plans. Maybe now he could learn.

He'd followed the wizard for half a furlong before he realized he was liable to get in trouble if Artapan did discover him dogging his tracks. He tried to be sneakier, keeping people and, once, a donkey cart between the mage and him, dodging from doorway to doorway.

After another couple of minutes, he concluded he could do just about anything short of walking up, tapping Artapan on the shoulder, and asking him for the time of day. Artapan plainly had something on his mind. He looked neither to the left nor to the right, and marched down the muddy streets of Etchmiadzin as if they were cobblestoned boulevards.

The wizard rapped on the door of a house separated from its neighbors by dank, narrow alleys. After a moment, he went inside. Phostis ducked into one of the alleys. He promptly regretted it: someone was in the habit of dumping slops there. The stink almost made him cough. He jammed a sleeve into his mouth and breathed hard through his nose till the spasm passed.

But he did not leave. A little slit window let him hear what was going on inside. He wouldn't have put a window there, but maybe it had been made before anyone started emptying chamber pots in the alley.

Artapan was saying, "How fare you today, supremely holy Tzepeas?"

The answer came in a dragging whisper: "Soon I shall be free. Skotos and his entrapping world cling hard to me; already most who abandon what is falsely called nourishment for as long as I have are on the journey behind the sun. But still I remain wrapped in the flesh that disfigures the soul."

*What do you want with one who has starved himself to the point of death?* Phostis almost shouted it at the Makuraner wizard. *If he's chosen to do it, let him alone with his choice.*

"You want, then, to leave this world?" Artapan's accented voice held wonder. Phostis wondered about that: the Four Prophets had their holy ascetics, too. "What will you find, do you think?"

"Light!" Just for a word, Tzepeas' voice came strong and clear, as if he were a well-fed man rather than a shivering bag of bones. As he continued, it faded again. "I shall be part of Phos' eternal light. Too long have I lingered in this sin-filled place."

"Would you seek help in leaving it?" Artapan had moved while Tzepeas was talking. Now he sounded as if he was right beside the starving Thanasiot.

"I don't know," Tzepeas said. "Is it permitted?"

"Of course," the wizard answered smoothly. "But a moment and you shall meet your good god face to face."

"*My* good god?" Tzepeas said indignantly. "He is *the* good god, the lord with the great and good mind. He—" The zealot's voice, which had risen again, suddenly broke off. Phostis heard a couple of very faint thumps, as if a man with no muscles left was trying to struggle against someone far stronger than he.

The thumps soon ceased. Artapan began a soft chant, partly in the Makuraner tongue—which Phostis did not understand—and partly in Videssian. Phostis knew he was missing some of what the mage said, but what he heard was quite enough: unless he'd gone completely mad, he could only conclude Artapan was using Tzepeas' death energy to further his own sorceries.

Phostis' stomach lurched harder than it ever had while sailing on the Videssian Sea. He sickly wondered how many starving Thanasioi hadn't finished the course they set out to travel, but were instead shoved from it by the Makuraner wizard for his own purposes. The one was bad enough; the other struck Phostis as altogether abominable. And who would ever know?

Artapan came out of the house. Phostis flattened himself against the wall. The wizard walked on by. He wasn't quite rubbing his hands with glee, but he gave that impression. Again, he had no time to look around for details as small as Phostis.

Phostis waited until he was sure Artapan was gone, then cautiously emerged from the alley. "What do I do now?" he said out loud. His first thought was to run to Livanios with the story as fast as his legs would carry him. A version of the tale he'd tell formed in his mind: *After I'd had your daughter, I found out your pet wizard was going around killing devout Thanasioi before they could die on their own.* He shook his head. Like a lot of first thoughts, that one needed some work.

All right, suppose he managed not to mention Olyvria and also managed to convince Livanios he was telling the truth about Artapan. What then? How much good would that do him? If Livanios didn't know what the mage was up to, maybe quite a lot. But what if he did?

In that case, the only thing Phostis saw in his own future

was a lot more trouble—something he'd not imagined possible when he woke up after Olyvria drugged him. And he could not tell whether Livanios knew or not.

It came down to the question he'd been asking himself ever since he learned Artapan's name: was Livanios the wizard's puppet, or the other way round? He didn't know the answer to that, either, or how to find out.

*From Olyvria,* he thought. But even she might well not know for certain. She'd know what her father thought, but that might not be what was so. Videssian history was littered with men who'd thought themselves in charge—until the worlds they'd made crashed down around them. Anthimos had been sure he held a firm grip on the Empire—until Krispos took it away from him.

And so, when Phostis got back to the fortress, he did not go looking for Livanios. Instead, he headed over to the corner where, as usual, several men gathered around a couple of players hunched over the game board.

The soldiers moved away from him, wrinkling their noses. One of them said, "You may have been born a toff, friend, but you smell like you've been wading in shit."

Phostis remembered the stinking alleyway where he'd stood. He should have done a better job of cleaning his shoes after he came out. Then he thought of what Artapan had done in the house by the alleyway. How was he supposed to clean that from his memory?

He looked at the soldier. "Maybe I have," he said.

# IX

WALL, ROOFS, STREETS, NEW LEAVES—ALL GLISTENED WITH rain under the bright sun. It made them seem to Krispos brighter and more vivid than they really were, as if the shower—or perhaps the season—had washed the whole world clean.

The clouds that had dropped the rain on Videssos the city were now just small, gray, fluffy lumps diminishing toward the east. The rest of the sky was the glorious blue the enamel makers kept trying—and failing—to match with glass paste.

With the wary eye of one who has had to watch the weather for the sake of his crops, Krispos looked not east at the receding rain clouds but west, whence new weather would come. He tasted the breeze between his tongue and the roof of his mouth. That it came straight off the sea gave it a salt tang he'd not had to worry about in his peasant days, but he'd learned to allow for that. He sucked in another breath, tasting that one, too.

When at last he spat it out, he'd made up his mind. "Spring is really here," he declared.

"Your Majesty has in the past been remarkably accurate with such predictions," Barsymes said, as close as he ever came to alluding to Krispos' decidedly unimperial birth.

"It matters more this year than most," Krispos said, "for as soon as I can be sure—or at least can expect—the roads will stay dry, I have to move against the Thanasioi. The less chance they have of getting loose and raiding, the better off the westlands and the whole Empire will be."

"The city has stayed quiet since Midwinter's Day, for which Phos be praised."

"Aye." Whenever Krispos prayed, he made a point of reminding the good god how grateful he was for that. He still did not completely trust the calm that had prevailed through winter and now up to the borderland of spring: he kept wondering whether he was walking on a thin crust of ice over freezing water—the images from Skotos' hell seemed particularly fitting. If the crust ever broke, he might be dragged down to doom. But so far it had held.

"I believe your Majesty handled the matter of the priest Digenis with as much discretion as was practicable," the vestiarios said.

"Just letting him go out like a guttering taper, you mean? All he wanted to do was raise a ruction. Smothering his end in silence is the best revenge on him; if Phos is kind, the chroniclers will forget his name as the people have—so far— forgotten to rally to the cause he preached."

Barsymes looked at him out of the corners of his eyes that had seen so much. "And when you fare forth on campaign, your Majesty, will you then leave Videssos the city ungarrisoned?"

"Oh, of course," Krispos answered, and laughed to make sure his vestiarios knew he was not in earnest. "Wouldn't that be lovely, beating the Thanasioi in the field and coming back to find my capital closed against me? It won't happen, not if I can find any way around it."

"Whom shall you name to command the city garrison?" Barsymes asked.

"Do you know, esteemed sir, I was thinking of giving the job to Evripos." Krispos spoke in a deliberately neutral tone. If Barsymes had anything to say against the appointment of his middle son, he didn't want to intimidate the eunuch into keeping his mouth shut.

Barsymes tasted the appointment with the same sort of thoughtful attention Krispos had given to the weather. After a similar pause for that consideration, the vestiarios answered, "That may serve very nicely, your Majesty. By all accounts, the young Majesty acquitted himself well in the westlands."

"He did," Krispos agreed. "Not only that, soldiers followed where he led, which is a magic that can't be taught. I'll also leave behind some steady officer who can try to keep him from doing anything too rash if the need arises."

"That's sensible," Barsymes replied, saying by not saying that he would have reckoned Krispos daft for doing anything else. "It will be valuable experience for the young Majesty, especially if—if other matters do not eventuate as we would desire."

"Phostis still lives," Krispos said suddenly. "Zaidas' sorcery continues to confirm that, and he's fairly sure Phostis is in Etchmiadzin, where the rebels seem to have their headquarters. He's made real headway in penetrating the masking sorcery since we realized it springs from Makuran." His briefly kindled enthusiasm faded fast. "Of course, he has no way of telling what Phostis believes these days."

There lay the nut of it, as was Krispos' way, in one sentence. The Avtokrator shook his head. Phostis was so young; who could say what latest enthusiasm he'd seized on? At that same age, Krispos knew he'd had a good core of solid sense. But at just past twenty, he'd been a peasant still, and he could imagine no stronger dose of reality than that. Phostis had grown up in the palaces, where flights of fancy were far more easily sustained. And Phostis had always taken pleasure in going dead against whatever Krispos had in mind.

"What of Katakolon?" Barsymes asked.

"I'll take him with me—I'll need one spatharios, at any rate," Krispos said. "He did tolerably well in the westlands himself, and rather better than that during the Midwinter's Day riots. One thing these past few months have taught me: all my sons need such training in command as I can give them. Counting on Phos' mercy instead of providing for the times to come is foolish and wasteful."

"Few have accused your Majesty of harboring those traits—none truthfully."

"For which, believe me, you have my thanks," Krispos said. "Find Evripos for me, would you? I've not yet told him what I have in mind."

"Of course, your Majesty." Barsymes went back inside the imperial residence. Krispos stood and enjoyed the sunshine. The cherry trees around the residence were putting on leaves; soon, for a few glorious weeks, they'd be a riot of sweet pink and white blossoms. Krispos' thoughts drifted away from them and back toward raising troops, moving troops, supplying troops . . .

He sighed. Being Avtokrator meant having to worry about things you'd rather ignore. He wondered if the rebels he'd put down ever realized how much work the job of ruling the Empire really was. He certainly hadn't, back when he took it away from Anthimos.

*If I thought Livanios wouldn't botch things, I ought to give him the crown and let him see how he likes it,* he thought angrily. But he knew that would never happen: the only way Livanios would take the crown from him was by prying it out of his dead fingers.

"What is it, Father?" Evripos asked, coming up in Barsymes' wake. The wariness in his voice was different from what Krispos was used to hearing from Phostis. Phostis and he simply disagreed every chance they got. Evripos resented being born second; it made his opinions not worth serious disagreement.

Or it had made them so. Now Krispos explained what he had in mind for his son. "This is serious business," he emphasized. "If real trouble does come, I won't want you throwing out orders at random. That's why I'll leave a steady captain with you. I expect you to heed his advice on matters military."

Evripos had puffed out his chest with pride at the trust Krispos placed in him. Now he said, "But what if I think he's wrong, Father?"

*Obey him anyhow,* Krispos started to say. But the words did not pass his lips. He remembered when Petronas had maneuvered him into the position of vestiarios for Anthimos. The then-Avtokrator's uncle had made it very clear that he expected nothing but obedience to him from Krispos. He remembered asking Petronas a question very similar to the one he'd just heard from Evripos.

"You have command," he said slowly. "If you think your advisor is wrong, you'd better do what you reckon right. But you have to remember, son, that with command comes responsibility. If you choose to go against the officer I give you and your course goes wrong, you will answer to me. Do you understand?"

"Aye, Father, I do. You're telling me I'd better be sure—and even if I am sure, I'd better be right. Is that the meat of it?"

"That's it exactly," Krispos agreed. "I'm not putting you in this place as part of a game, Evripos. The post is not only real but also important. A mistake would be important, too, in how much damage it could do. So if you go off on your own, against the advice of a man older and wiser than you are, what you do had better not turn out badly, for your sake and the Empire's both."

With the prickliness of youth, Evripos bristled like a hedgehog. "How do you know this officer you'll appoint for me will be smarter than I am?"

"I didn't say that. You're as smart as you'll ever be, son, and I have no reason to doubt that's very smart indeed. But you're not as wise as you're going to be, say, twenty years from now. Wisdom comes from using the wits you have to think on what's happened to you during your life, and you haven't lived long enough yet to have stored up much of it."

Evripos looked eloquently unconvinced. Krispos didn't blame him; at Evripos' age, he hadn't believed experience mattered, either. Now that he had a good deal of it, he was sure he'd been wrong before—but the only way for Evripos to come to the same conclusion was with the slow passage of the years. He couldn't afford to wait for that.

His middle son said, "Suppose this officer you name suggests a course I think is wrong, but I go along with it for fear of what you've just said. And suppose it does turn out to be the wrong course. What then, Father?"

"Maybe you should be pleading your case in the courts, not commanding men in the field," Krispos said. But the question was too much to the point to be answered with a sour joke. Slowly, the Avtokrator went on, "If I put you in the post, you will be the commander. When the time comes, making the judgment will be up to you. That's the hardest burden anyone can lay on a man. If you don't care to bear it, speak up now."

"Oh, I'll bear it, Father. I just wanted to be sure I understood what you were asking of me," Evripos said.

"Good," Krispos said. "I'll give you one piece of advice and one only—I know how you won't much care to listen. It's just this: if you have to decide, do it firmly. No matter how much doubt, no matter how much fear and trembling you feel, don't let it show. Half the business of leading people is just keeping up a solid front."

"That may be worth remembering," Evripos said, as big a concession as Krispos knew he was likely to get. His son asked, "What will Katakolon be doing while I'm here in the city?"

"He'll go the westlands as my spatharios. Another campaign will do him good, I think."

"Ah." If Evripos wanted to take issue with that, he didn't find any way to manage it. After a pause a tiny bit longer than a more experienced man would have given, he nodded brusquely and changed the subject. "I hope I'll serve as you'd have me do, Father."

"I hope you will, too. I don't see any reason why you shouldn't. If the lord with the great and good mind hears my prayers, you'll have a quiet time of it. I don't really *want* you to see action here; you'd better understand that. The less fighting there is, the happier I'll be."

"Then why take the army out?" Evripos asked.

Krispos sighed. "Because sometimes it's needful, as you know very well. If I don't go to the fighting this summer, it will come to me. Given that choice, I'd sooner do it on my own terms, or as nearly as I can."

"Aye, that makes sense," Evripos said after a moment's thought. "Sometimes the world won't let you have things all as you'd like them."

He was probably speaking from bitterness at not being first in line for the throne. Nonetheless, Krispos was moved to reach out and set a hand on his shoulder. "That's an important truth, son. You'd do well to remember it." It was, he thought, a truth Phostis hadn't fully grasped—but then Phostis, as firstborn, hadn't had the need. Each son was so different from the other two ... "Where's Katakolon? Do you know?"

Evripos pointed. "One of the rooms down that hallway: second or third on the left, I think."

"Thanks." Later, Krispos realized he hadn't asked what his youngest son was doing. If Evripos knew, he kept his mouth shut, a useful ploy he might well have picked up from his father. Krispos walked down the hallway. The second chamber on the left, a sewing room for the serving women, was empty.

The door to the third room on the left was closed. Krispos worked the latch. He saw a tangle of bare arms and legs, heard a couple of horrified squawks, and shut the door again in a hurry. He stood chuckling in the hall until Katakolon, his robe rumpled and his face red, came out a couple of minutes later.

He let Katakolon steer him down the corridor, and was anything but surprised to hear the door open and close behind him. He didn't look back, but started to laugh. Katakolon gave him a dirty look. "What's so funny?"

"You are," Krispos answered. "I do apologize for interrupting."

Katakolon's glare got blacker, but he seemed confused as well as annoyed. "Is that all you're going to say?"

"Yes, I think so. After all, it's nothing I haven't seen before. Remember, I was Anthimos' vestiarios." He decided not to go into detail about Anthimos' orgies. Katakolon was too likely to try imitating them.

Looking at his youngest son's face, Krispos had all he could do to keep from laughing again. Katakolon was obviously having heavy going imagining his rather paunchy, gray-bearded father reveling with an Avtokrator who, even after a generation, remained a byword for debauchery of all sorts.

Krispos patted his son on the back. "You have to bear in mind, lad, that once upon a time I wasn't a creaking elder. I had the same yen for good wine and bad women as any other young man."

"Yes, Father," Katakolon said, but not as if he believed it.

Sighing, Krispos said, "If you have too much trouble picturing me with a zest for life, try to imagine Iakovitzes, say, as a young man. The exercise will do your wits good."

He gave Katakolon credit: the youth visibly did try. After a few seconds, he whistled. "He'd have been something, wouldn't he?"

"Oh, he was," Krispos said. "He's still something, come to that."

All at once, he wondered if Iakovitzes had ever tried his blandishments on Katakolon. He didn't think the old lecher would have got anywhere; like his other two sons, his youngest seemed interested only in women. If Iakovitzes had ever tried to seduce Katakolon or one of the other boys, they'd never brought Krispos the tale.

"Now let me tell you why I interrupted you at a tender moment—" Krispos explained what he had in mind for the most junior Avtokrator.

"Of course, Father. I'll come with you, and help as I can," Katakolon said when he was done; of the three boys, he was the most tractable. Even the stubborn streak he shared with his brothers and Krispos was in him good-natured. "I don't expect I'll be busy every moment, and some of the provincial lasses last summer were tastier than I'd have expected away from the capital. When do we start out?"

"As soon as the roads are dry." Dry himself, Krispos added, "You won't be devastating the local girls by leaving quite yet."

"All right," Katakolon said. "In that case, if you'll excuse me—" He started down the hall, more purpose in his stride than on any mission for his father. Krispos wondered if he'd burned that hot at seventeen. He probably had, but he had almost as much trouble believing it as Katakolon did in placing him at one of Anthimos' revels.

Livanios addressed his assembled fighters: "Soon we fare forth, both to fight and to advance along the gleaming path. We shall not go alone. By the lord with the great and good mind, I swear our trouble will not be raising men but rather making sure we are not overwhelmed by those who would join us. We shall spread across the countryside like a fire through grassland; no one and nothing can hold us back."

The men cheered. By their look, a good many of them were herders from the westlands' central plateau: lean, weatherbeaten, sunbaked men intimately acquainted with grass fires. Now they carried javelins in their hands, not staves. They were not the best-disciplined troops in the world, but fanaticism went a long way toward making up for sloppy formations.

Phostis cheered when everyone else did. Standing there silent and glum would have got him noticed, and not in a way he wanted. He was trying to cultivate invisibility, the way a farmer cultivated radishes. He wished Livanios would forget he existed.

The heresiarch was in full spate: "The leeches who live in Videssos the city think they can suck our life's blood forever. We'll show them they're wrong, by the good god, and if the gleaming path leads through the smoking ruins of the palaces built from poor men's blood, why then, it does."

More cheers. Phostis didn't feel quite such a hypocrite in joining these: the ostentatious wealth the capital held was what had made him flirt with the doctrines of the Thanasioi in the first place. But Livanios' speech was a harangue and nothing more. If any Avtokrator of recent generations was sensitive to the peasant's plight, it was Krispos. Phostis was sick of hearing how his father had been taxed off his land, but he knew the experience made Krispos want not to visit it on anyone else.

"We'll hang up the fat ecclesiastics by their thumbs, too," Livanios shouted. "Whatever gold the Emperors don't get, the clerics do. Has Phos the need for fancy houses?"

"No!" the men roared back, and Phostis with them. In spite of everything, he still had some sympathy for what Thanasios had preached. He wondered if Livanios could truly say the same. And he wondered still more just how much hold Artapan had on the rebel leader. He was no closer to knowing that for certain than he had been on the day when he and Olyvria first became lovers.

Whenever she crossed his mind, his blood ran hotter. Digenis would have scolded him, or more likely given up on him as an incorrigible sinner and sensualist. He didn't care. He wanted her more with every passing day—and he knew she also wanted him.

They'd managed to join twice more since that first time: once late at night up in his little cell while the guard snored down the hall and once in a quiet corridor carved into the stone beneath the keep. Both couplings were almost as hurried and frantic as the first had been; neither was what Phostis had in mind when he thought of making love. But they inflamed him and Olyvria for more.

Was what he felt the love of which the romancers sang? He knew little firsthand of love; around the palaces, seduction and hedonism were more often on display. His own father and mother seemed to have got on well, but he'd still been a boy when Dara died. Zaidas and Aulissa were called a love match, but the wizard—aside from being Krispos' crony, which of itself made him suspect—had to be close to forty: could an old man really be in love?

Phostis couldn't tell if he was in love himself. All he knew was that he missed Olyvria desperately, that when they were apart every moment dragged as if it were an hour, that every stolen hour together somehow flashed by like a moment.

Lost in his own thoughts, he missed Livanios' last few sentences. They brought loud cheers from the assembled soldiers. Phostis cheered, too, as he had all through the heresiarch's speech.

Then one of the fighters who knew who he was turned round and slapped him on the back. "So you're going to fight with us for the gleaming path, are you, friend?" the fellow boomed. His grin had almost as many gaps as Syagrios'.

"I'm going to what?" Phostis said foolishly. It wasn't that he didn't believe his ears: more that he didn't want to.

"Sure—like Livanios said just now." The soldier wrinkled his brow, trying to recall his chief's exact words. "Take up the blade against maternalism—something like that, anyways."

"Materialism," Phostis corrected before he wondered why he bothered.

"Yeah, that's it," the soldier said happily. "Thank you, friend. By the good god, I'm right glad the Emperor's son's taken up with righteousness."

Moving as if in a daze, Phostis made his way toward the citadel. Fighters who recognized him kept coming up and congratulating him on taking up arms for the Thanasiot cause. By the time he got inside, he was sore and bruised, while his wits had taken a worse pummeling than his back.

Livanios was using his name to raise the spirits of the Thanasiot warriors: so much was clear. But life in the palace, while it left Phostis ignorant of love, made him look beneath the surface of machinations with as little effort as he used to breathe.

Not only would his name spur on the followers of the gleaming path, it would also dismay those who clove to his father. And if he fought alongside the Thanasioi, he might never be reconciled with Krispos.

Further, Livanios might arrange a hero's death for him. That would embarrass the Avtokrator as much as having him alive and fighting, and would hurt Krispos a good deal more. And it would serve Livanios' ends very well indeed.

Syagrios found Phostis. Phostis might have guessed the ruffian would come looking for him. From the nasty grin on Syagrios' face, he'd known about Livanios' scheme before the heresiarch announced it to his men. In fact, Phostis thought with the taut nerves of a man who genuinely has been persecuted, Syagrios might well have come up with it himself.

"So you're going to be a man before your mother, are you, stripling?" he said, making cut-and-thrust motions right in front of Phostis' face. "Go out there and make the gleaming path proud of you, boy."

"I'll do what I can." Phostis was aware of the ambiguity, but let it lay. He did not want to hear Syagrios speak of his mother. He wanted to smash the ruffian for presuming to speak of her. Only a well-founded apprehension that Syagrios would smash him instead kept him from trying it.

That was yet another thing the romances didn't talk about. Their heroes always beat the villains just because they *were* heroes. No writer of romances, Phostis was certain, had ever met Syagrios. For that matter, both sides here thought they were heroes and their foes villains. *I swear by the good god I'll never read another romance again as long as I live,* Phostis thought.

Syagrios said, "I don't know what you know about weapons, but whatever it is, you better practice it. Whoever you fight ain't gonna care that you're the Avtokrator's brat."

"I suppose not," Phostis said in a hollow voice that set Syagrios laughing anew. He'd actually had some training; his father had thought he'd find it useful. He didn't mention it. The more hopeless a dub everyone took him for, the less attention people would pay him.

He went up the black spiral stairway to his little chamber. When he opened the door, his mouth fell open in astonishment: Olyvria waited inside. He was not too surprised, however, to shut the door behind him as fast as he could. "What are you doing here?" he demanded. "Do you want to get us both caught?"

She grinned at him. "What could be safer?" she whispered back. "Everyone in the keep was down in the courtyard listening to my father."

Phostis wanted to rush to her and take her in his arms, but that brought him up short. "Yes, and do you know what your father said?" he whispered, and went on to explain exactly what Livanios had announced.

"Oh, no," Olyvria said, still in a tiny voice. "He wants you dead, then. I prayed he wouldn't."

"That's what I think, too," Phostis agreed bitterly. "But what can I do about it?"

"I don't know." Olyvria reached out to him. He hurried over to her. Her touch made him, if not forget everything else, then at least reckon it unimportant for as long as he held her. But he remembered how careful they had to be even while her thighs clasped his flanks; what should have been sighs of delight came from both of them as tiny hisses.

As they'd grown used to doing, they set their clothes to rights as fast as they could when they were through. Not for them the pleasure of lying lazily by each other afterward. "How will we get you out of here?" Phostis whispered. Before Olyvria could say anything, he found the answer for himself: "I'll go downstairs. Whoever's out there—probably Syagrios—will follow me. Once we're gone, you can come down, too."

Olyvria nodded. "Yes, that's very good. It should work; few of the rooms in this hallway have people in them, so I'm not likely to be seen till I'm safely down." She looked at him with some of her old calculation. He liked the soft looks he usually got from her these days better. But she said, "You wouldn't have found a plan so fast when we first brought you here."

"Maybe not," he admitted. "I've had to take care of a good many things I wasn't in the habit of doing for myself." He touched the very tip of her breast through her tunic, just for a moment. "Some of them I like better than others."

"You don't mean I'm your first?" That thought almost startled her into raising her voice; he made an alarmed gesture. But she was already shaking her head. "No, I couldn't have been."

"No, of course not," he said. "You're the first who matters, though."

She leaned forward and brushed her lips against his. "That's a sweet thing to say. It must not have been easy for you, growing up as you did."

He shrugged. He supposed the problem was that he just thought too much. Evripos and especially Katakolon seemed to have had no trouble enjoying themselves immensely. But all that was by the way. He got to his feet. "I'll leave you now. Listen to make sure everything's quiet before you come out." He took a step toward the door, stopped, then turned back to Olyvria. "I love you."

Her arched eyebrows lifted. "You hadn't said that before. I

love you—but then you know I must, or I wouldn't be here in spite of my father."

"Yes." Phostis thought he knew that, but he'd been raised to see plots, so sometimes he found them even when they weren't there. Here, though, he had to—and wanted to—take the chance.

He stepped into the hallway. Sure enough, there sat Syagrios. The ruffian leered at him. "So you found out you can't hide in there, did you? Now what are you going to do, head down and celebrate that you got turned into a soldier?"

"As a matter of fact, yes," Phostis answered. He had the somber satisfaction of seeing Syagrios' jaw sag. After lighting a taper to keep from killing himself on the dark stairway, he headed down toward the ground floor of the keep. Syagrios muttered under his breath but followed. Phostis had all he could do to keep from whistling on the stairs: letting Syagrios know he'd put one over on him wouldn't do.

Outside the southern end of the great double wall that warded the landward side of Videssos the city lay a broad stretch of meadow on which the Empire's cavalry practiced their maneuvers. Fresh new grass poked through the mud and the dead grayish remains of last year's growth as Krispos came out to watch his soldiers exercise.

"Don't be too hard on them too soon, your Majesty," Sarkis urged. "They're still ragged from being cooped up through the winter."

"I know that—we have done this business a few times before," Krispos answered, amiably enough. "But we'll go on campaign as soon as weather and supplies allow, and if they're still ragged then, it will cost lives and maybe battles."

"They won't be." Sarkis put grim promise into his voice. Krispos smiled; he'd hoped to hear that note.

A company rode hard toward upright bales of hay that simulated an enemy. They drew up eighty or ninety yards away, plied the targets with arrows as rapidly as they could draw bow, and then, at an officer's command, yanked out their swords and charged the imaginary foe with fierce and sanguinary roars.

The iron blades glittering in the bright sun made a fine martial spectacle. Nonetheless, Krispos turned to Sarkis and remarked, "This whole business of war would be a lot easier if the Thanasioi didn't fight back any harder than those bales."

Sarkis' doughy face twitched in a grin. "Isn't it the truth, your Majesty? Every general wants every campaign to be a walkover, but you can make yourself a reputation that will live forever if you get one of those in a lifetime. The trouble is, you see, the chap on the other side wants his walkover, too, and doesn't much care to cooperate in yours. Rude and inconsiderate of him, if you ask me."

"At the very least," Krispos agreed. After the company of archers reassembled well beyond the hay bales, another unit approached and pelted the targets with javelins. Farther away, a regiment split in two to get in some more realistic mounted swordwork. They tried not to hurt one another in practices like that, but Krispos knew the healers would have some extra work tonight.

"Their spirits seem as high as you could hope for," Sarkis said judiciously. "No hesitation about going out for another crack at the heretics, anyhow." He used the word with no irony whatever, though his own beliefs were anything but orthodox.

Krispos didn't twit him about it, not today. After some thought, he'd figured out the difference between the Vaspurakaners' heterodoxy and that of the Thanasioi. The "princes" might not want any part of that version of the faith that emanated from Videssos the city, but they also weren't interested in imposing their version on Videssos the city. Krispos could live with that.

He said, "Where do you suppose the Thanasioi will pop up this season?"

"Wherever they can make the worst nuisances of themselves," Sarkis answered at once. "Livanios proved how dangerous he is last year. He won't hurt us in a small way if he has the chance to hurt us in a big one."

Since that accorded all too well with Krispos' view of the situation, he only grunted by way of reply. Not far away, a youngster in gilded chain mail rode up to the hay-bale targets and flung light spears at them. Katakolon's aim wasn't bad, but could have been better.

Krispos cupped his hands to his mouth and yelled, "Everybody knows you can use your lance, son, but you've got to get the javelin down, too!"

Katakolon's head whipped around. He spotted his father and stuck out his tongue at him. Ribald howls rose from the horsemen who heard. Sarkis' chuckle held dry amusement. "You'll give him a reputation that way. I suppose it's what you have in mind."

"As a matter of fact, yes. If you're a lecher at my age, you're a laughingstock, but young men pride themselves on how hard they can go—so to speak."

"So to speak, indeed." Sarkis chuckled again, even more dryly than before. Then he sighed. "We ought to get some practice in ourselves. Battles take funny turns sometimes."

"So we should." Krispos sighed, too. "The good god knows I'll be sore for a long time after I start working, though. I begin to see I won't be able to go out on a campaign forever."

"You?" Sarkis ran a hand along his own corpulent frame. "Your Majesty, you're still svelte. I've put almost another me inside my mail here."

Krispos made an imperial decision. "I'll start exercising—tomorrow." The trouble with being Avtokrator was that none of the demands of the job went away when you concentrated on any one thing. You had to plug leaks everywhere at once, or some of them would get beyond the plugging stage while you weren't watching.

He went back to the palaces to make sure he didn't fall too far behind on matters of trade and commerce. He was examining customs reports from Prista, the imperial outpost on the northern shore of the Videssian Sea, when someone tapped on the door to the study. He glanced up, expecting to see Barsymes or another of the chamberlains. But it was none of them—it was Drina.

His frown was almost a scowl. She should have known better than to bother him while he was working. "Yes?" he said curtly.

Drina looked more than nervous—she looked frightened. She dropped to her knees and then to her belly in a full proskynesis. Krispos took a couple of seconds to wonder about the propriety of having the woman who warmed his bed prostrate herself before him. But by the time he decided she needn't bother, she was already rising. But she kept her eyes to the floor; her voice was small and her stammer large as she began, "May it p-please your Majesty—"

With that start, it probably wouldn't. Krispos almost said as much. The only thing that held him back was a strong suspicion she'd flee if he pressed her too hard. Since she'd braved bearding him at his work, whatever she had on her mind was important to her. Trying at least to sound neutral, he asked, "What's troubling you, Drina?"

"Your Majesty, I'm pregnant," she blurted.

He opened his mouth to answer her, but no words came out. After a little while, he realized she didn't need to keep looking at the back of his throat. He needed two tries to close his mouth, but managed in the end. "You're telling me it's mine?" he got out at last.

Drina nodded. "Your Majesty, I didn't—I mean, I haven't— so it must—" She spread her hands, as if that would help her explain better than her tongue, which seemed as fumbling as Krispos'.

"Well, well," he said, and then again, because it let him make noise without making sense, "Well, well." Another pause and he produced a coherent sentence, then a second one: "I didn't expect that to happen. If it was the night I think it was, I didn't expect anything to happen."

"People never do, your Majesty." Drina tried a wary smile, but still looked ready to run away. "But it does happen, or there wouldn't be any more people after a while."

*The Thanasioi would like that,* he thought. He shook his head. Drina was too much a creature of her body and her urges ever to make a Thanasiot, just as he was himself. "An imperial bastard," he said, more to himself than to her.

"Is it your first, your Majesty?" she asked. Now fear and a peculiar sort of pride warred in her voice. She held her chin a little higher.

"The first time I've fathered a child since Dara died, you mean? No," Krispos said. "It happened twice before, as a matter of fact, but once the mother miscarried and the other time the babe lived but a couple of days. Phos' choice, not mine, if that's what you're wondering. Both were years ago; I thought my seed had gone cold. I hope your luck will be better."

Hearing that, she let her face open up like a flower suddenly touched by the sun. "Oh, thank you, your Majesty!" she breathed.

"Neither you nor the child will ever want," Krispos promised. "If you don't know I care for my own, you don't know me." For the past twenty years, the whole Empire had been his own. Maybe that was why he worried so much about every detail of its life.

"Everyone knows your Majesty is kind and generous." Drina's smile got wider still.

"Everyone doesn't know any such thing," he answered sharply. "So you don't misunderstand, here are two things I won't do: number one, I won't marry you. I won't let this babe disturb the succession if it turns out to be a boy. Trying to get me to break my word about that will be the fastest way you can think of to make me angry. Do you have that?"

"Yes," she whispered. The smile flickered.

"I'm sorry to speak so plain to you, but I want to leave you in no doubt about these matters," Krispos said. "Here is the second thing: if you have a swarm of relatives who descend on me looking for jobs with no work for high pay, they'll go home to wherever they came from with stripes on their backs. I already told you I won't stint on what I give you, and of course you may share that with whomever you like. But the fisc is not a toy and it does have a bottom. All right?"

"Your Majesty, how can the likes of me argue with whatever you choose to do?" Drina sounded frightened again.

The plain answer was that she couldn't. Krispos didn't say that; it would just have alarmed her further. What he did say was: "Go and tell Barsymes what you've just told me. Tell him I said you're to be treated with every consideration, too."

"I will, your Majesty. Thank you. Uh, your Majesty—"

"What now?" Krispos asked when she showed no sign of saying anything more than *uh*.

"Will you still want me?" she said, and then stood there as if she wished the mosaic floor would open and swallow her up. Like most Videssians, she was olive-skinned; Krispos thought he saw her blush anyhow.

He got up, came around the desk, and put an arm around her. "I expect so, now and again," he said. "But if you have some young man waiting under the Amphitheater for the next race, so to speak, don't be shy about saying so. I wouldn't have you do anything you don't care to." He'd watched Anthimos take advantage of so many women that moderation came easy to him: anything Anthimos did was a good bet to have been wrong.

"It's not that," Drina said quickly. "I just—worry that you'll forget about me."

"I already said I wouldn't. I do keep my word." Thinking she needed more reassurance than words, he patted her on the backside. She sighed and snuggled against him. He let her stay for a bit, then said, "Go on, go see Barsymes. He'll take care of you."

Snuffling a little, Drina went. Krispos stood in the study, listening to her footsteps fade as she walked down the hall. When he couldn't hear them any more, he returned to his seat and to the customs reports he'd been reviewing. But he soon found he had to shove aside the parchments: he couldn't concentrate on what was in them.

"An imperial bastard," he said quietly. "*My* bastard. Well, well, what am I going to do about that?"

He was a man who believed in making plans as implicitly as he believed in Phos. Fathering a child at his age wasn't in any of those he'd made so far. *No help for it,* he told himself. *I'll have to come up with some new ones.*

He knew he might not need them; so many children never lived to grow up. As in so many things, though, better to have and not need than to need and not have. Besides, you always hoped your children lived unless you were a fanatical Thanasiot who thought all life ought to vanish from the earth and be quick about it, too.

If he had a daughter, things would stay simple. When she grew up, he'd do his best to make sure she married someone well disposed to him. That was what marriages were for, after all: joining together families that could be useful to each other.

If he had a son, now . . . He clicked his tongue between his teeth. That would complicate matters. Some Avtokrators had their bastards made into eunuchs; some had risen to high rank in the temples or at the palace. It was certainly one way of guaranteeing the boy would never challenge his legitimate sons for the throne: being physically imperfect, eunuchs could not claim imperial rank in Videssos or Makuran or any other country he knew of.

Krispos made that clicking noise again. He wasn't sure he had the stomach for that, no matter how expedient it might be.

He stared down at the delicately veined marble desktop, wondering what to do. He was so lost in his thoughts, the tap on the door frame made him jump. He looked up. This time it was Barsymes.

"I am given to understand congratulations are in order, your Majesty?" the vestiarios said carefully.

"Thank you, esteemed sir. I'm given to understand the same thing myself." Krispos managed a rueful laugh. "Life has a way of going off on its own path, not the one you'd choose for it."

"Very true. As you have requested, every care will be given to the mother-to-be. As part of that care, I gather you will want to ensure, so far as is feasible, that she does not acquire an exaggerated notion either of her own station or that of her offspring."

"You've hit in the center of the target, Barsymes. Can you imagine me, say, disinheriting the sons I have for the sake of a by-blow? Not a cook could find a better recipe for civil war after I'm gone."

"What you say is true, your Majesty. And yet—" Barsymes stepped out into the hallway, looked right and left. Even after he was sure no one save Krispos could hear him, he lowered his voice. "And yet, your Majesty, one of your sons may be lost to you, and you've not expressed entire satisfaction with any of them."

"But why should I expect the next one to be any better?" Krispos said. "Besides, I'd have to wait twenty years to have any idea what sort of man he is, and who says I have twenty years left? I might, aye, but the odds aren't the best. So I'd sooner discommode the one young bastard than the three older legitimate boys."

"I would not think of faulting the logic; I merely wondered if your Majesty had fully considered the situation. I see you have: well and good." The vestiarios ran pale tongue across paler lips. "I also wondered if you were, ah, besotted with the mother of the child-to-be."

"So I'd do stupid things to keep her happy, you mean?" Krispos said. Barsymes nodded. Krispos started to laugh, but restrained himself—that would have been cruel. "No, esteemed sir. Drina's very pleasant, but I've not lost my head."

"Ah," Barsymes said again. He seldom showed much emotion, and this moment was no exception to the rule; nonetheless, Krispos thought he heard relief in that single syllable.

*I've not lost my head.* That might have been the watchword for his reign, and for his life. If it had left him on the cold-blooded side, it had also given the Empire of Videssos more than two decades of steady, sensible rule. There were worse exchanges.

He remembered the thought he'd had before. "Esteemed sir, may I ask a question that might perturb you? Please understand my aim is not to cause you pain, but to learn."

"Ask, your Majesty," Barsymes replied at once. "You are the Avtokrator; you have the right."

"Very well, then. To make sure dynastic problems don't come up, Avtokrators have been known to make eunuchs of their bastard offspring. You know your life as only one who lives it can. What have you to say of it?"

The vestiarios gave the question his usual grave consideration. "The pain of the gelding does not last forever, of course. I have never known desire, so I do not particularly pine for it, though that is not true of all my kind. But being set aside forever from the general run of mankind—there is the true curse of the eunuch, your Majesty. So far as any of us knows, it has no balm."

"Thank you, esteemed sir." Krispos put the thought in the place where bad ideas belong. He felt an urgent need to change the subject. "By the good god!" he exclaimed, as heartily as he could. Barsymes raised an interrogative eyebrow. He explained: "No matter how smoothly things go, I'll never hear the end of teasing about this from my sons. I've given them a hard time about their affairs, but now I'm the one who's gone and put a loaf in a serving maid's oven."

"I pray your Majesty to forgive me, but you've forgotten something," Barsymes said. Now it was Krispos' turn to look puzzled. The vestiarios went on, "Think what the eminent Iakovitzes will say."

Krispos thought. After a moment, he pushed back his seat and hid under the desk. He'd seldom made Barsymes laugh, but he added one to the short list. He laughed, too, as he re-emerged, but he still dreaded what would happen the next time he saw his special envoy.

* * *

Phostis made sure the sword fit loose in its sheath. It was not a fancy weapon with a gold-chased hilt like the one he'd carried before he was kidnapped: just a curved blade, a leather-wrapped grip, and an iron hand guard. It would slice flesh as well as any other sword, though.

The horse they gave him wasn't fit to haul oats to the imperial stables. It was a scrawny, swaybacked gelding with scars on its knees and an evil glint in its eye. By the monster of a bit that went with the rest of its tack, it must have had a mouth made of wrought iron and a temper worthy of Skotos. But it was a horse, and the Thanasioi let him ride it. That marked a change for the better.

It would have been better still had Syagrios not joined the band to which Phostis had been attached. "What, you thought you'd be rid of me?" he boomed when Phostis could not quite hide his lack of enthusiasm. "Not so easy as that, boy."

Phostis shrugged, in control of himself again. "If nothing else, we can spar at the board game," he said.

Syagrios laughed in his face. "I never bother with that dung when I'm out fighting. It's for slack times, when there's no real blood to be spilled." His narrow eyes lit up with anticipation.

The raiders rode out of Etchmiadzin that afternoon, a party of about twenty-five heading south and east toward territory the men of the gleaming path did not control. Excitement ran high; everyone was eager to bring Thanasios' doctrines a step closer to reality by destroying the material goods of those who did not follow them.

The band's leader, a tough-looking fellow named Themistios, seemed almost as unsavory as Syagrios. He put the theology in terms no one could fail to follow: "Burn the farms, burn the monasteries, kill the animals, kill the people. They go straight to the ice. Any of us who fall, we walk the gleaming path beyond the sun and stay with Phos forever."

"The gleaming path!" the raiders bawled. "Phos bless the gleaming path!"

Phostis wondered how many such bands were sallying forth from Etchmiadzin and other Thanasiot strongholds, how many men stormed into the Empire with murder and martyrdom warring for the uppermost place in their minds. He also wondered where the main body of Livanios' men would fare. Syagrios knew. But Syagrios, however much he liked to brag and jeer, knew how to keep his mouth shut about things that mattered.

Soon Phostis' concerns became more immediate. Not least among them was seeing if he couldn't inconspicuously vanish from the raiding band. He couldn't. The horsemen kept him in their midst; Syagrios clung to him like a leech. *Maybe when the fighting starts,* he thought.

For the first day and a half of riding, they remained in territory under Thanasiot rule. Peasants waved from the fields and shouted slogans at the horsemen as they trotted past. The riders shouted back less often as time went by: muscles unused since fall were claiming their price. Phostis hadn't been so saddle sore in years.

Another day on horseback brought the raiders into country where, instead of cheering, the peasants fled at first sight of them. That occasioned argument among Phostis' companions: some wanted to scatter and destroy the peasants and their huts, while others preferred to press ahead without delay.

In the end, Themistios came down in favor of the second group. "There's a monastery outside Aptos I want to hit," he declared, "and I'm not going to waste my time with this riff-raff till it's smashed. We can nail peasants on the way home." With a large, juicy target thus set before them, the raiders stopped arguing. It would have taken a very bold man to quarrel with Themistios, anyhow.

They came to the monastery a little before sunset. Some of the monks were still in the fields. Howling like demons, the Thanasioi rode them down. Swords rose, fell, and rose again smeared with scarlet. Instead of prayers to Phos, screams rose into the reddening sky.

"We'll burn the building!" Themistios shouted. "Even monks have too fornicating much." He spurred his horse straight toward the monastery gate and got inside before the startled monks could slam it shut against him. His sword forced back the first blue-robe who came running up, and a moment later more of his wolves were in there with him.

Several of the raiders carried smoldering sticks of punk. Oil-soaked torches caught quickly. Syagrios pressed one into Phostis' hand. "Here," he growled. "Do some good with this." *Or else,* his voice warned. So did the way he cocked his sword.

Phostis threw the torch at a wall. He'd hoped it would fall short, and it did, but it rolled up against the wood. Flames crackled, caught, and began to spread. Syagrios pounded him on the back, as if he'd just been initiated into the brotherhood of wreckers. Shuddering, he realized he had.

A monk waving a cudgel rushed at him, shouting something incoherent. He wanted to tell the shaven-headed holy man it was all a dreadful mistake, that he didn't want to be here and hadn't truly intended to harm the monastery. But the monk didn't care about any of that. All he wanted to do was smash the closet invader—who happened to be Phostis.

He parried the blue-robe's first wild swipe, and his second. "By the good god, cut him!" Syagrios shouted in disgust. "What do you think—he's going to get tired and go away?"

Phostis didn't quite parry the third blow. It glanced off his shin, hard enough to make him bite his lip against the pain. He realized with growing dismay that he couldn't just try to hold off the monk, not when the fellow wanted nothing more than to kill him.

The monk drew back his club for yet another swing. Phostis slashed at him, feeling the blade bite. Behind him, Syagrios roared with glee. Phostis would cheerfully have killed the ruffian for forcing him into a position where he either had to hurt the monk or get himself maimed or killed.

None of the other raiders had any such compunctions. Several had dismounted, the better to torture the monks they overcame. Screams echoed down the halls that had resounded with hymns of praise to Phos. Watching the Thanasioi at their work—or was it better called sport?—Phostis felt his stomach lurch like a horse stepping into a snow-covered hole.

"Away! Away!" Themistios shouted. "It'll burn now, and we have more to do before we head home."

*What does he have in mind?* Phostis thought. About the only thing that fit in with what the raiders had done at the monastery was torching a home for penniless widows and orphans. Videssos the city had several such; he wondered if Aptos was a big enough town to boast any.

He never got the chance to find out, for as he and the Thanasioi rode away from the monastery, a troop of imperial soldiers came storming after them from out of Aptos. Faint in the distance but growing louder fast, Phostis heard a wary cry he'd never imagined could sound so welcome: "Krispos! The Avtokrator Krispos! Krispos!"

A good many of the Thanasioi had bows as well as sabers. They started shooting at the imperials. The garrison troops, like most imperial cavalry, were archers, too. They shot back. The advantage lay on their side, because they wore mail shirts and helmets while almost all the Thanasioi were unarmored.

Phostis yanked his horse's head around and booted the animal toward the imperials. All he thought about was giving himself up and doing whatever penance the patriarch or some other ecclesiastic set him for his sins in the monastery. Among the things he forgot was the saber he clutched in his right fist.

To the onrushing cavalrymen, he must have looked like a fanatical Thanasiot challenging them single-handed so he could go straight from death to the gleaming path beyond the sun. An arrow whistled past his ear. Another one buried itself in the ground by the horse's forefoot. Another one hit him in the shoulder.

At first he felt only the impact, and thought a kicked-up stone had grazed him. Then he looked down and saw the pale ash shaft sticking out of him. His eyes focused on the gray goose feathers of the fletching. *How stupid,* he thought. *I've been shot by my own father's men.*

All at once, the pain struck, and with it weakness. His own blood ran hot down his chest and began to stain his tunic. He swayed in the saddle. More arrows hissed past.

Syagrios came up beside him at a gallop. "Have you gone out of your head?" he yelled. "You can't fight them all by yourself." His eyes went wide when he saw Phostis was wounded. "See what I'm telling you? We got to get out of here."

Neither Phostis' wits nor his body was working very well. Syagrios saw that, too. He grabbed the reins away from the younger man and led Phostis' horse alongside his own. The horse was nasty, and tried to balk. Syagrios was nastier, and wouldn't let it. A couple of other Thanasioi came back to cover their retreat.

The weight of armor on the imperial cavalrymen slowed them in a long chase. The raiders managed to stay in front until darkness let them give the imperials the slip. Several were hurt by then, and a couple of others lost when their horses went down.

Phostis' world focused on the burning in his shoulder. Everything else seemed far away, unimportant. He scarcely noticed when the Thanasioi halted beside a little stream, though not having to fight to stay in the saddle was a relief.

Syagrios advanced on him with a knife. "We'll have to tend to that," he said. "Here, lie flat."

No one dared light a fire. Syagrios held his head close to Phostis to see what he was doing as he cut the tunic away from the arrow. He examined the wound, made an abstracted clucking noise, and pulled something out of the pouch he wore on his belt.

"What's that?" Phostis asked.

"Arrow-drawing spoon," Syagrios answered. "Can't just pull the fornicating thing out; the point'll have barbs. Hold still and shut up. Digging in there will hurt, but you won't be as torn up inside this way. Now—"

In spite of Syagrios' injunction, Phostis groaned. Nor were his the only cries that rose to the uncaring sky as the raiders did what they could for their wounded comrades. Now darkness didn't much matter; Syagrios was working more by feel than by sight as he forced the narrow, cupped end of the spoon down along the arrow's shaft toward the head.

Phostis felt the spoon grate on something. Syagrios grunted in satisfaction. "Here we go. Now we can get it out. Wasn't too deep—you're lucky."

The taste of blood filled Phostis' mouth: he'd bitten his lip while the ruffian guddled for the arrow. He could smell his own blood, too. He choked out, "If I were lucky, it would have missed me."

"Ha," Syagrios said. "Can't say you're wrong there. Hold on, now. Here it comes, here it comes—yes!" He got the spoon out of the wound, and the arrow with it. He grunted again. "No blood spurting—just a dribble. I'd say you'll make it."

In place of a canteen, the ruffian carried a wineskin on his belt. He poured a stream of wine onto Phostis' wound. After the probing with the spoon and the drawing of the arrow, the abused flesh felt as if it were being bathed with fire. Phostis thrashed and swore and clumsily tried to hit Syagrios left-handed.

"Easy there, curse you," Syagrios said. "Just hold still. You wash out a wound with wine, it's less likely to rot. You *want* pus and fever? You may get 'em anyways, mind, but wouldn't you rather bump up your odds?"

He wadded up a rag, pressed it to Phostis' shoulder to soak up the blood that still oozed from the wound, and tied it in place with another strip of cloth. "Thank you," Phostis got out, a little slower than he should have: he still struggled with the irony of being treated by a man he despised.

"Any time." Syagrios set a hand on his good shoulder. "I never would've thought it, but you really do want to walk the gleaming path, don't you? You laid out that monk fine as you please, and then you were ready to take on all the imperials at the same time. More brave than smart, maybe, but to the ice with smart, sometimes. You done better'n I would've dreamed."

"To the ice with smart, sometimes," Phostis repeated wearily. At last he'd found what it took to satisfy Syagrios: be too cowardly to refuse what he was ordered and then botch what he'd intended as a desertion. The moral there was too elusive for him. He let out a long, worn sigh.

"Yeah, sleep while you can," Syagrios said. "We'll have some fancy riding to do tomorrow before we're sure we've broken loose from the stinking imperials. But I've got to get you back to Etchmiadzin. Now that I know for sure you're with us, we'll have all kinds of things we can use you for."

Sleep? Phostis wouldn't have imagined it possible. Even though the worst of the agony had left his shoulder now that the arrow was out, it still ached like a rotting tooth and throbbed in time to his pulse. But as the wild excitement of the ride and the fight faded, exhaustion rolled over him like a great black tide. Rough ground, aching shoulder—no matter. He slept hard.

He woke from a dream where a wolf was alternately biting and kicking him to find Syagrios shaking him back to consciousness. The shoulder still hurt fiercely, but he managed a nod when the ruffian asked if he could ride.

He did his best to forget as much as he could of the journey back to Etchmiadzin. However much he tried, he couldn't forget the torment of more wine poured into his wound at every halt. The shoulder got hot, but only right around the hole in it, so he supposed the treatment, no matter how agonizing, did some good.

He wished a healer-priest would look at the wound, but had not seen any such among the Thanasioi. That made theological sense: if the body, like all things of this world, sprang from Skotos, what point to making any special effort to preserve it? Such an attitude was easy enough to maintain as an abstract principle. When it came down to Phostis' personal body and its pain, abstract principles got trivial fast.

The rising foothills ahead seemed welcome, not because Etchmiadzin was the home the Thanasioi had hoped it would become for him, but because they meant the imperial soldiers would not catch him on the road and finish the job of killing him. And, he reminded himself, Olyvria would be back at the fortress. The aching wound kept him from being as delighted about that as he would have been otherwise.

When the raiders drew near the valley that cupped Etchmiadzin, Themistios rode up to Syagrios and said, "My men and I will follow the gleaming path against the materialists now. Go as Phos wills you; we cannot follow any farther."

"I can take him in from here easy enough," Syagrios answered, nodding. "Do what you need to do, Themistios, and may the good god keep his eyes on you and your lads."

Singing a hymn with Thanasiot lyrics, the zealots wheeled their horses and rode back out of the holy work of slaughter and destruction. Syagrios and Phostis kept on toward the stronghold of Etchmiadzin.

"We'll get you patched up proper, make sure that arm's all right before we send you out again," Syagrios said as the gray stone mass of the fortress came in view. "Might be just as well I'm here, too, in case we need to settle anything while Livanios is in the field."

"Whatever you say." All Phostis wanted was a chance to get down from his horse and not have to mount again for, say, the next ten years.

Etchmiadzin seemed strangely spacious as he and Syagrios rode through the muddy streets toward the fortress. Wits dulled by pain and fatigue, Phostis needed longer than he should have to figure out why. At last he realized that most of the soldiers who had swelled the town through the winter were off glorifying the lord with the great and good mind by laying waste to what they reckoned the creations of his evil foe.

Only a couple of sentries stood guard at the fortress gate. The inner ward felt empty without warriors at weapons practice or listening to one of Livanios' orations. Most of the heresiarch's chief aides seemed to have gone with him; at least no one came out of the keep to take a report from Syagrios.

As Phostis soon discovered, that was because the keep was almost empty, too. His footsteps and Syagrios' echoed down the halls that had been crammed with soldiers. At least life did exist inside. A trooper came out of the chamber where Livanios had been wont to hold audiences as if he were Avtokrator. Seeing Phostis leaning on Syagrios, he asked the ruffian, "What happened to him?"

"What does it look like?" Syagrios growled. "He just found out he's been chosen patriarch and he can't even walk for the joy of it." The Thanasiot gaped; Phostis fought not to giggle as he watched the fellow realize Syagrios was being sarcastic. Syagrios pointed to the stained bandage on his shoulder. "He got shot in a scrape with the imperials—he did good."

"All right, but why bring him back here?" the soldier said. "He don't look like he's hurt too bad."

"You likely can't tell under all the dirt and stuff, but this is the Emperor's brat," Syagrios answered. "We need to take a little more care with him than with your regular fighter."

"Why?" Like any Videssian, the Thanasiot was ready to argue about his faith on any excuse or none. "We're all alike on the gleaming path."

"Yeah, but Phostis here has special worth," Syagrios returned. "If we use him right, he can help us put lots of new people on the gleaming path."

The soldier chewed on that: literally, for he gnawed at his lower lip while he thought. At last, grudgingly, he nodded. "The doctrine may be sound."

Syagrios turned his head to mutter into Phostis' ear, "The clincher is, I'd have chopped him into raven's meat if he said me nay." He gave his attention back to the trooper. "Is anybody left alive in the kitchens? We're starved, and not on purpose."

"Should be someone there," the fellow answered, though he frowned at Syagrios' levity.

Phostis had not had much appetite since he was wounded. Now his belly rumbled hungrily at the thought of food. Maybe that meant he was getting better.

The smell of bean porridge and onions and bread in the kitchens made his insides growl all over again. Bowls were piled in great stacks there, against a need that had for the moment gone. Only a handful of people sat at the long tables. Phostis' heart gave a lurch—one of them was Olyvria.

She looked around to see who the newcomers were. Phostis must have been as grimy as Syagrios had said, for she recognized the ruffian first. Then her eyes traveled from Phostis' face to the stained bandage on his shoulder and back again. He saw them widen. "What happened?" she exclaimed as she hurried over to the two men.

"I got shot," Phostis answered. Keeping his tone as light as he could, he went on, "I'll probably live." He couldn't say anything more, but did his silent best to urge her not to give anything away. Having Syagrios find out—or even suspect— they were lovers would be more likely fatal than the shaft the cavalryman had put into him.

They were lucky. Syagrios evidently didn't suspect, and so wasn't alert for any small clues they might have given him. He boomed, "Aye, he fought well—better'n I had any reason to think he would, my lady. He was riding toward the imperials when one of 'em got him. I drew the arrow myself and cleaned the wound. It seems to be healing well enough."

Now Olyvria looked at Phostis as if she didn't know what to make of him. She probably didn't: he hadn't gone out intending to fight, let alone well enough to draw praise from Syagrios. But self-preservation had made him swing his sword against the monk with the club, and the ruffian thought he'd been attacking the imperials, not trying to give himself up to them. The world got very strange sometimes.

"Could I please have some food before I fall over?" he asked plaintively.

Between them, Syagrios and Olyvria all but dragged him to a table, sat him down, and brought back bread, hard crumbly cheese, and wine he reckoned fit only for washing out wounded shoulders. He knocked back a hefty mug of it anyhow, and felt it mount quickly to his head. In between bites of bread and cheese, he gave Olyvria a carefully edited version of how he'd ended up on the pointed end of an arrow.

"I see," she said when he was through. He wasn't sure she did, but then he wasn't exactly sure himself of the wherefores of everything that had happened. She turned to Syagrios. Speaking carefully herself, and as if Phostis were not sitting across from her, she said, "When he was ordered to go out raiding, I thought the plan might be to expend him to bring woe to his father."

"That was in *your* father's mind, my lady," Syagrios agreed, also ignoring him, "but he doubted the lad's faith in the gleaming path. Since it's real, he becomes worth more to us alive than dead. That's what I figured, anyways."

"Let's hope you're right," Olyvria said with what Phostis hoped was a good imitation of dispassion.

He kept munching on the loaf of bread. The falser he was to what Syagrios thought him to be, the better off he did. What was the lesson there? That Syagrios was so wicked being false to him turned good? Then how to explain the way the ruffian had cared for him, brought him back to Etchmiadzin, and now poured more of that vile but potent wine into his mug?

He raised it left-handed. "Here's to—using my other arm soon."

Everyone drank.

# X

SCRIBBLING ON A MAP RUINED IT FOR FUTURE USE. SO DID POK-
ing pins into it. Krispos had prevailed upon Zaidas to magic
some red-painted pebbles so they behaved like lodestones and
clung to their appointed places on the parchment even when it
was rolled up. Now he wished he'd chosen some other color:
when the map was unrolled, it looked too much as if it were
suffering from smallpox.

And every time he unrolled it, he had to add more stones to
show fresh outbreaks of Thanasiot violence. Messengers
brought in a constant stream of such reports. Most, as had been
true the summer before, were in the northwest quadrant of the
westlands, but far from all. He glanced at dispatches and put
down two stones in the hill country in the southeastern part of
the gnarled peninsula that held the Empire's heartland.

That the map lay on a folding table in the imperial pavilion
rather than his study back at the palaces consoled him little.
The mere fact of being on campaign would have sufficed for
some Emperors, giving them the impression—justified or
not—they were doing something about the religious zealots.

But Krispos saw in his mind's eye fires rising up from the
map where every red pebble was placed, heard screams of triumph and of despair. Even one of those stones should have
been too many, yet several dozen measled the map.

At his side, Katakolon also stared glumly at the scarlet
stones. "They're everywhere," he said, shaking his head in dismay.

"They do seem that way, don't they?" Krispos said. He liked the picture no better than his son did.

"Aye, they do." Katakolon still eyed the stippled parchment. "Which of these shows where Livanios and his main band of fighters are lurking?"

"It's a good question," the Avtokrator admitted. "The Empire would be better off for a good answer. I wish I could give you one. Trouble is, the heresiarch is using all the little raids as cover to conceal that main band. They could be almost anywhere."

Put that way, the thought was especially disquieting. His own army was only a few days out of Videssos the city. If Livanios' fanatics fell on it before it was ready to fight— Krispos shook his head. It wasn't as if he didn't have sentries posted. Anyone who tried surprising him would be roughly handled. If he started jumping at shadows, Livanios was ahead of the game.

Katakolon looked from the map to him. "So you're going to have yourself another brat, are you, Father? At your age?"

"I've already had three brats. One more won't wreck Videssos, I expect, not if the lot of you haven't managed it. And yes, at my age, as I told you back in the city. The parts do still work, you see."

"Well, yes, I suppose so, but really . . ." Katakolon seemed to think that was a complete sentence. It probably meant something like *just because they work doesn't mean you have any business going around using them.*

Krispos parried, "Maybe you'll learn something watching how I handle things. The way you go on, boy, you're going to sire enough bastards to make up your own cavalry company. Katakolon's Whoresons they could call themselves, and be ferocious-sounding and truthful at the same time."

He'd hoped to abash his youngest son—he'd long since given up trying to shame him over venery—but the idea delighted Katakolon. He clapped his hands and exclaimed, "And if I sire a company, Father, the lads can father themselves a couple of regiments, and my great-grandsons will end up being the whole Videssian army."

Every so often with Iakovitzes, Krispos had to throw his hands in the air and own himself beaten. Now he found himself doing the same with Katakolon. "You're incorrigible. Go tell Sarkis I want to see him, and try not to seduce anyone between this tent and that one."

"Haloga guards are not to my taste," Katakolon replied with dignity bordering on hauteur. "Now, if their daughters and sisters took service with Videssos—" Krispos made as if to throw a folding chair at him. Laughing, the youth ducked out of the tent. Krispos remembered the exotically blond and pink Haloga doxy at a revel of Anthimos, a generation before. Katakolon surely would have liked her very well.

Krispos forced his wits away from lickerish memories and back toward the map. As best he could tell, the Thanasioi were popping up everywhere at once. That made it hard for him to figure out how to fight them.

One of the guards stuck his head into the tent. Krispos straightened, expecting him to announce Sarkis. But instead he said, "Your Majesty, the mage Zaidas would have speech wit' you."

"Would he? Yes, of course I'll listen to what he has to say."

As usual, Zaidas started to prostrate himself; as usual, Krispos waved for him not to bother. Both men smiled at the little ritual. But the wizard's lips quickly fell from their happy curve. He said, "May it please your Majesty, these past few days my magic has enabled me to track the whereabouts of the young Majesty Phostis."

"He's not stayed in the same place all the while?" Krispos asked. "I thought he was still at Etchmiadzin." Because Zaidas hadn't detected any motion from Phostis since he'd managed to pierce the screen of Makuraner magic, Krispos had dared hope his heir was prisoner rather than convert to the gleaming path.

"No, your Majesty, I'm afraid not. Here, let me show you." Zaidas drew from his belt pouch a square of leather. "This is from the tanned hide of a deer, the animal having been chosen because the melting tenderness of its gaze symbolically represents the affection you feel for your kidnapped son. See these marks—here, here, here?"

Krispos saw the marks: they looked as if the deerskin had been burned here and there with the end of a hot awl. "I see them, magical sir, but I must say I don't grasp what they mean."

"As you know, I've at last been able to locate Phostis

through the law of contagion. Were he remaining in
Etchmiadzin, the scorch marks you see would be virtually one
on top of the other. As it was, their dispersal indicates he
moved some considerable distance, most probably to the south
and east, and then returned to the place whence he had departed."

"I see." Krispos scowled down at the piece of deerskin.
"And why do you think he's been making these—move-
ments?"

"Your Majesty, I am sufficiently pleased to be able to infer
that he *has* moved, or rather moved and returned. Why he has
done so is beyond the scope of my art." Zaidas spoke with
quiet determination, as if to say he did not want to know why
Phostis had gone out from the Thanasiot stronghold and then
back to it.

The mage was both courtier and friend; no wonder he found
discretion the easier path to take. Krispos said harshly, "Magical sir, isn't the likeliest explanation that he went out on a raid
with the fanatics and then rode—rode home again?"

"That is certainly a possibility which must be considered,"
Zaidas admitted. "And yet, many other explanations are possible."

"Possible, yes, but likely? What I said fits the facts better
than anything else I can think of." Half a lifetime of judging
cases had convinced Krispos that the simplest explanation was
most often the right one. What could be simpler than Phostis'
joining the rebels and going out to fight for them? Krispos
crumbled the deerskin in his fist and threw it to the ground. "I
wish that cursed Digenis were still alive so I could have the
pleasure of executing him now."

"I sympathize, your Majesty, and believe me, I fully appreciate the gravity of the problem this presents."

"Problem, yes." That was a nice, bloodless way to put it.
What were you supposed to do when your son and heir turned
against you? However fond he was of making plans, Krispos
hadn't made one for that set of circumstances. Now, of neces-
sity, he began to. How would Evripos shape as heir? He'd be
delighted, certainly. But would he make a good Avtokrator?
Krispos didn't know.

Zaidas must have been thinking along with him. The wizard
said, "No need to deal with this on the instant, your Majesty.

Perhaps the campaign will reveal the full circumstances of what's gone on."

"It probably will," Krispos said gloomily. "The trouble is, the full circumstances may be ones I'd sooner not have learned."

Before Zaidas could answer that, Katakolon led Sarkis into the imperial pavilion. The youth nodded easily to the mage; Zaidas, having been around the palaces since before Katakolon was born, was familiar to him as the furniture. Sarkis sketched a salute, which Zaidas returned. They'd both prospered handsomely under Krispos; if either was jealous of the other, he hid it well.

"What's toward, your Majesty?" Sarkis said, and then, "Anything to eat in here? I'm peckish."

Krispos pointed to a bowl of salted olives. The cavalry general picked up a handful of them and popped them into his mouth one after another, spitting the seeds on the ground. As soon as he finished his first helping, he took another.

"Here." Krispos pointed to the map. "Some things occurred to me—late, perhaps, but better late than not at all. The trouble with this campaign is that the Thanasioi know just where we are. If they don't want to meet us in the field, they don't have to. They can just divide themselves up and raid endlessly: even if we smash some of their bands, we haven't done anything to break the back of the movement."

"Truth," Sarkis mumbled around an olive. "It's the curse of fighting folk who are only one step up from hill bandits. We move slow, with horns playing and banners waving, while they bounce over the landscape like fleas on a hot griddle. Belike they have spies in camp, too, to let them know right where we are at any hour of the day or night."

"I'm sure they do," Krispos said. "Here's what I have in mind, then: suppose we detach, say, fifteen hundred men from this force, take 'em back to the coast, and put 'em on board ship. Don't tell them where to land in advance; let the drungarios in charge of the fleet pick a coastal town—Tavas, Nakoleia, or Pityos—after they've set out. The detachment would be big enough to do us some good when it landed, maybe big enough to force Livanios to concentrate quickly against it . . . at which point, the good god willing, we'd be close enough to hit him with the rest of the army. Well?" He knew he was an amateur strategist, and wasn't in the habit of giving orders for major moves till he'd talked them over with professionals.

Sarkis absently popped another olive into his mouth. "It would keep the spies from knowing what was going on, which I like. But you ought to pick out the target town in advance and give it to the drungarios as a sealed order—"

"Sealed magically, too," Zaidas put in, "to prevent scrying as well as spying."

"Aye, sealed magically, by all means," Sarkis said. "No one would see the order save you and, say, one spatharios—" He glanced over at Katakolon. "—until the drungarios opened it. That way you could make sure the main army was at the right place at the right time."

"Thank you, eminent sir; you've closed a loophole. We'll do it as you suggest. What I mostly want is to make the Thanasioi react to us for once instead of the other way round. Let them counter our mischief for a change."

Krispos looked from Sarkis to Zaidas to Katakolon. They all nodded. His son asked, "Which town will you choose for the landing?"

Sarkis turned away from Katakolon so the youth would not see him smile. Krispos saw, though. Gently he answered, "I'm not going to tell you, because this tent just has cloth walls and I don't know who's walking by with his ear bent. The less we blab, the less there is for unfriendly people to learn from us."

"Oh." Katakolon still had trouble realizing this wasn't a large, elaborate game. Then he said, "Couldn't you have Zaidas create a zone of silence around the pavilion?"

"I could," Krispos said. "But I won't, because it's far more trouble than it's worth. Besides, another mage would be apt to notice the zone of silence and wonder what we were brewing up behind it. This way, everything stays nice and ordinary and no one suspects we have anything sneaky in mind—which is the best way to pull off something sneaky, assuming you want to."

"Oh," Katakolon said again.

Without warning, Syagrios came through the door into Phostis' little cubicle in the keep at Etchmiadzin. "Get your imperial backside out of bed," he growled. "You've got work to do."

Phostis' first muzzy thought on waking was relief that Olyvria wasn't lying on the pallet beside him. His next, as his head cleared a little, was curiosity. "Work?" he said. "What kind of work?" He crawled out from under the blanket, stretched, and tried to pull wrinkles out of his tunic. He'd slept on his beard wrong; parts of it were sticking out from his face like spikes.

"Come down and get some wine and porridge in you and we'll talk," Syagrios said. "No point to telling you anything now—you don't have any brains before breakfast."

Since that was more or less true, Phostis answered it with as dignified a silence as he could muster. The dignity would have been easier to maintain had he not made a hash of buckling one sandal. Syagrios laughed raucously.

On the way downstairs, the ruffian asked, "How's the arm?"

Phostis raised it and bent it at odd angles till he caught his breath at a sharp stab of pain. "It's still not perfect, not by a long shot," he answered, "but I'm getting to where I can use it well enough."

"Good," Syagrios said, and then nothing more until he and Phostis were down in the kitchens. If he'd hoped to pique Phostis' interest, he succeeded. The younger man would have gone through his morning porridge twice as fast had he not kept pestering Syagrios with questions. The ruffian, who drank more breakfast than he ate, was gleefully noncommunicative until Olyvria came in and joined the two of them at table. Seeing her made Phostis stop asking so many questions, but didn't make him eat any faster.

"Have you told him?" Olyvria asked Syagrios.

"No, he hasn't told me," Phostis said indignantly; were curiosity an itch, he would have been scratching with both hands.

Syagrios gave him an evil leer before he answered Olyvria. "Not a word. I figured I'd let him stew in his own juice a while longer."

"I think I'm done to a turn now," Phostis said. "What in the name of the lord with the great and good mind is going on? What *are* you supposed to tell me, Syagrios?" He knew he was being too eager, but couldn't help himself.

"All right, boy, you want to know that bad, you oughta

know," Syagrios said. But instead of telling Phostis whatever it was he wasn't saying, he got up and, with slow deliberation, poured himself another mug of wine. Phostis looked a mute appeal to Olyvria, but she didn't say anything, either. Syagrios came swaggering back, sat down again, and noisily swigged from the mug. Only when he was through did he come to the point. "Your father, lad, is getting cute."

Phostis had heard his father described in many ways. Till that moment, *cute* had never been one of them. Cautiously, he asked, "What's he done?"

"That's just it—we don't quite know." By Syagrios' scowl, he thought he had every right to know everything Krispos did. He went on, "He's sent a force out of the Videssian Sea, same as he did last fall when we snagged you. This time, though, we don't know ahead of time which town he's gonna land at."

"Ah." Phostis hoped he sounded wise. But he wasn't all that wise, for he had to ask another question. "What has that to do with me?"

"Suppose you're an imperial soldier," Syagrios said. "That makes you pretty fornicating dumb to start with, right? All right, now suppose you land in a town and you're getting ready to do whatever they tell you to do and here comes the Avtokrator's son, saying to the ice with your officers and come on and join the gleaming path. What you gonna do then?"

"I . . . see," Phostis said slowly. And he did, too; had he been as enamored of the gleaming path as Syagrios thought he was, he could have done his father a lot of harm. But he also saw a problem. "You said you didn't know where these troops are going to land?"

"Naah, we don't." No doubt about it: Syagrios was indignant about that. He continued, "But we think—and it's only a think, worse luck—like I say, we think he's gonna try and send 'em in at Pityos. It's what Livanios would do if he wore the red boots. He likes to strike for the heart, Livanios does."

Phostis nodded; the ruffian's reasoning made sense to him, too. He said, "So you'll send me to Pityos, then? Will I go alone?"

Syagrios and Olyvria both laughed at that. She said, "No, Phostis. While we're sure enough you follow the gleaming path to send you out, we're not sure enough to send you alone.

We have to be sure you will say what you're supposed to. So I shall accompany you to Pityos ... and so will Syagrios."

"All right," he answered mildly. He had no idea how things would go once he got to Pityos; he wasn't even sure whether Olyvria was on his side or her father's. He'd find out in due course, he supposed. Either way, he intended to try to escape. Etchmiadzin was in the heart of Thanasiot country—even if he got out of town, he'd be hunted down before he could go far.

But Pityos, now, Pityos lay by the sea. He was no great sailor, but he could manage a small boat. The good god willing, he wouldn't have to. If imperial soldiers were heading into the port, all he'd have to do was go over to them rather than persuade them to come over to the gleaming path. It seemed too easy to be true.

"When will we leave?" he asked, careful now to sound casual. "I'll need a little while to think about what I'm going to say. I don't suppose I'll be talking much to the officers?"

"Not bloody likely," Syagrios agreed, rumbling laughter. "You're after the odds and sods, the poor buggers who make a living—and a bad one—from soldiering. With any luck, they'll rise up and slaughter the proud bastards who give 'em orders. Most of those midwife's mistakes have it coming, anyways." While he might not have been a proper Thanasiot as far as theology went, Syagrios had unbounded contempt for anyone in authority.

Olyvria actually answered Phostis' question: "We want to leave tomorrow. It's several days' ride down to the coast; you can work on what you'll say as we go."

"However you like." Phostis laughed. "The lord with the great and good mind knows I haven't much to pack."

"Nor should you, if you follow the gleaming path," Olyvria said.

Phostis had to work hard not to stare at her. Now she sounded the way she had when she'd first fetched him to Etchmiadzin. What had become of the passion she'd shown? Was she dissembling now because Syagrios sat next to her? Or had she seduced Phostis to win him to the gleaming path when more honest methods failed?

He simply could not tell. In a certain sense, it didn't matter. When he got to Pityos, he was going to try to escape, no matter what. If she stood in his way then, he'd do it alone. But he knew some trust would go out of him forever if the girl he loved turned out only to have been using him for her own purposes.

He hoped she'd sneak up to his cubicle that night, both because he wanted her and so he could ask her the questions he couldn't speak with Syagrios listening. But she kept to herself. When morning came, Phostis packed a spare tunic he'd come by, belted on the sword he'd left in the little room ever since he came back from the raid on Aptos, and went downstairs.

Syagrios was already down in the kitchens eating. He flipped Phostis a wide-brimmed hat of woven straw like the one that sat at a jaunty angle on his own head. When Olyvria came down, she was wearing one like it, too, and mannish tunic and trousers suitable for riding.

"Good," Syagrios said, nodding approval when he saw her. "We'll take enough food here to keep us going till we get to Pityos, then stuff it into our saddlebags and be on our way. The bread'll go stale, but who cares?"

Phostis took several loaves, some cheese, some onions, and a length of hard, dry pork sausage flavored with fennel. He paused before some round pastries dusted with powdered sugar. "What's in these?" he asked.

"Take a few; they're good," Olyvria said. "They're made from chopped dates and nuts and honey. We must have a new cook out of Vaspurakan, because that's where they come from."

"True enough," Syagrios agreed. "You ever hear a Videssian who wants them, he'll call 'em 'princes' balls.' " He guffawed. Phostis smiled. Olyvria did her best to pretend she hadn't heard.

Phostis fed his foul-tempered horse one of the pastries in the hope of sweetening its disposition. The beast tried to bite his hand. He jerked it back just in time. Syagrios laughed again. Had Phostis been in any other company, he would have named his horse for the ruffian.

The ride into Pityos was a pleasant five days. The upland plateaus still wore their bright green coat of spring grass and shrubs; another month or two would go by before the vicious summer sun began baking everything brown. Fritillaries and hairstreaks flitted from one clump of red or yellow restharrow to another, and then on to white-flowered fenugreek. Swallows and skylarks swooped after the insects.

About halfway through the first day's ride, Syagrios dismounted to go off behind a bush some little distance from the road. Without turning her head toward Phostis, Olyvria said quietly, "It will be all right."

"Will it?" he answered. He wanted to believe her, but he'd grown chary of trusting anyone. If she meant what she'd said, she'd have the chance to prove it.

Before she could reply, back came Syagrios, buttoning the top button of his fly, rebuckling his belt, and whistling a marching song with more foul verses than clean ones. He grunted as he swung himself up into the saddle. "Off we go again," he declared.

The last day and a half of the journey were through the coastal lowlands. Peasants labored in the fields, plowing, planting, and pruning grape vines. Summer felt near in the lowlands, for the weather there was already hot and sticky. Phostis' shoulder twinged more than it had in the drier climate of the plateau.

As soon as Pityos came into view, the travelers all squinted and shaded their eyes to peer ahead. Phostis wondered how he'd feel to see a forest of masts in the harbor. But unless his eyes were tricking him, though the town seemed to boast fishing boats aplenty, none of them were the big imperial merchantmen that hauled troops and horses.

Syagrios grunted suspiciously. "Your old man is up to something sneaky," he told Phostis, as if it were the latter's fault. "Maybe the ships are lying out to sea so they can come in at nightfall and take folk by surprise, or maybe he's decided to have them make land at Tavas or Nakoleia after all."

"Livanios' Makuraner mage should have been able to divine where they'd put in," Phostis said.

"Naah." Syagrios made a slashing gesture of contempt with his hand. "Livanios took him on because his sorcery fuddles Videssian wizards, but it works the other way round, too, worse luck—some days he's lucky to find his way out of bed, that one is." He paused to give Phostis a meditative stare. "How did you know he's from Makuran?"

"By his accent," Phostis answered, as innocently as he

could. "And when I recognized that, I remembered I'd seen Makuraner envoys at court who wore caftans like his."

"Oh. All right." Syagrios relaxed. Phostis breathed easier, too; if he'd let Artapan's name fall from his lips, he'd have thrown himself straight into the soup pot.

The sentries lounging in front of the gates of Pityos were Thanasioi, longer on ferocity than discipline. When Syagrios greeted them in the name of the gleaming path, grins creased their grim faces in unexpected directions. They waved him and his companions into the city.

Pityos was smaller than Nakoleia; as Phostis had thought Nakoleia little better than a village, he'd expected to feel cramped in Pityos as well. But after some months in Etchmiadzin, much of that time mewed up inside the fortress, he found Pityos spacious enough to suit him.

Syagrios rented an upstairs room in a tavern near the harbor so he could keep lookout and spy imperial ships before they started spewing out their men. Olyvria stayed quiet all through the spirited haggle that got the room; Phostis couldn't tell whether the taverner thought her a beardless youth or knew she was a woman but didn't care.

The chamber got crowded when a potboy fetched in a third straw pallet, but remained roomier than Phostis' cubicle had been with him there by himself. He unslung his bedroll and, with a sigh of relief, let it fall to the mattress he'd chosen.

Syagrios leaned out the window to examine the harbor at close range. He shook his head. "Bugger me with a pinecone if I know where they are. They ought to be here, unless I miss my guess altogether." By a slight swagger, he managed to indicate how unlikely that was.

Olyvria picked up the chamber pot, which had been shoved into a corner when the new set of bedding arrived. She looked down into it, made a face, then walked over to the window as if to throw its contents out onto the street—and any unwary passersby below. Instead, when she came up behind Syagrios, she raised the chamber pot high and smashed it over his head.

The pot was of heavy earthenware; no doubt she'd hoped he would sag silently and easily into unconsciousness. But Syagrios was made of stern stuff. He staggered and groaned out, blood running down his face, turned shakily on Olyvria.

Phostis felt his heart beat—once, twice—while he gaped

dumbfounded on what she'd done. Then he unfroze. He grabbed Syagrios by the shoulder and hit the ruffian in the face as hard as he could with his left fist. Syagrios lurched backward. He tried to bring up his hands to protect himself or even to grapple with Phostis, but he moved as if in the slowness of a dream. Phostis hit him again, and again. His eyes rolled up in his head; he collapsed to the floor.

Olyvria seized the knife on his belt and held it above his neck. Phostis grabbed her wrist. "Have you gone mad?" she cried.

"No. We'll take his weapons and we'll tie him up," he answered. "But I owe him enough for this—" He touched his healing shoulder. "—that I don't care to slit his throat."

She made a face but didn't argue, instead turning the dagger on the linen mattress covers to cut strips of cloth for bonds. Syagrios grunted and stirred when Phostis rolled him over to tie his hands behind his back. Phostis hit him again, and also tied cloth strips over his mouth for a gag. Then he tied the ruffian's ankles together as tightly as he could.

"Give me the dagger," he said suddenly.

Olyvria pressed it into his hand. "Change your mind?"

"No." Phostis slit the money pouch Syagrios wore on his belt. Half a dozen goldpieces and a handful of silver spilled out. He scooped up the coins and stuffed them into his own belt pouch. "Now let's get out of here."

"All right," Olyvria said. "Whatever you intend to do, you'd best be quick about it. The good god only knows how long he'll lie quiet there, and he won't be pleased with us for what we've done."

That, Phostis was sure, was an understatement. "Come on," he said. They hurried out of the chamber. When they came down into the all-but-deserted taproom, the taverner raised an eyebrow but didn't say anything. Phostis walked over to him, took out a goldpiece, and set it on the bar. "You didn't see us come out. You were in the back room. You've never seen us."

The taverner's hand covered the coin. "Did somebody say something?" he asked, looking past Phostis. "This place is so empty, I'm starting to hear phantoms."

"I hope it's enough," Phostis said as he and Olyvria walked rapidly down to the harbor.

"So do I," Olyvria said. "Best if we don't have to find out. I hope you have something along those lines in mind."

"I do." Phostis took deep, happy gulps of seaside air. The salt tang and the aroma of stale fish reminded him at a level almost below consciousness of the way things smelled around the palaces. For the first time in months, he felt at home.

A fisherman leapt from the little boat he'd just tied to a pier. His catch was similarly minimal, a couple of buckets of mackerel and other, less interesting, fare. "Good day," Phostis called to him.

The fisherman was closer to sixty than fifty, and looked deathly tired. "Maybe you think so," he said. "It is a day. It is done. It is enough."

Phostis said, "I will give you two goldpieces for that boat, and another to forget you ever sold it to me." The boat could not have been worth more than a goldpiece and a half. Phostis didn't care. He had the money and he needed to be out of Pityos as fast as he could. He pressed ahead: "Does that make it a better day, if not a good one?"

He pulled out the three bright gold coins from his pouch and held them in the palm of his hand so they sparkled into the fisherman's face. The fellow stared as if he could not believe his eyes. He set down one of his buckets of fish. "Young man," he said slowly, "if you mock me, I shall thrash you, grizzled though I am. By the lord with the great and good mind I swear it."

"I don't mock," Phostis answered. "Have you hammocks aboard there, and your lines and nets?"

"Only one hammock—I fish alone," the fisherman answered, "but there are blankets so the other of you can bed down on deck. And aye, the rest of the tackle is there. See for yourself before you buy—I would not have you say I cheated you, though you must know you are cheating yourself. There's fresh water from yesterday in the tuns, too. You can sail a good ways without coming in to land, if that's what you aim to do."

"Never mind what I aim to do." The less Phostis told the fisherman, the better. He walked along the dock and peered into the boat. The nets lay neatly coiled at the bow; lines with hooks on them were wrapped between pegs on one side of the tiny cabin behind the mast. A pair of long sweeps lay on the deck. He nodded to himself and gave the fisherman the goldpieces. "You keep it shipshape."

"And if I don't, who'll do it for me?" the man answered.

Phostis handed Olyvria down into the boat, then got in himself and put the sweeps in the oarlocks. "Would you cast off the line?" he called to the fisherman.

The fellow was still staring at the gold coins. He started slightly before he obeyed. Grunting with effort, Phostis worked the sweeps. The fishing boat slowly backed away from the pier. Its former owned seemed glad to have seen the last of it. He picked up his buckets and walked into town without a backward glance.

When Phostis had put enough distance between himself and the dock, he let down the sail from its yard. It was, like most Videssian sails, a simple square rig, not much good for sailing against the wind but fine with it. The wind blew out of the west. Phostis wanted to sail east. As long as the wind held, he'd have no problems.

He turned to Olyvria. "Do you know anything about fishing?"

"No, not much, not boats, either," she answered. "Do you?"

"Enough," he said. "I can manage the boat as long as the weather doesn't get too rough. And I can fish, too, even if the gear here isn't exactly what I'm used to. I learned from my father." It was, he thought, the first time he'd ever simply acknowledged that Krispos had taught him something worth knowing.

"Good for him and good for you." Olyvria watched the harbor of Pityos recede off to the starboard side of the stern. "That means we won't starve right away?"

"I hope so," Phostis said, "though you never can tell with fish. If we have to put in to shore to feed ourselves, I still have some of Syagrios' money left." He slapped the pouch that hung from his belt.

Olyvria nodded. "That sounds fine to me. What do you plan to do? Sail along the coast until you find where the imperial fleet really is?"

"As a matter of fact, I'd intended to sail straight to Videssos the city. I can find out more about what's going on there than anywhere else, and then head straight out to the main body of the army. My father will be there, and I ought to join him. If

I hadn't intended to do that, what point to leaving the Thanasioi?"

"None, I suppose." Olyvria looked back at Pityos again. Already it seemed a toy town, the buildings shrunk to the size of those a woodcarver might shape for his children to play with. Quietly, without looking back to him, she asked, "And what do you intend to do about me?"

"Why—" Phostis shut his mouth with a snap. The question was too pointed to answer before he considered it. After a moment, he went on, "I hadn't thought so far ahead yet. The most that had occurred to me was that for the next few days we'd finally be able to make love without worry about someone catching us while we were at it."

She smiled, but her eyes were still on Pityos. "Yes, we'll be able to do that, if it's what you want. But what about afterwards? What happens when you go to the palaces in Videssos the city? What then, young Majesty?"

At Etchmiadzin, no one had called him that except in mockery or the false courtesy that was worse. Now Olyvria reminded him of everything to which he'd be returning: the eunuchs, the ceremonial, the rank. He also remembered, as he had not lately, that she'd kidnapped and humiliated him. She, plainly, had never forgotten. The question she'd asked him was pointed indeed.

Where she looked back across the water toward everything she was leaving, he looked out past the fishing boat's bow at what lay ahead. Slowly he said, "You stole me out of the camp, true. But if it hadn't been for you just now, I wouldn't have got free of Pityos, either. As far as I can reckon us, that puts us at quits there—but still leaves everything else between us."

"Which means?" Olyvria still sounded—*apprehensive* was the word, Phostis decided after a little thought. And no wonder. Until the fishing boat headed out onto the Videssian Sea, she'd been the dominant one, and set the terms of their dealings with each other. She'd kidnapped him, at Etchmiadzin she'd had the power of her father and the Thanasioi behind her . . . but now she'd committed herself to sailing into what literally was, or would be, his dominion. If he wanted vengeance, it was his for the taking.

"If you like," he said, "I'll put in to shore at any deserted beach you like and let you off there. I swear by the lord with the great and good mind I'll do everything in my power to keep my father from ever coming after you. Or—"

"Or what?" She fairly snapped at him. Yes, she was nervous about how things had changed.

He took a deep breath. "Or you can stay with me till we get to Videssos the city, and for as long as you care to after that. For the rest of our lives, I hope."

She studied him, wondering, no doubt, if this was but one more trap to make eventual revenge sweeter. "You mean it," she said at last, and then, "Of course I will," and then, "But what will your father say?"

"He'll probably have kittens," Phostis said cheerfully. "So what? I'm of a man's years, so he can't *make* me put you aside. And besides, people don't always remember these days—it's been a long time, after all—but my mother was Anthimos' Empress before she was my father's. Since I was born less than a year after my father took the throne, you can see his ways there weren't perfectly regular, either."

Phostis listened to that sentence again in his mind. As a matter of fact, he'd been born quite a bit less than a year after Krispos became Avtokrator. He hadn't really thought about how much less till just now. He wondered if Krispos had sired him . . . or Anthimos. By his birthdate, either was possible.

Maybe he frowned, for Olyvria said, "What's wrong?"

"Nothing," he said, and then again, more firmly, "Nothing." Anthimos wasn't around any more to claim him and, even if Krispos never had quite warmed to him—all at once, he wondered if he saw a new reason for that—he'd named him junior Avtokrator before he was out of swaddling clothes. Krispos wouldn't dispossess him of the succession now, especially when he'd escaped from danger by his own efforts—and those of Olyvria.

She was looking off to starboard again. Land now was just a strip of green and occasional brown on the horizon there; they were too far out to sea to make out any detail. Smiling, she turned to Phostis. "If nothing's wrong, you can prove it."

He started to say, "How am I supposed to do that?" Before he got out more than a couple of words, she took off her hat, shook down her hair, and then pulled her tunic up over her head. Sure enough, he found a way to show her everything was all right.

"Your Majesty!" That was Zaidas, calling from outside the imperial pavilion before the army got moving on a day full of muggy heat. "I've news, your Majesty!"

Inside the pavilion, Krispos was wearing a decidedly unimperial pair of linen drawers and nothing more. *To the ice with ceremony,* he thought, and called, "Well, come in and tell it, then." He smiled at Zaidas' pop-eyed expression. "Never mind the proskynesis, sorcerous sir. Just brush aside the mosquito netting and let me know what you've learned."

Zaidas inhaled portentously. "May it please your Majesty, my sorcery shows your son Phostis has traveled from Etchmiadzin down to Pityos on the coast."

"Has he?" Krispos growled. As usual with news prefaced by that formula, it pleased him not at all. "Bloody good thing I ordered the fleet to Tavas, then. The only reason I can find for him to go down to the port is to try and forestall us. But Livanios sent him to the wrong place, by Phos." He smacked one fist into the other palm. "The Thanasioi have spies among us, sure enough, but they didn't learn enough, not this time."

"No, your Majesty," Zaidas agreed. He hesitated, then went on, "Your Majesty, I might add that Phostis' sorcerous trace, if you will forgive an inexact expression, has itself become inexact."

"More interference from that accursed Makuraner." Krispos made it statement, not question.

But Zaidas shook his head. "I think not, your Majesty. It's almost as if the trace is attenuated by—water, perhaps. I'm puzzled to come up with any other explanation, yet the heretics would scarcely send Phostis out by sea, would they?"

"Not a chance," Krispos said, his voice flat. "Livanios isn't such a fool; I wish to Phos he were. Keep searching. The lord with the great and good mind willing, you'll come up with something that makes better sense. Believe me, sorcerous sir, I still have full confidence in you."

"More than I have in myself sometimes." Zaidas shook his head. "I'll do my best for you."

Krispos started sweating hard as soon as he put on his gilded mail shirt. He sighed; summer felt as if it were here already. He went out to stand in line with the soldiers for his morning bowl of porridge. The cooks never knew which line he'd pick. The food in all of them was better for it. This morning, for instance, the barley porridge was thick with onions and cloves of garlic, and almost every spoonful had a bit of chopped ham with an intensely smoky flavor.

He emptied the bowl. "If I'd eaten this well on my farm, I'd never have wanted to come to Videssos the city," he remarked.

Several of the soldiers nodded. Life on a farm, as Krispos knew, was seldom easy. That was one of the big reasons men left the country: if nothing else, soldiers ate regularly. But while farm work was harder day in and day out, soldiers sometimes earned their keep harder than any man who lived off the land.

The army's discipline, not bad when the men set out from the capital, had improved steadily since. Everyone knew his place, and went to it with a minimum of fuss. The cooks' kettles went back onto the supply wagons, the troopers mounted their horses, and the army pushed on through the lowlands toward Tavas.

Krispos rode at the head of the main body, a few hundred yards behind the vanguard. Peasants looked up from the fields in wonder as he went by, as if he were some kind of being altogether different from themselves. Had Anthimos' father Rhaptes ever happened to parade past the village where Krispos had grown to manhood, he was sure he would have gaped the same way.

A little before noon, a messenger on a lathered, blowing horse caught up with the army from behind. The animal gulped in great draughts of air as the fellow brought it down to a slow trot beside the Avtokrator's horse. He pulled out a sealed tube of oiled leather and handed it to Krispos. "From the city, your Majesty."

The seal was a sunburst stamped into the sky-blue wax that was an imperial prerogative, which meant the dispatch came from Evripos. Krispos could think of only one reason why his son would send out an urgent message. Filled with foreboding, he broke the seal.

His son's script still retained some of the copybook clarity that years of quickly scribbling will erode. The words were as legible as they were unwelcome: "Evripos to his father. Greetings. Riots flared here night before last, and have grown worse rather than better since. Forces under my command are doing all they can to restore order. I shall send more news as it becomes available. Phos guard you and this city both. Farewell."

"Do you know anything of this?" Krispos asked the messenger, waving the parchment in his direction.

"No, your Majesty, I'm sorry but I don't," the man answered. "I'm but the latest of a string of relay riders. I hear tell from the fellow who gave me the tube that there's some sort of trouble back at the city. Is that so?"

"Aye, that's so," Krispos answered grimly. He'd known the Thanasioi might try that ploy to distract him and, prepared for it as well as he could. Whether *well as he could* was *well enough* would come clear before long.

Then he thought of something else, something that chilled him: was Phostis on the sea to go to the capital and lead the rioters against loyal troops? If he was, he might throw the city into worse turmoil than even Krispos had expected. *Have to warn Evripos about that,* the Avtokrator thought.

"Is there a reply, your Majesty?" the messenger asked.

"Yes, by the good god, there is," Krispos said. But before he could give it, another dispatch rider rode up on an abused horse and waved a message tube in his face. He didn't like the fearful look in the newcomer's eyes. "Rest easy there, you. I've never been in the habit of blaming the messenger for the word he brings."

"Aye, your Majesty," the second rider said, but he didn't sound convinced. He thrust out the message tube as if it held poison.

Krispos took it, then asked, "You know what's in it?" The messenger nodded. Krispos said, "Speak it to me plain, then. By the lord with the great and good mind, I swear no harm nor blame shall fall on you because of it."

He'd never seen a man who so obviously wanted to be somewhere, anywhere, else. The dispatch rider licked his lips, looked this way and that, but found no escape. He sucked in a deep breath, then let it all out in five blurted words: "Your Majesty, Garsavra is fallen."

"What?" Krispos gaped at him, more in disbelief than horror. So did everyone close enough to hear. Lying where the Eriza and Arandos rivers came together, Garsavra was one of the two or three greatest towns in the westlands. The army was already west of it; they'd forded the northern reaches of the Eriza day before yesterday.

Krispos opened the message tube. It confirmed what the dispatch rider had said, and added details. Outriding news of their coming, the Thanasioi had swept down on the town at sunrise. They'd burned and killed and maimed; they'd thrown the local prelate headfirst off the roof of the temple by the central square, then set fire to the building. Few survivors would have their souls burdened by a surplus of material goods for years to come.

Krispos stared at the parchment in his left hand. He wanted to tear it into a thousand pieces. With a deliberate effort of will, he checked himself: some of the information it held might be valuable. As steadily as he could, he told the messenger, "You have my thanks for your courage in bringing this to me. What is your rank?"

"I'm on the books as a file closer, your Majesty," the man answered.

"You're a file leader now," Krispos told him.

One of the scouts from the vanguard came riding back to the main body. He waited to catch Krispos' eye, then said, "May it please your Majesty, we've rounded up a Thanasiot riding at us under shield of truce. He says he bears a message for you from Livanios."

Too much was falling on Krispos too fast. He had the feeling of a tavern juggler who has reached out for one plate he's tossed away, only to have all the others that were up in the air smash down on his head before he can snatch back his hand. "Bring me this Thanasiot," he said heavily. "Tell him I'll honor his truce sign, which is likely more courtesy than he'd give to one of ours. Tell him just that way."

The scout saluted and rode ahead. He came back a few minutes later with one of Livanios' irregulars. The Thanasiot carried a white-painted round target on his left arm. He smiled at Krispos' somber face and said, "I'd wager you have the news already. Am I right, friend?"

"I'm no friend of yours," Krispos said. "Give me your master's message."

The Thanasiot handed him a tube no different from those he'd had from his own couriers save in the seal: the image of a leaping flame stamped into scarlet wax. Krispos broke it and angrily threw the little pieces of wax down onto the ground. The parchment inside was sealed with the identical mark. Krispos cracked it, unrolled the parchment, and scanned the message it contained:

> *Livanios who treads the gleaming path to the false Avtokrator and servant of Skotos Krispos: Greetings. Know that I write this from the ruins of Garsavra, which city has been purified and cleansed of its sinful materialism by warriors true to the lord with the great and good mind. Know further that all cities of the westlands are liable to the same penalty, which Phos' soldiers may deliver at any time which suits them.*
>
> *And know further, miscalled ruler destined for the ice, your corrupt and gold-bloated regime is henceforward and ever after banished from these westlands. If you would preserve even a fragment of your illicit and tyrannical rule, withdraw at once over the Cattle-Crossing, yielding this land to those who shall hold it in triumph, peace, and piety. Repent of your wealth and other sins before Phos' final judgment descends upon you. Cast aside your greed and surrender yourself to the gleaming path. I am yours in Phos. Farewell.*

Krispos slowly and deliberately crumpled the parchment, then turned to the Thanasiot messenger and said, "My reply is one word: no. Take it and be thankful your life goes with it."

"I don't fear death—death liberates me from Skotos," the messenger retorted. "You call down doom on your own head." He twitched the reins, dug his heels into his horse's sides, and rode away singing a hymn.

"What did the whoreson want of you?" Sarkis asked. When Krispos told him, his fleshy face darkened with anger. "By the good god, a bragging fool ought to know better than to taunt a force that's bigger than his, especially when we stand closer to Etchmiadzin than he does."

"Maybe we stand closer to it," Krispos said bleakly. "You've said all along Livanios is no fool. Surely he'll have withdrawn after the rape of Garsavra. I don't want to chase him back to his stronghold; I want to force him to battle outside of it."

"How do you propose to do that?" Sarkis said. "The cursed Thanasioi move faster than we; they aren't even burdened by loot, because they burn it instead of carrying it along with them."

"I know." Krispos' scowl was black as winter midnight. "I suppose you were right before, though: We have to try. Livanios can't be smart all the time—I hope. If we march smartly, we may come to grips with him up on the plateau. Worth a try, anyhow."

"Aye." Sarkis nodded vigorously. "Our cavalry at Tavas can hold its own against anything the Thanasioi have around there—and now we know where their main force has been lurking."

"So we do," Krispos said. "It's a bloody big cloud for such a thin silver lining." He leaned over, spat down onto the ground as if in ritual rejection of Skotos, then began issuing the orders that would shift the army's line of march from the coast and up into the central highlands. Changing the troops' destination was the easy part. Making sure they would have food and their animals fodder along the new track was much more involved.

What with everything that came after, he forgot to send Evripos a reply.

Phostis guided the fishing boat up to the little quay from which his father would row out to see what he could catch. He threw out a line, scrambled up onto the dock, and made the boat fast.

He was just helping Olyvria up onto the planks when an indignant palace servitor opened the seawall gate and exclaimed, "Here, who do you think you are? This dock's not for just anyone. It's reserved for the Avtokrator, Phos bless him, so you can kindly take your smelly little boat somewhere else."

"It's all right, Soranos," Phostis answered. "I don't think Father will mind."

He wasn't in the least put out that Soranos hadn't recognized him. He was grimy, shaggy, wearing a cheap, ragged long tunic, and sunburned. In fact, he was sunburned in some tender spots under the tunic, too, thanks to frolicking with

Olyvria in broad, hot daylight. She was also sunburned; they'd shared misery and fish on the way back to the city.

The servitor put hands on hips. "Oh, your father won't mind, eh? And who, pray, is your father? Do you know yourself?"

Phostis had been wondering the same thing, but didn't let on. He said, "My father is Krispos son of Phostis, Avtokrator of the Videssians. I have, you will notice if you look closely, escaped from the Thanasioi."

Soranos started to give back another sharp answer, but paused and took a long look at Phostis. He was too swarthy to turn pale, but his jaw fell, his eyes widened, and his right hand, seemingly of its own accord, shaped the sun-circle above his heart. He prostrated himself, gabbling "Young Majesty, it is yourself—I mean, you are yourself! A thousand pardons, I pray, I beg! Phos be praised that he has granted you safe voyage home and blessed you with liberty once again."

Beside Phostis, Olyvria snickered. He shook his head reproachfully, then told the servitor, "Get up, get up. I forgive you. Now tell me at once what's going on, why I saw so much smoke in the sky as I was sailing down the Cattle-Crossing."

"The heretics have rioted again, young Majesty; they're trying to burn the city down around our heads," Soranos answered as he rose.

"I feared that's what it was. Take me to my father at once, then."

Soranos' face assumed the exaggerated mask of regret any sensible servant donned when saying no to a member of the imperial family. "Young Majesty, I cannot. He has left the city to campaign against the Thanasioi."

"Yes, of course he has," Phostis said, annoyed at himself. Had the imperial army not been on the move, he wouldn't have been sent to Pityos—or escaped. "Who is in command here in the city, then?"

"The young Majesty Evripos, your brother."

"Oh." Phostis bit down on that like a man finding a pebble in his lentil stew. From Krispos' point of view, the appointment made sense, especially with Phostis himself absent. But he could not imagine anyone who would be less delighted than Evripos at his sudden arrival. No help for it, though. "You'd best take me to him."

"Certainly, young Majesty. But would you and your, ah, companion—" Olyvria had her hair up under her hat and was in her baggy, mannish outfit, so Soranos could not be sure if she was woman or youth. "—not care first to refresh yourselves and change into, ah, more suitable garments?"

"No." Phostis made the single word as imperious—and imperial—as he could; not till it had passed his lips did he realize he'd taken his tone from Krispos.

Whatever its source, it worked wonders. Soranos said, "Of course, young Majesty. Follow me, if you would be so kind."

Phostis followed. No one came close to him, Olyvria, and Soranos as they walked through the palace compound. People who saw them at a distance no doubt thought Soranos was escorting a couple of day laborers to some job or other.

To Phostis, the palace compound was simply home. He took no special notice of the lawns and gardens and buildings among which he strode. To Olyvria, though, they all seemed new and marvelous. Watching her try to look every which way at once, seeing her awe at the Grand Courtroom, the cherry orchard that screened the imperial residence, and the Hall of the Nineteen Couches made him view them with fresh eyes, too.

Evripos was not conducting his fight against the rioters from the palaces. He'd set up a headquarters in the plaza of Palamas. People—some soldiers, some not—hurried in and out with news, orders, what-have-you. A big Haloga gave Phostis a first-rate dubious stare. "What you want here?" he asked in accented Videssian.

"I'd like to see my brother, Herwig," Phostis answered.

Herwig glowered at him, wondering who his brother might be—and who he was himself, to presume to address an imperial guardsman by name. Then the glower faded to wonderment. "Young Majesty!" the Haloga boomed, loud enough to cause heads to turn in the makeshift pavilion.

Among those heads was Evripos'. "Well, well," he said when he saw it truly was Phostis. "Look what the dog dragged to the doorstep."

"Hello, brother," Phostis said, more cautiously than he'd expected. In the bit more than half a year since he'd set eyes on his younger brother, Evripos had gone from youth to man. His features were sharper than they had been, his beard thicker and not so soft. He wore a man's expression, too, under a coat of smoke and dirt: tired, harassed, but determined to do what he'd set out to do.

Now he gave Phostis a hostile stare. It wasn't the stare Phostis was used to, the one that came because he was older. It was because he might be an enemy. Evripos barked, "Did the cursed Thanasioi send you here to stir up more trouble?"

"If they had, would I have tied up the fishing boat I sailed here over at Father's quay?" Phostis said. "Would I have come looking for you instead of Digenis?"

"Digenis is dead, and we don't miss him a bit," Evripos said, voice still harsh. "And who knows what you'd do? One of the things I know about the bloody heretics is that they're bloody sneaky. For all I know, you could have that doxy there by you just to fool me into thinking you're not off the pleasures of the flesh."

Unlike Soranos, Evripos knew a girl when he saw one, no matter what she wore. Phostis said, "Brother, I present to you Olyvria the daughter of Livanios, who helped me escape from the Thanasioi and rejects them as much as I do, which is to say altogether."

That succeeded in startling Evripos. Then Olyvria startled Phostis: She prostrated herself before his brother, murmuring, "Your Majesty." She probably should have said *young Majesty*, but Evripos had been left in command of the city, so she wasn't really wrong—and she was dead right to err on the side of flattery.

Evripos grunted. Before he could say more than "Get up," a messenger bleeding from a cut over one eye came up and gasped something Phostis didn't follow. Evripos said, "It's not hard unless you make it so. Push one troop down from Middle Street east of where those maniacs are holed up and another west of 'em. Then crush 'em between our men."

The messenger dashed away. Off to one side in the pavilion, Phostis saw Noetos bent over a map. But Noetos was not running the show. Evripos was. Phostis had watched Krispos exercise command too often to mistake it.

He said, "What can I do to help?"

"To take things away from me, you mean?" Evripos asked suspiciously.

"No. Father gave it to you, and you seem to be doing well

by it. I just got here, remember? I haven't the faintest idea what's going on. But if I can be of use, tell me how."

Evripos looked as if such cooperation were the last thing he wanted. Olyvria said, "If you like, we could speak to the mob and tell them why we care for the gleaming path no more."

"Not the least reason being that Makuran is behind the Thanasioi and supports them with a wizard and the good god only knows what all else," Phostis added.

"So you know about that, do you? We wondered, Father and I. We were afraid you knew and didn't care, afraid you'd thrown your lot in with the heretics. You hadn't seemed exactly eager when we went on campaign against them last year." Evripos' sarcasm stung like a whiplash.

"I wasn't eager then," Phostis admitted: No point denying it, for Evripos knew better. "It's different now. Fetch a mage for the two-mirror test if you don't believe me."

Evripos glowered at him. "The Thanasioi have tricks to beat the two-mirror test, as you'll recall from the delightful time Zaidas had trying to use it last year. And if Zaidas couldn't make it work, I doubt another mage would be able to, either. And so, brother of mine, I'll keep you and the heresiarch's daughter off the platform. I can't trust you, you see."

"Can't trust us how?" Phostis demanded.

"How d'you think? Suppose I let you go talk to the mob and instead of saying, 'The golden path is a midden full of dung,' you say, 'Hurrah for Thanasios! Now go out and burn the High Temple!'? That would spill the chamber pot into the stew, now wouldn't it?"

Noetos looked up from the map table and said, "Surely the young Majesty would commit no such outrage. He—"

Evripos cut him off with a sharp wave of the hand. "No." He sounded as imperial—and as much like his father—as Phostis had with the same word. "I will not take the chance. Have we not seen enough chaos in the city these past few days to fight shy of provoking more? I say again, no." He shifted his feet into a fighter's stance, as if defying Noetos to make him change his mind.

The general tamely yielded. "It shall be as you say, of course, young Majesty," he murmured, and went back to his map.

Phostis found himself furious enough to want to hit his

brother over the head with the nearest hard object he could find. "You're a fool," he growled.

"And you're a blockhead," Evripos retorted. "I'm not the one who let Digenis seduce him."

"How's this, then?" Phostis said. "Suppose you summon Oxeites the patriarch here to the plaza of Palamas or anyplace else you think would be a good idea, and he can marry me to Olyvria as publicly as possible. That ought to convince people I'm not a Thanasiot—they'd sooner starve than wive . . . Curse you, Evripos, I mean it. What's so bloody funny?"

"I'm sorry," Evripos said, the first concession Phostis had got from him. "I was just thinking it's too bad Father's gone on campaign. The two of you might don the crowns of marriage side by side. Do you remember the serving maid named Drina?"

"Of course. She's a pretty little thing, but—" Phostis gaped at his grinning brother. "Father's gone all soft in the head over her?"

"I doubt that," Evripos said judiciously. "When has Father ever gone soft in the head over anyone, us included? But she is pregnant by him. We'll have ourselves a little half brother or half sister before Midwinter's Day. Relax, Phostis—you don't need to go so white. Father truly doesn't plan on marrying her. Believe me, I'm as happy at that as you are."

"Yes. A new half brother or half sister, eh? Well, well." Phostis wondered if he was only half brother to Evripos and Katakolon as it was. He'd never know, not for certain. He said, "If you're done gossiping, I'm dead serious about what I said. If you think it will help end the riots, I'll wed in as open a ceremony as the chamberlains can dream up."

Beside him, Olyvria nodded vigorously. "That might be the best way to discredit the gleaming path: let those who think of following it see that their one-time leaders are abandoning it."

"The plan is sensible, young Majesty," Noetos said.

"Mmm—maybe it is." Evripos frowned in intense concentration. A messenger interrupted with a note. Evripos read it, snapped orders, and returned to study. At last he said, "No, I will not order it. One of the drawbacks of our rank, brother, is that we aren't always free to make the matches we would. I see nothing wrong with this one, but I'm slowly finding out—" His grin was rueful and disarming at the same time. "—I don't know everything there is to know. Too much rides here for me to say aye or nay."

"What then?" Phostis demanded.

"I'll send you along the courier route to Father. Tell him your tale. If he believes you, what can I possibly say? And if he thinks this marriage of yours a good idea, then married you shall be—and at a quickstep, if I know Father. Bargain?"

"Bargain," Phostis replied at once. A couple of orders from Evripos and he and Olyvria might have disappeared for good. If Krispos ever found out, Evripos could claim they were fanatical Thanasioi. Who would contradict him, especially after he became the primary heir? "It's . . . decent of you."

"Meaning you expect me to throw you into some dungeon or other and then forget which one it was?" Evripos asked.

"Well—yes." Phostis felt his face heat at being so obvious; had he made that kind of mistake at Etchmiadzin, he never would have got out of the fortress.

"If you think the notion didn't cross my mind, you're daft." Phostis needed a moment to realize the strangled noise Evripos made was intended as laughter. His younger brother went on, "Father always taught us to fear the ice, and I guess I listened to him. If you'd gone over to the gleaming path, nothing would have made me happier than hunting you down and taking your place. Always believe that, Phostis. But stealing it after you've got loose of the Thanasioi?" He made a wry face. "It's tempting, but I can resist it."

Phostis thought of the chamber under Digenis' tunnel, and of the naked and lovely temptation Olyvria had represented. He'd passed her by—then. Now he lay in her arms whenever he could. Had he yielded to temptation? Would Evripos, with some future chance to seize the throne, spring after it rather than turning his back?

As for the first question, Phostis told himself, the situation had changed by the time he and Olyvria became lovers. She wasn't just so much flesh set out for him to enjoy; she'd become his closest friend—almost his only friend—in Etchmiadzin. Were circumstances different, he'd gladly have paid her formal court.

As for the second question . . . the future would have to answer it. Phostis knew he'd be a fool to ignore the possibility of Evripos' trying to usurp him. In the future, though, he'd have the power, not his brother—as Evripos did today. And maybe today showed they had hope, at least, of working together.

Evripos said, "Come the day, brother, we may not make such a bad team. Even if you end up with the red boots on your feet, give me something to do with soldiers and I'll do well for Videssos with them."

Not *in your service*, Phostis noted. He didn't quibble. Among the other things Krispos had taught was that the Empire came first, that anyone who didn't put it ahead of everything else didn't deserve to have his fundament warm the throne in the Grand Courtroom. The lesson made more sense to Phostis than it ever had before.

"You know what?" he said. Evripos raised a questioning eyebrow. Phostis continued, "It'll be good to see Father. It's been too long." Phostis paused again. "I don't suppose I could bring Olyvria along?"

"No," Evripos said at once, but then added, "Wait. Maybe you should. She'll know a lot about the Thanasioi—"

"She does," Phostis said, at the same time as Olyvria was saying, "I do."

"Well then," Evripos said, as if that settled things, "if you don't bring her, Father will come down on me for making you leave her behind so he can't wring her dry with questions. Take her by all means."

"I shall obey your commands, young Majesty," Phostis said with a salute.

Evripos saluted in return. "I've obeyed yours a time or two, young Majesty," he answered.

"Brothers," Olyvria said; she might have been referring to some lower form of life. Phostis and Evripos looked at each other. Grinning, they both nodded.

# XI

KRISPOS SLAMMED HIS FOREHEAD WITH THE HEEL OF HIS HAND, hard enough to hurt. "By the good god, I'm an idiot," he exclaimed.

"No doubt, your Majesty," Sarkis agreed cheerfully; along with Iakovitzes, Zaidas, and Barsymes, he could say something like that without going up on charges of lese majesty. "In which particular matter are you being an idiot today?"

"With all the hoorah over Garsavra, I clean forgot to write to Evripos and warn him to be alert for Phostis," Krispos answered. He thumped himself again, in disgust. Characteristically, he wasted no more time on reproaches. Instead, he pulled a scrap of parchment and pen and ink from pouches on his belt, scrawled a few nearly illegible lines—the motion of the horse didn't help—and then called, "Katakolon!" After a moment, he called again, louder.

"Aye, Father? How can I help you?" His youngest son brought his own horse trotting up alongside Krispos' mount.

Krispos handed him the note. "Seal this, stick it in a message tube, and get it off to Videssos the city as fast as you can."

"Just as you say." The piece of parchment was too small to roll or fold conveniently. Katakolon read it before he took it to do as Krispos had commanded. His eyes were troubled when he raised them to look at his father again. "Surely it can't be as bad as—this?"

"I don't know whether it is or not," Krispos said. "But as to

301

whether it can be—by Phos, boy, it could be ten times worse. He might be landing in the city with a shipload of fanatics all hot to die for the gleaming path."

"Phostis?" Katakolon's voice rose. He shook his head. "I can't believe it."

"I can, which is what matters," Krispos answered. "Now get moving. I didn't give you that note to argue over it, just to have it start on its way to the city."

"Aye, Father," Katakolon said dolefully.

"You don't suppose he'll 'accidentally' lose that, do you?" Sarkis said.

"He'd better not," Krispos answered; the same thought had crossed his mind. He remembered his talk with Evripos back in the city. If his sons thought strongly enough that they were right, they would follow their own wills, not his. They were turning into men—at the most inconvenient time possible.

Had Phostis done that? When he chose to walk the gleaming path, was he making his own judgments as best he knew how, no matter how wrongheaded they seemed to Krispos? Or had he merely found someone whose lead he preferred to his father's? Krispos shook his head. He wondered if Phostis knew.

As he had so often over the years, he forced personal worries—and worries about which he could do nothing—to the back of his mind. Enough other business remained to occupy him. The army was up on the plateau now, with everyone a bit on the hungry side because supply arrangements hadn't kept up with the changed route.

Of Livanios' force there was no sign. That worried Krispos. If the Thanasioi scattered before he could smite them, what point to the campaign? How was he supposed to beat them if they turned back into harmless-looking herders and farmers and tanners and candlemakers and what-have-you? If he went back to Videssos the city, they'd be raiders again the moment his dust vanished over the horizon. He was bitterly certain of that.

The army camped for the night by a stream that wouldn't have water in it too much longer. Now, though, it would serve. The men saw to their horses before they cared for themselves. Krispos strolled through the encampment, checking to make sure his orders on that score were obeyed. He'd served as groom first for Iakovitzes and then for Petronas after he came to the imperial city; he knew what went into tending horses.

He was sound asleep on his folding cot in the imperial tent when a Haloga called "Your Majesty" over and over until it woke him. He groaned as he made himself sit; his eyes felt as if someone had poured sand into their sockets. The guardsman said, "Your pardon, Majesty, but out here waits a courier who must see you."

"Aye, send him in," Krispos said in a voice that sounded nothing like his own.

He waved for the courier not to bother prostrating himself; the sooner the fellow was gone, he thought, the sooner he could get back to sleep. "May it please your Majesty," the courier said, and Krispos braced himself for bad news. The man delivered it: "I have to report that the Thanasioi have fallen on and taken the city of Kyzikos."

"Kyzikos?" Still foggy, Krispos needed a moment to place the town on the map. It lay down in the coastal plain, east of Garsavra. "What's Livanios doing there?" As soon as he raised the question, the answer became obvious: "The imperial mint!"

"Aye, your Majesty, it's taken and burned," the courier said. "The temple is burned, as well, and so is much of the central part of the city—like many towns in the western lowlands, Kyzikos has, or rather had, no wall to hold invaders at bay. And the farmland round the city is ravaged as if locusts had been at it."

"Aye," Krispos said. "A heavy blow." If Livanios' warriors could ravage Kyzikos, no place in the westlands was safe from them. And if Livanios had the gold from the mint in Kyzikos, he could work untold mischief with it, too. Gold and the Thanasioi did not normally mix, but Krispos did not think Livanios was a typical Thanasiot. If he read the heresiarch aright, Livanios cared more about Livanios than about the gleaming path.

But no matter how much damage they had done—Krispos' wits began working a little faster—they'd also made what might prove a bad mistake: they'd given the imperial army the chance to interpose itself between them and their stronghold near the border with Vaspurakan.

"If you stick your neck out too far, it gets chopped," Krispos said.

"Your Majesty?" the courier asked.

"Never mind." Clad only in his linen drawers, the Avtokrator strode out into the night. Ignoring the grunts of surprise that rose from the Haloga guards, he started bawling for his generals. If he couldn't sleep, he wouldn't let them sleep, either, not with work to be done.

Two days later, Sarkis said, for about the dozenth time, "The trick, your Majesty, will be to make sure they don't get by us."

"Yes," Krispos said, also for the dozenth time. The westlands' central plateau was not flat like the lowlands; it was rough, broken country, gullies running into ravines running into valleys. If the imperial army didn't position itself correctly, slipping between the Thanasioi and Etchmiadzin wouldn't matter because the raiders would get past without being noticed till too late. That was probably the gamble Livanios had made when he decided to strike Kyzikos.

Sarkis found a new question to ask: "How will you choose the right spot?"

"The best way I can figure is this," Krispos said: "I'll station us near one of the central valleys and fan scouts out widely ahead of us and to either side. It's no guarantee of anything, of course, but it's what we'll do unless you have a better idea. I hope you will."

"I was thinking something along the same lines," Sarkis said. "The trouble is, it's what Livanios will think is in our minds, too."

"That's so," Krispos admitted. "But if we play the game of if-he-then-we and if-we-then-he, we're liable to get lost in the maze. I'll cut through it and just do what I think best under the circumstances."

"Against any other foe I would say you were wise, your Majesty, but Livanios ... Livanios never seems to do what you'd expect." Sarkis turned his head at the sound of galloping hoofbeats. So did Krispos. Sarkis said, "Looks like another courier coming up—no, two of 'em together."

"Oh, Phos, what now?" It was more a groan than a prayer. Every courier who'd ridden up to Krispos lately had brought bad news with him. How much longer could that go on?

Sure enough, the riders made straight for the imperial standard that marked Krispos' place in the line of march. *They're sending out babies,* he thought. One of the couriers had no beard. The other didn't seem much older.

Krispos braced for the call of "May it please your Majesty" and the displeasing message that would follow it. The bearded rider spotted him under the sunburst standard, then raised a hand to his mouth to make a shout carry farther. But he didn't yell "May it please your Majesty." Instead, he called, "Father!"

Krispos' first thought was that Katakolon was playing some kind of trick on him, and not a funny one. Then he recognized the voice. He hadn't been sure he'd ever hear that voice again, or want to. "Phostis," he whispered.

His son approached, and the other rider with him. Several Halogai quickly moved to put themselves between Phostis and Krispos—they knew where Phostis had been, and did not know what he'd become. Krispos wanted to thank them and punch them at the same time.

"It's all right, Father—I've escaped the gleaming path," Phostis said.

Before Krispos answered, one of the Halogai said, "What proof of this have you, young Majesty?" The big fair men from the north did not stand aside.

*What proof could Phostis possibly have?* Krispos wondered. But he produced some: "Allow me to present Olyvria, the daughter of Livanios."

By then, Krispos had figured out that Phostis' companion was a woman. To remove any doubt, she doffed her traveler's hat with a flourish and let her piled-up hair tumble out in a curly black waterfall. "Your Majesty," she said, bowing in the saddle to Krispos.

*She's not just accompanying Phostis,* Krispos realized. *She's with him.* Phostis' eyes did not want to leave her, even to look at his father. Katakolon got that mooncalf gaze, but never over the same girl for more than a couple of months. Krispos hadn't seen it on Phostis before. Olyvria looked at Phostis the same way.

Acting? Krispos didn't think so. He asked Olyvria, "Are you here of your own will, girl, or did he kidnap you?"

"As a matter of fact, your Majesty, I kidnapped him," Olyvria answered boldly. Krispos stared; that was not the reply he'd expected. Olyvria added, "We've made other arrangements since."

"So I gather." Krispos glanced over to Phostis, who was still grinning like a besotted schoolboy. The Avtokrator made his decision. He told the Haloga guards, "Stand aside." After a moment's hesitation, they obeyed. He urged his horse up alongside Phostis', held out his arms. The two men, one young, the other vividly remembering when he had been, embraced.

Phostis pulled away. "Sorry, Father, but hugging chain mail hurts. I have so much to tell you—did you know, for instance, that Makuran is aiding the Thanasioi?"

"As things turn out, I did," Krispos said. "I'm glad to hear you tell me as much all the same—it lets me know you are to be trusted indeed."

He wondered if he should have been so frank. He watched Phostis' face freeze into the mask he'd seen so often before, the one that concealed whatever went on behind it. Minutes into their reunion, would the two of them go back to misunderstanding each other?

But Olyvria said, "I don't blame you for being wary of us, your Majesty. Truly, though, the gleaming path lures us no more."

To Krispos' relief, Phostis' face cleared. "That's so," he said. "I've seen more along those lines than I can stomach. And Father!—is Zaidas with you?"

"Aye, he is," Krispos answered. "Why?"

"I have much to tell him—and little of it good—of Artapan, the Makuraner mage who aids Livanios' schemes."

"All that can wait till tonight when we camp," Krispos said. "For now, it's enough to see you again." *And to see you here as something besides a Thanasiot fanatic,* he thought. He kept that to himself, though Phostis would have to be a fool if he couldn't figure it out. Let the lad have his time in Phos' sun now, though. "How did you escape the zealots' clutches, then?"

Phostis and Olyvria took turns telling the tale, which, as it unfolded, seemed only fair to Krispos. Phostis didn't try to minimize what he'd done as an unwilling Thanasiot raider; if anything, he dwelt on it with pained guilt. "How are your arm and shoulder now?" Krispos asked.

"They still pain me now and again," Phostis said, working the arm. "I can use them, though. Anyhow, Father, getting wounded helped convince Syagrios I could be trusted, and prompted him to let me go to Pityos—"

Olyvria took over then with the story of how she'd smashed the chamber pot on Syagrios' head. "Fitting enough," Krispos agreed. Then Phostis told of buying the fishing boat and sailing to Videssos the city. That made Krispos laugh out loud. "There—you see? All that time you passed on the water with me wasn't wasted after all."

"I suppose not," Phostis said; he was, if nothing else, more patient around Krispos than he had been before he was kidnapped. Krispos watched his mirth fade as he continued, "I found riots in the city when I got there."

"Yes, I knew of them," Krispos said, nodding. "I knew you were on the way to the city, too; Zaidas' magic told me as much. I feared you were traveling as provocateur, not escapee. I meant to write Evripos and tell him as much, but it slipped my mind until yesterday in the midst of everything else that's been going on."

"It didn't matter," Phostis answered. "He thought of it for himself."

"Good," Krispos said, to see how Phostis would react. Phostis didn't react much at all, certainly not with the anger he would have shown a few months before. He just nodded and went on with his story. When he was finished, Krispos said, "So our troops have the upper hand?"

"They did when Olyvria and I left to join you," Phostis said. "Uh, Father . . ."

"Yes?"

"What *do* you think of the suggestion I made to Evripos, that Olyvria and I should marry at once to show the Thanasioi we've renounced their sect?"

"Imperial marriages have a way of being made for reasons of state, but till now I'd never heard of one made for reasons of doctrine," Krispos answered. "Were the emergency worse, I might send the two of you back there to be wedded forthwith. As it is, I think you can wait till the campaign is over before you marry—assuming you still want to by then."

Their expressions said they could imagine no other possibility. Krispos had a deeper imagination. If they still wanted to go through with it come fall, he didn't think he'd object—or that Phostis would listen if he tried. The lad had needed to take care of himself lately, and had discovered he could do it. Few discoveries were more important.

Krispos said, "If you two like, you can spend the night in my pavilion." Then he saw their faces and laughed at himself. "No, you'll want a tent for yourselves, won't you? I would have, at your age."

"Well, yes," Phostis said. "Thank you, Father."

"It's all right," Krispos answered. At that moment, having Phostis back not only in one piece but opposed to the gleaming path, he could have refused him very little. He did add, "Before you repair to that tent, I trust you'll do me the honor of dining on army food and bad wine in the pavilion. I'll have Zaidas there, too; you said you wanted to talk with him, didn't you, Phostis? I'll see you around sunset."

Even with Olyvria's hand warm in his, Phostis approached Krispos' tent with considerable trepidation. When he set sail for Videssos the city, she'd feared he would remember he was junior Avtokrator and forget he was her lover. Now, as the bright silks of the imperial pavilion drew near, he was afraid his father would turn him into a boy again, simply by refusing to imagine he could be anything else.

The Halogai outside the entrance to the tent saluted him in imperial style, clenched right fists over their hearts. He watched them discreetly look Olyvria up and down, as men of any nation will when they see a pretty girl. One of them said something in his own language. Phostis understood it was about Olyvria but not what it meant; he had only a smattering of the Haloga tongue. He almost asked the guardsmen what it meant, but at the last minute decided not to make an issue of it—Haloga candor could be brutal.

Inside the tent waited Krispos, Katakolon, Zaidas, Sarkis, and half a dozen helpings of bread and onions and sausage and salted olives. Olyvria's smile puzzled Phostis till he remembered she was an officer's daughter. No doubt the fare looked familiar.

As they ate, Phostis and Olyvria retold their story for Zaidas; Sarkis and Katakolon had heard most of it in the afternoon. The mage, as usual, made a good audience. He clapped his hands when Olyvria again recounted knocking Syagrios out with the chamber pot, and when Phostis told how they'd decamped immediately thereafter.

"That's the way to do it," he said approvingly. "When you need to get out in a hurry, spend what you have to and leave. What's the point to saving your gold but failing of your purpose? Which reminds me . . ." He abruptly went serious and intent. "His Majesty the Avtokrator—"

"Oh, just say, 'your father' and have done," Krispos broke in. "Otherwise you'll waste half the night in useless blathering."

"As your Majesty the Avtokrator commands," Zaidas said. Krispos made as if to throw a crust of bread at him. Grinning, Zaidas turned back to Phostis. "Your father, I should say, tells me you learned something of importance about the techniques of Livanios' Makuraner wizard."

"That's true, sorcerous sir." Phostis had to work to stay formal; he'd almost called the mage Uncle Zaidas. "One day—this was after I learned Artapan was from Makuran—I followed him and—" He described how he'd learned Artapan fortified his power with the death energies of Thanasioi who starved themselves to complete their renunciation of the world. "And if they weren't quite dead when he needed them so, he wasn't averse to holding a pillow over their heads, either."

"That's disgusting," Katakolon said, sick horror in his voice.

Zaidas, by contrast, sounded eager, like a hunting dog just catching a scent. "Tell me more," he urged.

Olyvria gave Phostis a curious look. "You never spoke to me of this before," she said.

"I know I didn't. I didn't even like to think about it. And besides, I didn't think saying anything would be safe in Etchmiadzin. Too many ears around." And even after they became lovers, he hadn't trusted her, not completely, not until she set upon Syagrios. That, though, he kept to himself.

"Go on," Zaidas said. "All the ears here are friendly."

In as much detail as he could, prompted by sharp questions from the mage, Phostis recounted following Artapan down the street, standing in the stinking alley listening to him talk with Tzepeas, and the Thanasiot's premature and assisted death. "That isn't the only time I saw him hovering over people who were on the point of starving, either," he said. "Remember,

Olyvria? He kept hanging around Strabon's house while he was dying."

"He did," she said, nodding. "With Strabon and others. I never thought much about it—wizards have their ways, that's all."

Zaidas stirred in his seat, but didn't say anything. For a man of his age he was, Phostis thought, reasonably normal save for his sorcerous talent. But then, he was the only wizard Phostis knew well. Who could say what others were like?

"Did he pray as he—ended—this heretic's life?" Zaidas asked. "Either to Phos or to the Four Prophets, I mean?"

"He spoke some in Makuraner, but since I don't understand it, I don't know what he said. I'm sorry," Phostis answered.

"Can't be helped," the mage said. "It probably doesn't matter in any case. As you've noted for yourself, the transition from life to death is a powerful source of magical energy. We who follow Phos are forbidden to exploit it, lest we grow to esteem the power so much that we fall into injustice, slaying for the sake of magic alone. I was given to understand that prohibition also applied to followers of the Prophets Four, but I may be wrong. On the other hand, Artapan—that was the name, not so?—may be as much a heretic by Mashiz's standards as the Thanasioi are by ours."

Krispos said, "This would all be very interesting if we were hashing it out as an exercise at the Sorcerers' Collegium, sorcerous sir, but how does it affect us here in the wider world? Suppose Artapan is using magic fueled by death? Does that make him more dangerous? How do we counteract his magic if it does?"

Behind her hand, Olyvria whispered, "Your father drives straight for the heart of a question."

"That he does." Phostis scratched at the side of his jaw. "He gets frustrated when others don't follow as quickly, as they often don't." He wondered if that accounted for some of his father's impatience with him. But how could someone just coming into manhood be expected to stay with the schemes of a grown man with the full power of experience who was also one of the master schemers that Videssos, a nation of schemers, had ever known?

Zaidas missed the byplay and spoke straight to Krispos: "Your Majesty, a mage who uses death energy in his thaumaturgy gains strength, aye, but he also becomes more vulnerable to others' magic. That sort of compensation is nothing surprising. Wizardry, no matter what the ignorant may think, offers no free miracles. What you gain in one area, you lose in another."

"That's not just wizardry—that's life," Krispos said. "If you've chosen to take on a big flock of sheep, you won't be able to plant as much barley."

Sarkis chuckled. "How many years on the throne, your Majesty, to have you still talking like a peasant? A proper Emperor now, one from the romances, would say you can't war in east and west at the same time, or some such."

"To the ice with the romances," Phostis broke in. "The next one that tells a copper's worth of truth will be the first."

He caught Krispos watching him with eyebrow upraised in speculation. Unabashed, the Avtokrator gave him a sober nod. "You're learning, lad."

"I will speak for the romances," Olyvria said. "Where but in them does the prisoner escape with the heresiarch's daughter who's fallen in love with him?"

Now Sarkis laughed out loud. "By the good god, she's caught father and son in the same net." He swigged wine, refilled his mug, and swigged again.

When Krispos turned his gaze on Olyvria, amusement sparked in his eyes. He dipped his head, as if she'd made a clever move at the board game. "There is something to what you say, lady."

"No, there's not," Phostis insisted. "In what romance isn't the woman a quivering wreck who requires some bold hero to rescue her? And in which of them does *she* rescue the hero by clouting the villain with a thundermug?"

"It seemed the handiest thing in the room," Olyvria said amid general laughter. "Besides, you can't expect a romance to have *all* the details straight."

"You have to watch this one, brother," Katakolon said. "She's quick."

The only things Katakolon looked for in his companions were looks and willingness. No wonder he went through them like a drunkard through a wine cellar, Phostis thought. But he didn't feel like quarreling with Katakolon, not tonight. "I'll take my chances," he said, and let it go at that.

Sarkis looked at the jar of wine in front of him, yawned, and shook his head. He climbed to his feet. "I'm for bed, your Majesty," he announced. He turned to Phostis. "Good to have you back, and your *quick* lady." He walked out into the night.

Zaidas also rose. "I'm for bed, too. Would I had the power to store up sleep as a dormouse stores fat for its winter rest. Spurred not least by what you've said tonight, young Majesty, I think I shall be engaged in serious sorcery soon, at which time I will call on all my bodily reserves. The good god grant that they suffice."

"How cozy—it's a family gathering now," Krispos said when the mage left. He was not being sardonic; he beamed from Katakolon to Phostis and on to Olyvria. That took a weight of worry from Phostis; a young man will seldom turn aside from his beloved at his father's urging, but that is not an urging he ever cares to hear.

Then Katakolon also stood up. He clapped Phostis on the back, careful to stay away from the wounded shoulder. "Wonderful you're here and mostly intact," he said. He nodded to Olyvria and Krispos, then followed Sarkis and Zaidas out of the pavilion.

"He didn't say anything about bed," Krispos said, half laughing, half sighing. "He's probably out prowling for a friendly wench among the camp followers. He'll probably find one, too."

"Now I know you believe our tale, your Majesty," Olyvria said.

"How's that?" Krispos asked. Phostis recognized his tone; it was the one he always used when he was finding out what his sons had learned of their lessons.

"If you didn't, you'd not be sitting here with the two of us closer to you than your guards are," she answered. "We're desperate characters, after all, and if we can turn a chamber pot into a weapon, who knows what we might do with a spoon or an inkwell?"

"Who indeed?" Krispos said with a small chuckle. He turned to Phostis. "She is quick—you'd better take good care of her." He was quick himself; he didn't miss the yawn Olyvria tried to hide. "Now you'd better take her back to your tent. Riding the courier circuit is wearing—I remember."

"I'll do that, Father," Phostis said. "But may I come back here for a few minutes afterward?" Both Olyvria and Krispos looked at him in surprise. "Something I want to ask you," he said, knowing it was not an explanation.

Krispos had to know that, too, but he nodded. "Whatever you like, of course."

Olyvria asked questions all the way to the tent that had been set up for them. Phostis didn't answer any of them. He knew how much that irked her, but held his course regardless. The most he would say was, "It's nothing to do with you."

He walked back to the imperial pavilion almost as warily as he'd entered the tunnel that ran under Videssos the city. What he found here might be as dangerous as anything that had lurked there.

Salutes from the Halogai didn't make him any less nervous as he ducked his way into the pavilion. Krispos waited at the map table, a wine cup in his hand and curiosity on his face. Despite that curiosity, he waited quietly until Phostis had also filled a cup and taken a long draft. Then wine ran sweet down his throat, but gave him no extra courage. *Too bad,* he thought.

"Well," Krispos said when Phostis lowered the wine cup from his lips, "what's such a deep, dark secret that you can't speak of it in front of your lady love?"

Had Krispos sounded sarcastic, Phostis would have turned on his heel and strode out of the pavilion without answering. But he just seemed inquisitive—and friendly, too, which Phostis wasn't used to. He'd tried a dozen different ways of framing his question. When it escaped his lips, though, it did so without any fancy frame whatever: "Are you my father?"

He watched Krispos suddenly seem to freeze in place, all except his eyes, which grew very wide. Then, as if to give himself time to think, the Avtokrator lifted his cup and drained it dry. "I'd wondered what you wanted," he said at last. "I didn't expect you to ask me that."

"Are you?" Phostis pressed.

As young men will of their fathers—or those they believe their fathers—he'd always thought of Krispos as old, but old in the sense of conservative and powerful rather than actually elderly. Now, as the lines on Krispos' face deepened harshly, Phostis saw with eerie certainty what he would look like as an old man.

"*Are* you?" Phostis said again.

Krispos sighed. His shoulders sagged. He laughed for a moment, quietly and to himself. Phostis almost hit him then. Krispos walked over to the wine jar, poured himself another cup from it, then peered into the dark ruby depths. When he looked up toward Phostis, he spoke in what was almost a whisper: "Not a week's gone by, I think, since I took the crown that I haven't asked myself the same question . . . and I just don't know."

Phostis had expected a *yes* or *no*, something he could get his teeth into either way. Being left with more uncertainty was— maddening. "How can you *not* know?" he cried.

"If you thought to ask the question, son, the answer should be plain enough," Krispos said. He drank some of the wine— maybe he was looking for courage there, too. "Your mother was Anthimos' Empress; if it hadn't been for her, Anthimos would have slain me by magic the night I took the throne. She'd been his Empress for some years before she was mine, and never conceived. None of the other women he had—and believe me, he had a great flock of them—ever quickened, ei- ther. But what does that prove? Nothing for certain. I think you're likely to be mine, but that's the most I can say with any hope for truth."

Phostis did some more quiet calculating. If Krispos had sired him, he'd likely done it before he took the throne from Anthimos . . . and before he'd married Dara. He'd done it adulterously, in other words—and so had Phostis' mother.

He shied away from that thought; it was too uncomfortable to examine straight on. Instead, he said, "You always say I look like Mother."

"Oh, you do, lad—the eyes especially. That tiny fold of skin on the inner corner comes straight from her. So does the shape of your face, and so does your nose. She's the reason you don't have a great beak like mine." Krispos put thumb and forefinger on the tip of his nose.

"Unless you had nothing to do with the way my nose looks at all," Phostis said.

"There is that chance," Krispos agreed. "But if you don't take after me, you don't look like Anthimos, either. You might be handsomer if you did; nothing wrong with the way he looked. You favor Dara, though. You always have, ever since you were a baby."

In his mind's eye, Phostis had a sudden, vivid picture of

Krispos studying the infant he'd been, trying to trace resemblances. "No wonder you sometimes treated me as if I were the cuckoo's egg," he said.

"Did I?" Krispos peered down into his wine cup again. He sighed deeply. "I'm sorry, son; I truly am. I've always tried to be just with you, to put aside whatever doubts I had."

"Just? I'd say you were that," Phostis answered. "But you didn't often—" He broke off. How was he supposed to explain to Krispos that justice sufficed in the courts, but families needed more? The closest he could come was to say, "You always did seem easier with Evripos and Katakolon."

"Maybe I was . . . maybe I am. Not your fault, though—the trouble's been mine." If without great warmth, Krispos had the strength to meet troubles head on. "Where do we go from here?" he asked. "What would you have of me?"

"Can you take me for what I am instead of for whose son I might be?" Phostis said. "In every way that matters, I'm yours." He told Krispos how he'd found himself imitating him while a prisoner, and how so much of what Krispos said made more sense afterward.

"I know why that is," Krispos said. Phostis made a questioning noise. Krispos went on, "It's because the only experience anyone can really learn from is his own. I was probably just wasting breath beforehand when I preached at you: you couldn't have had any idea what I was talking about. And when my words did prove of some use to you—nothing could make me prouder."

He folded Phostis into a bear hug. For a moment, resentment flared in the younger man: where had embraces like this been when he was a boy and needed them most? But he'd already worked out the answer to that for himself. He wasn't pleased with Krispos for acting as he had over the years, but now that, too, made more sense.

Phostis said, "Can we go on as we did before? Even with doubts, I can't think of anyone I'd rather have for my father than you—and that includes Anthimos."

"That cuts both ways—son," Krispos said. "With me or in spite of me, you've made yourself a man. Let's hope it's not as it was. Let's hope it's better. So it may prove, for much of the poison between us is out in the open now."

"Phos grant that it be so—Father," Phostis said. They embraced again. When they separated, Phostis found himself yawning. He said, "Now I'm going back to my tent for the night."

Krispos gave him a sly look. "Will you tell your lady what passed here?"

"One of these days, maybe," Phostis said after a little thought. "Not just yet."

"That's what I'd say in your sandals," Krispos agreed. "You think like one of mine, all right. Good night, son."

"Good night," Phostis said. He yawned again, then headed back to the tent where Olyvria was waiting. When he walked in, he found that, almost certainly against her best intentions, she'd fallen asleep. He was careful not to wake her when he lay down himself.

"All right, sorcerous sir," Krispos said to Zaidas, "having learned what you did from my son, how do you propose to exploit it to our best advantage?"

He felt a stab when he spoke thus of Phostis, but it was not the usual stab of suspicious fear, merely one of curiosity. He was beginning to see he had a man there to reckon with, and if perchance Phostis was not his by blood, he certainly was by turn of mind. What more could any ruler—any father—want?

Zaidas said, "I will show you what I can do, your Majesty. Not least by using the power he has gained from the transition of fanatical Thanasioi out of life and into death, this Makuraner wizard, this Artapan, has built his magic to a point where it is difficult to assail. This much, to my discomfiture, you have seen."

"Yes," Krispos said. Many times he'd resolved to treat Phostis as if he were certain of his parentage; as many times, till now, he'd failed. This time, he thought he might succeed.

"An arch has a keystone," Zaidas went on. "Take it out and the whole thing crashes to the ground. So with Artapan's magic. Take away this power he has wrongfully arrogated to himself and he will be weaker than if he never meddled where he should not have. This is what I aim to do."

Krispos recognized the didactic tone in the sorcerer's voice. It suited him: though he had no sorcerous talent himself, he was always interested in hearing how wizards did what they did. Today, moreover, it would influence how he conducted his campaign. And so he asked, "How will you manage it, sorcerous sir?"

"By opposing the power of death with the power of life," Zaidas answered. "The sorcery is prepared, your Majesty. I shall essay it tomorrow at dawn, when the rising of Phos' sun, most powerful symbol of light and life and rebirth, shall add its influence to that of my magic. And your son, too, shall play a role, as shall Livanios' daughter Olyvria."

"Shall they?" Krispos said. "Will it endanger them? I'd not care to have Phostis restored to me only to lose him two days later in a war of sorcerers."

"No, no." Zaidas shook his head. "The good god willing—and so I believe the case to be—the procedure I have in mind will take Artapan altogether by surprise. And even if he knows Phostis has escaped and joined you here, your son gives the strong impression the Makuraner does not know his technique has been discovered."

"Until the dawn, then," Krispos said. He wanted immediate action, but Zaidas' reason for delay struck him as good. It also let the imperial army advance farther onto the westlands' central plateau—with luck, positioning the force to exploit whatever success against Artapan that Zaidas achieved.

Krispos wondered how much faith to place in his chief mage. Zaidas hadn't had much luck against the Thanasioi. Before, though, he hadn't known what he was opposing. Now he did. If he couldn't do something useful with that advantage . . . "Then he won't be any help at all," Krispos said aloud. He breathed a silent prayer for Zaidas up to the watching sky.

Red as blood, the sun crawled up over the eastern horizon. Zaidas greeted it by raising his hands to the heavens and intoning Phos' creed: "We bless thee, Phos, lord with the great and good mind, by thy grace our protector, watchful beforehand that the great test of life may be decided in our favor."

Phostis imitated the gesture and echoed the creed. He fought to stifle a yawn; yawning during the creed struck him as faintly blasphemous. But getting up well before sunrise as spring grew toward summer was anything but easy.

Beside him, Olyvria shifted from foot to foot. She looked awake enough, but nervous nonetheless. She kept stealing glances at Krispos. Being around the Avtokrator had to add to her unease. To Phostis, his father—for so he still supposed Krispos to be—was family first and ruler second; familiarity overcame awe. It was just the other way round for Olyvria.

"Get on with it," Krispos said harshly.

Used to any other man, it would have been a heads-will-roll tone. Zaidas merely nodded and said, "All in good time, your Majesty . . . Ah, now we see the entire disk of the sun. We may proceed."

A few hundred yards away, sunrise made the imperial army begin to stir in camp. Almost all the Haloga bodyguards stood between the camp and this little hillock, to make sure no one blundered up while Zaidas was at his magic. The rest were between the sorcerer and Krispos. Phostis didn't know what their axes could do against magic gone wrong. He didn't think they knew, either, but they were ready to try.

Zaidas lighted a sliver of wood from one of the torches that had illuminated the hillock before the day began. He used the flame to light a stout candle of sky-blue wax, one fat and tall enough to have provided imperial sealing wax for the next fifty years. As the flame slid down the wick and caught in the wax, he spoke the creed again, this time softly to himself.

Candles in daylight were normally overwhelmed by the sun. Somehow this one was not. Though when seen directly its flame was no brighter than that of an ordinary candle, yet its glow caught and held on Zaidas' face, and Krispos', and Olyvria's. Though he could not see himself, Phostis supposed the light lingered on him, as well.

Zaidas said, "This light symbolizes the long and great life of the Empire of Videssos, and of the faith that it has sustained and that has sustained it across the centuries. Long may Empire and faith flourish."

From under a silk cloth he took out another candle, this one hardly better than a tiny taper, a thin layer of bright red wax around a wick.

"That's the same color as the sealing wax on that vaunting letter Livanios sent me," Krispos said.

Zaidas smiled. "Your Majesty lacks only the gift to be a first-rate wizard. Your instincts are perfectly sound." He raised his voice to the half-chanting tone he used when incanting. "This small, brief candle stands for the Thanasioi, whose foolish heresy will soon fail and be forgotten."

Almost as soon as he spoke the last words, the little red candle guttered out. A thin spiral of smoke rose from it. When the breeze blew that away, nothing showed that the candle representing the Thanasioi had ever existed. The larger light, the one symbolizing Videssos as a whole, burned on.

"Now what?" Krispos demanded. "This should be the time to settle accounts with that Makuraner mage."

"Yes, your Majesty." Zaidas was a patient man. Sometimes even the most patient of men finds it necessary to let his patience show. He said, "I could proceed even more expeditiously if I did not have to pause and respond to inquiries and comments. Now—"

Krispos chuckled, quite unabashed. This time Zaidas ignored him. He took a large silk cloth, big enough for a wall hanging, and draped it over both Phostis and Olyvria. The cloth was of the same sky blue as the candle that stood for the Empire and the orthodox faith. The silk's fine weave let Phostis see through it mistily, as if through fog.

He watched Zaidas take up yet another cloth, this one striped in bright colors. It reminded him of the caftans Artapan had worn. No sooner had the thought crossed his mind than Zaidas declared, "Now we shall sorcerously show the wicked wizard of Makuran that he shall profit nothing from his courtship of death!" He dropped out of that impressive tone and into ordinary speech for a moment: "Now, young Majesty, comes your time to contribute to this magic. Take your intended in your arms, kiss her, and think on all you might be doing were the rest of us not standing around here making nuisances of ourselves."

Phostis stared at him through the thin silk cloth. "Are you sure that's what you want of us, Uncle Z—uh, sorcerous sir?"

"Do that alone and do it properly, young Majesty, and no one could do more this day. Think of it, if you must, as duty rather than pleasure."

Kissing Olyvria was not a duty, and Phostis refused to consider it one. Her sweet lips and tongue, the soft firmness of her body pressed against his, argued that she, too, enjoyed the task Zaidas had set them. So tightly did Phostis hold her against him that she could not have doubted what he wanted to do with her. He heard her laugh softly, back in her throat.

After a while, he opened his eyes. He'd kissed Olyvria a lot lately, and while he thoroughly enjoyed it, he'd never been part of a major conjuration before. He wanted to see what Zaidas was up to. The first thing he saw was that Olyvria's eyes were already open. That made him laugh.

Zaidas was holding the piece of striped fabric above the flame of the blue candle. He intoned, "As they celebrate life under their cloth, so may that overturn the Makuraner mage who would strengthen himself through death. Let his sorcery be consumed as Videssos' light consumes the cloth of his country." He thrust the fabric into the fire.

Phostis always regretted the silk cloth that hazed his vision; it made him doubt his own eyes. The striped square of fabric flared up brightly the moment the candle flame touched it. For that instant, it burned as if it had been soaked in oil; Phostis wondered if Zaidas could drop it fast enough to save his fingers.

But then the burning cloth flickered and almost went out. Not only that, the part that had been consumed seemed restored, so that the cloth looked bigger than it had when it burned brightest. Zaidas stumbled and almost took it out of the candle flame.

He stood steady, though, and repeated the incantation he'd used when he first put the cloth in the flame. To it he added other muttered charms that Phostis heard only indistinctly. The striped cloth began to burn again, hesitantly at first but then with greater vigor. "You have it, sorcerous sir!" Krispos breathed.

Though he spoke softly, he must have distracted Zaidas, for the flame on the cloth shrank and the cloth itself seemed to expand once more. But Zaidas rallied again. More and more of the cloth burned away. Finally, with a puff of smoke like the one from the expiring Thanasiot candle, it was gone. Zaidas stuck the thumb and forefinger of his right hand into his mouth. They shouldn't have been scorched, though—they should have been burned to the bone.

When he took the fingers out, the wizard said in a worn voice, "What magic can do, magic has done. The good god willing, I have struck Artapan a heavy blow this day."

"How shall you know whether the good god was willing?" Krispos asked.

Instead of answering directly, Zaidas swept the filmy silk

cloth away from Phostis and Olyvria and said, "You two can detach yourselves from each other now."

They shook their heads at the same time and both started to laugh. That was what made them break apart. Phostis said, "We liked what we were doing."

"I noticed that, yes," Zaidas said, so dryly it might have been Krispos talking.

Krispos repeated, "How will you know whether you smote Artapan?"

"Your Majesty, I am about to find that out, for which purpose I require your eldest son once more."

"Me?" Phostis said. "What do I need to do now?"

"What I tell you." Before explaining what that was, the mage turned to Olyvria and bowed. "My lady, I am grateful for your services against the Makuraner. Your presence is not required for this next conjuration." He made it sound as if her presence was not desired. Though that miffed Phostis, Olyvria nodded and swept down the little hillock. A couple of Halogai trailed after her; the northerners seemed to have accepted her as part of the imperial family.

"Why don't you want her to watch what we're doing?" Phostis asked Zaidas.

"Because I am going to use you to help locate her father Livanios," Zaidas answered. "You were in contact with him; by the law of contagion, you remain in contact. So, for that matter, does she, but no matter how she loves you, I would not use her as the instrument of her father's betrayal."

"A nicety of sentiment the Thanasioi wouldn't give back to us," Krispos said. "But you're right to use it. Carry on, sorcerous sir."

"I shall, never fear," Zaidas answered. "I was just about to explain that Artapan's magic has up to this point shielded the Thanasioi from such direct sorcerous scrutiny. If, however, we have weakened him with the conjuration just completed, this next spell should also succeed."

"Very neat," Krispos said approvingly. "You use the same magic to learn whether the previous one worked and where the heresiarch's main force is. That's economical enough to have sprung from the brain of a treasury logothete."

"I shall construe that as a compliment, and hope it was

meant so," Zaidas said, which squeezed a chuckle out of Krispos.

The conjuration the sorcerer had in mind seemed simple in the extreme. He took some loose, crumbly dirt from the top of the hillock and put it in a large, low bowl. Then he called Phostis over and had him press his hand down onto the dirt. As soon as Phostis drew back a pace, Zaidas began to chant. His left hand moved in quick passes over the bowl.

A few seconds later, hair prickled up on the back of Phostis' neck. The dirt was stirring, shifting, humping itself up into a ridge—no, not a ridge, an arrow, for one end showed an unmistakable point.

"East and a little south," Zaidas said.

"Very, very good," Krispos breathed; as usual, he was quietest when he felt most triumphant. "The mask is down, then—we can see the moves Livanios makes. Have you any idea how far away his force lies?"

"Not precisely, no," the mage answered. "By the speed with which the arrow formed, I should say he is not close. It gives but a rough measure, though."

"A rough measure is all we need for now. You and Phostis will work this magic every morning from now on, to give us the foe's bearing and your rough measure of how far away he is. Will Artapan know his magic has failed him?"

"I'm afraid so, your Majesty," Zaidas said. "Did you see how the cloth representing Makuran tried a couple of times to reconstitute itself? That was my opponent, attempting to resist and undo my spell. But he failed as I thought he would, for the power of life is stronger than that of death."

Krispos walked over to Phostis and clapped him on the back hard enough to stagger him. "And all of it thanks to you, son. I owe you a great deal; you've done me as much good by returning and aiding me as I feared you'd do me harm had you stayed with the Thanasioi. And besides that, I'm glad you're back."

"I'm glad I'm back, too, Father," Phostis said. If Krispos claimed the relationship despite his doubts, Phostis would not quarrel with it. He went on, "And what's this I hear about your missing me so much that you decided to sire a bastard"—He carefully did not say *another bastard*—"to take my place?" The year before, he couldn't have bantered so with Krispos.

The Avtokrator looked startled, then laughed. "Which of your brothers told you that?"

"Evripos, back at Videssos the city."

"Aye, it's true. I hope he also said I didn't intend to let it compromise the rights you three enjoy, even if it is a son."

"He did," Phostis said, nodding. "But really, Father, at your age—"

"That's all of you who've said that now," Krispos broke in. "To the ice with your teasing. As you'll find out, gray in your beard doesn't stop you from being a man. It may slow you down, but it doesn't stop you." He looked defiant, as if waiting for Phostis to find that funny.

But Phostis didn't feel like provoking him any further. Having just found his way onto good terms with Krispos, he wouldn't risk throwing that away for the sake of a few minutes' amusement. He probably wouldn't have made such a calculation the year before; two or three years earlier, he was sure he wouldn't have.

*What does that signify?* he wondered. *Is it what they mean by growing up?* But he already was grown up. He had been for years—hadn't he? Scratching his head, he walked back to the tent he shared with Olyvria.

"Due east now, your Majesty," Zaidas reported. "They're getting close, too; the arrow formed almost as soon as Phostis took his hand from the ensorceled soil."

"All right, sorcerous sir, and thank you," Krispos answered. For the last week he'd been maneuvering to place the imperial army square in the path of the withdrawing Thanasioi. "If the lord with the great and good mind is kind to us, we'll swoop down on them before they even know we're in the neighborhood."

"May it be so," Zaidas said.

"Due east, you say?" Krispos went on musingly. "They'd be somewhere not far from, hmm, Aptos, I'd say. Is that about right?"

"Given where we are now—" The mage frowned in concentration, then nodded. "Somewhere not far from there, yes."

"Uh, Father . . . ?" Phostis began in a tentative voice.

He hadn't sounded tentative since he'd escaped from the

Thanasioi. Krispos gave him a curious look, wondering why he did now. "What's wrong?" he asked.

"Uh," Phostis said again. By the hangdog look on his face, he regretted having spoke up. He needed a very visible rally before he continued. "When I had to go out on that Thanasiot raiding party, Father—remember? I told you of that."

"I remember," Krispos said. He also remembered what a turn news of Phostis' movement had given him, and how much he'd feared the youth really had decided to follow the gleaming path.

"When I was on that raid," Phostis resumed, "to my shame, I had to join in attacking a monastery. I know I wounded one of the holy monks; if I hadn't, he'd have broken my bones with his cudgel. And my torch was one that helped fire the place."

"Why are you telling me this?" Krispos asked. "Oxeites the patriarch is a better one to hear it if you're after the forgiveness of your sin."

"I wasn't thinking of that so much—more of making amends," Phostis said. "By your leave, I'd like to set aside a third of my allowance for the next couple of years and devote it to the monastery."

"You don't need my leave; the gold I give you each month is yours to do with as you will," Krispos said. "But this I will say to you: I'm proud of you for having the idea." He thought for a moment. "So you'd give them eighty goldpieces a year, would you? How would it be if I matched that?"

He watched Phostis' face catch fire. "Thank you, Father! That would be wonderful."

"I'll leave my name off the money," Krispos said. "Let them think it all comes from you."

"Uh," Phostis said for a third time. "I hadn't planned on putting my name on, either."

"Really?" Krispos said. "The most holy Oxeites would tell you an anonymous gift finds twice as much favor with Phos as the other kind, for it must be given for its own sake rather than to gain acclaim. I don't know about that, but I admit it sounds reasonable. I know I'm all the prouder of you, though."

"You know, you tell me that now twice in the space of a couple of minutes, but I'm not sure you ever said it to me before," Phostis said.

Had he spoken with intent to wound, he would have infuriated Krispos. But he had the air of a man just stating a fact. And it *was* a fact; Krispos' memory confirmed that too well. He hung his head. "You shame me."

"I didn't mean to."

"I know," Krispos said. "That makes it worse."

Sarkis rode up then, rather to Krispos' relief. After saluting, the cavalry general asked, "Now that the heretics are drawing near, shall we send out scouts to learn exactly where they are?"

Instead of answering at once, Krispos turned to Phostis. "Your store of wisdom seems bigger than usual this morning. What would *you* do?"

"Urk," Phostis said.

Krispos shook a finger at him. "You have to answer without the foolish noises. When the red boots are on your feet, these are the questions you must deal with. You can't waste time, either." He studied the youth, wondering how he'd do.

As if to redeem that startled squawk, Phostis made his voice as deep and serious as he could: "Were the command mine, I'd say no. We're tracking the Thanasioi well by magic, so why let them blunder against our men before the last possible moment? If Zaidas' magic has worked as well as he hopes, Artapan should be nearly blind to us. The more surprise we have, the better."

Sarkis glanced toward Krispos. The Avtokrator spoke six words: "As he said, for his reasons." Phostis looked even more pleased at that indirect praise than he had when Krispos said he was proud of him.

"Aye, it does make sense." Sarkis chuckled. "Your Majesty, you were a pretty fair strategist yourself before you really knew what you were doing. It must run in the blood."

"Well, maybe." Krispos and Phostis said it in the same breath and in the same tone. They looked at each other. The Avtokrator started to laugh. A moment later, so did Phostis. Neither one seemed able to stop.

Now Sarkis studied them as if wondering whether they'd lost their wits. "I didn't think it was that funny," he said plaintively.

"Maybe it's not," Krispos said.

"On the other hand, maybe it is," Phostis said. Thinking

back to the grueling and in the end uncertain talk they'd had a few nights before, the Avtokrator found himself nodding. If they could laugh about it, that probably boded well for the future.

"I still say you've gone mad in the morning," Sarkis rumbled. "I'll try one of you or the other this afternoon and see if you make any sense then." He rode off, beak of a nose in the air.

The tent was small and close. The warm night made it seem even closer. So did the stink of hot tallow from the candle stuck in the ground where its flame couldn't reach anything burnable. As she had for the past several nights, Olyvria asked, "What *did* you go back to talk about with your father?"

"I don't want to tell you," Phostis said. He'd been saying that ever since he'd come back from Krispos' pavilion. It was not an answer calculated to stifle curiosity, but he knew no better to give.

"Why don't you?" Olyvria demanded. "If it had to do with me, I have a right to know."

"It had nothing to do with you." Phostis had repeated that a good many times, too. It was even true. The only trouble was, Olyvria didn't believe him.

Tonight she seemed to have decided to argue like a canon lawyer. "Well, if it has nothing to do with me, then what possible harm could there be to my knowing it?" She grinned smugly, pleased with herself; she'd put him in a logician's classic double bind.

But he refused to be bound. "If it were your business, I wouldn't have wanted the talk to be private."

"That's not right." She glared, angry now.

"I think it is." Phostis didn't want anyone wondering who his father was. He wished he didn't have to wonder himself. One person could keep a secret—Krispos had, after all. Two people might keep a secret. More than two people . . . he supposed it was possible, but it didn't seem likely.

"*Why* won't you tell me?" Olyvria tried a new tack. "You've given me no reason."

"If I tell you why I won't tell you, that would be about the same as telling you," Phostis had to listen to that sentence again in his head before he was sure it had come out the way he wanted it. He went on, "It has nothing to do with you and me."

"What you talked about may not have, but that you won't tell me certainly does." Olyvria needed a moment's hesitation, too. "What could you possibly want to keep to yourself that way?"

"It's none of your concern." Phostis ground out the words one at a time. Olyvria glowered at him. He glowered back; these arguments got him angry, too. His hissed exhale was almost a snarl. He said, "All right, by the good god, I'll tell you what: suppose you go over to the Avtokrator's pavilion and ask him. If he doesn't mind telling you what we talked about, I suppose it's all right with me."

She had spirit. He'd known that from the day he first encountered her, naked and lovely and tempting, under Videssos the city. For a moment he thought she'd do as he'd dared and storm out of the tent. He wondered what Krispos would make of that, how he'd handle it.

But even Olyvria's nerve could fray. She said, "It's not just that he's your father—he's the Avtokrator, too."

"I know," Phostis said dryly. "I've had to deal with that my whole life. You'd best get used to it, too. Phos is the only true judge, of course, but my guess is that he'll be Avtokrator a good many years yet."

Videssian history knew instances of imperial heirs who grew impatient waiting for their fathers to die and helped the process along. It also knew rather more instances of impatient imperial heirs who tried to help the process along, failed, and never, ever got a second chance. Phostis had no interest in raising a sedition against Krispos for, among others, the most practical of good reasons: he was convinced the Avtokrator would smell out the plot and use him for it as a failed rebel deserved. He counted himself lucky that Krispos had forgiven him after his involuntary sojourn among the Thanasioi.

Probing still, Olyvria said, "Is it something that discredits you or your father? Is that why you don't want to talk about it?"

"I won't answer questions like that, either," Phostis said. Not answering was another trick he'd learned from Krispos. If you started responding the questions around the edge of the

one you didn't want to discuss, before long the exact shape
and size of the answer to that one came clear.

"I think you're being hateful," Olyvria said.

Phostis stared down his nose at her. It wasn't quite as long
and impressive as Krispos', but it served well enough. "I'm
doing what I think I need to do. You're Livanios' daughter, but
no one has tried to tear out of you any of his secrets that you
didn't care to give. Seems to me I ought to be allowed a secret
or two of my own."

"It just strikes me as foolish, that's all," Olyvria said. "How
could telling whatever it is possibly hurt you?"

"Maybe it couldn't," Phostis said, though he wondered how
much hay Evripos might make out of knowing how uncertain
his paternity was. Then he started to laugh.

"What's funny?" Olyvria's voice turned dangerous. "You're
not laughing at me, are you?"

Phostis drew the sun-circle over his heart. "By the good
god, I swear I'm not." His obvious sincerity mollified Olyvria.
Better still, he'd not taken a false oath. When he thought of
Evripos making hay, whose perspective was he borrowing but
that of Krispos the ex-peasant? Even if Krispos hadn't sired
him, he'd certainly shaped the way he thought, at levels so
deep Phostis rarely noticed them.

Olyvria remained mulish. "How can I trust you if you keep
secrets from me?"

"If you don't think you can trust me, you should have let
me put you ashore at some deserted beach." Now Phostis grew
angry. "And if you still don't trust me, I daresay my father will
give you a safe conduct to leave camp and go back to
Etchmiadzin or wherever else you'd like."

"No, I don't want that." Olyvria studied him curiously.
"You're not the same as you were last summer under the temple or even last fall after you—came to Etchmiadzin. Then you
weren't sure of what you wanted or how to go about getting it.
You're harder now—and don't make lewd jokes. You trust
your own judgment more than you did before."

"Do I?" Phostis thought about it. "Perhaps I do. I'd better,
don't you think? In the end, it's all I have."

"I hadn't thought you could be so stubborn," Olyvria said.
"Now that I know, I'll have to deal with you a little differently." She laughed in small embarrassment. "Maybe I

shouldn't have said that. It sounds as if I'm giving away some special womanly secret."

"No, I don't think so," Phostis said; he was happy to steer the conversation away from what he and Krispos had talked about. "Men also have to change the way they treat women as they come to know them better—or so I'm finding out, anyway."

"You don't mean *men*, you mean *you*," Olyvria said with a catlike pounce. Phostis spread his hands, conceding the point. He didn't mind yielding on small things if that let him keep hold of the big ones. He slowly nodded—Krispos would have handled this the same way.

Someone rode up to the nearby imperial pavilion in a tearing hurry. A moment later, Krispos started yelling for Sarkis. Not long after that, the Avtokrator and his general both yelled for messengers. And not long after *that*, the whole camp started stirring, though it had to be well into the third hour of the night.

"What do you suppose that's all about?" Olyvria asked.

Phostis had an idea of what it might be about, but before he could answer, someone called from outside the tent, "Are you two decent in there?"

Olyvria looked offended. Phostis didn't—he recognized the voice. "Aye, decent enough," he called back. "Come on in, Katakolon."

His younger brother pushed aside the entry flap. "If you are decent, you've probably been listening to all the fuss outside." Katakolon's eyes gleamed with excitement.

"So we have," Phostis said. "What is it? Have scouts brought back word that they've run into the Thanasioi?"

"Oh, to the ice with you," Katakolon said indignantly. "I was hoping to bring a surprise, and here you've gone and figured it out."

"Never mind that," Phostis said. "The fuss means we fight tomorrow?"

"Aye," Katakolon answered. "We fight tomorrow."

# XII

K<small>ATAKOLON POINTED TO THE RISING CLOUD OF DUST AHEAD.</small>
"Soon now, Father," he said.

"Aye, very soon," Krispos agreed. Through the dust, the early morning sun sparkled off the iron heads of arrows and javelins, off chain mail shirts, off the polished edges of sword blades. The Thanasioi were hurrying through the pass, heading back toward Etchmiadzin after a raid that had spanned most of the length of the westlands.

Sarkis said, "Now, your Majesty?"

Krispos tasted the moment. "Aye, now," he said.

Sarkis waved. Quietly, without the trumpet calls that usually would have ordered them into action, two regiments of cavalry rode up the pass from the imperial lines. Sarkis' grin filled his fat face. "That should give them something new to think about. If Zaidas spoke truly, they don't know we're anywhere nearby, let alone in front of them."

"I hope he spoke truly," Krispos said. "I think he did. By all the signs his magic could give, their Makuraner mage is altogether stifled."

"The good god grant it be so," Sarkis said. "I have no love for Makuraners; every so often they take it into their heads that the princes of Vaspurakan should be forced to reverence their Prophets Four rather than Phos."

"One day, maybe, Videssos can do something about that," Krispos said. The Empire, he thought, ought to protect all those who followed the lord with the great and good mind. But

Vaspurakan had lain under the rule of the Kings of Kings of Makuran for a couple of hundred years.

"Begging your pardon, your Majesty, but I'd sooner we were free altogether," Sarkis said. "Likely your hierarchs would make spiritual masters no more pleasant than the men from Mashiz. Your folk would be as harsh on us as heretics as the Makuraners are on us as infidels."

"Seems to me you're both quarreling over the taste of a loaf you don't have," Katakolon said.

Krispos laughed. "You're probably right, son—no, you *are* right." Thin in the distance, shouts said that the Thanasioi and the regiments Krispos had sent out to delay them were knocking heads.

This time, Krispos waved. Now trumpets and drums and pipes rang loud. The imperial force that had been aligned parallel to the direction of the pass swung in a great left wheel to block its mouth and keep the heretics from breaking through.

As the imperials raised their own dust and then as they came into view, the shouts from the Thanasioi got louder. Their red banners waved furiously. They might have been taken by surprise, but there was no quit in them. On they came, driving the lead regiments back on the main body of Krispos' force.

The Avtokrator, who now stood at his army's extreme right rather than to the fore, admired the bravery of the Thanasioi. He would have admired it even more had it been aimed at the Empire's foreign enemies rather than against him.

Phostis tapped him on the shoulder, pointing to the center of the heretics' line. "That's Livanios, Father: the fellow in the gilded shirt between those two flags there."

Krispos' eye followed Phostis' finger. "I see the man you mean. His helm is gilded, too, isn't it? For someone who leads a heresy where all men are condemned to the least they can stand, he likes imperial trappings well, doesn't he?"

"He does," Phostis agreed. "That's one of the reasons I decided I couldn't stomach the Thanasioi: too much hypocrisy there for me to stand."

"I see," Krispos said slowly. Had Livanios been a sincere fanatic rather than an opportunist, then, he might have used Phostis' self-righteousness to draw him deep into the Thanasiot movement. But a sincerely destructive fanatic would not have gone after the imperial mint at Kyzikos. Had Krispos needed any further explication of Livanios' character, that raid would have given it to him.

Which was not to say he lacked courage. He threw himself into the thick of the fighting, flinging javelins and slashing with his saber when the battle came to close quarters.

It was, to all appearances, a fight devoid of tactical subtlety. The Thanasioi wanted to break through the imperial line; Krispos' soldiers aimed to keep them bottled up inside the pass. They plied the heretics with arrows from a line several men deep. Even when the first ranks had to struggle hand to hand, those behind them kept shooting at the Thanasioi who piled up ever tighter against the barrier the imperials had formed.

Fewer Thanasioi were archers. In any case, archery by itself would not sweep aside Krispos' men. In spite of the galling wounds they received, the heretics charged again and again, seeking to hew a path through their foes. "The path!" they cried. "The gleaming path!"

Along with trying to break through in the center, the Thanasioi also sent wave after wave of fighters against Krispos and his retinue. With their shields, mail shirts, and heavy axes, the Halogai stood like a dam between the Avtokrator and the fighters who sought to lay him low. But the northerners could not hold all arrows away from him. He had a shield of his own, and needed it to protect his face.

His horse let out a frightened squeal and tried to rear. Krispos fought the animal back under control. An arrow protruded from its rump. *Poor beast*, he thought—it knew nothing of the differences in worship because of which it had been wounded.

The Thanasioi charged again. This time some of them broke through his screen of bodyguards. Phostis traded saber strokes with one, Katakolon with another. That left Krispos facing two at once. He slashed at the one on his right side, used his shield to hold off the blows of the one to his left, and hoped someone would come to his aid soon.

Suddenly the horse of the Thanasiot to his right screamed, far louder and more terribly than his own mount had a few minutes before. A Haloga axe had bitten into its spine, just behind its rider. The horse foundered. The Haloga raised his axe again and slew the Thanasiot.

That let Krispos turn against his other foe. He still remembered how to use a sword himself, and slashed the fellow on the forearm. Another Haloga guard, his axe dripping gore, bore down on the heretic. The Thanasiot ignored him, bending every effort toward slaying the Avtokrator. He paid the price for his fanaticism: the guardsman hacked him out of the saddle.

"Thanks." Krispos panted. Sweat ran down his forehead and stung his eyes. "I'm getting old for this business, much as I hate to admit it."

"No man is young enough to be happy fighting two," the Haloga said, which made him feel a little better.

Among them, his sons and the northerners had put an end to the other Thanasioi who'd broken through. Katakolon had a cut that stretched halfway across one cheek, but managed a blood-spattered smile for Krispos. "Iakovitzes won't like me so well anymore," he shouted.

"Ah, but all the girls will sigh over how brave you are," Krispos answered, which made his youngest son's smile wider.

Another Thanasiot surge. The Halogai on foot and Videssians on horseback contained it. Krispos gauged the fighting. He had not asked a great deal of his men, only that they hold their place against the onslaught of the Thanasioi. So much had they done. The heretics were bunched against them, still trying to force their way out of the valley.

"Send for Zaidas," Krispos commanded. A messenger rode off.

He soon returned with the wizard, who had not been far away. "Now, your Majesty?" Zaidas asked.

"The time will never be better," Krispos said.

Zaidas set to work. Most of his preparations for this magic had been made ahead of time. It was not, properly speaking, battle magic, nor directed against the Thanasioi. Battle magic had a way of failing; the stress of fighting raised emotions to such a pitch that a spell which might otherwise have been fatal failed to bite at all.

"Let it come forth!" Zaidas cried, and stabbed a finger up toward the sky. From his fingertip sprang a glowing green fireball that rose high above the heaving battle line, growing and getting brighter as it climbed. A few soldiers from both sides paused for an instant to call Phos' name or sketch the sun-sign above their hearts. Most, however, were too busy fighting for their lives to exclaim over the fireball or to notice it at all.

Zaidas turned to Krispos. "What magic may do, magic has done," he said. His voice was ragged and worn; sorcery cost those who worked it dear.

Little by little, the green fireball faded. Before too long, it was gone. Watching the indecisive fight to which he had committed his army, Krispos wondered if it had been sent skyward in vain. Men should have been watching for its flare ... but one of the lessons he'd learned after close to half a lifetime on the throne was the chasm that sometimes yawned between *should have been* and *were*.

His head went rapidly back and forth from one side of the valley to the other. "Where are they?" he demanded, not of anyone in particular but of the world at large.

As if that had been a cue, martial music rang out in the distance. Soldiers in the imperial army cheered like men possessed; the Thanasioi stared about in sudden confusion and alarm. Down into the valley from left and right rode fresh regiments of horsemen in line. "Krispos!" they cried as they bent their bows.

"Taken in both flanks, by the good god!" Sarkis exclaimed. "Your Majesty, my hat's off to you." He doffed the iron pot he wore on his head to show he meant his words literally.

"You helped come up with the plan," Krispos said. "Besides, we both ought to thank Zaidas for giving a signal the watchers from both concealed flanking parties could see and use. Better by far than trying to gauge when to come in by the sandglass or any other way I could think of."

"Very well." Sarkis took off his helmet for Zaidas, too.

The wizard's grin took years off his age and reminded Krispos of the eager, almost painfully bright youngster he'd been when he began his sorcerous service. That had been in the last campaign against Harvas, till now the hardest one Krispos had known. But civil war—and religious civil war at that—was worse than any attack from a foreign foe.

Where the Avtokrator and the general had praised his sorcery, Zaidas thought about the fighting that remained ahead. "We still have to win the battle," he said. "Fail in that and the best plan in the world counts for nothing."

Krispos studied the field. Had the Thanasioi been professional soldiers, they might have salvaged something by retreating as soon as they discovered themselves so disastrously outflanked. But all they understood of the military art was going forward no matter what. That only got them more thoroughly trapped.

For the first time since fighting began, Krispos turned loose a smile. "This is a battle we are going to win," he said.

Phostis was only a few feet from his father when Krispos claimed victory. He was no practiced strategist himself, but he could see that a foe attacked on three sides at once was on the way to destruction. He was glad Olyvria had stayed back at the camp. Though she'd given herself to him without reservation, seeing all her father's hopes go down in ruin could only bring her pain.

Phostis knew pain, too, but of a purely physical sort. His shoulder ached with the effort it took to hold up a shield against arrows and saber slashes. In another couple of weeks it could have borne the burden without complaint, but not yet.

Screeching "The gleaming path!" for all they were worth, the Thanasioi mounted yet another charge. And from the midst of the fanatics' ranks, Phostis heard another cry, one not fanatical at all: "If we slay the Avtokrator, lads, it's all up for grabs!"

Fueled by desperation, fervor, and that coldly rational cry, the heretics surged against the right wing of the imperial line. As they had once before, they shot and hacked their way through the Halogai and Videssians protecting Krispos. All at once, being of high rank stopped mattering.

Off to one side of Phostis, Sarkis laid about him with a vigor that denied his bulk. To the other, Krispos and Katakolon were both engaged. Before Phostis could spur his horse to their aid, someone landed what felt like a hammer blow to his shield.

He twisted in the saddle. His foe was yelling at the top of his lungs; his was the voice that had urged the Thanasioi against Krispos. "Syagrios!" Phostis yelled.

The ruffian's face screwed into a gap-toothed grimace of hate. "You, eh?" he said. "I'd rather carve you than your old man—I owe you plenty, by the good god." He sent a vicious cut at Phostis' head.

Just staying alive through the next minute or so was as hard as anything Phostis had ever done. He didn't so much as think of attack; defense was enough and more. Intellectually, he knew that was a mistake—if all he did was try to block Syagrios' blows, sooner or later one would get through. But they came in such unrelenting torrents that he could do nothing else. Syagrios was twice his age and more, but fought with the vigor of a tireless youth.

As he slashed, he taunted Phostis: "After I'm done with you, I'll settle accounts with that little whore who crowned me. Pity you won't be around to watch, on account of it'd be worth seeing. First I'll cut her a few times, just so she hurts while I'm—" He went into deliberately obscene detail.

Fury all but blinded Phostis. The only thing that kept him from attacking wildly, foolishly, was the calculating look in Syagrios' eyes as he went through his speech. He was working to enrage, to provoke. Refusing to give him what he wanted was the best thing Phostis saw to do.

A Haloga came up on Syagrios' left side. The ruffian had no shield, but managed to turn aside the guardsman's axe with the flat of his blade. That wouldn't work every time, and he knew it. He spurred his horse away from the northerner—and from Phostis.

As he drew back, Phostis cut at him. The stroke missed. Phostis laughed. In the romances, the hero always slashed the villain into steaks. In real life, you were lucky if you didn't get hacked to bits yourself.

Since he was for the moment not beset, Phostis looked around to see how his comrades were faring. He found Krispos in the midst of a sea of shouting Thanasioi. The Avtokrator, badly beset, slashed frantically this way and that.

Phostis spurred toward him. To the Thanasioi, he was nothing—just another soldier, a nuisance, not a vital target like Krispos. He wounded three heretics from behind in quick succession. That sort of thing wasn't in the romances, either; they went on and on about glory and duels and fair fights. Real war, Phostis was discovering in a hurry, didn't concern itself with such niceties. If you stayed alive and the other fellow didn't, that was a triumph of strategy.

The Halogai also fought their way in Krispos' direction. So did all the reserves who saw he was in danger. Quite suddenly, no living Thanasioi were near the Avtokrator. Krispos' helmet had been battered so that it sat at a crazy angle on his head. He had a cut on his cheek—almost a match for Katakolon's—and another on his sword arm. His gilded mail shirt and shield were splashed with sticky red.

"Hello, everyone," he said. "Rather to my surprise, I find myself still in one piece."

Several variations of *Glad you are* rose into the air, Phostis' among them. He looked round for Syagrios, but did not see him. Real battle lacked the romances' neat resolutions, too.

Krispos went in the blink of an eye from a horseman fighting wildly for his life to the commander of a great host. "Drive them hard!" he shouted, pointing toward the center of the line. "See them waver? One good push and they'll break."

Had Zaidas not said Krispos lacked all talent for magic, Phostis might have believed him a wizard then. No sooner had he called attention to the sagging Thanasiot line than crimson banners began falling or being wrested from the hands of the heretics who bore them. The roar that went up from the imperials at that rang through the valley like a great horn call.

"How could you tell?" Phostis demanded.

"What? That?" Krispos thought for a moment, then looked sheepish. "Part of it comes from seeing a lot of fights. My eye knows the signs even if my mouth doesn't. And part of it—sometimes, don't ask me how, you can make your will reach over a whole battlefield."

"Maybe it *is* magic."

Phostis didn't realize he'd spoken out loud until Krispos nodded soberly. "Aye, it is, but not of the sort Zaidas practices. Evripos has a touch of it; I've seen that. You haven't yet had the chance to find out. You can rule without it, not doubt of that, but it makes life easier if it's there."

*One more thing to worry about,* Phostis thought. Then he shook his head. He needed to worry about two things, not one: whether he had the magic of leadership, and how vulnerable he would be if Evripos had it and he didn't.

At any other time, he might have occupied himself for hours, maybe days, with worries over those two. Now, with the battle swinging the imperials' way at last—could it be past noon already?—he had no leisure for fretting.

"Forward!" came the cry all along the line. Phostis was glad to press the fighting. It relieved him of having to think. As he'd found in Olyvria's arms, that could be a blessing of sorts. The only trouble was, worries didn't go away. When the fighting or the loving was done, they reared their heads again.

But not now. Shouting "Forward!" with the rest, he rode against the crumbling resistance of the Thanasioi.

Krispos looked out at victory and found it as appalling as it usually is. Pierced and mangled men and horses were the building blocks of what the chroniclers would one day call a splendid triumph of arms. At the moment, it reminded Krispos of nothing so much as an open-air slaughterhouse, down to the stink of entrails and the buzz of hungry flies.

Healer-priests wandered through the carnage, now and then stooping to aid some desperately wounded man. Their calling did not let them discriminate between Krispos' followers and the Thanasioi. Once, though, Krispos saw a blue-robe stand up and walk away from someone, shaking his shaven head in bewilderment. He wondered if a dying Thanasiot had possessed the courage to tell the healer he would sooner walk the gleaming path.

Most of the heretics, though, were glad enough to get any help the imperials gave them. They held out gashed arms and legs for bandages and obeyed their captors' commands with the alacrity of men who knew they might suffer for any transgression. In short, they behaved like other prisoners of war Krispos had seen over the years.

Katakolon rode up to the Avtokrator. "Father, they've run down the heretics' baggage train. In it they found some of the gold, ah, abstracted from the mint at Kyzikos."

"Did they? That's good news," Krispos said. "How much of the gold gold was recovered?"

"Something less than half the amount reported taken," Katakolon answered.

"More than I expected," Krispos said. Nevertheless, he suspected the troopers who'd captured the baggage train were richer now than when they'd started their pursuit. That was part of the price the Empire paid for civil war. If he tried to squeeze the gold out of them, he'd get a name for niggardliness that might lead to another revolt a year or three down the line.

"Your Majesty!" Another messenger waved frantically. "Your Majesty, we think we have Livanios!"

The gilded mail shirt that weighed on Krispos' shoulders all at once seemed lighter. "Fetch him here," the Avtokrator ordered. Then he raised his voice. "Phostis!"

"Aye, Father?" His eldest looked worn, but so did everyone else in the army.

"Did you hear that? They think they've caught Livanios. Will you identify him for me? You've see him often enough."

Phostis thought for a moment, then shook his head. "No," he said firmly.

"What?" Krispos glared at him. "Why not?"

"He's Olyvria's father," Phostis said. "How am I to live with her if I point the finger at him for the headsman?"

"Your mother's father plotted against me when you were a baby, do you know that?" Krispos said. "I exiled him to a monastery at Prista." The outpost on the northern shore of the Videssian Sea was as grim a place of exile as the Empire had.

"But did Mother tell you of his plot?" Phostis demanded. "And would you have taken his head if he'd not been her father?"

The questions, Krispos admitted to himself, were to the point. "No and yes, in that order," he said. Even after exiling Rhisoulphos, he'd been nervous about sleeping in the same bed with Dara for a while.

"There, you see?" Phostis said. "Livanios was an officer of ours. You'll have others here who can name him for you."

Krispos thought about ordering Phostis to do as he'd said, but not for long. He had learned better than to give orders that had no hope of being obeyed—and in any case, Phostis was right. "Let it be as you say, son," the Avtokrator said.

He watched in some amusement as Phostis, obviously ready to argue more, deflated. "Thank you," the younger man said, his voice full of relief.

Krispos nodded, then called, "Who among my soldiers knows the traitor and rebel Livanios by sight?"

The question ran rapidly through the army. Before long, several men sat their horses close by Krispos. Among them was Gainas, the officer who'd sent back to Videssos the city the dispatch warning of Livanios' defection to the gleaming path.

The prisoner himself took a while to arrive. When he did,

Krispos saw why: he was afoot, one of several captives with hands tied behind their backs so they could not even walk quickly. Phostis said, "The one on the left there, Father, is the mage Artapan."

"Very good," Krispos said quietly. If Artapan was in this group, then Livanios probably was, too. Phostis had, in fact, all but said he was. Here, though, the *all but* was important. Krispos turned to the men he'd assembled. "Which of them is Livanios?"

Without hesitation, they all pointed to the fellow two men away from Artapan. The captive straightened and glared at Krispos. He was doing his best to keep up a brave front. "I am Livanios. Do as you please with my body. My soul will walk the gleaming path beyond the sun and dwell with Phos forever."

"If you were so set on walking the gleaming path, why did you rob the mint at Kyzikos and not just burn it?" Phostis asked. "You didn't despise material things enough to keep from dirtying your hands with them."

"I do not claim to be the purest among the followers of the holy Thanasios," Livanios said. "Nevertheless, I follow the truth he preached."

"The only place you'll follow him, I think, is to the ice," Krispos said. "And since I've beaten you and taken you in arms against me, I don't need to argue with you." He turned to one of the Halogai. "Trygve, you're still carrying your axe. Strike off his head and have done."

"Aye, Majesty." The big blond northerner strode over to Livanios and pushed him so he went to his knees. Trygve spoke with neither cruelty nor any great compassion, merely a sense of what needed doing: "Bend your neck, you. It will be over soonest then."

Livanios started to obey, but then his eyes found Phostis. With a quick glance toward Krispos, he asked, "May I put a last question?"

Krispos thought he knew what that question would be. "Be quick about it."

"Yes, your Majesty." Livanios did not sound sarcastic—but then, Krispos did not have to give him an easy end, and he knew it. He turned to Phostis. "D'you have my daughter? Syagrios said he thought you did, but—"

"Yes, I have her," Phostis said.

Livanios bowed his head. "I die content. My blood goes on."

Krispos did not want him having the last word. "My father-in-law died in exile up in Prista, a traitor," he said. "My son's father-in-law will die before he even properly gains that title, also a traitor. Temptation, it seems, rides Emperors' fathers-in-law hard—too hard." He gestured to Trygve.

The axe came down. It wasn't a broad-bladed, long-handled headsman's weapon, but the big man who wielded it was strong enough that that didn't matter. Krispos turned his head away from the convulsions of Livanios' corpse. Phostis, who had watched, looked green. Executions were harder to stomach than deaths in combat.

Unfortunately, they were also sometimes necessary. Krispos turned to Artapan. "If your hands were free, sirrah, I daresay you'd be making magic from his death agony there."

"I would try." Artapan's mouth twisted. "You have a strong mage at your side, Videssian Emperor. With him opposing, perhaps I'd not succeed."

"Did Rubyab King of Kings know you were a death-drinker when he sent you forth to help our heretics?" Krispos asked.

"Oh, indeed." The Makuraner magician's mouth twisted again, this time in a different way—wry amusement. "I was under sentence of death from the *Mobedham-mobedh*—the high patriarch, you would say—when the King of Kings plucked me from my cell and told me what he required. I had nothing to lose by the arrangement. Nor did he."

"True enough," Krispos said. If Artapan had failed in the mission Rubyab set him, he would die—but he was condemned to die anyhow. And if he succeeded, he would do more good for Makuran than for himself. Rubyab had never been anything but a wily foe to Videssos, but this piece of double-dealing was as devious as any Krispos had ever imagined.

He nodded again to Trygve. Artapan jerked free of his captors and tried to run. With his hands bound behind him, with so many men chasing him, he didn't get more than a couple of paces. The meaty sound of the axe striking cut off his last scream.

"Foolishness," Trygve said from where he cleaned the blade

on the wizard's caftan. "Better to die well, since die he would. Livanios did it properly."

Katakolon pointed to the other two captive Thanasioi, who stood in glum and shaky silence. "Will you take their heads, too, Father?"

Krispos started to ask if they would abandon their heresy, then remembered the answer meant little: the Thanasioi felt no shame at lying to save their skins, and might keep their beliefs in secret. Instead, the Avtokrator turned to Phostis and asked, "How big are these fish we've caught?"

"Medium size," Phostis answered. "They're officers, but they weren't part of Livanios' inner circle."

"Take them away and put them with the rest of the prisoners, then," Krispos said to the guards who stood behind the captives. "I'll figure out what to do with them later."

"I've never seen—I've never imagined—so many captives." Katakolon pointed toward long rows of Thanasiot prisoners, each bound to the man in front of him by a line that wrapped round his wrists and then his neck: any effort to flee would only choke those near him. Katakolon went on, "What will you do with them all?"

"I'll figure that out later, too," Krispos said. His memory went back across two decades, to the fearsome massacres Harvas Black-Robe had worked among the captives he'd taken. Seeing those pathetic corpses, even so long ago, had burned away forever any inclination toward slaughter Krispos might have had. He could imagine no surer road to the eternal ice.

"You can't just send them back to their villages," Phostis said. "I did come to know them while I was in their hands. They'll promise anything, and then a year from now, or two, or three, they'll find themselves a new leader and start raiding again."

"I know that," Krispos said. "I'm glad to see you do, too."

Sarkis rode up. In spite of bloody bandages, the cavalry general seemed in high spirits. "We shattered 'em and scattered 'em, your Majesty," he boomed.

"Aye, so we did." Krispos sounded less gleeful. He'd learned to think in bigger terms than battles, or even campaigns. He wanted more from this victory than the two years' respite Phostis had suggested. He scratched his nose, which wasn't as impressive as Sarkis' but did exceed the Videssian norm. "By the good god," he said softly.

"What is it?" Katakolon asked.

"My father—after whom you're named, Phostis—always said we had Vaspurakaner blood in us, even though we lived far from here, up by—and sometimes over—what used to be the border with Kubrat. My guess is that our ancestors had been resettled there on account of some crime or other."

"Very likely," Sarkis said, as if that were a matter for pride.

"We could do the same with the Thanasioi," Krispos said. "If we uproot the villages where the heresy flourishes most and transplant those people over near Opsikion in the far east, say, and up near the Istros—what used to be Kubrat still needs more folk to work the land—those Thanasioi would be likely to lose their beliefs in a generation or two among so many orthodox folk, just as a pinch of salt loses itself in a big jug of water."

"It might work," Sarkis said. "Videssos has done such things before—else, as you say, your Majesty, your own forebears would not have ended up where they did."

"So I've read," Krispos said. "We can even run the transfer both ways, sending in orthodox villagers to loosen the hold the Thanasioi have on the region round Etchmiadzin. It will mean a great lot of work, but if the good god is willing it will put an end to the Thanasiot problem once and for all."

"Moving whole villages—thousands, tens of thousands of people—from one end of the Empire to the other? Moving more thousands back the other way?" Phostis said. "Not the work alone—think of the hardships you'll be making."

Krispos exhaled in exasperation. "Remember, these men we just beat down have sacked and ravaged Kyzikos and Garsavra just lately, Pityos last year, and the lord with the great and good mind only knows how many smaller places. How much hardship did they make? How much more would they have made if we hadn't beaten them? Put that in the balance against moving villagers around and tell me which side of the scale goes down."

"They believe in the Balance in Khatrish and Thatagush," Phostis said. "Have you beaten one heresy, Father, only to join another?"

"I wasn't talking about Phos' Balance, only the one any

man with a dram of sense can form in his own mind," Krispos said irritably. Then he saw Phostis was laughing at him. "You scamp! I didn't think you'd stoop to baiting me."

As was his way, Phostis quickly turned serious again. "I'm sorry. I'll build that balance and tell you what I think."

"That's fair," Krispos said. "Meanwhile, no need to apologize. I can stand being twitted. If I couldn't, Sarkis here would have spent these last many years in a cell under the government office buildings—assuming he'd fit into one."

The cavalry commander assumed an injured expression. "If you'd jailed me many years ago, your Majesty, I shouldn't have attained to my present size. Not on what you feed your miscreants, I shouldn't."

"Hrmph." Krispos turned back to Phostis. "What did your balance tell you?"

"If it must be done, then it must." Phostis neither looked nor sounded happy. Krispos didn't mind that. He wasn't happy himself. He and his village had been resettled twice when he was a boy, once forcibly by Kubrati raiders, and then again after the Empire ransomed them from the nomads. He knew the hardship relocating entailed. Phostis went on, "I wish it didn't have to be done."

"So do I," Krispos said. Phostis blinked, which made Krispos snort. "Son, if you think I enjoy doing this, you're daft. But I see that it has to be done, and I don't shrink from it. Liking all of what you do when you wear the red boots is altogether different from doing what needs doing whether you like it or not."

Phostis thought about that. It was a very visible process. Krispos gave him credit for it; before he'd been snatched, he would have been more likely to dismiss out of hand anything Krispos said. At last, biting his lip, Phostis nodded. Krispos nodded back, well pleased. He'd actually managed to get a lesson home to his hardheaded son.

"Come on, move!" a soldier shouted, with the air of a man who's already shouted the same thing twenty times and expects to shout it another twenty before the day is through.

The woman in faded gray wool, her head covered by a white scarf, sent the horseman a look of hatred. Back bent under the bundle she bore, she trudged away from the thatch-roofed hut that had housed her since she wed, away from the village that had housed her family for untold generations. Tears carved tracks through the dust on her cheeks. "The good god curse you to the ice forever," she snarled.

The imperial trooper said, "If I had a goldpiece for every time I've been cursed these past weeks, I'd be rich enough to buy this whole province."

"And heartless enough to rule it," the peasant woman retorted.

To her obvious dismay, the trooper thought that was funny. Having no choice—the soldier and his comrades confronted the villagers with sabers and drawn bows and implacable purpose—she kept walking, three children trailing behind her, and then her husband, who carried an even bigger pack on his back and held lead ropes for a couple of scrawny goats.

Phostis watched the family join the stream of unwilling peasants shambling east. Soon they were gone from sight, as one drop of water loses itself in a river. For a little while longer, he could hear the goats bleating. Then their voices, too, were lost amid murmurs and complaints and lowing cattle and creaking axles from richer farmers' carts and the endless shuffle of feet.

This had to be the dozenth village he'd watched empty. He wondered why he kept making himself witness the process over and over again. The best answer he came up with was that he was partly responsible for what was happening to these people, and so he had the obligation to understand it to the fullest, no matter how pained and uncomfortable it made him.

That afternoon, as the sun sank toward the not so distant mountains of Vaspurakan, he rode with another company that descended on another village. As the peasants were forcibly assembled in the marketplace, a woman screamed, "You have no right to treat us so. We're orthodox, by the good god. This for the gleaming path!" She spat in the dust.

"Is that so?" Phostis worriedly asked the officer in charge of the company.

"Young Majesty, you just wait till they're all gathered here and then you'll see for yourself," the captain answered.

The people kept coming until at last the village marketplace was full. Phostis frowned. He told the officer, "I don't see anything that makes them look either orthodox or Thanasiot."

"You don't know what to look for, then," the man replied. He waved at the glum crowd. "Do you see more men or women, young Majesty?"

Phostis hadn't noticed one way or the other. Now he examined villagers with a new eye. "More women, I'd say."

"I'd say so, too, young Majesty," the captain said, nodding. "And note the men, how many of them are either graybeards or else striplings with the down just sprouting on their cheeks and chins. Not a lot of fellows in their prime, are there? Why do you suppose that is?"

Phostis studied the shouting, sweating crowd once more. "I see what you're saying. Why, though?"

The officer glanced upward for a moment, perhaps in lieu of calling the heir to the imperial throne dense. "Young Majesty, it's on account of most of the men in their prime were in Livanios' army, and we either killed 'em or caught 'em. So you can believe that skirt is orthodox if you choose, but me, I have to doubt it."

Orthodox or heretic—and Phostis found the company commander's logic compelling—the villagers, carrying and leading what they could, shuffled away on the first stage of their journey to new homes at the far end of the Empire. Some of the company quartered themselves in abandoned houses. Phostis went back with the rest to the main imperial camp.

The place was becoming more like a semipermanent town than the encampment of an army on the march. Krispos' men fanned out from it every day to resettle villagers who followed—or might follow—the gleaming path. Supply wagons rumbled in every day—with occasional lapses as unsubdued Thanasioi raided them—to keep the army fed. Tents were not pitched at random, but in clumps with ways—almost streets—through them. Phostis had no trouble finding his way to the tent he shared with Olyvria.

When he ducked through the flap, she was lying on her bedroll. Her eyes were closed, but came open as soon as he walked in, so he did not think she'd been asleep. "How are you?" she asked listlessly.

"Worn," he answered. "Saying you're going to resettle some peasants is one thing; it sounds simple and practical enough. But seeing what it entails—" He shook his head. "Ruling is a hard, cruel business."

"I suppose so." Olyvria sounded indifferent.

Phostis asked, "How are *you*?" She'd wept through the night when she learned her father's fate. In the days since then, she'd been like this—very quiet, more than a little withdrawn from what happened around her. He hadn't touched her, except accidentally, since he'd held her while she cried herself out that night.

Now she answered, "All right," as she had whenever he'd asked her since then. The response was as flat and unemphatic as everything else she'd said lately.

He wanted to shake her, to force some life into her. He did not think that was a good idea. Instead, he unrolled his own blanket. Under a surcoat, his mail shirt jingled as he sat down beside her. He said, "How are you really?"

"All right," she repeated, as indifferently as before. But now a small spark came into her eyes. "I'll truly be all right in time; I'm sure I will. It's just that . . . my life has turned upside down these past weeks. No, even that's not right. First it turned upside down—I turned it upside down—and then it flipped again, when, when—"

She didn't go on, not with words, but she started to cry again, as she had not done since Krispos, sparing Phostis that duty, brought her word of what he'd ordered done to Livanios. Phostis thought there might be healing in these tears. He held his arms open, hoping she would come to him. After a few seconds, she did.

When she was through, she dried her eyes on the fabric of his surcoat. "Better?" he asked, patting her back as if she were a child.

"Who can say?" she answered. "I made the choice; I have to live with it. I love you. Phostis, I do, but I hadn't thought through everything that might happen after I got onto that fishing boat with you. My father—" She started to cry again.

"That would have happened anyhow, I think," he said. "You didn't have anything to do with it. Even when we were on the worst of terms—which seemed like much of the time—I knew my father did what he did well. I doubt the Thanasioi would have won the civil war even with us, and if they lost it . . . Early in his reign, my father paid a price for showing his enemies more mercy than they deserved. One of the things that set him apart from most people is that he learns from his mistakes. He gives rebels no second chance these days."

"But my father wasn't just a rebel," she said. "He was my father."

To that, Phostis had no good answer. Luckily for him, he didn't have to grope for a poor one. From outside the tent, a Haloga guard called, "Young Majesty, here's a man would have speech with you."

"I'm coming," Phostis answered. To Olyvria, he added in a low voice, "Probably a messenger from my father. Who else would disturb me?"

He climbed to his feet. Tired as he was, the iron he wore felt doubly heavy. He blinked against the bright afternoon sunshine as he stepped outside, then stopped in surprise and horror. "You!" he gasped.

"You!" Syagrios roared. The ruffian wore a long-sleeved tunic to cover the knife he'd strapped to his forearm. He flipped it into his hand now, and stabbed Phostis in the belly with it before the Haloga guard could spring between them.

As Phostis remembered, Syagrios was strong as a bear. He cried out when the tip of the knife bit him and grabbed Syagrios' right arm with both hands.

"I'll get you," Syagrios panted. "I'll get you and then I'll get that little whore you're swiving. I'll—"

Phostis never did find out what Syagrios would do next. The guardsman's frozen surprise did not last longer than a heartbeat. Syagrios screamed hoarsely as the Haloga's axe went into his back. He broke free of Phostis and whirled, trying to come to grips with the northerner. The Haloga struck him again, this time full in the face. Blood sprayed over Phostis. Syagrios crumpled. The guardsman methodically smote him again and again until he stopped twitching.

Olyvria burst out of the tent, a knife in her hand, her eyes wild. The guardsman, however, needed no help. Olyvria gulped at Syagrios' dreadful wounds. Though an officer's daughter, she wasn't altogether accustomed to fighting's grim aftermath.

Then the Haloga turned to Phostis. "Are you yet hale, young Majesty?"

"I don't know." Phostis yanked up his mail shirt and surcoat together. He had a bleeding scratch a couple of inches above his navel, but nothing worse. He let the mail shirt fall back down with a clink of iron rings.

"Aye, here we are. Look, young Majesty." The northerner poked the mail shirt with a forefinger. "You had luck with you. The knife went into a ring—see the bright cuts here and here? It went in, but could go no farther. Had it slid between two rings, more of your gore would have spilled."

"Yes." Phostis started to shake. So much luck in life—a fingernail's breadth to either side and he'd be lying on the ground beside dead Syagrios, trying to hold his guts in. Maybe a healer-priest would have been able to save him, but he was ever so glad he didn't have to make the test. He told the guard, "My thanks for slaying him, Viggo."

The Haloga guardsman looked disgusted with himself. "I should never have let him draw near enough to stab you. I thank the gods you were not worse hurt." He lifted Syagrios' corpse by the heels and dragged it away. The ruffian's blood soaked blackly into the thirsty soil.

By then, curious and concerned faces pressed close; the fight and the outcries had raised a crowd as if by magic. Phostis waved to show he was all right. "No harm done," he called, "and the madman got what he deserved." He pointed to the trail Syagrios left behind, as if he were a snail filled with blood rather than slime. The soldiers cheered.

Phostis waved again, then ducked back into the tent. Olyvria followed. Phostis looked again at the little cut he'd taken. He didn't require much imagination to make it bigger in his mind's eye. If the knife had slipped between rings, or if he'd taken off the mail shirt, the better to comfort Olyvria . . . He shuddered. He didn't even want to think about that.

"I fought with him during the battle," he said. "I guessed he'd flee, but he must have been wild for revenge."

"You never wanted to cross Syagrios," Olyvria agreed soberly. "And—" She hesitated, then went on, "And I'd known he wanted me for a long time."

"Oh." Phostis made a sour face at that. But it made sense—how doubly mortifying and infuriating to be struck down by someone you lusted after. "No wonder he didn't run, then." His laugh was shaky. "I wish he would have—he came too close to getting his vengeance and letting the air out of me in the process."

Katakolon stuck his head into the tent. "Ah, good, you still have your clothes on," he said. "Father's right behind me, and I don't suppose you'd care to be caught as I was."

Before Phostis could do more than gape at that or ask any of the myriad questions that suggested themselves, Krispos came in. "I'm glad you're all right," he said, folding Phostis into a bear hug. When he let Phostis go, he stood back and eyed him quizzically. "Someone didn't care for you there, son."

"No, he didn't," Phostis agreed. "He helped kidnap me—" He watched Krispos, but the Avtokrator's eyes never moved toward Olyvria: discipline and style. "—and he was my, I guess you'd say keeper, in Etchmiadzin. He couldn't have been very happy when I escaped."

"Your keeper, eh? So that was Syagrios?" Krispos asked.

Phostis nodded, impressed at his memory for detail. He said, "He was a bad man, but not of the worst. He played the board game well, and he drew the arrow from my shoulder when I got shot while I was along with the Thanasiot raiding party."

"A slim enough eulogy, but the best he'll get, and likely better than he deserves, too," Krispos said. "If you think I'll say I'm sorry he's gone, you can think again: good riddance, say I. I just praise the good god that you weren't hurt." He embraced Phostis again.

"I'm glad you're not ventilated, too," Katakolon said. "It's good having you back, especially in one piece." He ducked to get out of the tent. Krispos followed a moment later.

"What was that your brother said about getting caught with his clothes off?" Olyvria kept her voice low so no one but Phostis would hear, but she couldn't stop the giggle that welled up from deep inside.

"I don't know," Phostis said. "As a matter of fact, I don't think I want to know. Knowing Katakolon, it was probably something spectacular. Sometimes I think he takes after Anthimos, even if—" He'd been about to say something like *even if I'm the one Anthimos might have fathered.* That was just what he didn't want to say to Olyvria.

"Even if what?" she asked.

"Even if Anthimos was four years dead before Katakolon was born," Phostis finished, more smoothly than he would have thought possible.

"Oh." Olyvria sounded disappointed, which meant his answer had convinced her. He nodded to himself. Krispos would have approved. And he'd lived through a completely unexpected attack. He approved of that himself.

Krispos studied the gloomy stone pile of Etchmiadzin. It had been built to hold off men at arms, but the ones its designers had in mind came from Makuran. The stone, however, knew nothing of that. It would—and did—defy Videssians as readily as any others.

The fanatics on those grim stone walls still screamed defiance at the imperial army below. Most of the territory the Thanasioi had once held was back in Krispos' hands again. Dozens of villages were empty; he'd given the orders to send streams of orthodox peasants on the way to replace those uprooted from the area. Pityos and its hinterland had fallen to Noetos' cavalry, advancing west along the coast from Nakoleia.

But if Etchmiadzin held until the advancing season made Krispos withdraw, much of what he'd accomplished was likely to unravel. The Thanasioi would still have a base from which to grow once more. He'd already seen the consequences of their growth. He didn't care for them.

Storming the fortress, though, was easier to talk about than to do. Videssian engineers had labored mightily to make it as near impregnable as they could. So far as Krispos knew, it had never fallen to the Makuraners, despite several sieges. It didn't look likely to fall to his army, either.

"If they won't fall, maybe I can trip them," Krispos muttered.

"How's that, your Majesty?"

Krispos jumped. There beside him stood Sarkis. "I'm sorry—I didn't notice you'd come up. I was trying to work out some way to inveigle the cursed Thanasioi into coming out of Etchmiadzin without storming the place."

"Good luck to you," Sarkis said skeptically. "Hard enough to trick a foe in the confusion of the battlefield. Why should the heretics come out from their citadel for anything you do short of leaving? Even if they stand and fight and die, they think they go up their gleaming path to heaven. Next to that, any promise you can make is a small loaf."

"Aye, they're solidly against me, stiff-necked as they are." Krispos' voice was gloomy—but only for a moment. He turned to Sarkis. "They're solidly against me—for now. But tell me, eminent sir, what do you have if you put three Videssians together and tell them to talk about their faith for a day?"

"Six heresies," Sarkis answered at once. "Each one's view of his two comrades. Also a big brawl, probably a knifing or two, a couple of slit purses. Begging your pardon, Majesty, but that's how it looks to a poor stolid prince from Vaspurakan, anyhow."

"That's how it looks to me, too," Krispos said, smiling, "even if I have only a touch of princes' blood in me. I think like a Videssian, no matter whose blood I have, and I know full well that if you give Videssians a chance to argue about religion, they're sure to take it."

"I don't hold your breeding against you, your Majesty," Sarkis said generously, "but how do you propose to get the Thanasioi squabbling among themselves when to them you're the impious heretic they've all joined together to fight?"

"It's not even my idea," Krispos said. "Phostis thought of it and gave it to Evripos."

"To Evripos?" Sarkis scratched his head. "But he's back in Videssos the city. How could anything there have to do with the Thanasioi here? Did Evripos write you a letter and—" The cavalry commander stopped. His black, black eyes sparkled. Just for a moment, through the sheath of heavy flesh, Krispos saw the eager young scout with whom he'd ridden like a madman back to the imperial capital in the days when his reign was new. He said, "Wait a minute. You're not going to—"

"Oh, yes, I am," Krispos said. "Right out there where they can all watch from the walls. If it wouldn't brew more scandal than it was worth, I'd have them consummate it out there, too, not that it hasn't been consummated already."

"You're a demon, you are—but then, you used to revel with Anthimos, now that I think of it." Sarkis let out a theatrical sigh. "Too bad you couldn't get by with that. She's a fine-looking young woman. I wouldn't mind watching that marriage consummated, not one bit I wouldn't."

"Shameless old stallion." Krispos lowered his voice. "I wouldn't, either." They both laughed.

* * *

For a day, the imperial army besieging Etchmiadzin had sent no darts, no arrows, no stones against those frowning gray walls. Instead, heralds bearing white-painted shields of truce had approached the walls, bidding the Thanasioi also desist from battle "so that you may join us in observing a celebration at noon."

The choice of words must have intrigued the heretics; they had gone along with the heralds' suggestion, at least thus far. Phostis wondered how long they would remain calm when they observed what was about to happen. *Not long,* he thought.

He'd suggested to Evripos that he marry Olyvria to help calm the rampaging Thanasioi of the city. Trust Krispos to take his suggestion and turn it into a weapon of war against the belligerent heretics here at Etchmiadzin.

"Noon" was an approximation; the only sundial in the imperial army was a little brass one that belonged to Zaidas. But men accustomed to gauging the apex of the sun's path when they were working in the fields had no trouble doing the same while on campaign. Imperial soldiers gathered to protect the wooden platform that had been built safely out of bowshot of Etchmiadzin's walls. On those walls, the Thanasioi also gathered.

A herald with a shield of truce strode from the imperial lines toward the rebel-held fortress. In a huge bass voice, he called to the Thanasioi: "His imperial Majesty the Avtokrator Krispos bids you welcome to the marriage of his son Phostis to the lady Olyvria, daughter of the late Livanios."

Phostis wished the herald had omitted *the late*; the words would hurt Olyvria. But at the same time, he understood why Krispos had told the man to include them: they would remind Etchmiadzin's defenders of the defeats their cause had already suffered.

The Thanasioi rained curses on the herald's head. A couple of them shot at him, too. He lifted the shield of truce to protect his face; he wore a helmet and a mail shirt that covered him down to the knee.

When the arrows stopped coming, the man lowered the white-faced shield and resumed: "The Avtokrator bids you ponder the import of this wedding: not only what it says about your fortune in battle, but how it reminds you of the joy that life holds and the way it continues—and should continue— from one generation to the next."

More curses—and more arrows—flew at him. Having delivered his message, he needed to stand up under them no more, but hastily drew back out of range.

The wedding party ascended to the makeshift stage. It was not a large group, certainly not the horde that would have been involved had the marriage taken place at the High Temple in Videssos the city. Ahead of Phostis and Olyvria came a healerpriest named Glavas, who would perform the ceremony. Behind them walked Krispos, Katakolon, and Zaidas. That was all.

Even Zaidas' presence was not directly required by the ceremony, though Phostis was glad to have him close by. But the wizard was there mainly because he owned a small magic that would let the voices of the people on the platform carry farther than they would have without it: Krispos wanted the Thanasioi to listen to all that passed here.

The priest said, "Let us praise the lord with the great and good mind." He recited Phos' creed. So did Phostis and Olyvria; so as well did Krispos, Katakolon, and Zaidas. Phostis also heard the watching soldiers echo the prayer they made several times every day of their lives.

"We are come together in this unusual place to celebrate an unusual union," Glavas said. "After the boon of many healthful years, the greatest gift the good god can grant his worshipers is continuance of their line. A marriage is a time of rejoicing not least because it marks hope and expectation for that continuance.

"When the marriage comes from the imperial family, more hopes ride on it than those of the family alone. Continuance of the dynasty, generation upon generation, is our best guarantee against the disaster of civil war."

Phostis noticed he did not mention that Krispos was the first member of his family to hold the imperial throne, or indeed anything more than a peasant plot. The priest went on, "And with this marriage, we also have the chance to heal a rift that has opened among the faithful of Videssos, to symbolize the return to their familiar faith by those who for a time thought differently in the union of the young majesty Phostis to Olyvria the daughter of Livanios."

That, Phostis thought, was as conciliatory toward the Thanasioi as Krispos could be without following the gleaming path himself. He hadn't even had Glavas call them heretics. He wanted to make them forget their beliefs, not stubbornly cling to them.

The priest went on for some time about the qualities bride and groom should bring to a marriage to ensure its success. Phostis' mind wandered. He was taken unawares when Glavas asked, "Are the two of you prepared to cleave to these virtues, and to each other, so long as you both may live?"

From behind, Krispos nudged Phostis. He realized he had to speak first. "Yes," he said, and was glad Zaidas' magic made his voice larger than it was.

"Yes, for all my life—*this* is the path I will walk," Olyvria responded firmly.

Krispos and Katakolon set on her head and Phostis' garlands of sweet-smelling herbs—the crown of marriage that completed the ceremony. The priest stepped down from the platform. As quickly as that, it was over. "I'm married," Phostis said. Even to himself, he sounded surprised.

The Thanasioi on the wall screamed insults and catcalls for all they were worth. Ignoring them, Krispos slapped Phostis on the back and said, "So you are, son—and to a wise woman, too." He turned to Olyvria and added, "That last touch was perfect. Phos willing, they'll do a lot of stewing over it."

Katakolon poked Phostis in the ribs. "Now you're supposed to grab her and carry her off to your—well, to your tent it would be here."

Phostis had a well-founded suspicion that Olyvria would not permit any such thing. He glanced over to her. Sure enough, a steely glint in her eye warned him he'd better not try it.

"I've heard ideas that sounded more practical," Krispos said; the amusement in his voice said he'd seen that glint, too. "But do go on back to your tent. You would anyhow—that's what the day is for—but you should do it now, while you're still decked in the crowns of marriage."

That tickled Phostis' curiosity. He extended his arm to Olyvria. She took it. As they headed away from the hastily built platform, some of the soldiers cheered and others called lewd advice. Phostis smiled foolishly at Olyvria. She smiled back. Lewd advice from the bystanders came with every wedding celebration.

A grinning Haloga held the tent flap wide, then let it fall behind the newlyweds. "We'll not see you for a while, I think," he said.

"Will you look at that?" Olyvria exclaimed.

Phostis looked. At the top corners of their unfolded blankets, someone—maybe Krispos himself, maybe a man acting at his orders—had driven stout sticks into the ground to stimulate bedposts. "It's good luck to hang the crowns on them," Phostis said. He doffed his and carefully set it on top of one post.

Olyvria did the same on the other side. "It starts to feel real," she said.

"It is real." Phostis lowered his voice so the guardsmen outside would not hear—not that they wouldn't know perfectly well what was going on in there, but the forms had to be observed. "As long as it's real, and as long as we're here by ourselves and no battle's going on right this moment—"

"Yes? What then?" Olyvria played the game with him. She spoke quietly, too; her hands worked at the catch of the white linen dress Krispos had given her for the wedding. It came open. "What then?" she repeated softly.

Between the two of them, they figured out what then. Because Phostis was still quite a young man, they got to try again soon, and again after that. Phostis had lost track of the hour by then, though the sun still lit one side of the tent. He yawned, wiped his sweaty forehead with a sweaty forearm, and dozed off. Beside him, Olyvria had already fallen asleep.

It was dark when a horrible racket woke him. He sat up and looked around, blinking. Olyvria lay beside him, still sleeping—snoring just a little—a small smile on her face. Carefully, so as not to disturb her, he put on a robe and walked outside. A new shift of Halogai ringed his tent. "What's toward?" he asked one of them.

The northerner pointed toward Etchmiadzin. The ruddy light of campfires and torches gave him the look of a man made of bronze. "Fighting in there," he said.

"By Phos," Phostis murmured, smacking a fist into the other palm. He looked over toward the imperial pavilion not far away. Krispos was outside, too, watching. Phostis felt a surge of relief that he'd not thrown in his lot with the Thanasioi. One

way or another, he was more sure now than ever, Krispos
would have found a way to beat them no matter what they did.

Inside Etchmiadzin, they sounded as if they were going at
each other with everything they had. *They probably were,*
Phostis thought. The men and women who followed the
gleaming path were fanatics—whatever views they held, they
held with all their hearts and all their souls. If Krispos had
managed to drive a wedge between two groups of them over
the propriety of Olyvria's marriage, they'd fight each other as
savagely as—maybe more savagely than—they'd opposed the
imperial army.

The Haloga pointed again. "Ha! Look, young Majesty—
smoke. With blazing brand they burn their burg."

Sure enough, a thick column of smoke rose from inside the
walls, orange-tinted gray against the black of the night sky.
Phostis tried to figure out where in the town the fire had flared.
His best guess was that it wasn't far from the Vaspurakaner
cobbler's shop where he and Olyvria had first made love.

Another plume of smoke sprang up, and a few minutes later
yet another. A tongue of yellow fire, perhaps from a burning
roof, leapt into sight above the walls like a live thing, then sul-
lenly fell back.

Before long, more and more flames sprang into view, and
not all of them died down again. Fire was a terror in any city;
it could so easily race ahead of anything men were able to do
to hold it back. Fire in a city at war with itself was a horror
to rank with the ice in Skotos' hell: how could you hope to
fight it when your hand was turned against your neighbor, your
friend—and his against you?

The answer was, you couldn't. The fires in Etchmiadzin
burned on and on. The air of the imperial camp grew thick
with the stink of smoke and, now and again, of burned flesh.
Screams rent the air, some of terror, some of agony, but most
of hate. In the burning streets, the battle among the Thanasioi
went on.

After a while, Olyvria came out of the tent to stand beside
Phostis. She slipped her hand into his without saying anything.
Silently, they watched Etchmiadzin burn. Olyvria wiped at her
eyes. The smoke made Phostis' sting, too. For the sake of his
own peace of mind, he assumed that smoke was why she
dabbed at hers.

He yawned and said, "I'm going back inside the tent. Maybe the air will be fresher in there."

Olyvria followed him in, still without speaking. Only when they were away from the guards did she say in a low voice, "There is the dowry I bring to you and your father—Etchmiadzin."

"You knew that," he answered. "You must have known it, or you'd not have answered the priest as you did."

"I suppose I did know, in a way. But knowing in advance what a thing is and seeing what it looks like when it comes to pass are not the same. Tonight I'm finding out how different they can be." She shook her head.

Had Krispos been in the tent, Phostis suspected he would have said that was one of the lessons of growing up. Phostis couldn't put a middle-aged rasp in his voice to make that sound convincing. He asked, "If you'd known, would you have done differently?"

Olyvria stayed quiet so long, he wondered if she'd heard. At last she said, "No, I suppose I would have left things as they were, but I'd have thought about them more beforehand."

"That's fair," Phostis agreed. He yawned again. "Shall we try to get some more sleep? I don't think they're going to sally against us; they're too busy warring with each other."

"I suppose so." Olyvria lay down and closed her eyes. Phostis lay down beside her. To his surprise, he dropped off almost at once.

Olyvria must have fallen asleep, too, for she jerked up at the same time as he when a great cheer roared through the encampment. He needed a moment to realize what time it was—sunshine against the east side of the tent meant dawn had broken.

As he had the night before, he poked out his head and asked a Haloga what was going on. The northerner answered, "Those in there, they have yielded themselves. The gates are thrown wide."

"Then the war is over," Phostis blurted. When he realized what he'd said, he repeated it: "The war is over." He wanted to say it again and again; he couldn't imagine four more wonderful words.

# XIII

A LINE OF MEN AND WOMEN AND CHILDREN TRUDGING WEARILY down a dirt track, carrying such belongings as they could, the cows and goats and donkeys with them as thin and worn as they were. The only difference Krispos could see between them and the uprooted Thanasioi was the direction of their journey: they were moving west, not east.

No, there was another: they'd not rebelled to give him a reason to remove them from their old homes. But the land from which war and policy had removed the Thanasioi could not stay empty. That was asking for trouble. And so peasants who lived in a relatively crowded—and safely loyal—stretch of territory between Develtos and Opsikion east of Videssos the city were taking the place of the Thanasioi whether they liked the idea or not.

Phostis rode up alongside Krispos and pointed to the villagers on the way to resettlement. "Is that justice?" he asked.

"I just put the same question to myself," Krispos answered. "I don't think the answer is clear or easy. If you asked any one of them now, no doubt they'd curse me to the skies. But after two years, who can say? I've granted them tax exemptions for that long, and put them on half rates for three years more. I'm not moving them just to fill space—I want them to thrive."

"It may work out well enough for them," Phostis persisted, "but is it justice?"

"Probably not," Krispos answered, sighing. He fought back a smile; he'd managed to surprise Phostis. "Probably not," he repeated, "but is it justice to empty a land so no crops to speak of are raised on it, so it becomes a haven for brigands and outlaws, so it tempts the Makuraners to try to gobble it up? Makuran hasn't much troubled us lately, but that's because Rubyab King of Kings sees me as strong. It hasn't always been so."

"How do you aim to pay Rubyab back for sponsoring the Thanasioi?" Phostis asked.

Krispos took the change of subject to mean that Phostis thought he had a point. He answered, "I don't know right now. A big war, like the one we fought with Makuran a century and a half ago, could leave both lands prostrate for years. I don't want that. But believe me, that's not a debt to forget. Maybe it'll be one I leave to you to repay."

Phostis responded to that with a calculating look Krispos had seldom seen on him before he was kidnapped. "Fomenting the Vaspurakaners against Mashiz is likely to be worth trying."

"Aye, maybe, if the Makuraners commit some outrage in the princes' lands, or they're troubled with foes farther west," Krispos said. "But that's not as sure a bet as it looks, because the Makuraners are always on the watch for it. The beauty of Rubyab's ploy was that it used our own people against us: Videssos has known so much religious strife over the years that for a long time I didn't see the Makuraner hand in the Thanasiot glove."

"The beauty of it?" Phostis shook his head. "I don't see how you can use that word for something that caused so much trouble and death."

"It's like an unexpected clever move at the board game," Krispos said. "The board here, though, stretches all the way across the world, and you can change the rules you play by."

"And the pieces you take off the board are real people," Phostis said, "and you can't bring them back again and play them somewhere else."

"Can't I?" Krispos said. "What do you think this resettlement is, if not capturing a piece and playing it on a better square?"

He watched Phostis chew on that. The young man said, "I suppose I should have learned to stop arguing with you. No matter how well I start out, most of the time you end up turning things your way. Experience." By the way that sounded in his mouth, it might as well have been a filthy word. It was something he lacked, at any rate, which of itself made its possession suspect.

Krispos pulled a silk handkerchief from a pocket of his surcoat and dabbed at his dripping forehead. He'd left some of the imperial army back in and around Etchmiadzin, both to watch the border with Makuraner-held Vaspurakan and to help uprooted arrivals settle in. More troops were strung out along the line of travel between west and east. With what remained, he was drawing near Videssos the city.

That meant, of course, that he and his men were passing through the coastal lowlands. In late summer, there were other places he'd sooner have been; at the moment, he would have welcomed some of Skotos' ice, so long as he did not have to meet its master. It was so hot and sticky that sweat wouldn't dry; it just clung to you and rolled greasily along your skin.

"By the good god, I wish I didn't have to wear the imperial regalia," he said. "In this country, I'd sooner be dressed like them." He pointed to the peasants working in the fields to either side of the road. Some of them were in thin linen tunics that came down about half the distance from buttocks to knee. Others didn't even bother with that, but were content to wrap a loincloth around their middles.

Phostis shook his head. "If I dressed like that, it would mean I lived here all year around. I don't think I could stand that."

"You'd best be glad someone can," Krispos said. "The soil here is wonderful, and they get plenty of rain. The crops they bring in are bigger than anywhere else in the Empire. If it weren't for the lowlands, Videssos the city wouldn't have enough to eat."

"The peasants aren't fleeing from us the way they did when we set out," Katakolon said, stopping his horse by his father and brother.

"A good thing, too," Krispos answered. "One reason we have an army is to protect them. If they think soldiers are something they need to be protected from, we aren't doing the job as we should." He knew as well as anyone else that soldiers plundered peasants when they got the chance. The trick was not giving them the chance and making the peasants know they wouldn't get it. He wouldn't have to worry about that much longer on this campaign—almost home now. He said that aloud.

Katakolon leered at him. "You needn't be in such a swivet to get back to Drina, Father. Remember, she'll be out to here by now." He held a hand a couple of feet in front of his belly.

"She's not giving birth to a foal, by the good god," Krispos said. "If she were out to *there*, I might think you meant an elephant." He glared at his youngest, but couldn't help snorting as he went on, "And I'll thank you not to twit me any more about her having my by-blow. Only fool luck I'm not paying for six or seven of yours; Phos knows it's not your lack of effort."

"He's just giving you twit for twat, Father," Phostis said helpfully.

Beset from both sides, Krispos threw his hands in the air. "The two of you will be the death of me. If Evripos were here, I'd be altogether surrounded. I expect I shall be when we get back to the palaces. That's the first decent argument I've heard for making this march take longer."

"I thought it was an indecent argument," Katakolon said, not willing to be outdone by Phostis.

"Enough, enough!" Krispos groaned. "Have mercy on your poor decrepit father. I've got softening of the brain from too many years of staring at tax receipts and edicts; you can't expect me to throw puns about the way you do."

Just then, the scouts up ahead started raising a racket. One of them rode back to the van of the main body. Saluting Krispos, he said, "Your Majesty, the sharp-eyed among us have spied the sun glinting off the temple domes of Videssos the city."

Krispos peered ahead. He wasn't particularly sharp-sighted any longer; things in the distance got blurry for him. But whether he could see them or not, knowing the temples and their domes were so close made him feel the journey was coming to its end.

"Almost home," he said again. He looked from Phostis to Katakolon, daring them to make more wisecracks. They both kept quiet. He nodded, pleased with himself: the young bulls still respected the old bull's horns.

* * *

The folk of Videssos the city packed the colonnaded sidewalks of Middle Street, cheering as the triumphal procession made its way toward the plaza of Palamas. Phostis rode near the head of the procession, Olyvria at his side. He wore a gilded mail shirt and helmet to let the people know who he was—and to make sure no diehard Thanasiot assassinated him for the greater glory of the gleaming path.

As he rode, he waved, which brought fresh applause from the crowd. He turned to Olyvria and said quietly, "I wonder how many of these same people were screaming for Thanasios and trying to burn down the city not long ago."

"A fair number, I'd say," she answered.

He nodded. "I think you're right." Rooting Thanasioi out from Videssos the city wasn't nearly so straightforward as uprooting and transplanting villages. Unless you caught someone setting fires or wrecking, how could you know what was in his heart? You couldn't; that was the long and short of it. Thanasios' followers surely lingered here. If they stayed quiet, they might go unnoticed for generations—those who cared to raise new generations, at any rate.

Middle Street showed few scars from the rioting. Countless fires burned in the city every day, for cooking and heating and at smithies and other workplaces. Whitewashed buildings were usually gray with soot in a few months' time. The soot that came from the rioters' blazes looked no different from any other after the fact.

The procession passed through the Forum of the Ox, about a third of the way from the Silver Gate in the great land wall to the plaza of Palamas. The stalls in the Forum of the Ox sold cheap goods to people who could afford no better. Most of the folk who packed the square wore either ragged tunics or gaudy finery whose "gold" threads were apt to turn green in a matter of days. Phostis would have bet that plenty of them had bawled for the gleaming path.

Now, though, they cried out Krispos' name as loudly as anyone else—and that despite some former market stalls that were now only charred ruins. "Maybe they'll come back to orthodoxy now that they've really seen what their heresy leads to," Phostis said. He spoke more softly still: "That's more or less what I did, after all."

"Maybe," Olyvria said, her voice so neutral he couldn't tell whether she agreed with him or not.

*We'll know twenty years from now,* he thought. Looking about as far ahead as he'd already lived felt strange, almost unnatural, to him, but he was beginning to do it. He didn't know whether that was because he'd started taking seriously the idea of ruling or simply because he was getting older.

Off to the north of Middle Street, between the Forum of the Ox and the plaza of Palamas, stood the huge mass of the High Temple. It was undamaged, not from any lack of malevolence on the part of the Thanasioi but because soldiers and ecclesiastics armed with stout staves had ringed it day and night until rioting subsided.

Phostis still felt uncomfortable as he rode past the High Temple: He looked on it as an enormous sponge that had soaked up endless gold that might have been better spent elsewhere. But he had returned to the faith that found deepest expression beneath that marvelous dome. He shook his head. Not all puzzles had neat solutions. This one, too, would have to wait for more years to do their work in defining his views.

The red granite facing of the government office building caught his eye and told him the plaza of Palamas was drawing near. Somewhere under there, in the jail levels below ground, Digenis the priest had starved himself to death.

"Digenis might have been right to be angry about how the rich have too much, but I don't think making everyone poor is the right answer," Phostis said to Olyvria. "Still, I can't hate him, not when I met you through him."

She smiled at that, but answered, "Aren't you putting your own affairs above those of the Empire there?"

He needed a moment to realize she was teasing. "As a matter of fact, yes," he said. "Or at least one affair. Katakolon's the fellow who keeps four of them in the air at the same time." She made a face at him, which let him think he'd come out best in that little skirmish.

Up ahead, a great roar announced that Krispos had entered the packed plaza of Palamas. With the Avtokrator marched servitors armed not with weapons but with sacks of gold and silver. Many an Emperor had kept the city mob happy with largess, and Krispos had shown over and over that he was able to profit from others' examples. Letting people squabble over money flung among them might keep them from more serious uprisings like the one Videssos the city had just seen.

Sky-blue ribbons—and Haloga guardsmen—kept the crowds from swamping the route the procession took to the western edge of the plaza. Krispos had ascended to a wooden platform whose pieces were stored in a palace outbuilding against time of need. Phostis wondered how many times Krispos had mounted that platform to speak to the people of the city. *Quite a few,* he thought.

He dismounted, then reached out to help Olyvria do the same. Grooms took their horses. Hand in hand, the two of them went up onto the platform themselves.

"It's a sea of people out there," Phostis exclaimed, looking out at the restless mass. Their noise rose and fell in almost regular waves, like the surf.

For the first time, Phostis had a chance to see that part of the procession which had been behind him. A parade was not a parade without soldiers. A company of Halogai marched around Krispos, Phostis, and Olyvria, for protection and show both. Behind them came several regiments of Videssians, some mounted, others afoot. They tramped along looking neither right nor left, as if the people of the city were not worth their notice. Not only were they part of the spectacle, they also served as a reminder that Krispos had powerful forces ready at hand should rioting break out again.

The Halogai formed up in front of the platform. The rest of the troops headed past the plaza of Palamas and into the palace quarter. Some had barracks there; others would be dismissed back to the countryside after the celebration was over.

Between one regiment and the next walked dejected Thanasiot prisoners. Some of them still showed the marks of wounds; none wore anything more than ragged drawers; all had their hands tied behind their backs. The crowd jeered them and pelted them with eggs and rotten fruit and the occasional stone.

Olyvria said, "A lot of Avtokrators would have capped this parade with a massacre."

"I know," Phostis said. "But Father has seen real massacres—ask him about Harvas Black-Robe some time. Having seen the beast, he doesn't want to give birth to it."

The prisoners took the same route out of the plaza as had

the soldiers. Their fate would not be much different: they'd be sent off to live on the land with the rest of the uprooted Thanasioi, with luck in peace. Unlike the soldiers, though, they would get no choice about where they went.

Another contingent of Halogai entered the plaza of Palamas. The noise from the crowd grew quieter and took on a rougher edge. Behind the front of axe-bearing northerners rode Evripos. By the reaction, not everyone in Videssos the city was happy with the way he had put down the riots.

He rode as if blithely unaware of that, waving to the people as Krispos and Phostis had before him. The guardsmen who had surrounded him took their places with their countrymen while he climbed up to stand by Phostis and Olyvria.

Without turning his head toward Phostis, he said, "They're not pleased that I didn't give them all a kiss and send them to bed with a mug of milk and a spiced bun. Well, I wasn't any too pleased that they did their best to bring the city down around my ears."

"I can understand that," Phostis answered, also looking straight ahead.

Evripos' lip curled. "And you, brother, you come through this everyone's hero. You've married the beautiful girl, like someone out of a romance. Hardly seems fair, somehow." He did not try to hide his bitterness.

"To the ice with the romances," Phostis said, but that wasn't what was bothering Evripos, and he knew it.

The low-voiced argument stopped then, because someone else ascended to the platform: Iakovitzes, gorgeous in robes just short in imperial splendor. He would not make a speech, of course, not without a tongue, but he had served in so many different roles during Krispos' reign that excluding him would have seemed unnatural.

He smiled at Olyvria, politely enough but without real interest. As he walked past Phostis and Evripos toward Krispos, he managed to pat each of them on the behind. Olyvria's eyes went wide. The two brothers looked at Iakovitzes, looked at each other, and started to laugh. "He's been doing that for as long as we've been alive," Phostis said.

"For a lot longer than that," Evripos said. "Father always tells of how Iakovitzes tried to seduce him when he was a boy, and then later when he was a groom in Iakovitzes' service, and even after he donned the red boots."

"He knows we care nothing for men," Phostis said. "If we ever made as if we wanted to go along, the shock might kill him. He's anything but young, even if he dyes his hairs and powders over his wrinkles to try to hide his years."

"I don't think you're right, Phostis," Evripos said. "If he thought we wanted to go along, he'd have our robes up and our drawers down before we could say 'I was only joking.' "

Phostis considered. "You may have something there." On a matter like that, he was willing to concede a point to his brother.

Olyvria stared at both of them, then at Iakovitzes. "That's—terrible," she exclaimed. "Why does your father keep him around?"

She made the mistake of speaking as if Iakovitzes couldn't hear her. He strolled back toward her, smiling now in a way that said he meant mischief. Alarmed, Phostis tried to head him off. Iakovitzes opened the tablet he always carried, wrote rapidly on the wax, and showed it to Phostis. "Does she read?"

"Yes, of course she does," Phostis said, whereupon Iakovitzes pushed past him toward Olyvria, scribbling as he walked.

He handed her the tablet. She took it with some apprehension, read aloud: "His Majesty keeps me around, as you say, for two reasons: first, because I am slyer than any three men you can name, including your father before and after he lost his head; and second, because he knows I would never try to seduce any wives of the imperial family."

Iakovitzes' smile got wider, and therefore more unnerving. He took back the tablet and started away. "Wait," Olyvria said sharply. Iakovitzes turned back, stylus poised like a sting. Phostis started to step between them again. But Olyvria said, "I wanted to apologize. I was cruel without thinking."

Iakovitzes chewed on that. He scribbled again, then proffered the tablet to her with a bow. Phostis looked over her shoulder. Iakovitzes had written, "So was I, to speak of your father so. In my book, the honors—or rather, dishonors—are even."

To Phostis' relief, Olyvria said, "Let it be so." Generations of sharp wits had picked quarrels with Iakovitzes, generally to end up in disarray. Phostis was glad Olyvria did not propose to make the attempt.

Iakovitzes nodded and walked back to Krispos' side. The Avtokrator held up a hand, waited for quiet. It came slowly, but did at length arrive. Into it Krispos said, "Let us have peace: peace in Videssos the city, peace in the Empire of Videssos. Civil war is nothing the Empire needs. The lord with the great and good mind knows I undertook it unwillingly. Only when those who followed what they called the gleaming path rose in rebellion, first in the westlands and then here in Videssos the city, did I take up arms against them."

"Does that mean you father would have let the Thanasioi alone if they'd been quiet, peaceful heretics?" Olyvria asked.

"I don't know. Maybe," Phostis said. "He's never persecuted the Vaspurakaners, that's certain." Phostis puzzled over that: Krispos always said religious unity was vital to holding the Empire together, but he didn't necessarily practice what he preached. Was that hypocrisy, or just pragmatism? Phostis couldn't answer, not without more thought.

He'd missed a few sentences. Krispos was saying "—shall rebuild the city so that no one may know it has come to harm. We shall rebuild the fabric of our lives in the same fashion. It will not be quick, not all of it, but Videssos is no child, to need everything on the instant. What we do, we do for generations."

Phostis still had trouble thinking in those terms. Next year felt a long way away to him; worrying about what would happen when his grandchildren were old felt as strange as worrying about what was on the other side of the moon.

He'd fallen behind again. "—but so long as you live at peace with one another, you need not fear spies will seek you out to do you harm," Krispos declared.

"What about tax collectors?" a safely anonymous wit roared from the crowd.

Krispos took no notice of him. "People of the city," he said earnestly, "if you so choose, you can be at one another's throats for longer than you care to imagine. If you start feuds now, they may last for generations after you are gone. I pray to Phos this does not happen." He let iron show in his voice: "I do not intend to let it happen. If you try to fight among yourselves, first you must overcome the soldiers of the Empire.

I say this as warning, not as threat. My view is that we have had enough of strife. May we be free of it for years to come."

He did not say "forever," Phostis noted, and wondered why. He decided Krispos didn't believe such things endured forever. By everything the Avtokrator had shown, he worked to build a framework for what would come after him, but did not necessarily expect that framework to become a solid wall: he knew too well that history gave no assurance of success.

"We shall rebuild, as I said, and we shall go on," Krispos said. "Together, we shall do as well as we can for as long as we can. The good god knows we can do no more." He stepped back on the platform, his speech done.

Applause filled the plaza of Palamas, more than polite, less than ecstatic. Along with Olyvria and Evripos, Phostis joined it. *As well as we can for as long as we can,* he thought. If Krispos had picked a phrase to summarize himself, he couldn't have found a better one.

Though Krispos waved for him not to bother, Barsymes performed a full proskynesis. "I welcome you back to the imperial residence, your Majesty," he said from the pavement. Then, still spry, he rose as gracefully as he had prostrated himself and added, "The truth is, life is on the boring side here when you take the field."

Krispos snorted. "I'm glad to be back, then, if only to give you something interesting to do."

"The cooks are also glad you've returned," the vestiarios said.

"They're looking for a chance to spread themselves, you mean," Krispos said. "Too bad. They can wait until the next time I dine with Iakovitzes; he'll appreciate it properly. As for me, I've got used to eating like a soldier. A bowl of stew, a heel of bread, and a mug of wine will suit me nicely."

Barsymes' shoulders moved slightly in what would have been a sigh in someone less exquisitely polite than the eunuch. "I shall inform the kitchens of your desires," he said. "The cooks will be disappointed, but perhaps not surprised. You have a habit of acting thus whenever you return from campaign."

"Do I?" Krispos said, irked at being so predictable. He was

tempted to demand a fancy feast just to keep people guessing about him. The only trouble was, he really did want stew.

Barsymes said, "Perhaps your Majesty will not take it too much amiss if the stew be of lobster and mullet, though I know that diverges from what the army cooks ladled into your bowl."

"Perhaps I won't," Krispos admitted. "I did miss seafood." Barsymes nodded in satisfaction; Krispos might rule the Empire, but the vestiarios held sway here. Unlike some vestiarioi, he had the sense not to flaunt his power or push it beyond its limits—or perhaps he had simply decided Krispos would not let him get away with the liberties some vestiarioi had taken.

"The hour remains young," Barsymes said after a glance at the shadows. "Would your Majesty care for an early supper?"

"Thank you, no," Krispos said. "I could plunge into the pile of parchments that no doubt reaches tall as the apex of the High Temple's dome. I will do that . . . tomorrow, or perhaps the day after. The pile won't be much taller by then. For now, though, I am going to march to the imperial bedchamber and do the one thing I couldn't in the field: relax." He paused. "No. I'm not."

"Your Majesty?" Barsymes said. "What, then?"

"I am going to the bedchamber," Krispos said. "I may even rest . . . presently. But first, please tell Drina I want to see her."

"Ah," Barsymes said; Krispos read approval in the nondescript noise. The vestiarios added, "It shall be just as you say, of course."

In the privacy of the bedchamber, Krispos took off his own boots. When his feet were free, he happily wiggled his toes. In the palaces, his doing something for himself rather than summoning a servant was as much an act of rebellion as a Thanasiot's taking a torch to a rich man's house. Barsymes had needed quite a while before he accepted that the Avtokrator was sometimes stubborn enough to insist on having his own way in such matters.

A tapping at the door sounded so tentative that Krispos wondered if he'd really heard it. He walked over and opened the door anyhow. Drina stood in the hall, looking nervous. "I'm not going to bite you," Krispos said. "It would spoil my appetite for the supper the esteemed Barsymes wants to stuff down me." She didn't laugh; he concluded she didn't get the joke. Swallowing a sigh, he waved her into the bedchamber.

She walked slowly. She was still a couple of months from giving birth, but her belly bulged quite noticeably even though she wore a loose-fitting linen smock. Krispos leaned forward over that belly to give her a light kiss, hoping to put her more at ease.

He succeeded, if not quite the way he thought he would. She smiled and said, "You didn't bump into my middle there. You know how to kiss a woman who's big with child."

"I should," Krispos said. "I've had practice, even if it was years ago. Sit if you care to; I know your feet won't be happy now. How are you feeling?"

"Well enough, thank you, your Majesty," Drina answered, sinking with a grateful sigh into a chair. "I only lost my breakfast once or twice, and but for needing the chamber pot all the time, I'm pretty well."

Krispos paced back and forth, wondering what to say next. He hadn't been in this situation for a long time, and had never expected to find himself in it again. It wasn't as if he loved Drina, or even as if he knew her well. He wished it were that way, but it wasn't. He'd just found her convenient for relieving the lust he still sometimes felt. Now he was discovering that convenience for the moment could turn into something else over the long haul. He used that principle every day in the way he ruled; he realized he should have applied it to his own life, too.

Well, he hadn't. Now he had to make the best of it. After a couple of more back and forths, he settled on, "Is everyone treating you well?"

"Oh, yes, your Majesty." Drina nodded eagerly. "Better than I've ever been treated before. Plenty of nice food—not that I haven't always eaten well, but more and better—and I haven't had to work too hard, especially since I started getting big." Her hands cupped her belly. She gave Krispos a very serious look. "And you warned me about putting on airs, so I haven't. I've been careful about that."

"Good. I wish everyone paid as much attention to what I say," Krispos said. Drina nodded, serious still. Even with that intent expression, even pregnant as she was, she looked very young. Suddenly he asked, "How many years do you have, Drina?"

She counted on her fingers before she answered: "Twenty-two, I think, your Majesty, but I may be out one or two either way."

Krispos started pacing again. It wasn't that she didn't know her exact age; he wasn't precisely sure of his own. Peasants such as he and his family had been didn't worry over such things: you were as old as the work you could do. But twenty-two, more or less? She'd been born right around the time he took the throne.

"What am I to do with you?" he asked, aiming the question as much at himself, or possibly at Phos, as at her.

"Your Majesty?" Her eyes got large and frightened. "You said I'd not lack for anything . . ." Her voice trailed away, as if reminding him of his own promise took all the courage she had, and as if she'd not be surprised if he broke it.

"You won't—by the good god I swear it. " He sketched the sun-circle over his heart to reinforce his words. "But that's not what I meant."

"What then?" Drina's horizons, like his when he'd been a peasant, reached no farther than plenty of food and not too much work. "All I want to do is take care of the baby."

"You'll do that, and with as much help as you need," he said. He scratched his head. "Do you read?"

"No, your Majesty."

"Do you want to learn how?"

"Not especially, your Majesty," Drina said. "Can't see that I'd ever have much call to use it."

Krispos clucked disapprovingly. A veteran resettled to his village had taught him his letters before his beard sprouted, and his world was never the same again. Written words bound time and space together in a way mere talk could never match. But if Drina did not care to acquire the skill, forcing it on her would not bring her pleasure. He scratched his head again.

"Your Majesty?" she asked. He raised an eyebrow and waited for her to go on. She did, nervously: "Your Majesty, after the baby's born, will you—will you want me again?"

It was a good question, Krispos admitted to himself. From Drina's point of view, it probably looked like the most important question in the world. She wanted to know whether she'd stay close to the source of power and influence in the Empire. The trouble was, Krispos had no idea what reply to give her. He couldn't pretend, to himself or to her, that he'd fallen wildly in love, not when he was more than old enough to be her father. And even if he had fallen wildly in love with her, the result would only have been grotesque. Older men who fell in love with girls got laughed at behind their backs.

She waited for his answer. "We'll have to see," he said at last. He wished he could do better than that, but he didn't want to lie to her, either.

"Yes, your Majesty," she said. The pained resignation in her voice cut like a knife. He wished he hadn't bedded her at all. But he hadn't the nature or temperament to make a monk. What was he supposed to do?

*I should have remarried after Dara died,* he thought. But he hadn't wanted to do that then, and a second wife might have created more problems—dynastic ones—than she solved. So he'd taken serving maids to bed every now and then . . . and so he had his present problem.

"I told you before that I'd settle a fine dowry on you when you find yourself someone who can give you all the love and caring you deserve," he said. "I don't think you'll find an Emperor's bastard any obstacle to that."

"No, I don't think so, either," she agreed; she was ignorant, but not stupid. "The trouble is, I don't have anyone like that in mind right now."

*Not right now.* She was twenty-two; *not right now* didn't look that different from *forever* to her. Nor, in fairness, could she look past her confinement. Her whole world would turn upside down once she held her baby in her arms. She'd need time to see how things had changed.

"We'll see," Krispos said again.

"All right," She accepted that; she had no choice.

Krispos knew it wasn't fair for her. Most Avtokrators would not have given that a first thought, let alone a second, but he knew about unfairness from having been on the receiving end. If he hadn't been unjustly taxed off his farm, he never would have come to Videssos the city and started on the road that led to a crown.

But what was he to do? Say he loved her when he didn't? That wouldn't be right—or fair—either. He was uneasily aware that providing for Drina and her child wasn't enough, but he didn't see what else he could do.

She wasn't a helpless maiden, not by a long shot. Her eyes twinkled as she asked, "What do the young Majesties think of all this? Evripos has known for a long time, of course; he just laughs whenever he sees me."

"Does he?" Krispos didn't know whether to be miffed or to laugh himself. "If you must know, Phostis and Katakolon seem to be of a mind that I'm a disgusting old lecher who should keep his drawers on when he goes to bed."

Drina dismissed that with one word: "Pooh."

Krispos couldn't even glow with pride, as another man might have. He'd spent too many years on the throne weighing everything he heard for flattery, doing his best not to believe all the praise that poured over him like honey, thick and sweet. He thought some of the man he had been still remained behind the imperial façade he'd built up—but how could you be sure?

He started pacing again. *Sometimes you think too much,* he told himself. He knew it was true, but it was so ingrained in him that he couldn't change. At last, too late, he told Drina, "Thank you."

"I should thank you, your Majesty, for not ignoring me or casting me out of the palaces or putting me in a sack and throwing me into the Cattle-Crossing because my belly made me a nuisance to you," Drina said.

"You shame me," Krispos said. He saw she didn't understand, and felt bound to explain: "When I'm thanked for not being a monster, it tells me I've not been all the man I might be."

"Who is?" she said. "And you're the Avtokrator. All the things you keep in your head, your Majesty—I'd go mad if I tried it for a day. I was just glad you saw fit to remember me at all, and do what you can for me."

Krispos pondered that. An Avtokrator could do what he chose—he needed to look no further than Anthimos' antics to be reminded of that. The power made responsibility hard to remember. Seen from that viewpoint, maybe he wasn't doing so badly after all.

"Thank you," he said to Drina again, this time with no hesitation at all.

\* \* \*

A boys' choir sang hymns of thanksgiving. The sweet, almost unearthly notes came echoing back from the dome of the High Temple, filing the worship area below with joyous sound.

Phostis, however, listened without joy. He knew he was no Thanasiot. All the same, the countless wealth lavished on the High Temple still struck him as excessive. And when Oxeites lifted up his hands to beseech Phos' favor, all Phostis could think of was the ecumenical patriarch's cloth-of-gold sleeves and the pearls and precious gems mounted on them.

Only because of the peace he'd made with Krispos had he come here. He recognized that celebrating his safe return to Videssos the city at the most holy shrine of the Empire's faith was politically and theologically valuable, so he endured it. That did not mean he liked it.

Beside him, though, awe turned Olyvria's face almost into that of a stranger. Her eyes flew like butterflies, landing now here, now there, marveling at the patriarch's regalia, at the moss-agate and marble columns, at the altar, at the rich woods of the pews, and most of all, inevitably, at the mosaic image of Phos, stern in judgment, that looked down on his worshipers from the dome.

"It's so marvelous," she whispered to Phostis for the third time since the service began. "Every city in the provinces says its main temple is modeled after this one. What none of them says is that all their models are toys."

Phostis grunted softly, back in his throat. What she found wondrous was cloying to him. Then, of themselves, his eyes too went up to the dome. No man could be easy meeting the gaze of that Phos: the image seemed to see inside his head, to know and note every stain on his soul. Even Thanasios would have quailed under that inspection. For the sake of the image in the dome, Phostis forgave the rest of the temple.

The choirmaster brought down his hands. The boys fell silent. Their blue silk robes shimmered in the lamplight as the echoes of their music slowly faded. Oxeites recited Phos' creed. The notables who filled the temple joined him at prayer. Those echoes also reverberated from the dome.

The patriarch said, "Not only do we seek thy blessing, Phos, we also humbly send up to thee our thanks for returning to us Phostis son of Krispos, heir to the throne of Videssos, and granting him thine aid through all the troubles he has so bravely endured."

"He's never been humble in his life, surely not since he donned the blue boots," Phostis murmured to Olyvria.

"Hush," she murmured back; the Temple had her in its spell.

Oxeites went on, "Surely, lord with the great and good mind, thou also viewest with favor the ending of the Empire's trial of heresy, and the way in which its passing was symbolized by the recent union of the young Majesty and his lovely bride."

A spattering of applause rose from the assembled worshipers, vigorously led by Krispos. Phostis was convinced Oxeites would not know a symbol if it reached up and yanked him by the beard; he suspected the Avtokrator of putting words in his patriarch's mouth.

"We thank thee, Phos, for thy blessings of peace and prosperity, and once more for the restoration of the young Majesty to the bosom of his family and to Videssos the city," Oxeites said in ringing tones.

The choir burst into song again. When the hymn was finished, the patriarch dismissed the congregation: the thanksgiving service was not a full and formal liturgy. Phostis blinked against the late summer sun as he walked down the broad, wide stairs outside the High Temple. Katakolon poked him in the ribs and said, "The only bosom you care about in your family is Olyvria's."

"By the good god, you're shameless," Phostis said. He couldn't help laughing, even so. Because Katakolon had no malice in him, he could get away with outrages that would have landed either of his brothers in trouble.

In the courtyard outside the High Temple, people of rank insufficient to get them into the thanksgiving service cheered as Phostis came down from the steps and walked over to his horse. He waved to them, all the while wondering how many had shouted for the gleaming path not long before.

The Haloga guard who held the horse's head said, "You talk to your god only a little while today." He sounded approving, or at least relieved.

Phostis handed Olyvria up onto her mount, then swung into the saddle himself. The Halogai formed up around the imperial party for the return to the palaces. Olyvria rode at Phostis' left.

To his right was Evripos. His older younger brother curled his lip and said, "You're back. Hurrah." Then he looked straight ahead and seemed to concentrate solely on his horsemanship.

"Wait a minute," Phostis said harshly. "I'm sick of cracks like that from you. If you wanted me to be gone and stay gone, you had your chance to do something about it."

"I told you then, I don't have that kind of butchery in me," Evripos answered.

"Well then, quit talking to me as if you wish you did."

That made Evripos look his way again, though still without anything that could be called friendliness. "Brother of mine, just because I won't shed blood of my blood, that doesn't mean I want to clasp you to my bosom, if I can steal the patriarch's phrase."

"That's not enough," Phostis said.

"It's all I care to make it," Evripos answered.

"It's not enough, I tell you," Phostis said, which succeeded in gaining Evripos' undivided attention. Phostis went on, "One of these days, if I live, I'm going to wear the red boots. Unless Olyvria and I have a son of our own, you'll be next in line for them. Even if we do, he'd be small for a long time. The day may come when you decide blood doesn't matter, or maybe you'll think you can just shave my head and pack me off to a monastery: you'd get the throne and salve your tender conscience at the same time."

Evripos scowled. "I wouldn't do that. As you said, I had my chance."

"You wouldn't do it *now*," Phostis returned. "What about ten years from now, or twenty, when you feel you can't stand being second in line for another heartbeat? Or what happens if I decide I can't trust you to stay in your proper place? I might strike first, little brother. Did you ever think of that?"

Evripos was good at using his face to mask his thoughts. But Phostis had watched him all his life, and saw he'd succeeded in surprising him. The surprise faded quickly. Evripos studied Phostis as closely as he was studied in turn. Slowly, he said, "You've changed." It sounded like an accusation.

"Have I, now?" Phostis tried to keep anything but the words themselves from his voice.

"Aye, you have." It *was* accusation. "Before you got kidnapped, you didn't have the slightest notion what you were for, what you wanted. You knew what you were against—"

"Anything that had to do with Father," Phostis interrupted.

"Just so," Evripos agreed with a thin smile. "But being against is easy. Finding, knowing, what you truly do want is harder."

"You know what you want," Olyvria put in.

"Of course I do," Evripos said. *The red boots* hung unspoken in the air. "But it looks like I can't have that. And now that Phostis knows what he wants, too, and what it means to him, it makes him ever so much more dangerous to me than he was before."

"So it does," Phostis said. "You can do one of two things about it, as far as I can see: you can try to take me out, which you say you don't want to do, or you can work with me. We spoke of that before I got kidnapped; maybe you remember. You scoffed at me then. Do you sing a different tune now? The second man in all the Empire can find or make a great part for himself."

"But it's not the first part," Evripos said.

"I know that's what you want," Phostis answered, saying it for his brother. "If you look one way, you see one person ahead of you. But if you look in the other direction, you see everyone else behind. Isn't that enough?"

Enough to make Evripos thoughtful, at any rate. When he answered, "It's not what I want," the words lacked the hostility with which he'd spoken before.

Krispos rode ahead of the younger members of the imperial family. As he clattered down the cobblestones in front of the government office building where Digenis had been confined, a man strolling along the sidewalk sang out, "Phos bless you, your Majesty!" Krispos sent him a wave and kept on riding.

"*That's* what I want." Now Evripos' voice ached with envy. "Who's going to cheer a general or a minister? It's the Avtokrator who gets the glory, by the good god."

"He gets the blame, too," Phostis pointed out. "If I could, I'd give you all the glory, Evripos; for all I care, it can go straight to the ice. But there's more to running the Empire than having people cheer you in the streets. I didn't take it seriously before I got snatched, but my eyes have been opened since then."

He wondered if that would mean anything to his brother. It seemed to, for Evripos said, "So have mine. Don't forget, I was running Videssos the city while Father went on campaign. Even without the riots, I'll not deny that was a great bloody lot of work. All jots and tittles and parchments that didn't mean anything till you'd read them five times, and sometimes not then."

Phostis nodded. He often wondered if he wanted to walk in Krispos' footsteps and pore over documents into the middle of the night. That, surely, was why the Empire of Videssos had developed so large and thorough a bureaucracy over the centuries: to keep the Avtokrator from having to shoulder such burdens.

As if Krispos had spoken aloud, Phostis heard his opinion of that: *Aye, and if you let the pen-pushers and seal-stampers run affairs without checking up on them, how do you know when they're bungling things or cheating you? The good god knows we need them, and he also knows they need someone looking over them. Anthimos almost brought the Empire to ruin because he wouldn't attend to his ruling.*

"I wouldn't be Anthimos," Phostis protested, just as if Krispos *had* spoken out loud. Olyvria, Evripos, and Katakolon all gave him curious looks. He felt his cheeks heat.

Evripos said, "Well, I wouldn't, either. If I tried to live that life after Father died, I expect he'd climb out of the tomb and wring my neck with bony fingers." He dropped his voice and sent a nervous glance up ahead toward Krispos; Phostis guessed he was only half joking.

"Me, I'm just as glad I'm not likely to wear the red boots," Katakolon said. "I like a good carouse now and then; it keeps you from going stale."

"A good carouse now and then is one thing," Phostis said. "From all the tales, though, Anthimos never stopped, or even slowed down."

"A short life but a merry one," Katakolon said, grinning.

"You let Father hear that from you and your life may be short, but it won't be merry," Phostis answered. "He's not what you'd call fond of Anthimos' memory."

Katakolon looked forward again; he did not want to rouse Krispos' wrath. Phostis suddenly grasped another reason why Krispos so despised the predecessor whose throne and wife

he'd taken: no doubt he'd wondered all the years since
Anthimos had left behind a cuckoo's egg for him to raise as
his own.

And yet, of the three young men, Phostis was probably most
like Krispos in character, if perhaps more inclined to reflection
and less to action. Evripos was devious in a different way, and
his resentment that he hadn't been born first left him sour. And
Katakolon—Katakolon had a blithe disregard for consequences
that set him apart from both his brothers.

Without warning, Evripos said, "You'll give me room to
make something for myself, make something of myself, when
the red boots go on your feet?"

"I've said so all along," Phostis answered. "Would an oath
make you happier?"

"Nothing along those lines would truly make me happy,"
Evripos said. "But one of the things I've seen is that sometimes there's nothing to be done about the way things are . . .
or nothing that isn't worse, anyhow. Let it be as you say,
brother of mine; I'll serve you, and do my best to recall that
everyone else serves me as well as you."

The two of them solemnly clasped hands. Olyvria exclaimed
in delight; even Katakolon looked unwontedly sober. Evripos'
palm was warm in Phostis'. By her expression, Olyvria
thought all the troubles between them were over. Phostis
wished he thought the same. As far as he could see, he and
Evripos would be watching each other for the rest of their
lives, no matter what promises they made each other. That, too,
came with being part of the imperial family.

Had Evripos said something like *Good to have that settled
once and for all*, Phostis would have suspected him more, not
less. As it was, his younger brother just flicked him a glance
to see how seriously he took the gesture of reconciliation. For
a moment, their eyes met. They both smiled, again for a moment only. They might not trust each other, but they understood each other.

Along with the rest of the imperial party, they rode through
the plaza of Palamas and into the palace quarter. After the raucous bustle of the rest of the city, quiet enfolded them there
like a cloak. Phostis felt he was coming home. That had special meaning to him after what he'd gone through the past few
months.

He'd always used his bedchamber in the imperial residence as a refuge from Krispos. Now that Olyvria shared it with him, he sometimes thought he never wanted to come out again. It wasn't that they spent all their time making love, delightful though that was. But he'd also found in her somebody he liked talking with more than anyone else he'd ever known.

He let himself tip over backward onto the bed like a falling tree. The thick goose down of the mattress absorbed his weight; it was like falling into a warm, dry snowbank. With him sprawled across the middle of the bed, Olyvria sat at its foot. She said, "All of this—" She waved to show she meant not just the room, not just the palace, but also the service and the procession through the streets of the city. "—still feels unreal to me."

"You'll have the rest of your days to get used to it," Phostis answered. "A lot of it is foolish and boring to go through; even Father thinks so. But ceremony is the glue that holds Videssos together, so he does go through with it, and then grumbles when no one outside the palaces can hear him."

"That's hypocrisy," Olyvria frowned; like Phostis, she still had some Thanasiot righteousness clinging to her.

"I've told him as much," Phostis said. "He just shrugs and says things would go worse if he didn't give the people what they expected of him." Before he'd been kidnapped, he would have rolled his eyes at that. Now, after a small pause for thought, he admitted, "There may be something to it."

"I don't know." Olyvria's frown deepened. "How can you live with yourself after doing things you don't believe in year after year after year?"

"I didn't say Father doesn't believe in them. He does, for the sake of the Empire. I said he doesn't like them. It's not quite the same thing."

"Close enough, for anyone who's not a theologian and used to splitting hairs." But Olyvria changed the subject, which might have meant she yielded the point. "I'm glad you made peace with your brother—or he with you, however you want to look at it."

"So am I," Phostis said. Not wanting to deceive Olyvria about his judgment of that peace, he added, "Now we'll see how long it lasts."

She took his meaning at once. "Oh," she said in a crestfallen voice. "I'd thought you put more faith in it than that."

"Hope, yes. Faith?" He shrugged, then repeated, "We'll see how long it lasts. The good god willing, it'll hold forever. If it doesn't—"

"If it doesn't, you'll do what you have to do," Olyvria said.

"Aye, what I have to do," Phostis echoed. He'd come safe out of Etchmiadzin by that rule, but if you cared to, you could use it to justify anything. He sighed, then said, "You know what the real trouble with Thanasiot doctrine is?"

"What?" Olyvria asked. "The ecumenical patriarch could come up with a hundred without thinking."

"Oxeites does quite a lot without thinking," Phostis said. "He's not good at it."

Olyvria giggled, deliciously scandalized. "But what's yours?" she asked.

"The real trouble with Thanasiot doctrine," Phostis declared, as if pontificating before a synod, "is that it makes the world and life out to be simpler than they are. Burn and wreck and starve and you've somehow made the world a better place? But what about the people who don't want to be burned out and who like to eat till they're fat? What about the Makuraners, who would pick up the pieces if Videssos fell apart—and who tried to make it fall apart? The gleaming path takes none of them into account. It just goes on along the track it thinks right, regardless of any complications."

"That's all true enough," Olyvria said.

"In fact," Phostis went on, "following the gleaming path is almost like getting caught up in a new love affair, where you just notice everything that's good and kind about the person you love, but none of the flaws."

Olyvria gave him an unfathomable look. His analogy pleased him so much that he wondered what was troubling her until she asked, in rather a small voice, "And what does that say about us?"

"It says—uh—" Feeling his mouth hanging foolishly open, Phostis shut it. He kept it shut while he did some hard thinking. At last, much less sure of himself than he had been a moment before, he answered, "I think it says that we can't afford to take us for granted, or to think that, because we're happy now, we're always going to be happy unless we work to make that happen. The romances talk a lot about living happily ever after, but they don't say how it's done. We have to find that out for ourselves."

"I wish you'd stop poking fun at the romances, seeing as we're living one," Olyvria said, but she smiled to take any sting from her words. "Other than that, though, you make good sense. You seem to have a way of doing that."

"Thank you," he said seriously. Then he reached out and poked her in the ribs. She squawked and whipped her head around, curls flying. He drew her to him and drowned the squawk in a kiss. When at last he had to breathe, he asked her softly, "How are we doing now?"

"Now, well." This time, she kissed him. "As for the rest, ask me in twenty years."

He glanced up, just for a moment, to make sure the door was barred. "I will."


Imperial crown heavy on his head, Krispos sat on the throne in the Grand Courtroom, awaiting the approach of the ambassador for Khatrish. In front of the throne stood Barsymes, Iakovitzes, and Zaidas. Krispos hoped the three of them would be enough to protect him from Tribo's pungent sarcasm.

The fuzzy-bearded envoy advanced down the long central aisle of the courtroom between ranks of courtiers who scorned him as both barbarian and heretic. He managed to give the impression that their scorn amused him, which only irked them the more.

He prostrated himself at the proper place before Krispos' throne. Krispos had debated whether to have the throne rise while Tribo's head rested on the gleaming marble floor. In the end, he'd decided against it.

As before, when Tribo rose, he asked, "Has the gearing broken down, your Majesty, or are you just not bothering?"

"I'm not bothering." Krispos swallowed a sigh. So much for the fond hope Avtokrators nursed of overawing envoys from less sophisticated lands. He inclined his head to Tribo. "I've waited in eager curiosity for your words since you requested this audience, honored ambassador."

"You're wondering how I'll get on your nerves now, you mean." Mutters rose at Tribo's undiplomatic language. By his foxy grin, he reveled in them. But when he resumed, he spoke more formally: "I am bidden by the puissant khagan Nobad son of Gumush to extend Khatrish's congratulations to your Majesty for your victory over the Thanasiot heretics."

"The puissant khagan is gracious," Krispos said.

"The puissant khagan, for all his congratulations, is unhappy with your Majesty," Tribo said. "You've put out the fire in your own house, but sparks caught in the thatch of ours, and they're liable to burn down the roof. We still have plenty of trouble from the Thanasioi in Khatrish."

"I'm sorry to hear that." Krispos reflected that he wasn't even lying. Just as Videssian Thanasioi had spread the heresy to Khatrish, so foreign followers of the gleaming path might one day bring it back to the Empire. Krispos resumed, "I don't know what the khagan would have me do now, though, beyond what I've already done here in my own realm."

"He thinks it hardly just for you to export your problems and then forget about them when they trouble you no more," Tribo said.

"What would he have me do?" Krispos repeated. "Shall I ship imperial troops to your ports to help your soldiers root out the heretics? Shall I send in priests I reckon orthodox to uphold the pure and true doctrines?"

Tribo made a sour face. "Shall Videssos swallow up Khatrish, you mean. Thank you, your Majesty, but no. If I said aye to that, my khagan would likely tie me between horses and whip them to a gallop, one going one way and one the other . . . unless he paused to think up a truly interesting and creative end for me. Khatrish has been free of the imperial yoke for more than three hundred years. For reasons you may not understand, we'd sooner keep it that way."

"As you will," Krispos said. "Your land and mine are at peace, and I'm happy with that. But if you don't want our warriors and you don't want our priests, honored ambassador, what do you expect us to do about the Thanasioi in Khatrish?"

"You ought to pay us an indemnity for inflicting the heresy on us," Tribo said. "The gold would help us take care of the problem for ourselves."

Krispos shook his head. "If we'd deliberately set the Thanasioi on you, that would be a just claim. But Videssos just fought a war to put them down here: we didn't want them around, either. I'm sorry they spread to Khatrish, but it was no fault of ours. Shall I bill the puissant khagan every time the Balancer heresy you love so well shows its head here in the Empire?"

"Your Majesty, I know you imperials have a saying, 'When in Videssos the city, eat fish.' But till now I hadn't known you hid a shark's dorsal fin under those fancy robes."

"From you, honored ambassador, that's high praise indeed," Krispos said, which only made Tribo look unhappier still. The Avtokrator went on, "Does your puissant khagan have any other business for you to set before me?"

"No, your Majesty," Tribo answered. "I shall convey to him your stubborn refusal to act as justice would dictate, and warn you that I cannot answer for the consequences."

From the Makuraner ambassador, that would have meant war. But Videssos badly outweighed Khatrish, and the two nations, despite bickering, had not fought for generations. So Krispos said, "Do tell his puissant self that I admire his gall, and that if I could afford to subsidize it, I would. As is, he'll just have to smuggle more and hope he makes it up that way."

"I shall convey your insulting and degrading remarks along with your refusal." Tribo paused. "He may take you up on that smuggling scheme."

"I know. I'll stop him if I can." Krispos mentally began framing orders for more customs inspectors and tighter vigilance along the Khatrisher border. All the same, he knew the easterners would get some untaxed amber through.

Tribo prostrated himself again, then rose and walked away from the throne backward until he'd withdrawn far enough to turn around without offending court etiquette. He was too accomplished a diplomat to do anything so rude as sticking his nose in the air as he marched off, but so accomplished a mime that he managed to create that impression without the reality.

The courtiers began streaming out after the ambassador left the Grand Courtroom. Their robes and capes of bright, glistening silk made them seem a moving field of springtime flowers.

Zaidas turned to Krispos and made small, silent clapping motions. "Well done, your Majesty," he said. "It's not every day that the envoy from Khatrish, whoever he may be, leaves an audience in such dismay."

"Khatrishers are insolent louts with no respect for their betters," Barsymes said. "They disrupt ceremonial merely for the sake of disruption." By his tone, the offense ranked somewhere between heresy and infanticide on his scale of enormities.

"I don't mind them that much," Krispos said. "They just have a hard time taking anything seriously." He'd lost his own war against ceremonial years before; if he needed a reminder, the weight of the crown on his head gave him one. Seeing other folk strike blows against the foe—the only foe, in the Empire or out of it that had overcome him—let him dream about renewing the struggle himself one day. He was, sadly, realist enough to know he did but dream.

Iakovitzes opened his table, plucked out a stylus, and wrote busily: "I don't like Khatrishers because they're too apt to cheat when they dicker with us. Of course, they say the same of Videssos."

"And they're probably as right as we are," Zaidas murmured.

Krispos suspected Iakovitzes didn't like Khatrishers because they took the same glee he did in flouting staid Videssian custom—and sometimes upstaged him while they were at it. That was something he wouldn't say out loud, for fear of finding out he was right and wounding Iakovitzes in the process.

The Grand Courtroom continued to empty. A couple of men came forward instead of leaving; they carried rolled and sealed parchments in their outstretched right hands. Haloga guardsmen kept them from getting too close. One of the northerners glanced back at Krispos. He nodded. The Haloga took the petitions and carried them over to him. They'd go into one of the piles on his desk. He wondered when he'd have the chance to read them. *They'll reach the top one of these days,* he thought.

The petitioners walked down the long aisle toward the doorway. Krispos rose, stretched, and descended the stairs from the throne. Iakovitzes wrote another note: "You know, it might not be so bad if the Thanasioi give the Khatrishers all the trouble they can handle and a bit more besides. Let Tribo say what he will; the day may come when the khagan really has to choose between going under and calling on Videssos for aid."

"That would be excellent," Barsymes said. "Krispos brought Kubrat back under Videssian rule; why not Khatrish, as well?"

*Why not?* Krispos thought. Videssos had never abandoned her claim to Kubrat or Khatrish or Thatagush, all lands overwhelmed by Khamorth nomads off the plains of Pardraya three hundred years before. To restore two of them to the Empire . . . he might go down in the chronicles as Krispos the Conqueror.

That, however, assumed the Khatrishers were ripe to be conquered. "I don't see it," Krispos said, not altogether regretfully. "Khatrish somehow has a way of fumbling through troubles and coming out on the other side stronger than it has any business being. They're more easygoing about their religion than we are, too, so heresy has a harder time inciting them."

"They certainly didn't—don't—care for the Thanasioi," Zaidas said. Krispos guessed the idea of conquest appealed to him, too.

"We'll see what happens, that's all," the Avtokrator said. "If it turns to chaos, we may try going in. We'd have to be careful even so, though, to make sure the Khatrishers don't unite again—against us. Nothing like a foreign foe to make the problems you have with your neighbors look small."

"Remember also, your Majesty, the Thanasioi dissemble," Barsymes said. "Even if the Khatrishers seem to put down the heresy of the gleaming path for the time being, it may yet spring to life a generation from now."

"A generation from now?" Krispos snorted. "Odds are that'll be Phostis' worry, not mine." A year before, the idea of passing the Empire on to his eldest—if Phostis was *his* eldest—had filled him with dread. Now . . . "I expect he'll take care of it," he said.

## ABOUT THE AUTHOR

Harry Turtledove has lived in Southern California all his life. He has a Ph.D. in history from UCLA and has taught at UCLA, California State, Fullerton, and California State University, Los Angeles. He has published in both history and speculative fiction. He is married to novelist Laura Frankos. They have three daughters: Alison, Rachel, and Rebecca.